Here is the [   ]D0628291[   ] history of the frontier. Here is the struggle that
broke the red man's hold on the way west.
Here is the remarkable tale of a war party,
over a thousand warriors strong, traveling
over a hundred miles undetected to strike
with fury at the heart of helpless white settlements, destroying two towns and killing
untold numbers of besieged pioneers.

It is also the story of breaking the powerful
Comanche-Kiowa hold of the southern
plains, with a death toll higher than
Wounded Knee. It is the tale of the Texas
Rangers, who, always outnumbered, at
Plum Creek in August of 1840, finally
checked the massive Indian threat and kept
a vengeful Mexico, anxious to reclaim the
Lone Star State, at bay.

Other Avon Books by
David William Ross

EYE OF THE HAWK

WAR CRIES

DAVID WILLIAM ROSS

AVON BOOKS ⬥ NEW YORK

WAR CRIES is an original publication of Avon Books. This work has never before appeared in book form. This work is a novel. Any similarity to actual persons or events is purely coincidental.

AVON BOOKS
A division of
The Hearst Corporation
1350 Avenue of the Americas
New York, New York 10019

First Avon Books Printing: October 1995

AVON TRADEMARK REG. U.S. PAT. OFF. AND IN OTHER COUNTRIES, MARCA REGISTRADA, HECHO EN U.S.A.

Printed in the U.S.A.

RA 10 9 8 7 6 5 4 3 2 1

To Clifford, Valerie, Darielle and David,
in hopes they will follow in the steps of Libby Holister

Chapter 1

THE MORNING BROKE overcast, with dark roiling clouds threatening. Damp winds brought a heavy mist over the valley as thunder sounded to the north, its echo adding to its distant rumble. Sudden gusts swept along the river, rattling the roof and bringing rivulets of rain against the windows, stopping only for brief moments of silence broken by a clocklike dripping from the eaves.

The Holister brothers had been trying to shake off a feeling of danger that arose earlier when Kyle thought he heard gunshots, muffled by thunder, coming from up-river. But after a period of silence they nodded reassuringly to one another. Like every morning, they drank coffee and remarked about crops, yet the vague anxiety, fueled by some curious tension in the air, refused to dispel. By noon their quick movements and response to every sound coming downwind betrayed a fear now visible in the tightness about Kyle's eyes.

Matt, older of the two, suddenly rose to glance out the window, quietly mumbling to himself. The rain had let up enough to see a galloping horse splashing along the river's edge, turning finally at the mouth of the brook

1

and coming in their direction. He glanced at Kyle. "Damn . . . looks like Pete Spevy. Could be trouble."

Kyle hurried over to peer across the damp fields. "That's Pete sure enough." His voice fought to stay normal. "If he keeps pushing that mare thataway, she won't hardly last." They were both tall men with pronounced features, their skin ruddy brown from constant sun and wind. They were struggling to farm a claim on the Guadalupe and had just finished the house, a barn, an outhouse, and had dug a deep well. They were not young; both were in their late forties. Both were hardworking, making a new start here after giving up the few acres of exhausted soil their family owned for generations in hilly Missouri. Arriving a year ago, they had worked seven days a week to finish building and to get a crop in. Now they watched Pete Spevy ride up and jump from his mare, his hands gesturing upriver as he shouted, "By Jesus, it's Injuns again! You best git over to the mission. They're butchering every soul they catch! The Reillys are dead . . . Got old Jake, damn it . . . For certain there's smoke risin' over to Chauncy's place."

"How many are there?" asked Kyle, rubbing his sides like a man quietly fighting fear.

"Too many to argue with . . . Folks is grabbing what they can and clearing out."

"We gettin' any help from San Antonio?" asked Matt.

"Not likely and sure as hell not soon. We'd be best off fetching help from Lavaca Flats." Spevy caught his breath as he slapped his mare on the flank. "I'm going to have to borrow a horse. Betsy here is near done in. I got two more families to warn."

Matt waved to an old Negro who had come to the barn door, attracted by the sound of Spevy's horse. "Josiah, bring up Blackie," he shouted. The Negro nodded and disappeared.

Spevy started stripping the saddle and bridle from his mare. "Yer kinfolk still coming?"

"Reckon so," replied Matt, a worried frown now clamped about his eyes. "They gonna be warned?"

"Figure so . . . Riders are covering every trail eastways. Those damn Comanches . . . Jesus, I hope those Chauncy kids got clear in time."

They stood in silence as Josiah brought the black around, helping Pete to throw the saddle on him. As he tightened the cinches, Spevy glanced quizzically at the brothers. "Shouldn't you folks be fixing to hightail? . . . They're a'ready this side of the river . . . Don't believe you've got more 'n half an hour."

Matt nodded. "Thanks, Pete, appreciate your trouble. Reckon we'll be along."

Spevy mounted and cut diagonally across the field to the river; it was another four miles to the Sutters'. They watched him go, not moving till Blackie's hoofbeats faded away.

Kyle's voice betrayed the pain beneath his words. "They're gonna burn us out, Matt."

Matt looked at the small wooden house, caulked with adobe, the tall narrow barn, even the outhouse, all built with such effort, all built with the hope that Jody and his new wife were coming to join them. Now they were going to be burned out, now a year of backbreaking labor would just disappear. Now Jody and Libby wouldn't stay; his dream of having his son and his coming grandchild with him would die in the ashes of this farm. Was there no God to strike these red devils, no merciful spirit to spare the few dreams a lifetime of grubby hardship allowed? Kyle and Josiah watched him shake his head and stare at the ground. Matt's mind couldn't deal with the thought of starting over again; he ended by covering his eyes with one hand and moaning quietly before dropping it hopelessly at his side. "I can't leave," he murmured. "I just can't give it up."

"We can't hardly hold it if they come," muttered Kyle, his expression as bleak as Matt's.

"Reckon we got us plenty misery a-comin'," muttered old Josiah, tense and looking doubtful of what to do with Spevy's mare.

Matt gazed at the stretch of river running beyond their plowed fields, a desperate hope alive in his words. "Maybe they won't come down this far."

"Maybe," quickly echoed Kyle, revealing he, too, was desperately seeking a way out of leaving. The Holisters were not men who frightened easily; life had been hard and it had hardened them, but they knew desperation was pulling their minds toward a dangerous, likely fatal, gamble. Yet they weren't a breed that displayed emotion; only their tightened lips gave any hint of the stress they were under.

It was long moments before Matt once again looked about the stretch of land they had labored over for a year, then turned to his brother. "Well, Kyle, what do you think?"

Kyle knew his answer could lead to life or death for both of them, but he knew the answer Matt wanted, the answer his own heart wanted, and taking a deep breath, he said, "Why don't we chance it, Matt. Hell, if there ain't too many, maybe we could fight 'em off."

Matt took a moment before he nodded and patted him on the shoulder. Then he turned to Josiah. "Josiah, you'd best take that mare to the barn, saddle up Beauty, and get south of here. Take old Tom and Spevy's horse with you. If we're not here when you get back, our horses are yours."

Josiah looked startled. "Yo sho enough fixin' to stay?" he asked, his eyes growing larger as he spoke.

"Yep, and you better get movin'; they might be pretty close."

"Yes'r," mumbled Josiah, moving uncertainly with the mare toward the barn. "Dis tarnation foolish," he whispered to himself, beginning to shake as he led Beauty from her stall. "What fo' dey want to mess with dat passel of Injuns? Why dey sendin' ole Josiah 'way?"

Back at the house Matt and Kyle got their rifles out.

They set up small piles of ammunition beneath the windows and on a shelf beside the door. They didn't talk. The house could only be defended from three sides; the back was a thin wall of stones with no openings. Both knew the front of the house was the most vulnerable, and Kyle, who was the best shot, set his rifle down by the door. Matt put out a pail of water and some bread for each of them. A tub of water was set in the middle of the main room with two pots to deal with fire. From time to time they glanced at each other, knowing time was passing, knowing if an attack was coming, it was getting close.

With their minds on each other, they had forgotten Josiah; in surprise they heard him knocking on the door. Josiah had been standing in the barn looking toward the river for a time. He had readied the horses but found his heart wasn't in leaving. He was an old man, older than the brothers, and had been with the Holisters since he was ten. He was neither slave nor free but just stayed with this family, having none of his own. He rubbed his wrinkled face with hands gnarled and near crippled from work. He lived in the barn and, except when he worked with the brothers in the field, ate alone. There were few Negroes in that part of Texas and he had no friends. Matt had told him to go and take the horses, but where was he to take them? Who would take him in? Now that he could only work a few hours at a time, who was there to feed him, let him live in their barn? He stood in the doorway, one hand holding the other, the old discarded homespun clothes hanging on his meager frame. The brothers looked at him, waiting for him to speak.

"Reckon Ah could stay y'here wid y'all?" he half whispered.

Frowning, Matt crossed over to him. "Josiah, you heard Spevy. Injuns are raiding down the river. We're hoping to hold out here . . . but maybe . . ."

"Ah knows . . . figure the Lord knows too . . . Maybe Ah could fight a little . . . Let me stay!"

The brothers looked at each other. Matt picked up an old pistol and studied it for a moment. "Josiah, the Sutters will take you in, take good care of you; they're fine people."

"Dis my home."

Kyle took him by the shoulder. "You only have a barn here; they have a nice big stable, even a bunkhouse."

"Ah know, reckon dat just look like duh barn . . . but das my home."

Matt sighed and shrugged, then reluctantly gave him the pistol. "Well, Josiah, where do you figure to fight?"

Josiah managed a half smile. "Y'all fight for dis house . . . Dis your home. Ah fights fo' duh barn . . . Dat mine."

Matt began to reason if Indians struck the house, a shot from the barn might distract them, it could help. But there was no time to discuss it; something told him the faint movements he now caught beyond the field were dim figures coming through a heavy mist that had formed over the river.

"Get over there," he said firmly, "and good luck!"

Josiah left smiling. He hurried over to the barn content. "Ole Josiah comin' home," he muttered as its familiar smells greeted his nostrils.

Two of the warriors had dismounted to crawl up behind the line of brush that rimmed the river. They had seen the old Negro hustling back to the barn. One made a hand signal behind him and over thirty mounted braves, led by a warrior whose red and yellow face paint marked him as a war leader, rode out of a stand of trees filling a bend of the river upstream from the farm. At a signal from the leader, the two dismounted braves ran for their horses. The rain had stopped, but a mist had formed like thick fog along the river. They rode out of it, coming across the plowed fields, beginning their war cries as they reached and circled the house. They had been trying to set the dwellings they came upon afire, but unless they broke in, the rain made the task difficult. But they had taken several scalps, tortured three people to death, and seized two captives. It was time to withdraw to the buffalo plains. Their war leader, *Isi-man-ica*, Hears-the-Wolf, knew the whites were gathering at the mission. With walls to fight behind, they would be too costly to attack. This would be his last assault.

The Holisters, like hundreds of settlers along the verdant Guadalupe valley, had come to Texas to find a home and a future, willing to pay for both with honest labor and fervent hopes. But they had misjudged the price of this land. The brothers fought valiantly, killing two Comanches and wounding a third before Kyle received an arrow in his throat. Matt watched him die, praying over him as the Comanches withdrew to prepare for a second charge. Knowing he was going to die, he tried to scribble a note to his son, but then he saw them coming with firebrands and knew it was no use. He lasted longer than he thought, but fire forced him to the side he couldn't protect and he fell as two arrows tore into his back.

With the house in flames, they turned to the barn. Only a shot or two had been fired from there, for the old pistol had jammed on Josiah. Yet it made little difference; he couldn't see well enough to aim. They broke in and seized him. They could have killed him with a shot or a hatchet blow, but these were Comanches. They tied him to a beam, surrounded him with heaps of dry straw, and setting them aflame, closed the barn door. Josiah watched the flames mounting about him, somehow not sad to leave his dismal life behind. In his final moments he looked up and smiled. Somewhere Lord Jesus was up there, somewhere He was waiting and would know this time old Josiah was sure enough coming home.

With the mist lifting and rain trailing off, young Jody Holister knew they were nearing Gonzales when he caught a glimpse of the Guadalupe. He pulled the wagon to a stop to rest the team and jumped down to stretch his legs. He was tall like his father and walked with the same determined stride, as though he were starting up-hill. He had his family's prominent features and deep hazel eyes under straw-colored hair. His wife, Libby, at seventeen a beauty with oval green eyes and coal black hair, watched him come around the wagon and offer to help her down. She declined. Eight months pregnant, she just wanted to sit and enjoy the stationary wagon for a few moments. Besides, she had sighted a rider coming toward them at a gallop. "Jody," she said, "look yonder, someone's coming."

Jody studied the trail ahead for a moment, then pulled a rifle from the wagon scabbard. "Probably just a mail carrier," he said quietly. He glanced at the two saddle horses he had tied to the rear of the wagon. "We must be pretty close to town."

"Whoever it is," answered Libby, "he's waving his hat and making for us."

They both watched the rider coming up, discovering he was an old man, thin but wiry-looking, his face dominated by a firm protruding jaw. "There's been an Indian raid ahead," he shouted. "Best you folks wait here for a spell . . . Better still, take that turn just beyond and hole up with the Bishops. They fine people . . . make yuh feel t'home."

"Indian raid?" said Jody, his tone inquiring.

"That's right! Came down the river, burning and killing to beat hell. Best you do like I say . . . Don't believe they figure to come this far." With that he was off, eastward toward Shiner Crossing.

Jody and Libby watched him go, remaining silent for a moment, looking at each other till Jody reached up to take her hand. "We knew there might be Injun trouble, Lib . . . Likely it won't last."

Libby stared at his hand holding hers as though accepting his assurance, but then she said, "Jody, we'd

best fetch those Bishop folks . . . This land is too scary
to be alone.''

"We will,'' he answered, climbing back on the
wagon. "Likely they'll know Dad and uncle Kyle,'' he
added comfortingly. "We can't be more than half a day
from the farm.''

By nightfall the small settlement of Gonzales would
find two of its children missing, three men tortured to
death, their tongues and genitals cut off. They would
find two women stripped, raped, and impaled on fence
posts. Farther out they would find the mutilated bodies
of the Holister brothers and the burnt husk of a half-
blind old Negro. They would spend that night looking
into the darkness, their outrage muted, knowing their
demands for vengeance were beyond the lonely settlement's strength. Like the Holisters, they had come thinking the cost of this land was hard work and a faith in
the future, but discovered the soil wasn't theirs for the
taking. It proved to be the fief of a savage warlike people, conquerors of the southern buffalo range, masters
of the hardy mustang and the deadly bois d'arc bow.
They were the Penateka Comanches, largest tribe of the
Nerm, whose warriors were the most arrogant, aggressive, and sanguinary on the continent. This was deep
Comanche country, and those aspiring to it faced mortal
combat, without hope of truces or honorable surrender.
The Texas frontier was about to burst into flames. Two
assertive and dominant peoples, whose ways of life
could never be reconciled, had met. Victory would go
to the one who first destroyed the other.

Chapter 2

THE WINTER SUN was still throwing welcome heat on the low rolling hills along the Nueces when *Isi-man-ica*, Hears-the-Wolf, the famous war leader, led his party into camp. They had several scalps and two captives, a boy of six and a girl of eight. The young ones had been stripped and examined to see if their bodies were injured or malformed. Being neither, they were spared the hatchet and abducted instead. He had watched them on the journey back. After some trials of courage, he planned to adopt the boy, who looked well built and could already ride with some skill. The girl would be turned over to the squaws to be trained or whipped, depending on her willingness to work. When she was big enough he would take her into his robe or trade her off. He neither knew nor cared that their names were Tad and Liza Chauncy. It meant nothing to him that their parents, missing them, had collapsed in shock and grief. He was a Comanche warrior, born to conflict and embittered by the knowledge that his people's long history of conquest and rule was threatening to end. His usual stony expression concealed sudden violent emotions, making many followers wary. He was the spawn of that hostile arid wilderness, the Southwest plains, where all forms of life killed to survive. His faith lay in his weapons, and his scarred body was testimony to the ceaseless fighting and marauding that was life for warriors of Nerm. He had only one passion that matched his hatred of *tejanos*, and this one carried equal risks. It was Blue Hawk, wife of the aging chief, Rising Buffalo, a strange, strong-willed woman, whose light skin betrayed her strain of white blood. She aroused emotions in him that were leading to trouble, but like his hatred of *tejanos*, it was not a thing he could control, especially since in her tall stately way she had signaled, after his last raid, her robe lay open for such a dauntless war leader.

As his war party arrived, a frowning camp caller was making his way about with words that were spreading tension over the encampment. Drums were beginning to sound, and here and there a medicine man softly lowered his chant. Hears-the-Wolf noticed braves, aware of why the council was being called, grunting with irritation. There were whispers of three chieftains returning from a peace-seeking talk at San Antonio, when everyone knew the Penateka, the most powerful of the southern Comanches, had no need of peace, especially with the hated *tejanos*. Some, coming forward slowly, glared mutely into the fire as young boys throwing brush on the flames built a roaring blaze in the camp's center. A large party led by Black Tail, just returning from Mexico, laden with booty and slaves, stood apart. They had been preparing for a victory dance, followed by feasting, and here they found their chiefs calling a council to talk of peace. Was there wisdom in this thing?

There were many white captives in the camp, mostly women and teenage girls, their bodies showing long abuse by the braves, their haggard features long enslavement by the squaws. There were several small children, ritually adopted into families to be raised as Comanches. The camp, like most Comanche camps, was a war camp, the terror its warriors were inflicting on nearby settlements hanging in the air. Half-decayed heads were left impaled on spears before painted tepees, surrounded with freshly taken scalps stretched out to dry. Cackling squaws squatted proudly among these trophies as they cooked at smoky fires and scolded thieving camp dogs. Yet they were the mighty Nerm, the real People, fiercely proud, arrogant, ever defiant horsemen, nomads from the far mountains who had come to rule the southern plains.

Hears-the-Wolf approached his longtime friend, Black Tail, whose dark looks revealed how distasteful he found this council where the chiefs were already settling. The war leader, though already feeling the rage any talk of peace with *tejanos* incited in him, was still careful his words reached Black Tail alone. "Peace!" he snarled in a half whisper. "The *tejanos* will give us the same peace hungry wolves give the crippled calf!"

Black Tail nodded in agreement. "It is Spirit Talker, *Muk-wah-rah*, who tells them much is to be gained. He is the one who had us smoke with the whites two summers ago, when the treaty of false promises was offered. Now he asks us to smoke with them again."

Hears-the-Wolf shook his head. "Our chiefs cannot save our winter camps. They think another season of foolish talk will protect them, a thing only our war hatchets can do! Hear my words. Our chiefs are wrong; hope clouds their eyes and blinds them to the treachery that follows the whites like a shadow." Looking up at the darkening sky, he grunted with vexation. "Like the snake that lets the rabbit feed nearby until it loses all fear of it, they will sit and smoke with those *tejanos* once too often."

Ranger Captain Henry Karnes stood on the corner of San Antonio's Main Plaza and Market Street and watched the three Comanche warriors ride away. Even the sight of them revived a long-standing bitterness in his heart. He would have welcomed a chance to jail them, hold them as hostages for the white captives enduring a shameful existence in their camps. Young girls and women particularly disturbed him. That these filthy foul-smelling savages abducted and violated helpless white females rankled him, as it did every Anglo Texan male. Children were a special source of fury. When they were not killed, they were adopted into far-ranging tribes, and few ever saw their devastated parents again. Karnes knew a day of reckoning had to come. For his part, it couldn't come soon enough.

But these three messengers posed a problem. They said their chiefs wanted peace and would attend truce talks if the *tejanos* were willing. Karnes, a redhead known for blunt talk, immediately saw this as a sign the Ranger forays against Indian winter quarters were taking their toll. The avenging Rangers had surprised and destroyed more than one camp. There would be no peace talks, he declared, until all white captives were returned. But it was known there were well over two hundred captives in Comanche hands. It would not be a simple undertaking, for Karnes made it clear he wanted them all. The braves whispered together, then, staring back at him, agreed to bring as many as they could, the rest to be sent for. They promised to return with their chiefs in twenty days.

Karnes had absolutely no faith in Comanche promises, but such an offer had to be reported to his superiors. He wrote to Albert Sidney Johnston, Texas secretary of war, a man who shared his repugnance and skepticism about Indians in general and Comanches in particular. With typical candor Karnes stated the three braves avoided his jail, if not worse, only because three hostages were not enough to force Comanche compliance. But if a delegation of chiefs was coming, he wanted enough troops on hand to ensure "cooperation."

As he wrote, word came in about a murder raid along the banks of the Guadalupe. Five minutes after he had laid down his pen, he was mounted and leading his

Ranger troop eastward. With every raid in sparsely populated West Texas, a man had to wonder whether he had
lost kith or kin. Though it was nearly sixty miles away,
he knew the country well. His thoughts went immediately to the Chauncy family, Pete Spevy, and those Holister brothers. Surely they had all got to the mission in
time. Together they should have been able to stand off
a fair-sized war party. But even as he rode, he knew this
wasn't true. The Sutter youth, who alerted a mail carrier
to hurry word to San Antonio, reported shots were being
fired at the Holister farm as he passed. Apparently there
were Comanches who weren't yet ready to treat for
peace.

When Jess Bishop returned from a scout to report the
Indian raid was over, Jody and Libby, the young couple
seeking refuge in his home, thanked him and continued
on their way to Gonzales. Old Jess heard the Holister
place had been wiped out but didn't have the heart to
tell these frightened youngsters headed there. That job
fell to Karnes, who, finding the Indian tracks breaking
up into single trails, making pursuit impossible, turned
to burying bodies and getting the names of citizens who
were wounded or abducted. It was a scene he had witnessed before, and confirmed his long suspicion of Comanche barbarity and bad faith.

He stood by their wagon looking up, his weathered
face concealing emotions he knew wouldn't help. If
these young people were going to live in this country,
they had better learn its perils, its hardships, its sacrifices. He saw no point in extending sympathy; in West
Texas you had to learn to get along without it.

Jody looked at him in disbelief. "You mean they're
all dead?"

" 'Fraid so. Sorry."

Jody could only gasp, "Why?"

"Because they figured to fight for their farm rather

than run for the mission. Spevy says they were warned in time.''

"My God!'' sighed Jody. Libby looked at him, lines of fear and uncertainty gathering about her eyes. She felt herself getting ill.

"How do I get to the farm?'' asked Jody, manfully trying to mask his shock and confusion.

Karnes gave him directions. ''There's not much left,'' he said somewhat more softly, his eyes now on Libby, who he finally noticed was pregnant. ''You might have to live in the wagon for a spell. If the weather turns poor, you'd best get back to town.''

Jody thanked him and urged the team on. As they pulled away, Libby buried her head in her hands and wept. They rode the four miles in almost complete silence till they came upon the farm site with its black patches where the few structures had stood, and the freshly turned earth where three badly burned bodies had been buried.

Lieutenant Colonel Fisher of the Texas Army, a veteran Indian fighter, studied the highly classified dispatch from Secretary of War Johnston in silence, then, folding it slowly, rubbed his lean jaw and stared at the surface of his desk. In spite of its careful wording, he had more than an inkling of what it meant. He didn't like it. He had dealt with Comanches many times before. They weren't sheep; he could hardly think of a more dangerous bunch to play false with. If he were called upon to disarm and detain seasoned warriors, which most Comanche chiefs were, his troops would have to carry live ammunition. He smiled cynically at Johnston's suggestion that he take three full companies; there was to be no doubt, if trouble came, who would be holding the big baton. He sighed, weighing the possible outcome of this hazardous situation, which ignored the fact that the Comanches were still a formidable force on the plains. To arouse their anger beyond its already smoldering point meant more trouble for lonely white settlements, spread over thousands of square miles of territory, well beyond the army's power to patrol, let alone protect.

But Fisher was a soldier, paid to fight, not think.

Dutifully he called in his adjutant and, showing him the dispatch, ordered him to prepare three companies of the First Regiment to march to San Antonio.

The adjutant nodded and asked quietly, "For how long, sir?"

"For as long as it takes this risky business to work . . . or until we find ourselves in the biggest God-damn Indian mess since Tippecanoe."

That first frightening night Jody and Libby slept in their wagon. Jody, at twenty-two, was a well-built six-footer who could swing an ax or handle a squirrel rifle with the precision that comes only with mountain training. But at first glance the job of rebuilding his dead father's farm seemed, if not beyond his strength, beyond his building skills. Libby could not help sobbing off and on throughout the long bitter night. Jody, comforting her, had to keep reminding himself she was only seventeen and faced not only with this barren earth, marked with death and desolation, but the knowledge that her first child was about to enter life in this terrifying wilderness.

Well before dawn he built a fire and was preparing some coffee, but just before sunup he heard hoofbeats. Taking the rifle from the wagon scabbard, he waited till two riders took shape from out of the gloom. They jumped down to shake his hand and introduce themselves. They were his two closest neighbors, Race and Dale Sutter, powerfully built men with handshakes to match. "Came by to give a hand," said Race. "Have some lumber over t'home if you're anyways needin'."

Jody thought of waking Libby up and telling her they weren't as alone as they thought, but before he could climb into the wagon, he heard more hoofbeats. It was

Pete Spevy returning Blackie. Jody could see in the meager light that the horse had a pack on its back holding several tools. It was clear these men had agreed to meet here, for before he could finish the coffee, Jess Bishop arrived. He brought a team of horses and news that Buck Chauncy would have come, but, upon hearing a new treaty being talked about, which carried the hope the Comanches might return their children, he and his stricken wife, Maude, had traveled with their youngest son, Lucas, to San Antonio.

But by then Libby didn't need to be awakened. She heard the strange voices outside and quickly gathered they were friendly. Somehow it helped her muster the strength to pull herself together. She tensely washed her face in the little pot of water Jody had left for her. These were surely her new neighbors, and Jody would want her to make a good impression. She heard talk of pulling away the burnt remnants of the house and knew they had come to help. That lifted her spirits a little. She listened for female voices but heard none. Oh well, they were bound to come. Her mother had trained her to feed men who came to work on her father's farm, and she began to wonder where she might get some food. She had nothing to offer these kind folks, coming with their offers of help at this early hour.

Making sure everyone had coffee, Jody started calling out to her, finally pulling the canvas back and reaching in with a few whispered words and gestures to help her down. Feeling her pregnant stomach had grown larger overnight, she awkwardly lowered herself on the tailgate and, trying to smile, allowed herself to be lifted to the ground. The hard-fisted men standing about in the still meager light immediately whipped off their hats and make little bows.

"Mighty pleased to meet you, ma'am" and "Pleasure to make yer acquaintance" rolled by her ears without knowing which one said what. Jody went over their names, but she was too shy to remember any except Jess

Bishop's, whom she had met the day before. Jess could
see she was feeling strange standing in the near darkness
with so many unfamiliar males about and said, "Best
tell you, Libby, Becky should be along after
chores . . . plans to bring some food." Suddenly the
grimness of the situation dissolved a little at this spark
of warmth.

"So does my sister, Kate," drawled Race Sutter.
"You folks needn't worry for a spell; we're all used to
helping one another round here."

Curiously, Libby didn't feel strange anymore. Suddenly she knew from the look on Jody's face that his
hopes for a home here, kindled by offerings of friendship
from these emerging faces about her, had risen in the
last few minutes. She could have cried with relief but
knew that might embarrass Jody. He would want his
neighbors to think well of his wife, think she was a
strong woman, a match for this raw, threatening country.

After they had all gulped down hot coffee, they turned
to the work. Race Sutter and Jess Bishop both agreed
they should clear the well and start the house around it.
With the help of the team, they soon had it cleared. Dale
Sutter, who wanted to be a surveyor, began to pace off
dimensions suitable for a small house. Libby got interested when she heard them talking about a bedroom and
a stone fireplace. Everyone came up with ideas except
Pete Spevy, who seemed oddly silent. In time he drifted
off to start clearing the barn, his mind unable to escape
the memory of Matt, Kyle, and old Josiah, standing on
this very ground the year before, eagerly planning a
home. Those few pathetic structures had cost them their
lives. Old-timers like himself knew this country was far
from settled. What might this house now being planned
cost that young couple trying to smile bravely into the
dawn?

Chapter 3

THE COUNCIL LASTED well into the night, with many chiefs speaking, and most in the end, like Iron Eagle, the tribal leader, opting for peace. Though none chose to voice it, all knew the deadly winter attacks were taking their toll. Women and children were dying; the Nerm needed time to deal with this new weapon the Rangers were using from horseback, a gun firing many times without reloading. The days when the whites were easily outmaneuvered and forced to run or fight from cover were over. The ones called Rangers, the ''killer ones,'' were coming during the winter moons. Guided by Apache or Tonkawa scouts, they assaulted small unwary camps, sparing no one. Last season Hears-the-Wolf's mother and sisters had been cut down without mercy, as were many Indian children too young to escape into the brush.

Hears-the-Wolf remained fiercely against any talk of peace. His granite face darkened with fury as he rose to speak. ''Are we fools that we listen to a tongue that is the mother of all lies, that we take the hand of men who with every sun steal more of our hunting grounds, plowing up the earth where our fathers sleep? Are you giving them this truce so they can travel freely through our lands, killing our buffalo, driving their great wagons that scare the antelope, the deer, even the birds that warn our people in times of danger? Are you opening our lodge flaps to cowards who have murdered our old ones, our weak ones? I say if you give these *tejanos* peace, you are only giving them time for more treachery, more betrayals, more shameful defeats for the Nerm. Our answer should be all-out war, slaying them as they slay us, burning their dwellings and destroying their crops. There will be no peace until their scalps line our tepees and their wagons have all been turned back to where the sun rises!''

There were a few wild shouts of agreement from the warriors, but the solemn chiefs continued to suck their pipes and study the fire in silence. Brave talk did not remove the growing threat to their hard-pressed winter camps. The Nerm were numerous but, like all nomads, had to hunt in small groups, particularly when game was scarce. Cold-weather camps were usually strung out along a river or a stream, within riding distance of each other but poorly arranged for defense.

Black Tail, knowing Hears-the-Wolf could not stand alone, was getting ready to rise, for he, too, was against this peace. But in his heart he knew the chiefs, urged on by the sly *Muk-wah-rah* and seriously troubled by events, were inclining toward the truce. Like Hears-the-Wolf, he carried a deep hatred of the *tejanos*, but unlike the famous war leader, he knew raids, which killed only a handful of settlers, would not stop the wave of whites breaking across their buffalo plains from the east. But as he waited for the council to settle again, for the defiant words of Hears-the-Wolf hung like arid smoke in the air, he sensed the presence of a dim figure standing in the shadows behind the chiefs. Strangely, without looking, he knew it was the tall-walking Blue Hawk, wife of Rising Buffalo, a woman many men desired and not a few women regarded with envy and perhaps suspicion. She had been standing listening to Hears-the-Wolf, her expression containing something beyond interest. It made Black Tail uncomfortable. He had heard rumors. Hears-the-Wolf was a powerful and highly respected war leader, but one with a reputation for taking what he wanted, including squaws who belonged to others. Yet old Rising Buffalo was sitting across the fire next to Iron Eagle, and old as he was, he was still a man of enormous power and many important friends. Black Tail lowered his eyes, frowning with concern. Was his good friend, *Isi-man-ica*, whose awesome reputation had drawn many comely squaws to his blanket, now reaching for one too many?

Buck Chauncy saw his wife, Maude, coming toward him, her eyes swollen and heavy with that dull inflamed redness that comes from days of weeping. He wanted to comfort her, but there was little he could say. The passing days made it clear Tad and Liza were really gone. His mind at first, refusing to accept it, kept going back, like a recurring nightmare, to that moment when, returning from Gonzales with Maude and little Lucas, he spotted smoke over his farm. In panic he had rushed the wagon forward to find the barn and smokehouse in ashes and their two older children missing. Their house, because of its stone and adobe walls and heavy rains that day, had not continued to burn and could be repaired. But Maude began to rant frantically as they made their way to the mission, the shock of losing her children already threatening her sanity. Nothing else mattered. The barn, the smokehouse, the entire farm, could be replaced; their children couldn't. Buck never told her he was secretly frozen with fear he would find their dead bodies, scalped or charred by fire. That he hadn't left hope they were still alive, a hope that even brightened when Karnes told them there was talk of a peace treaty, with Comanches agreeing to return all captives.

But poor Maude was inconsolable; at night she sat at the edge of the bed wringing her hands. "Buck, I can't live without my children . . . Why doesn't God help us? . . . Make them bring my Liza back . . . little Tad." She buried her head in the rumpled bedclothes and tear-soaked pillows at each new outburst.

His own heart was too heavy to make comforting her easy. "God is a-watchin' over them," he murmured quietly, thankful she couldn't see the lack of conviction in his eyes.

Poor Maude had always been a tense, nervous woman, clutching to others when trouble threatened. Anxious to be a dutiful wife, she had followed her husband, with his hopes for a bright future, to the Texas frontier. She had tried to adjust to life here, but in her heart she hated it, hated its ceaseless hardships, its changeable, often violent weather, its endless mud. Above all she hated its pall of fear. And now her children were gone, gone in a living death that was too much for a mind all too ready to retreat from reality. Buck spent night after night holding her, reassuring her, helping to sustain a lingering hold on her sanity. All farm work was at a standstill. In some deep way even life itself had been suspended until those promised peace talks, their only hope, came about.

Blue Hawk, holding a blanket about her, watched the council from the shadow of a shield rack rising behind the chiefs. As the night progressed, she wondered at this long talking about a matter that spoke plainly for itself. The Nerm needed peace, needed it more than the hated *tejanos*. As a woman, she dared not speak, but the somber faces along the long line of squatting chiefs betrayed a growing concern over losses many feared the tribe, large as it was, could not make up.

Tall, made striking by a lighter skin and a strange violet tint in her eyes that marked her strain of white blood, Blue Hawk was the envy of many women, secretly annoyed at how men's eyes followed her about the camp. That she was the wife of old Rising Buffalo should have removed her as a threat, but Blue Hawk did not have a married squaw's usual restraints, burdensome care of a lodge or the taboo against returning other men's glances. She lived with her aged husband and his two younger brothers, along with their many wives. Even without slaves, there were plenty of hands to deal with the work, and her attentions went to her two children. But Blue Hawk, in spite of her seeming wisdom, was fast courting trouble in an already agitated and divided camp. She was a fiercely proud, plucky, if deeply sensuous woman, who had endured the frustrations of a docile, dutiful squaw long enough.

Rising Buffalo, once a powerful warrior, was a very old man. The magic muscle between his legs had long since shriveled up and lay limp under his robe. He was like an aged bull no longer aroused by the mating call of cows. Often he reminded her of a grandfather buffalo, gaunt with age, standing with its legs braced on the prairie waiting for death. Under Comanche custom, brothers shared wives, and sleeping with his had led to the birth of two children. But his brothers were weak men, loud-talking parasites enjoying the power and largesse Rising Buffalo's reputation brought them. Secretly she held them in contempt. Long resentment of her lot had brought firmness to a desperate and dangerous decision. Unashamed of her healthy female lust, she had searched for a man worthy to share and return it. With that ingrained sense by which women register the strength and vibrancy of men's masculinity, she had chosen Hears-the-Wolf, who now, standing tall and defiant before the council, once again awakened that tingling sensation that swelled warmly between her thighs.

San Antonio had been the loneliest and most perilous outpost of the Southwest for over a hundred years. It was desperately isolated, difficult to protect, and under frequent attack. Catholic Spain struggled but failed to maintain vestiges of Christianity in its surrounding wastes, dry arid plains populated by warlike nomads bent on murder and plunder. With the coming of the Anglos, defense of this hazardous bastion might have fallen to a veteran commander, one tutored by military training and seasoned in frontier campaigns. But it fell to a slim, slightly built young man, only five foot ten and weighing only a hundred sixty pounds. This soft-spoken Tennessean, with a full forehead crowned with jet black hair over flashing dark eyes, was named Jack Coffee Hays. He was appointed to replace Karnes, who had been drawn back to Louisiana by a family death. His choice was no accident. Hays's reputation was well established. More than once he had succeeded in turning and successfully attacking Comanche bands who had his small troop not only outnumbered but caught in situations dangerous beyond belief. He was a natural leader; men twice his size and known for their truculent natures obeyed him without question. Even a few Comanche chiefs had begun to think of him as an evil spirit they'd rather not fight.

Most Ranger captains were quiet taciturn men, learning their job in the saddle and having little use for military protocol. Hays had expected the hard-pressed Comanches to sue for peace, but this demand for the return of all captives, he knew would be a tricky business. Captives did not belong to tribes but to individual warriors. Getting them to surrender females serving as slaves or young children already adopted into families was no simple matter. Word of troops marching into San Antonio quickly raised his eyebrows. Was the government hoping to achieve this by force?

Hays, long convinced their bloody winter campaigns of extinction would finally defeat the Comanches, had been keeping his eyes on the Rio Grande. To his thinking, Mexico still loomed as the major threat to the young republic. San Antonio was still largely a Mexican town of questionable loyalty, its adobe walls difficult to defend against organized troops armed with artillery.

He was glad Matt Caldwell, another Ranger captain with a reputation for killing Indians whenever and wherever he found them, had just struck town. Now he sighted Matt standing at the door of the Rangers' favorite saloon, signaling him in. Because of his messily streaked beard and mottled complexion, Caldwell had won himself the nickname "Old Paint."

Hays, crossing the planked sidewalk to join him, said quietly as they shook hands, "Guess you've heard they're promising to bring in all their captives."

Caldwell sent a long stream of tobacco juice toward the street. "Comanches promising to do somethin' always reminds me of a drunken whore promisin' to be true," he answered. "Come, have a drink. With what I'm fixin' to tell you, you'll likely need it."

The council lasted far into the night, but the watching Blue Hawk could see those choosing peace were winning. Yet it was clear the growing bitterness of the debate was worrying Iron Eagle. He did not like dissension or bitter feelings in the camp. He rose now, gathering his robe about him. "The night is growing weary of our talk," he began, looking over at the grim Hears-the-Wolf. "More words will not join our hearts; now we must decide and our people must move as one. Those who choose this peace will remain here in council; those who do not must walk away. Let a pipe be filled and smoked while you decide. I, Iron Eagle, have spoken." The great medicine pipe was lit and passed around. When it was finally put down, only four warriors, the fuming Hears-the-Wolf and Black Tail among them, had sullenly walked away.

Many gathered at the council were ready to return to their lodges, but Iron Eagle knew an equally thorny issue still faced them. Wisdom led him to place it before them now so that by the next council they would have time to consider and perhaps resign themselves to the price of peace. "We have told the *tejanos* we will bring all their people we have captured to the peace talks," he said, measuring his words and glancing at faces that visibly tightened and darkened under his eyes, *"Muk-wah-rah* will tell us of the many good things they will offer us in return."

There was an ominous silence, but Iron Eagle quickly threw a handful of medicine grass upon the fire to signal the council was over. Then, followed by several chiefs, he strode away to his lodge.

Later that night Hears-the-Wolf found Blue Hawk coming toward him in the darkness. Both knew these nocturnal trysts were fraught with danger, but Blue Hawk was hoping it would not always be so. In the wickiup she had prepared beyond the outskirts of camp, they made abandoned, often frenzied love, until, exhausted, they sank together in the blanket she had spirited from her lodge. It was only their third wild secret mating, but it left them knowing whatever risks they were running, there was no longer a choice; a deep drug-like need of each other's flesh could no longer be denied.

Chapter 4

IT WAS ONLY a few days before the little house began to take form. Jody and Libby were kept too busy to mourn the loss that still slipped in like the tip of an icy tentacle to touch their hearts every time they glanced at the little crosses, sitting on a rise toward the river. Becky Bishop, whose broad shoulders and firm bosom easily filled her husband, Jesse's, shirts, put it plainly one night at mealtime. ''Don't pay to get to fussin' about what's done and can't be changed. No matter how bad things get out here, a buddy ain't got but two choices, die or go on.'' Libby was feeling overwrought, her body weary from trying to help the men with her baby only a week or two away.

Kate Sutter, with her trim figure and cluster of blond curls, was stirring a great pot of soup. ''When my ma first came out here,'' she exclaimed, ''she swore she'd at last found out where the Devil lived, but by God, if that critter could live here, she could too.''

Libby couldn't help feeling the quiet strength of these women, the faith with which they followed their venturous men, the fortitude that dissolved fears she herself

.. about the future. Could she ever match it? Though she knew boys had always found her pretty, she was still just a simple farm girl, used to hard work and the warmth of a large family in a household where love and good cooking abounded. She had been secretly homesick for some time, torn between telling Jody how miserable she was or just weeping in silence. Now sitting here, watching the grove of pale green trees beyond the river, and hearing the wind sighing high above the rude plank structure that was to be her home, she felt the first faint stirrings of a desire to be one of these plucky females, to be a "Texian," as they called themselves. She decided these women must never be allowed to know the anxieties that continually made her clutch her breast or cause her breath to come in little uneven starts. For her husband, Jody's, sake she must earn and keep their neighbors' respect, she must deserve and return their offers of friendship and strive to take up their confident ways.

She had heard the Chauncy children were missing, that the parents had gone to San Antonio in hopes of getting them back. Strangely enough, neither Becky nor Kate mentioned it, and when she brought it up, Becky simply said, " 'Taint a subject for easy talkin'. If poor Maude doesn't fetch her young 'uns back from San Antonio, Lord knows what we'll do . . . She's never had a right good hold on things."

Kate sighed. "Buck shouldn't have ever brought her out here . . . Woman never seemed at peace with these parts. Reckon she'll be wanting back east again if they ever find Liza and Tad."

"Reckon," answered Becky, but her tone dismissed the subject.

Suddenly Kate was saying, "When we get you folks set up, with a roof over your heads and all, we just got to have us a gathering." She chuckled to herself. "Race and Dale sure love to swing girls off the floor at a good hoedown. Libby, you won't believe the wild times we've had here.''

Now Becky laughed as though she were remembering some particularly joyous night. "If we can get Marylou to bring her fiddle and Pete Spevy to play that banjo, we'll surely get some of our bowlegged men up to dance.''

Both women laughed heartily, and Libby, feeling the baby kicking playfully, found herself managing a smile.

Liza and Tad Chauncy were two woefully frightened children. Liza hugged her brother and whispered quietly not to cry. After two days of travel, instinct told this scared yet watchful young girl they were not going to die. These fierce-looking people, now brusquely ignoring them, had something else in mind. When she and Tad were given food and left alone in a lodge, she decided from the looks and gestures that greeted them as they arrived in camp that little pity could be expected here. She had already noticed while traveling that crying or other signs of their suffering only annoyed the braves.

Though they could see nothing, they knew a council was being held, for loud voices were heard and many rumblings of discontent were reaching their ears. They were also reaching the ears of two other children, who sat in a large decorated lodge closer to the camp center. They were a girl of five and a boy of four whose names were Blossom and Bright Arrow. They belonged to Blue Hawk, and she was sitting with her arms around them as they stared through the lodge flap at the noisy gathering beyond.

The question of which captives should be given up for the coming peace talks was being argued, and Iron Eagle's fears were proving well founded. At first not one captive was offered for surrender, and the chief, becoming angry, pointed out there would be no peace if the *tejanos*' demands were not met, at least in part, while *Muk-wah-rah*, slapping his immense stomach, kept re-

minding them important presents were sure to be
received in return. After hours of wrangling, the council
broke up, with Iron Eagle saying at least one captive
must be supplied by sundown, and *Muk-wah-rah* adding
that a single captive was needed to begin negotiations.
After the tribe saw what presents were being offered in
return, they could start bargaining for their other captives, one by one, raising their demands each time.

It was a strange day with storms building in the west
and a high wind herding dark clouds across the sky.
Hears-the-Wolf, still secretly furious at the council's decision, wanted to leave camp again, taking the silent,
embittered Black Tail with him. But he was torn by in-
decision. He could not believe Blue Hawk's assurances
that Rising Buffalo's pride alone had to be assuaged,
that the old chief no longer wanted her under his robe.
All his possessions were not enough to barter for her,
and any offer, especially if refused, would make known
their secret and the whole camp would be aware and
watching.

But at that very moment Blue Hawk, silently dealing
with her own fears, was hoping he would move and
move quickly. Time was running out. She could tell
from the sly yet sharp looks thrown at her by other wives
in the lodge that suspicions were mounting; soon mali-
cious whispers would be reaching the ears of Rising
Buffalo. Adulterous women were punished by disfigure-
ment among the Nerm. Blue Hawk's fine features would
be slashed and cut until her once-striking and attractive
face was a horror of scar tissue. Yet, sitting with her
children and holding them close, she had a fear even
greater than that. Her sensual nature extended beyond
her need for a virile mate; she dearly loved her children
and embraced them often. Unlike most mothers of the
Nerm, she was not anxious for her little ones to be
taught, at an early age, the endless rigors of Comanche
life: Bright Arrow the brutal fighting skills of a warrior,
Blossom the taxing and near oppressive duties of the

lodge. She had long decided this desire for a man worthy of her must not separate her from her children. Secretly she was counting on Rising Buffalo's stoic indifference to offspring he knew were not his own to keep them hers.

Hears-the-Wolf entered Black Tail's lodge as the threatening storm finally broke. "The Penateka have learned to sit and talk rather than fight," he muttered, his head inclining to where the council was breaking up at the sudden downpour.

"The chiefs need captives to take to the peace parley," said Black Tail sourly.

"They will not get mine."

Black Tail looked at him peculiarly. "My friend, there are captives no warrior would willingly give up, just as there are squaws no man of power surrenders."

Hears-the-Wolf knew he was referring to Blue Hawk and sat in silence for a moment, the gray wrinkled face of Rising Buffalo hanging like a specter between them. "I am not afraid of his power," he muttered. "There are warriors who will stand with me in this thing."

Black Tail looked at him, slowly shaking his head. Would this brave, daring, near fearless man ever learn that power could not resolve every human problem? There were other forces at work. "Do not waste time worrying about his power; it is not what makes this folly dangerous."

"What then?"

"He is a chief who has been long honored by our people. He must keep the respect of other chiefs or lose his place at the council. Beware of his pride; it is a much more subtle and difficult thing to deal with than power."

Hears-the-Wolf looked down and fixed his gaze on the pipe Black Tail had started to fill. Could Blue Hawk be right? Could the old chief be more concerned about his dignity than an impassioned wife he could no longer enjoy? But the issue was fraught with trouble, danger,

and the possible wrath of many. He took the pipe from
Black Tail and puffed on it, staring at his friend as the
storm pounded against the lodge skins, and the wind
drove in an ominous whine through the smoke hole
above.

Sixteen-year-old Matilda Lockhart, being led before
the council, quickly realized she had been chosen to be
returned to her people. Yet in her misery she hardly
cared. Two years of captivity had been a nightmare of
torment and torture. Her body was now scarred and dis-
colored from brutal handling, her face hideous from cuts
and burns. The thought of being restored to civilization
was tempered by shame at her appearance and the memory of sexual abuses too degrading to describe. But Matilda was to prove a surprisingly intelligent girl. Like few
other captives, she had mastered much of the Comanche
tongue. She knew there were thirteen other captives in
the camp, and she had heard how the chiefs planned to
barter them to the whites. She also heard a Mexican boy,
whose owner was killed in a recent raid and whom no
one else wanted, was to be sent along with her. Oddly
enough, this youth, thinking that he had been safely
adopted into the tribe, was the only captive who did not
wish to go.

The violent storm had cleared in time for a sacred
ritual to be held. By sundown a medicine man was leading the warriors in a dance, chanting medicine words to
draw favor from the spirits. With the drums beating rapidly and their feet pounding the earth, the braves began
shouting, echoing the magic words. Many of them
sported great horned headdresses, with fox tails tied to
their arms and legs and little hawk bells fixed to their
knees and ankles. The medicine man kept chanting, calling for powerful medicine that would keep the tribe
strong and its peace party successful. The dance ended
with a long thrilling cry, joined by the entire encampment, with all arms extended upward toward the setting

sun, now disappearing behind a brilliant canvas of lavender and orange. A final flurry of drums ended with a deep silence as warriors made their way back to their tepees.

With darkness the great camp was finally hushed, but in the lodge of Rising Buffalo the old chief was quietly glaring at the near naked body of Blue Hawk, self-consciously tying her braids and settling her children to sleep. A strange air had claimed the lodge that evening. The other squaws were keeping their eyes down, their usual chatter curiously muted. The old chief's normally stern but composed features had visibly tightened around the mouth and eyes, and though he uttered no words, under his blanket his hand had found and was idly clutching the handle of his knife.

Chapter 5

ON THE VERY morning the house was finished, Libby went to the Sutters to have her baby. A widow everyone called Marylou acted as midwife. Kate comforted her by holding her hands while the contractions mounted, and bathing her face with cool water from the well until, with a final scream and hard pressing on Libby's part, the baby arrived. It was a fine-looking boy, and Jody coming in to see his new son wanted to name him Matthew, after his grandfather, but Libby only smiled. She had a name she had liked since childhood, Lance, for it reminded her of a picture in her mother's old but treasured storybook of a brave and romantic knight called Sir Lancelot. So the baby would be christened Lance Holister, and Libby took her son into her new home and, settling him on some blankets and pillows from the wagon, threw herself into Jody's arms and wept for joy.

Later, when Jody went with the other men to work on the barn, she took out the square mirror they had carried from Missouri and placed it with its thin iron frame against the wall. She took off her clothes and looked at her body. Her breasts, filling with milk, were

34

now very prominent. Her stomach was down, but her hips seemed rounder and fuller. She was a mother now and would soon be eighteen. If only her own mother could see her, but Missouri was many miles and many years away. She would write her family and describe the baby; that would surely help. Comforted by the thought, she lifted her tiny son and hugged him in sudden ecstasy. Ah, motherhood was surely exciting. It was a joy just to be alive.

In San Antonio the days had turned clear with winds from the Pecos range turning soft and a scent of sage bringing the first hint of spring. Though little was officially known, tensions were growing in the winding clay streets and weathered stone plazas of the old settlement. Word that the Comanches were coming for a peace parley had spread to the surrounding countryside. Soldiers had been noticed marching into town. Government and military men of high rank, the Texas adjutant general, the acting secretary of war, and Lieutenant Colonel Fisher, were there, reported to be commissioners preparing to present the government's terms to a great assemblage of Penateka chiefs. Yet many who heard these terms responded with wiry smiles. Such terms had been offered before. *Comanches to stay behind prescribed boundaries, never to enter white settlements again.* All such terms had been arrogantly, even disdainfully, ignored. But now these truce talks promised something different. It was rumored the Comanches had agreed to bring in all white captives, a merciful deliverance for which hundreds of grieving families throughout the Lone Star Republic had prayed.

Ranger captains were steadily appearing, saying little but meeting quietly with Colonel Fisher. Every one of Karnes's proposals was being carried out, but there was a growing concern about the government's intent. The Comanches were a testy and touchy bunch. The visible presence of so many troops was itself of questionable wisdom. Hays and Caldwell could not agree with government bureaucrats who felt the issue was simply a matter of Anglo Texan jurisprudence. In Texas, as in all western-style nations, rules of law were territorial. Comanches on Texas soil had to obey Texas laws. Indians were brazenly committing crimes for which whites would be summarily hung. Swayed by such reasoning, many new to the frontier did not feel murdering savages, who deserve to be convicts if not facing a gallows, were entitled to honorable treatment. But experienced Indian fighters knew this notion was a blunt invitation to disaster.

Still excitement continued to grow as the warming days slipped by until runners finally arrived, announcing the chiefs were approaching. Scouts, sent out to report the makeup of the party, came back saying over sixty were coming, some of them warriors but all heavily decorated, even the squaws and children. A few read this as a sign the Comanches truly wanted peace, but the watchful Ranger captains weren't so sure. They cautioned Fisher against taking anything for granted. "Comanches ain't like normal folks," they advised warily. "Whenever they tell you they're speaking from the heart, likely they're eyeing your scalp."

The one-story limestone house in which they were to meet had been used for years as a courthouse and sat next to the town jail. It had been cleared to make room for the many chiefs to squat on their blankets and the commissioners to sit on low stools. The escorting Indians were to camp just beyond, close to the river.

It was a memorable sight, this arrival of no fewer than twelve Comanche chiefs. It was an event that would be remembered, sadly or bitterly by many. Chief after chief paraded by on his favorite warhorse, followed by his wife and children, all decked out in outlandish colors and headgear. They wore either wildly painted buffalo skulls or long strings of feathers that trailed down their horses' backs. A medicine man who led them kept tapping a little drum fixed to his saddle, and the mounts behind him seemed to be keeping step to its beat. Colonel Fisher directed them to their campsite, which the chiefs carefully studied before dismounting. Then, with the aide of an interpreter, who had once been a Comanche captive, a few words of greeting were offered. A welcoming feast had been prepared, but before they fell to eating, Iron Eagle, using *Muk-wah-rah* to interpret, made a short address. In spite of both sides trying to put a cordial face on things, there was little warmth in this meeting. Both parties were still secretly seething over past and all too recent murders, too indelible in their memories to erase.

Muk-rah-wah, sitting with his bald head and big belly, smiled at Texan children, who ran up to take a peek at these ferocious people their parents warned would come if they didn't behave. Though the conference was not slated to begin until the following morning, already Ranger captains were looking on uneasily and frowning at what they saw. Studying the Indian encampment, they saw no sign of white captives, but lost among the squaws, a single girl wrapped in a blanket was noticed, and beside her a Mexican boy who looked with indifference at the many Mexicans who came to smile at him from beneath their wide sombreros.

After long minutes of staring, Hays, standing with Old Paint, muttered, "I don't think it's gonna work."

"Never thought it would," answered Caldwell. "Figured the army was too smart to listen to them anymore."

"From the looks of things, the army has quit listening."

"Well, it's sure time. Come on, Jack, we'd best have a little drink and get some sleep. Don't 'spect tomorrow will be a good day for church."

Hays, hitching his gun belt up, was anxious to get back to his lodging house. "Don't have much of a dry tonight, Matt, but reckon I could use some sleep." With his lips now tight with concern, he threw a parting glance at Caldwell. "See you in the morning."

Caldwell nodded, his eyes still on the Indian camp,
but now wondering which saloon Big Foot Wallace, a
colorful character from Virginia and a veteran Ranger,
had wandered into. Being a sociable man, he wanted
some companionship for his nightly belt of bourbon.

Across the way poor Matilda Lockhart stayed buried
in her blanket. She was keeping it closely wrapped
around her, thanking God she was back with her own
people, but praying as hard as she could He would help
her find a way to hide her disfigured face and scarred
body for the rest of her life.

The startling presence of military troops milling about
town was not wasted on the chiefs. Armed men appearing at peace talks clashed with their notions of a proper
setting for forging friendships, particularly one rising
from years of deception and mutual atrocities. Yet Iron
Eagle and *Muk-wah-rah* refused to be alarmed. The tradition that banned participants in truce talks from re-
sorting to arms was strong, almost sacred. But some
soldiers were noticed standing guard with fixed bayonets, and a few of the chiefs began to wonder.

"Is there not a distant storm sleeping in this unexpected wind?" questioned the hulking Red Crow. He
was drawing a pipe from beneath his blanket, an action
that made it clear he had raised a point deserving to be
smoked over.

Another chief, Shields-the-Squaw, spotted two Ranger
captains standing by and held a cautioning hand to his
mouth to murmur, "Ah, the killer ones are also here;
strange faces walk the path of peace."

There was silence for a few moments. In retrospect
the chiefs were beginning to recall matters that the council in its angry controversy had overlooked. But the raw
facts now rose to be faced, their minds compelled toward
them by some menace in the air. "Were not the whites

promised all our captives in return for these peace talks?'' queried Red Crow.

"Those were our promises of yesterday," muttered Iron Eagle, grimly remembering how difficult it was to get even one captive. His mouth tightened with aggravation, his eyes becoming troubled with this new concern. "We must tell them as we do the squawlike Mexicans, it's the promises the Penateka bring with them today that count."

Shields-the-Squaw shook his head. "It is not good. We should have brought more warriors," he muttered, "or left our weak ones at home."

"Rest your pipe," reassured stout *Muk-wah-rah.* "The *tejanos* must still bargain with us. If not, the Penateka will keep their captives and seize many more."

The others looked at him in silence. There seemed little point in more words, but as the pipe was put down, more than one chief sat wondering if their Spirit Talker had forgotten it was the Penateka who were suing for peace.

It was beginning to feel like home. There were only two small rooms beside the kitchen, but the larger of the two rooms, which she dubbed "the parlor," had a fireplace and a screen door leading out to a tiny porch where Libby rocked her baby and sang to the early morn. Jody was still working on the barn, but it was nearing completion, and the outhouse was finally getting walls so that Libby no longer waited till dark to use it. The bedding, brought in from the wagon to the smaller room, lay across an ancient box spring contributed by the Sutters. It was there that Libby slept, dreamed, nursed her baby, and Jody, full of plans for his son, Lance, and already talking about having more children, made love to her. She had begun to like making love since Jody, during her pregnancy, had become more patient, more tender. But it was all her doing. In the beginning she had not hesitated to pound his long muscular body with her little fists and squeal in his ear when he hurt her. When alone during the day, she fussed with the few pieces of furniture they brought along or Jody hammered together, put up sheets of yellow paper for curtains, looked forward to a gathering planned at the Sutters' to celebrate resurrection of their farm, and took in the waist on one of her pale cotton dresses, making sure her slightly more buxom figure would show and Jody would be proud of her.

In spite of the grim news that seemed to be forever coming from San Antonio, and the saddening thought of the grieving Chauncys, Libby couldn't help feeling this land was filled with promise. Though the Indians were a constant threat, the people, though concerned, were amazingly confident, even buoyant, as though they could easily see approaching years of peace and prosperity. The Lord alone knew what sustained such optimism. The farm work was brutal and unending, the earth only begrudgingly giving up its fruits. Necessities such as candles and soap had to be made by hand. Water away from the rivers was a problem, and livestock was preyed upon by wolves, cougars, bears, and endless bands of coyotes. Snakes, particularly rattlers, were everywhere, and the summer sun hung angrily in the sky, evaporating the last drops of moisture and leaving long stretches of marginal soil parched. Most settlers were subsistence farmers, though a few, like the Sutters, raised horses and a few cattle. Many of the people she met were no longer young, but curiously, she felt this to be a young land, and Libby decided young lands infuse people's spirits with energy and hope. If there was neither leisure nor luxury to ease this life, at least tension and excitement rode every wind. If it was a land where courage was needed to settle, it was also a land where dreams were needed to survive.

By now Kate Sutter and Becky Bishop were close and comforting friends, coming by often in the afternoon, bringing things they had cooked, holding her baby, passing judgment on the clothes she was altering. It was they who told her the Chauncys were still in San Antonio, along with rumors of peace talks under way. Kate also smilingly advised her Ben McCulloch, the local Ranger captain, was coming to the gathering with his brother, Henry, and a new couple, the Munsters, with their strange New England accent, had also promised to attend. Libby could not keep them from treating her like a little sister, but secretly she promised herself, as soon as she was able, she would return these thoughtful visits, bringing some cooking of her own.

On the long-awaited evening of the gathering, she and Jody, like their neighbors, took their baby with them, for since the last raid, and the abduction of Liza and Tad, parents refused to let children out of sight. It was an evening Libby would always remember, for it was there in the midst of merriment she first glimpsed the harsh and secretly bitter heart of the frontier.

Buck Chauncy could get no rest in the boardinghouse he had managed to find for Maude and young Lucas, on a back street off Buena Vista. They had spent several days waiting for the peace talks to begin, and now that the chiefs in all their ceremonial pomp had arrived, he and Maude, like so many others, still saw no sign of their loved ones. Strangers they met, men desperate for wives or children, relatives praying some kin had survived massacres when all bodies could not be accounted for, only depressed them more. Scenes of rage and frustration were becoming as common as tearful scenes of helplessness and despair. One young farmer, whose bride of two months had been swept away in a dawn attack while he searched the brush for stray cattle, kept shaking his fists at heaven. "Those sinful bastards," he roared over and over again. "May God burn them in hell for their wickedness!"

Maude remained inconsolable; only through exhaustion could she collapse into brief spells of sleep. Buck found himself seizing such moments to slip away to preserve his sanity. People in the boardinghouse were quietly avoiding them, not out of rudeness but because nothing one could say could help, and faced with Maude's paralyzing despair, the usual platitudes sounded cant.

The morning the conference started, Buck had watched the chiefs entering the old courthouse. There seemed little to do but wait, grimacing at some of the Indian children who began to play in the street, shooting their little bows and arrows or wrestling one another. In time he strayed back to the boardinghouse to report the parley was on. Himself despondent and almost ill from fatigue, he lay on the bed next to Maude and helplessly fell asleep. It was many hours before he awoke with a frightening start, knowing he was hearing gunshots, rising in a swelling clamor from the direction of the courthouse.

Libby loved to dance and found the Sutter boys, and a lengthy string of shyly bowing young men, vying for her as a partner. Jody had never managed to look graceful in a waltz, his big muscular body looking ungainly beside the willowy sweep of his pretty and now noticeably fetching wife. Dancing was popular on the frontier; it was one of the few joyous outlets for the endless energy required for every day's demanding toil. Almost all the women along with their grown children and most of the men joined in. Waltzes were well liked, but settlers from the tidewater had brought west the Virginia reels, and old-timers had gotten up their own version of a Mexican dance they insisted on calling the fandango. Pete Spevy with his banjo, the widowed Marylou with her violin, and a young man with a foreign instrument called the concertina provided the music. Kate Sutter had the first dance with Ben McCulloch, who was a bachelor and one of the handsomest men there. But he seemed preoccupied; some said it was because of news from San Antonio, which was always bad.

There was plenty of fruit punch to drink, but there must have been two punch bowls, because some men were displaying an intoxication different from the one claiming Libby, who was heady with excitement and secretly pleased at the attention she was getting. She hoped Jody would notice and be proud that his wife was so sought after. She prayed it didn't show, but it was beginning to make her feel a little more assured and relaxed, a little more like Kate Sutter, who was shaking her golden curls loose as she twirled around the dance floor. But it was soon apparent Jody was neither pleased nor proud, having sulkily decided she must be flirting to get that much attention. He sat in the corner frowning at her till she sat down, and from that nettlesome moment on, the evening, so glorious till then, began to change.

Settling demurely beside Jess Bishop, she didn't realize, until he turned to her, that he had been drinking; not only drinking but embroiled in an argument with the Munsters, the couple from New England. Word had gotten around that afternoon that an Indian boy, caught stealing a pig, had been shot and killed by a farmer west of the settlement. The Munsters were appalled at the cruelty of the act, while Jess was arguing that there was no other way to teach thieving heathens to behave.

"Back home we'd a' just taken a switch to him," maintained Nat Munster, "aiming to teach that boy some gospel living."

"You've got plenty to learn 'bout Comanches," said Jess insistently. "The sooner we kill off the lot of them, the sooner this country will be fit to live in."

Nellie Munster lifted her nose slightly. To Libby she looked bookish and likely a women of strong opinions. "From what I hear, you folks have been settling on their land and shooting at them because they resent it."

Jess Bishop was suddenly on his feet and his voice

was rising. People were beginning to turn toward him. Libby wished she had sat somewhere else. "If yer so damned fond of 'em, maybe you better fetch yourself a tepee and squat down beside 'em!"

A vexed and flustered Becky Bishop came rushing up to seize her husband's arm. "Jess, you've been drinking again!" She turned to the Munsters. "Don't pay him no heed; he's upset about the Chauncy children. We're fixin' a prayer meeting for them come Sunday."

Nellie Munster turned to her, her arched eyes signaling she was far from placated. "Where we come from, we don't believe killing is righteous. It's unchristian . . . sinful!"

"Nellie, let it be," said her husband. It was evident Nat Munster was afraid of where this tense and embarrassing situation might lead.

One of the farmers sitting nearby spoke up. "Lady, you'd best see some of these Comanches' doings before you get to settin' up and judging 'em. If there be a snake pit in hell most folks 'round here reckon it would be too good for them."

There were spontaneous murmurs of assent.

Nellie Munster jerked away from her husband, who was trying to take her aside. "When you deal with simple ignorant people . . . shoot their children for stealing pigs . . . what do you expect?"

Ben McCulloch strode over and stopped the argument, firmly sending Jess off, then whispered to Nat and Nellie before nodding to Pete Spevy to start another dance.

Later, he told Jody and Libby the boy was not a Comanche but a Wichita, though few farmers knew the difference. The boy was with his mother, who was hungry and trying to get to her people farther north. Ben had helped her bury his body.

The next time Libby looked around the Munsters were gone, but she soon realized the incident had triggered strong feelings that had been simmering below the party's gaiety. Some people continued laughing and talking, but as the effects of liquor spread their attempts at enjoyment appeared strained, forced. It bewildered her. The dancing no longer seemed exhilarating and she became annoyed by Jody's constant scowling at her from across the floor. In the end a peculiar fear, frightening in its very strangeness, began claiming her. As the evening drew on, more and more angry voices could be heard, more and more faces seemed to turn baneful. She only knew she was experiencing an icy chill as she saw surfacing the deep soul-scarring hatred that obsessed and preyed upon this frontier like a diabolical curse. Libby, her heart jumping, heard an old embittered farmer, whose only daughter had been carried off, standing up to exclaim if he could get the whole damn Comanche nation over his sights, he'd solve all their problems and answer every settler's prayer. The tone of those chiming in, already strident, kept sounding more and more menacing. Incidents wherein Comanches had been cornered and mercilessly killed, even women and children, were brought up to audible grunts and knee slaps of satisfaction. Murders that Comanches had committed against friends and relatives were, in shameless and profane language, sworn to be avenged. The rape of helpless women and seizure of children brought the most vicious and rancorous remarks of all, prompting such terrifying vows of vengeance that Libby had to close her ears and turn to helping Kate clean up. The party wasn't over, it would go on till dawn, but Libby, looking pleadingly at Jody, wanted to go home. She had heard enough about hatred, and the horrors it wrought in the human mind, to keep her for a lifetime.

Chapter 6

THE MEETING OPENED with *Muk-wah-rah* leading the way into the Council House, his heavy body wrapped in a bright red robe, a decorative pipe in his hand and a bold look of confidence on his face. As spokesman, he sat in the middle of the floor; Iron Eagle sat behind him, and the other chiefs formed a semicircle facing the commissioners. The commissioners were already on hand when they arrived. Predictably, the atmosphere was hardly cordial—expressions on both sides were tense, watchful—but the formalities of truce talks were carefully observed. The commissioners, two dressed in uniforms, were well prepared. The Texas adjutant general was seated in the middle, the acting secretary of war was on his right, with Colonel Fisher on his left.

Custom gave the opening speech at truce talks to the host party. Traditionally it was to be a speech of welcome with presents distributed to establish goodwill. But instead of the blandishments usually showered on visiting delegations, the Texas adjutant general's opening speech was a model of brevity. Through the interpreter he thanked the chiefs for coming and said he was looking forward to the meeting's successful conclusion. Then soldier hats, covered with different colored braids, were offered to the chiefs.

There should have been an interlude here, an opportunity for the chiefs to express thanks for the presents and offer a token few of their own. But the adjutant general, an impatient man, did not come to exchange presents, he came to declare terms under which the Penateka could have peace. Mindless of the affront his hurried manner was causing, he brusquely plunged into the government's demands as its price for signing the truce. The interpreter, who had been abducted in his youth and held by the Comanches for many years, actually softened many of the adjutant general's remarks, for no one talked to the Penateka like that, not if they were interested in peace. After a charge that they had not lived up to their promises on previous occasions, a practice often complained about by Mexicans, *Muk-wah-rah* roused himself in anger, defiantly conceding that was true, but this time it would be different.

The government's terms, they had heard many times before. They sat stoically facing the commissioners, saying nothing. Comanches were to stay behind designated borders; entry into or trespassing across settled areas was prohibited. Without explanation, a new one had been added, and it had the chiefs grunting to each other. There was to be no interference with settlers coming into and settling on land not presently in use. The land "not presently in use" was their hunting grounds, their only source of food and very much in use. It was not an auspicious start. The air in the Council House was increasingly charged with tension, and as yet, no mention had been made of white captives.

At the interpreter's suggestion, backed by Fisher's feeling the situation was getting out of hand, it was decided to allow the chiefs time to start responding. It was surely a wise decision. *Muk-wah-rah,* no longer smiling, rose to his feet, his manner almost aggressive. The grave peril that had always hung over this conference was beginning to surface. If the Texans thought to intimidate the Penateka, they had badly misjudged. Comanches were a proud and remarkably self-confident people. The assertive Texans would find they had met their equal in assumptions of superiority, both in fighting ability and audacity. *Muk-wah-rah* complained that many whites were regularly crossing their buffalo range in violation of previous treaties. He called upon the commissioners to deny it. The adjutant general pointed out this was Texas's soil; many traversing it were Texas citizens carrying out official duties. Only the government could prohibit entry into territory under the republic's flag. This had the chiefs staring at each other. Over what lands, *Muk-wah-rah* wanted to know, did Indians have a say about the right of way? The adjutant general began to explain they would have to form a sovereign state, territory that others agreed was exclusively theirs. The chiefs grunted; they had achieved that status long before anyone there could remember.

By midmorning trouble was brewing and Fisher began to insist they get to the captives; the mood of the meeting was growing ugly. He had orders to follow and, as a good soldier, wanted to carry them out. These troubled exchanges were clearly jeopardizing his very reason for coming. The other commissioners, finally aware of the dangerously rising tension, agreed.

Outside, Indian children were playing in the roadway and nearby yard. Some of them were shooting arrows at coins citizens were throwing in the air. From everywhere people came to see the dreaded Comanches who had plagued west Texas for so long and were still far from subdued. Among these onlookers were many like the Chauncys, silently praying they would get their loved ones back. But inside, for another hour, red and white men continued to sit facing each other, neither understanding the life view of the other, neither trusting the other to perform in good faith, neither feeling any peace would last. The fated borderland could not be shared. The cultural gap was too wide, the racial and ethnic hatred too deep, the record too bloodstained. The answer had long been recognized by both sides, and there could be no other. Peace would only come when one or the other was destroyed.

Blue Hawk could not conceal the fear stamped on her face. Rising Buffalo had not taken her to the peace parley, a most dangerous sign. She was left to tend the lodge and had to listen to his other squaws snickering behind her back as they decorated themselves and talked of presents offered at peace parleys. Blossom and Bright Arrow, not understanding but in the way of children aware something was wrong, stood together staring at the ground. Most ominous of all was the parting look Rising Buffalo had given her. He had stood whispering to his brothers, words that brought their eyes to her and smirks of suspicion to their lips. Since he had left, one or the other had watched her, even when she went to relieve herself in the brush beyond the camp. She had to find a way to reach Hears-the-Wolf; he had to know of this imminent threat suddenly hanging over them. They could not be seen together again until the old chief's pride had been dealt with. But it wasn't until late afternoon, when a wave of heavy spring storms rolled in from the west, that she had her chance. The brothers, probably figuring a tryst was not likely in such a heavy downpour, had gone to a nearby lodge to gamble, a vice they indulged behind the chief's back. Still it was a terrible risk, and Hears-the-Wolf's startled eyes widened with concern as he saw Blue Hawk's pale and frightened face coming through the rain.

Black Tail was not the renowned warrior Hears-the-Wolf was, but neither was he as burdened with pride nor as blinded by vengeance, things that made Black Tail wonder about his friend, *Isi-man-ica*. Black Tail had spent many years raiding in Mexico, and though he knew only a few words of English, he spoke a rudimentary Spanish. From the very beginning he had been suspicious of several things surrounding the parley in San Antonio. They were suing for a truce, and the *tejanos* had named its price. A single sickly and scarred female hardly met it. They would soon be sending back for more.

Over a pipe Black Tail confided these thoughts to Hears-the-Wolf, who, still furious about this move for peace, was determined no captives of his would ever be offered. He had been studying Liza and Tad. The little girl with the pigtails and pert nose would make a fine squaw one day, and the boy with his little freckled face and wiry body was showing a defiant spirit that hinted at a warrior's heart. He had noticed the little girl watching and occasionally whispering to other captives in camp, while the young boy trailed shyly behind her, only looking up and becoming wide-eyed when sleek war ponies raced by. Perhaps they would make good Comanches.

As the first storm let up, Hears-the-Wolf approached his cousin, Elk Slayer, one of his favorite warriors. The tall, muscular Elk Slayer, a man of prodigious size and strength, was devoted to Hears-the-Wolf. He readily agreed to take the two white children and, leaving under the cover of the weather, lead them to the Tenawas, another tribe of southern Comanches. There they would stay with *Isi-man-ica*'s relatives until he sent for them. As the second storm broke, the war leader stood watching Elk Slayer leading a tight-lipped Liza and a puzzled Tad off and vanishing behind a roaring curtain of rain.

Little Lance was still sleeping in the wagon as Jody and Libby headed back to the farm. A brittle silence had developed between them. Jody was still smarting over his suspicion that Libby had been flirting. But she ignored him; she knew she hadn't been flirting, and what's more, she was still shocked by what the evening revealed. Some remarks she had heard kept going through her head. She found herself repeating them under her breath. Long minutes went by as the wagon creaked over the rough earth. After a time Jody began to look at her. Secretly he was becoming convinced she hadn't been flirting after all; she didn't look like someone coming from a party she had enjoyed. Finally, still mumbling to herself, she suddenly became audible. ". . . For stealing a pig . . . He was killed for stealing a pig!"

Jody, in a sudden change of moods, decided to answer her. "Stealin' is stealin'," he mumbled with a touch of sullenness to save face.

"The boy wasn't a Comanche . . . He was with his mother."

"He was an Injun."

She turned to him. "Jody, you're not like those other men, are you?"

"What d'you mean?"

"I mean what they said about the Indians and everything, about hating them."

"They killed my pa and uncle Kyle . . . Did you expect me to love 'em?"

Libby grew silent. The Indians did hideous things, but what appalled her was how these terrible acts were turning her neighbors into near barbarians. Some of their remarks had left her frightened. Surely they were going to be strange people to have as neighbors, as friends.

Ignoring the driving rain, Blue Hawk found him returning to his lodge. "We have waited too long," she began breathlessly, her words almost lost in the heavy downpour. "His brothers are only waiting to see us together."

Hears-the-Wolf, taking her hand, found it trembling. "His brothers are not warriors . . . There is more to fear from camp dogs."

"They will tell Rising Buffalo! . . . His knife will leave an ugly trail upon my face!"

Hears-the-Wolf, wanting out of the soaking rain, pulled her into his lodge. "I will speak to Iron Eagle and Rising Buffalo when they return, but you must shake off this blanket of fear." He drew her closer and slipped his hand under her robe. "Have courage, woman, the spirits are with us . . . If not . . ." His eyes sought and held hers. "Rising Buffalo's knife is no sharper than mine."

Normally she would have responded to the feel of his hand on her breasts, but her mind froze at the thought of a fight. Even if *Isi-man-ica* won, Rising Buffalo or his brothers would surely keep her children as punishment. But other doubts, doubts about this proud war leader, weighed upon her. She allowed him to reach below her waist before whispering in his ear. "The lodge that holds me must also hold my children." For a moment he held her back and stared at her, her heart ticking off one or two tense beats, but then he pulled her to him again, and slowly they sank together on the buffalo robe covered by soft skins that at darkness became his bed. There, while the rain pounded against the lodge covers and the wind whined through the smoke hole like a low lament, that passion, only heightened now by her imminent peril, rose once again like a fever, raising their pulses and heating the quivering flesh of their loins with invisible fire.

Colonel Fisher, at the adjutant general's suggestion, took over the meeting. Unlike the others, he was experienced in dealing with Indians, particularly Comanches. He was wise enough to start out saying he knew the Penateka were men of honor. After they'd given their word to bring in all their white captives, even their enemies knew they would honor it. Would the Penateka now wish to present the white captives or explain how they were to be returned?

There was a brief silence, then *Muk-wah-rah* rose to say they had brought in one girl to show goodwill. If the commissioners wished, they would send for her.

The secretary of war had to struggle to keep himself from shouting, "You've brought only one girl?" But Fisher knew Comanches couldn't be rushed. Their sober faces warned him the earlier brusque handling had put their dignity on edge. If this was the only way to start negotiations, they would have to accept it. Fisher indicated he wanted the girl sent for, and one of the chiefs rose and moved silently to the door. While they waited, *Muk-wah-rah* said the girl was only partly a gift; it would make her owner's heart happy to receive some presents in return.

Fisher, beginning to sense this cunning Indian's strategy, only smiled. He was anxious to know the girl's name and where she was from; it would tell a great deal. But a disturbing sensation began to stir in a far corner of his mind when he saw her coming in covered by a blanket. Her steps were shaky and uncertain as she was led before him, and she continued to hold a flap of blanket over her face when he said, "What is your name, miss?"

"Matilda Lockhart," came the weak reply.

Fisher lifted the flap of blanket to see her and had to step back in shock. Her face was cruelly disfigured, scabbed, scarred. The other two commissioners rose to their feet. "Good heavens!" exploded the adjutant general. "What have you done to her?"

The Penateka chiefs sat with stony but grimly resolute faces. What was the commissioner shouting about? She was a prisoner of war! How she was treated was up to her captors. The reactions of these big-talking whites were beginning to anger them. At least she was alive. How many Indians remained alive in white hands? But the commissioners were stunned into silence. Even Fisher did not know how to proceed. After a few mumbled words between them, the adjutant general an-

nounced they would have to delay the meeting until the
Texans could decide on the issuing of presents. The interpreter wisely made this sound an innocuous matter, a
harmless oversight the whites would correct while the
chiefs enjoyed coffee with large lumps of sugar.

Fisher wanted to open the girl's blanket to look at her
body, but he, like the other commissioners, was a Christian gentleman and acutely aware of this poor girl's humiliation and shame. He was now desperately anxious
to get her into the care of women. But this marked the
end of Fisher's patience. It also marked the beginning
of a disaster few in San Antonio that day would ever
forget.

As fast as the commissioners could give instructions,
Matilda Lockhart was taken to a house a short distance
away in which several women were gathered. One was
Mary Maverick, wife of Samuel Maverick, one of San
Antonio's biggest and best-known merchants. The
women could not conceal their shock. Though they
worked delicately to bathe her and tend to her sores,
many could not look at her without wincing. That evening Mary wrote, "The sight of this girl turned the day
into a day of horrors. Her head, arms, and face were full
of bruises and sores, and her nose was actually burnt off
to the bone. Both nostrils were wide open and denuded
of flesh. A large scab hung over the bone. Apart from
her sexual humiliations, she told of having been tortured
terribly by the women, who awakened her by placing
burning sticks on her face." Mary, among others, went
outside to Colonel Fisher, pleading with him to demand
that all captured females be returned at once. Colonel
Fisher needed no urging. Matilda had told the women
she had heard the Comanches say they were planning to
return the captives one at a time so they could bargain
for each and get a better price.

                    *   *   *

In the council house the chiefs drank their coffee and grunted to each other. "It is not going well," mumbled Shields-the-Squaw. "It is the thing I feared." His frowning face settled on *Muk-wah-rah*.

Red Crow nodded at Iron Eagle. "Let us send for more white captives. We came for peace . . . My ears are hearing words that belong to war."

An old chief whose face was grim for reasons beyond the conference began to light a medicine pipe he had just taken from its beaded sheath. He spoke slowly. "We should send for our warriors or hurry our weak ones away. There are no spirits friendly to the Nerm here." It was Buffalo Rising, the husband of Blue Hawk, a man whom age had drained of his powers. He was aware the notorious war leader Hears-the-Wolf was said to be cuckolding him, but only pride made it matter. His teeth were gone, his joints ached, and in bad weather his old wounds raged with pain. For a man who had once been a great warrior, it was a bitter end. Thoughtfully he puffed on the pipe, then passed it to Iron Eagle. Since the sly whispers of his other squaws told him his shame was no longer a secret, he had to act. If his brothers caught her with *Isi-man-ica*, she would suffer the fate of all adulterous squaws, after which no man would want her, and Rising Buffalo would then use his power to see that Hears-the-Wolf paid heavily in horses and other valuables for this offense.

Though growing agitated, *Muk-wah-rah* waited until the interpreter discreetly moved away before he said, "Wait till we receive more presents before your worries weaken my words." He was fingering the braid on the hatband before him. "We did not come here for this single *tejano* soldier hat."

"We came here for peace," growled Shields-the-Squaw.

Iron Eagle passed the pipe and raised his hand for silence. "There will be no peace if these *tejanos* do not want it. Let us send for more captives. My heart tells me the whites are angry; anger is the scout of war." He looked up at the grim brick walls and ceiling enclosing them. "We should not have met them in this place; a warrior's heart is troubled when he cannot see the sky."

"We have brought strong medicine," grunted *Muk-wah-rah* to the stolid faces around him. "The *tejanos* are now deciding on more presents; you will see all will be well."

Knowing what was coming and bringing with him his newly arrived superior, Colonel Cooke, Fisher returned to the Council House to find all the whites there as aroused and infuriated as himself. It was only with a great effort at civility that he was able to start the parley again. But Fisher, impelled by his anger, came directly to the point. Turning to Iron Eagle, he almost shouted, "Where are the white captives you promised to bring to this meeting?"

As the frightened interpreter started to translate, *Muk-wah-rah* leaned forward boldly and answered. "We have them in different camps of our people; we will bring them when we hear what you offer for them." Then settling back, pleased with himself, he finished with, "How do you like that answer?"

Iron Eagle glanced nervously at the other chiefs as his eye caught Colonel Fisher signaling someone at the door. In that terribly fateful moment a long line of soldiers with fixed bayonets solemnly entered the room and stationed themselves around the chiefs. Every face in the room drew taut. The long-threatening crisis, simmering for so long at the heart of this confrontation, had surfaced. Colonel Cooke, a gruff veteran of many Indian wars, pulled the interpreter to his feet. "Tell them," he said in a low commanding voice, "they're all prisoners and will be held until every white captive has been returned!"

The interpreter turned pale. "Colonel, I can't do that.

They will fight! This is a peace parley. I know these Comanches; they will die first!''

Colonel Cooke drew his pistol and held it slack in his hand. "Tell them! That's an order!"

The interpreter pulled away and, breathlessly rambling the words, hurried to the door at the back of the room and fled. But now, though agape, *Muk-wah-rah* was also translating the words. Astonishment followed by explosive outrage was suddenly warping the chiefs' faces. This was unheard-of . . . a betrayal of trust beyond belief! Prisoners! Had he forgotten they were Comanches?! The chiefs began to draw their weapons; some had them out before they got to their knees. One chief in the rear, rising and rushing over, plunged his knife into the soldier guarding the door. A sergeant nearby fired at him point-blank and the chief crumpled.

In desperation these old men, once powerful and agile warriors, tried to match the feats of their youth. Some almost succeeded. In spite of stumbling feet and shaking hands, one soldier went down with a tomahawk wound in his head, and another had two stab wounds in his stomach as the dying Red Crow slipped down his body. Very aged ones like Iron Eagle and Buffalo Rising were shot trying to wrestle guns from the soldiers' hands. Ranger Captain Matt Caldwell, who had just wandered in unarmed, was shot in the leg. He pulled a musket from an Indian chief and blew his head off with it, then beat another to death with the stock. Even though some of their voices were creaky and often broke, the dying chiefs raised the Comanche war cry that Penaketa warriors ritually screamed as they fought and killed. This nightmarish sound emanating from the Council House brought gasps of alarm from Indian women and children loitering outside.

But shocking as the sudden sprays of blood that stained the choking clouds of gunpowder in the courthouse were, the real carnage was only beginning. As the surviving chiefs, many wounded, tumbled through the

door, fear and panic spread like wildfire. Not every Comanche nearby knew what was happening, but they
heard the shots and their chiefs giving death cries.
Armed warriors started streaming from the encampment;
citizens seeing them running sensed excitement and followed. An Indian boy who had been firing arrows at
coins suddenly fired one at a circuit judge standing
nearby and killed him. The town sheriff, coming up
thinking this clamor might mean trouble, was hit by a
stray bullet as soldiers on guard outside the building entered the fray. He was dead within seconds. Like an
upswell of lava from a fast-erupting volcano, the fighting
spread. The warriors might have had a chance against
the troops, but now they saw confused civilians and soldiers frantically shouting to each other and decided all
tejanos were attacking. The Texans standing near, wit-
nessing both judge and sheriff being struck down before
their startled eyes, drew guns to protect themselves.
When screeching squaws started attacking a passing
wagon driver with skinning knives, the chaos was complete.

The stark suddenness of it made Fisher's plans for
controlling the situation impossible. Many chiefs were
already dead or dying; the breach of faith was irrepa-
rable. In the Council House *Muh-wah-rah* sat slumped
with his skull caved in, some saying it was done by
Shields-the-Squaw's hatchet before he struggled through
the door. Shields-the-Squaw had actually reached some
of his warriors outside and took refuge with them under
the stalled wagon, but by now Rangers were coming up,
joining the fight. Within moments the warriors were shot
down and the chief killed.

Terrible as the scene around the Council House was,
a more ominous one threatened as the townspeople began reacting to the sight of innocent bystanders being
gunned down or wounded. On this troubled frontier
every male went armed. Not only did passing Texans
feel themselves threatened, but many carried a deeply

embedded hatred for these painted hellions who smelled
like rotting carrion and had the morals of hyenas. After
the first few shots, there was no earthly way it could be
stopped. As shrieking Indians flocked from the encampment, more and more citizens joined the frenzied struggle.

But the odds were appalling. What started as a fight
soon became a massacre. Indian women and children,
howling at the sight of their dead chiefs or brandishing
knives or clubs, were shot down indiscriminately. Indian
warriors trying to find cover were killed entering houses
or stables. More and more civilians were wounded and
not a few killed, but the whites had now become an
enraged mob. Every last Indian who did not swiftly surrender—and for this aroused populace, no warrior
proved swift enough—was shot or feverishly hunted
down. With soldiers and civilians shooting from every
side, no stand was possible, no amount of bravery even
delayed the onslaught. The last two braves took refuge
in a cookhouse, which was soaked with turpentine and
set on fire. As they emerged, one's head was split open
with an ax, the other's body was riddled with lead. Only
some twenty-odd women and children, many of them
wounded, were taken prisoner and thrown in jail. The
rest, to a soul, perished.

So ended the long-awaited parley, and with it all hope
of peace between Texan and Comanche. A few thoughtful citizens, viewing the devastation, suspected this day's
sad legacy would haunt the frontier for years. One such
was the soft-spoken Jack Hays. Wounded Matt Caldwell, a borrowed gun still smoking in his hand and
glancing at the bodies of Indians lying along the roadway in those awkward positions only death can impose,
came by to mutter, "Damn red bastards sure die hard
enough . . . but reckon that's an end to it, Jack."

Hays was looking at the sky, which had turned a faint
bronze, streaked with ribbons of gray as the only warning of an approaching storm. The town had grown

weirdly silent in the wake of the havoc. The young Ranger captain's face was grim but resigned, matching his thoughts, but his voice was sadly laconic when he finally answered. "Don't bet on it, Matt. I've got a hunch folks will find out afore long it's only the beginning."

Chapter 7

LIBBY DISCOVERED PRAYER meetings were held at the campgrounds, a stretch along the river where early settlers camped while staking out claims and planning dwellings. There was a small mound at its center. It was from this mound that fiery-eyed Bible thumpers raised the clarion call for righteousness and in sonorous tones, ominous as drum rolls, described the damnation awaiting sin. Many thought Reverend Bumeister was possibly a reincarnation of Moses, with his prodigious white beard and thundering voice. He had come to the West Texas frontier knowing the deviltry of heathen power demanded his missionary zeal. Now he stood on the mound, his arms upraised, a red shawl over his long black coat, a dramatic touch for special occasions. With effort he kept his arms raised in supplication as the congregation flocked before him to settle on the hillside, symbolically at his feet.

Jody and Libby, carrying Lance, had come with the Sutters. They saw the Bishops sitting down beside the grieving Maude and Buck Chauncy. Libby, walking in front, found herself approaching the Munsters, whom

she hadn't seen since the party. It was clear that Nat
Munster was about to offer his hand, but Libby suddenly
found Kate's arm about her, steering her away. With this
obvious avoidance of the Munsters she found herself
puzzled but suddenly nearing the wretched-looking
Maude and the grim-faced Buck. The Bishops quietly
motioned them down as the Reverend Bumeister was
about to begin his sermon. Libby, settling with her baby
but still confused, caught, out of the corner of her eye,
Nat Munster looking toward her uncomfortably and Nellie deliberately staring the other way. She looked questioningly at Becky Bishop, who she knew had seen this
deliberate snub. "They're not our kind," Becky whispered, her eyes now fixed on Bumeister on the mound.

Libby felt her cheeks reddening with embarrassment;
she had never done anything so rude before. A little
choking pain started in her throat. If this was fitting be-
havior, she couldn't help wondering if maybe she wasn't
their "kind" either. But it wasn't over. As people continued to arrive, even after the sermon had begun, they
eyed the Munsters, then drifted to the right or left. When
finally a crowd covered the hillside, the Munsters still
sat in glaring isolation. Shortly thereafter Libby, still
troubled, peeked in their direction. The Munsters were
gone.

The Reverend Bumeister's booming voice, heavily in-
flected with his Pennsylvania Dutch accent, pulled all
eyes to him. "Christians! Christians!" he bellowed. "Ye
have come here to pray, have ye not? Ye have come to
pray for two children swept off by red infidels, by the
ungodly, by worshipers of Moloch and Belial. You have
come to pray to the God Who smites the wicked and
raises to everlasting glory those who believe in Him. The
savages may desecrate the body, but they cannot touch
the soul. Let us turn, in these cruel days of trial, to the
God of Abraham. Let us pray Jehovah walks once again
amongst the Host, that He will raise His fiery sword
against these heathens who abduct our children, defile

our women, and break His Holy Commandments. Let us pray He will sweep them from the earth as He did the Amorites, Canaanites, and the prideful Philistines. Let Him burn these sinners in a fiery hell as He did the evil of Sodom and Gomorrah!''

Libby listen to him call upon Jehovah to lay waste the red man, likening Joshua's struggle for the promised land to their struggle for West Texas. Libby, still thinking of the Munsters, wondered, is this really a man of peace? But whatever emotions he stirred in her, there was little doubt he was reaching the hearts of the congregation. They were gratefully drinking in his prophecy that divine retribution would bring total destruction to the tribes. An airy euphoria, matching that of wine, had many eyes shining as he described Joshua's army of rude herdsmen and farmers sweeping indigenous barbarians from the valleys of Judea and the plains of Galilee.

Libby, who had only been exposed to simple sermons about charity and grace in a small rural church in Missouri, found it a peculiar message from a man who had started out hailing them as Christians. It troubled her. For now she sensed, in spite of her desire to be like those around her, an uneasy feeling of estrangement. She wondered if she dared admit this new burden to Jody.

An hour passed before Bumeister led the prayer for Liza and little Tad. Maude sobbed throughout it, and Buck tightened his fists till his knuckles showed white. Bumeister prayed for their deliverance, their comfort and care in captivity, but if denied those, he prayed for their salvation. Shouts of ''Amen'' followed many of his closing lines, one woman punctuating his last words with a screeching ''Hallelujah!'' The congregation then stood and sang an old hymn as the standard collection for the preacher began.

Fluttering about with her usual candor, Kate Sutter selected and invited several friends and Preacher Bumeister to her place for refreshments and a midday meal.

There was much talk about the sermon, although Libby discovered not everyone found either his sermon or Bumeister himself particularly uplifting. Out of the preacher's hearing, Pete Spevy mumbled that "Joshua never locked horns with red hellions on horseback." Becky Bishop screwed her mouth up as she caught Bumeister holding forth across the room. "Didn't care much for his red shawl, something papist about it."

Violence was fast sowing its legacy in San Antonio. A strange mood hung over the town. Everyone knew any chance for peace was gone, and with it, all hope of recovering loved ones. But a long-mounting fury and outrage soon swept aside grief. Citizens stood at bars and street corners, declaring there was no making peace with wild savages, a war of extermination was the only answer. Yet in the end this proved only talk; the young republic lacked the means for a decisive military effort. Colonel Cooke inadvertently played their last card; he mounted one of the captive squaws on a pinto horse and sent her off to tell the Penaketa camp they had twelve days to deliver all whites in their custody. If this was not complied with, the squaws and children now being held would never be released. Jack Hays, watching this, smiled grimly. Would no one remember they were dealing with Comanches? The woman was never seen again, but she was the spark that started a conflagration that would turn West Texas into a landscape of smoking ruins and lonely graves.

Yet for several days only a peculiar silence prevailed, almost eerie in its completeness. But after the first tense week slipped by and there was no sign of Comanches, Colonel Fisher, hearing of civil trouble on the Sabine, started his troops back east. He left one contingent behind under the command of Captain Red. Regrettably, he had little choice. Life was quietly returning to normal; the far frontier, as before, had to deal with its own problems. Yet old-timers knew all along that Indian captives were a poor bargaining chip; Comanche mentality would consider these squaws and children already lost.

Late the following day, the lonely half-demented squaw, Colonel Cooke's fateful messenger, had made her way through heavy rains and was nearing camp. Her face was haunted and her hands were bloodless from squeezing the reins. She was one of Rising Buffalo's old wives and the bearer of ghastly news. So wretched in heart was she that she was looking forward to her own death, which she had already planned. Though she had been traveling for many, many hours, she was still partly paralyzed with shock, still having trouble formulating words. She knew what her mouth was to bring forth would destroy her people, that after her terrible tidings, the Penateka would never be the same again.

An old medicine man relieving himself behind his lodge saw her first. Though she was almost incoherent, the shaman soon realized, in spite of her hysterical screeching, that every chief in the delegation and all the warriors that accompanied them, along with many of their women and children, were dead. At first he could only cry out in shock, but faces were appearing in the flaps of tepees, and the sound of feet beginning to run toward them began to swell. A pall quickly seized but as quickly relinquished its morbid hold on the campsite, for the wailing of one squaw after the other started a hellish chorus that kept growing louder and louder till hunting parties, still miles away, heard the clamor and spurred their horses into camp. The endless swelling of shrill screaming women, falling to their knees, was a grotesque if pitiable sight, for their anguish was being expressed with skinning knives that slashed their arms and breasts, cut off fingers, disfigured their faces and bodies, and left their torsos bathed in their own blood. The old wife of Rising Buffalo who brought the horrifying news was the first to collapse and die from cuts she made across her own veins. Others were joining her as warriors, drifting to the outskirts of camp, began slashing at and cutting their sacred hair. Confusion and near panic reigned, for this was a blow to the Penateka beyond the comprehension of any white. Many warriors, including Hears-the-Wolf, took several minutes to grasp the immensity of their loss, for at first, hearing it seemed too terrible to be true. The tribe's leaders, civil, military, and spiritual, had been wiped out. The most capable men of the Penateka were gone. For a primitive people, this was a tragedy equaling the death of the sun.

Blue Hawk, because of her half-breed mother, was not as bound by Comanche traditions as were her full-blooded neighbors, though there had been a quiet movement among the tribes to do away with such extreme measures of expressing grief. That tradition from the dim past, when the hungry tribes wandered on foot through the barren northern mountains, and the loss of a warrior meant starvation for his family, now seemed pointless. Certainly the immolation of valuable horseflesh, even for chiefs, was disappearing, though it was revived here. This calamity was too great; the terror of an unknown and evil spirit had descended upon them. People were stunned; abandoning themselves to mindless, explosive destruction seemed the only way to relieve their grief. It took two days to sacrifice all the mounts that were led up to the dead chiefs' biers, made up of their lances and shields and, where available, a string of scalps or other war trophies they had won. Blood soon lay in pools on the ground, the smell of slaughtered animals sickening the stomach and gagging the throat. But the most macabre scenes were yet to come.

Hatred of the *tejanos* now fixed itself on the helpless captives. Only the adopted children were spared. Women and young girls were taken, stripped and tied down near the fires where the squaws bent over them with knives, flaying them, slicing off toes, fingers, tongues, eyelids, thrusting burning sticks into their ori-

fices and forcing out every last gasp of pain. Matilda
Lockhart's younger sister died this way, writhing in agony under the merciless faces of her tormentors.

But all such torture was left to the squaws; by now
the camp had swollen in size with every hunting and
raiding party coming in. Hears-the-Wolf was rallying the
warriors, already numbering over three hundred, and
was soon leading them in full war regalia to San Antonio. The whites would quickly learn the cost of betraying
the trust of the proud, now enraged and vengeful, Penaketa.

More than a week had passed before Libby discovered
Ben McCulloch had spoken to Jody at the party about
joining his Ranger troop. Secretly shocked, she looked
at him askance. "You really fixing to go off fighting
Indians?"

"It's expected of me. Everybody's got to do their
share."

Masking her irritation, Libby still hardened her mouth
in a pout. "Didn't know he was there recruiting."

"He wasn't. They only want volunteers."

"Oh, you volunteered!"

"Libby, what a-troubling you? You know we can't
do no different from other folks."

Libby avoided answering by bending over the baby;
it was clear she now had something else to stew about.
"You be gone a lot?" she finally started again.

"Iffen I'm needed, reckon I got to go."

Libby picked up the baby and walked to the door. She
stared toward the river, her eyes seemingly drawn to
something on the first rise. She stared at it for long
minutes before Jody realized she was staring at the white
cross that marked his father's grave.

Chapter 8

AFTER THE STORMS, San Antonio began to enjoy a spell of fine weather. Flights of birds were seen passing over from the south, and foliage along the river was turning a leafy green. Few people bothered to count the days the Indians had been given to return their captives; few believed any would ever be returned. Ranger scouts had been watching the Penateka camp and grimly surmised what a failure to sight any white prisoners meant. It was finally reported that a great war party had formed and even now was approaching the town.

Captain Red heard these tidings with concern. There were still three days to go before the period allowed the tribe to return their captives expired. It was his problem, as Fisher had fallen ill with a dangerously high fever and Cooke had departed with the troops returning east. Rumors of a large war party coming their way aroused the men, many of whom were spoiling for a fight. After the one-sided massacre, there were brags that they could wipe out the entire tribe. Red, a career army officer, warily consulted his second-in-command, the debonair, stylishly dressed Lysander Wells. Wells, who had pis-

toled down at least one chief in the Council House fight,
now argued that the men should be allowed to open fire
if the Indians came into town. Red insisted that would
be a violation of orders, a fact to which Wells finally if
reluctantly agreed. Because of their natures, Red, the
stolid by-the-book commander, and Wells, the impetu-
ous, and some thought too cavalier, subordinate, had developed uneasy blood between them. It was subtly
polarizing the men. Sensing this unrest among his
troops, and suspecting the war party would be after the
Indian prisoners, Red ordered both behind the walls of
the San Jose mission, issuing a strict command that no
guns were to be fired without his permission. Captain
Wells made no comment; he begrudgingly acknowledged it was Red's responsibility to keep open whatever
chance the captives had of returning, but like the Ranger
captains, he suspected any captives in Indian hands were
already dead. Yet this couldn't be proven, and Red was
clearly not going to risk a court-martial by irresponsibly
risking lives.

The sun was high in the sky when the warning bells
of San Fernando began to ring. From any elevated spot
the Comanches could be seen massing at the western
edge of town. People rushed indoors to pull rifles from
the wall, bar windows, and quench stoves. In the bars
and cantinas in the center of town, men congregated; all
were armed, but not all were looking for a fight. There
were shady types who took no risks defending other people's property, and Mexicans who, with hardly concealed glee, declared this a gringo problem. When had
the Texas government moved a finger to recover their
captives?

It was a tense moment. San Antonio, as a frontier
town, had seen perilous days, but never anything quite
like this. The Comanches came on slowly. Fortunately
horse Indians were never comfortable in towns. Walls
and elevated windows bothered them. Their strength was
on the open prairie, where they could maneuver and see

clearly in all directions. Hears-the-Wolf, with Black Tail at his side, rode ahead. As they approached the town's center, they began to shout. "Where are the cowardly *tejanos* who strike like low crawling snakes? Where are the dogs without honor, the squaw killers, the eaters of filth?" Hears-the-Wolf was shouting in Comanche, which few understood, but Black Tail was also shouting in his rough border Spanish, which many followed. "Give us our people or we will scalp you all! Our squaws will cut out your hearts! Our brave children will eat them!" roared Hears-the-Wolf. Black Tail was repeating much of this in crude Spanish. As they passed a Mexican cantina, a voice suddenly shouted back, "Go to the Mission San Jose. Your people are there!"

Black Tail, who knew San Antonio, now led the way as Hears-the-Wolf signaled the great war party to close up. Within minutes three hundred shouting warriors were massed outside the mission walls. Hears-the-Wolf told Black Tail to demand the garrison come out and fight. Captain Red stood beside a soldier who spoke Spanish and had him shout back, if they returned in three days, he would accommodate them. Hears-the-Wolf snorted in derision. Did the whites expect Comanches to sit their horses for three days waiting for a fight? The situation grew hotter. The soldiers looked on as the warriors drew their hands across their loincloths, making cutting motions, a way of telling the soldiers they were emasculated and no longer men. There were seventy-two soldiers inside the mission, and with their rifles braced behind mission walls, they could have inflicted grievous losses on the Comanches, but Red doggedly refused permission to fire. Outside, warriors were crying to Hears-the-Wolf that by standing on their horses' backs, they could reach the top of the walls on one side. But glancing at the threatening line of rifles, he knew this could only be done at a price that might make any victory an ultimate defeat. The Penateka could not afford to squander manpower; all war leaders understood there were no expendable warriors. Against the ever-rising tide of *tejanos*, every brave was needed. The Penateka had learned the hard way not only strong medicine but an increasing mastery of guerrilla warfare was required to match the whites' numbers and increasing firepower.

But if challenges and insults could not bring the garrison out to fight, they were causing rising dissension within the mission itself. Spirited southerners like Wells and two of his lieutenants were mortified that a band of ignorant painted savages was intimidating the Texas Army. A whole town was watching this disgrace. They demanded that Red open fire. They were sure one or two volleys would scatter the Indians and send them howling for the hills. But Red stared them down. He had his orders. He was responsible; they weren't.

The breaking point came when a pole holding a Texas flag, placed at the mission's entrance to indicate the presence of the military, was lifted by a warrior, broken in two, and hurled over the wall. Several soldiers cocked their guns as Red cried out, "Don't shoot!"

"Goddamn it! Captain, they're attacking us!" bawled a flush-faced sergeant.

"He's right," said Wells, coming up, no longer hiding his irritation. "This demonstration is outrageous . . . It's Goddamn humiliating. Open fire!"

Red confronted him, pistol in hand. "You know our orders, Wells. For Christ's sake, don't incite the men!"

Impulsively Wells shot back a heated response. "Orders don't remove the right of soldiers to defend their flag when it's attacked!"

Red's weathered face was suddenly trenched with his own anger; tight white lines rimmed his mouth. "Captain Wells, only a damn fool would consider the breaking of a flagpole an attack!"

Wells, under the eyes of the men and growing more incensed by the second, became choleric. "Captain Red, some of us who came to fight think only a coward wouldn't!"

The fateful words were said; it hushed the men and threw a strange calm over the assembled force. Now Red grimly approached Wells, pulling his military gloves from his belt as he did, using them to strike his second-in-command across the face with a smack that resounded across the courtyard. "That remark, sir, you will have to prove!"

Even after the Indians, with Hears-the-Wolf deciding to find a simpler but surer way of punishing these *tejanos*, headed down the Sequin road toward settlements farther east, a sudden sense of tragedy hung over the mission. Insults between men who held their personal honor sacred had but one end.

Before sundown, both lay dead, dueling pistols in their hands, as the garrison stood silenced by this "honorable" end to a gentlemen's argument.

Libby never liked it when Jody went away. As long as she could hear him working in the barn or see him following a team of horses in the fields, she was content to sit with her baby and sing, or dance lightly around her tiny rooms hugging Lance and enjoying her favorite fantasies. Often she visualized herself going home to her family, particularly her mother, showing off her baby, perhaps being taken through her hometown in a sulky as neighbors stood along the way and smiled in admiration. Her dreams sometimes mounted to having several babies, all beautiful, all resembling Lance. Once in a while her dreams spiraled off to where she had six grown sons, all handsome, all gallantly protecting their mother, all the envy of girls she had grown up with.

It was the day Jody had gone into town and got back late that Libby began to worry. She had seen him talking to Dale Sutter, who had come riding up the river the day before. Later that afternoon he returned from the fields silent and thoughtful. She had watched him leaving in the morning with his guns and the spirited Blackie, their fleetest horse. Not surprisingly, talkative Kate came to visit a few hours later, knowing her youngest brother, Dale, had gone with Jody, and Libby would be alone. "There's been a lot of fighting," she said candidly. "McCulloch has been gone for a spell . . . Hear he's back. Likely he's looking for more help."

"My God!" exclaimed Libby. "You mean those boys have gone to join the Rangers!"

"Certainly," responded Kate. "Someone's got to up and punish these red devils for the hellish things they do."

"But Jody is no fighter."

"He soon will be."

"Oh, Kate, this is terrible."

"Libby, stop talking that way! If our menfolk lose their grit for fighting, we'll all be murdered in our beds! If I didn't need Race to help me run the ranch, he'd be gone too." Kate, older than her two brothers, could ride and even break horses as well as any man, but the ranch was too big, with colts beginning to drop in the far pastures, for one person to handle.

Libby went to change the baby and came back frowning. Kate, who had been watching her, spoke first. "Libby, be careful what you say around here. Most folks, like the Chauncys, are sore put about Injuns . . . Most figure killing is too good for 'em." She paused to sip the coffee Libby had put on but Kate served herself. "Remember, Injuns don't clear out for the asking . . . We ain't a-gonna have any peace hereabouts till every last one of them filthy painted varmits is dead."

"Kate, that's dreadful!"

"Not as dreadful as what they'll do to you and your baby if they come a-raidin' this way again. Libby, you better get rid of those genteel eastern airs of yours and learn to shoot and maybe even use a hunting knife. This ain't no country for folks who haven't got the brisket to fight."

Libby turned away from her, hugging Lance and

heaving a big sigh. "Heavens! And just when will this dreadful fighting be over?"

"When we've killed them all . . . or we lie scalped in our graves."

"Kate, Kate, it really can't be that bad."

" 'Fraid 'tis. Jawing 'bout it is nothing but a waste of breath. It's them or us!"

Jody had always thought he could ride well, but young Dale Sutter was raised with horses, and it showed in his style. Yet as they rode up to the mission, where they were told to report, Ben McCulloch, watching them ride in, didn't seem impressed with either. He questioned them without ceremony. "Can you shoot?"

Jody held up his squirrel gun, and Dale raised his long-barrel rifle. "Not with those." McCulloch showed them a six-gun.

"With this."

Jody and Dale looked at each other. "I'll be glad to jump down and try," said Jody agreeably.

"Not on the ground," corrected McCulloch, "from the saddle."

"We can learn," said Dale, looking slightly offended.

"Better start," responded McCulloch. His tone was blunt, but his eyes were serious, and both boys began to realize he was trying to tell them fighting Comanches could be tricky for a beginner. Within a few moments McCulloch made it clear that only those who were capable of riding and shooting like Rangers could join. Oddly enough, this daunting but prudent standard gave them confidence. "We'll work at it," offered Jody. Dale nodded.

McCulloch continued, his eyes level with theirs, his tone frank, unwavering, "I know you think you can ride, but Comanches do things with horses that will keep you awake nights. And while we're at it, don't underestimate what they can do with a bow. They can fire ten arrows hard enough to go straight through you while you're still trying to reload one of those rifles. That's why you've got to use six-guns and from the saddle. There aren't many orders given around here, but every one has to be obeyed. Every life in the troop could depend upon it. We can't use men who are queasy about killing redskins or who have to think before they shoot. If any of this is interfering with your digestion, you'd better quit now.'' There was a long moment as Jody and Dale flicked a look at each other from the corners of their eyes. "Reckon I can handle it," breathed Jody.

"Likewise," added Dale hurriedly.

McCulloch gave them both a six-gun and told them to scratch their initials on it. "You only get one, so don't lose it," he cautioned. "If we get into a fight, don't drop it. Injuns will be learning how to use these soon enough. When you hear these mission bells, day or night, come a-running. There'll be riders out, but they may not get to all of you. You'll get a supply of shells here, but tote enough grub for a day or two. After that, we live off the land. Any questions?"

"Do we get some shells to practice with?" inquired Dale.

"Pick 'em up in back," answered McCulloch. "And incidentally, since they cost money, we always favor getting close enough to make every one count."

Libby had been very tired that night, for Becky Bishop showed up while Kate was still there, and both women began to teach her how to make soap and candles, two items necessary to life on the frontier but available only if homemade.

Thoughtfully Becky brought her old candle mold along, but the beeswax had to be melted and the cotton wicks twisted and settled in at the right stage. They built a large fire in a rain barrel behind the house, preparing to leach lye from the ashes, which would later be joined with animal fat to make the rough brown soap needed to clean the homespun and linsey-woolsey clothing. The fire had to burn for hours, and wood had to be gathered. By dark Libby was exhausted and her hands were rough and sore. She understood now why the other women's grips always seemed so coarse. But she refused to let up until the others agreed it was too dark to work. Then she settled down with little Lance feeding at her breast and the women, seeing Jody approaching, preparing to leave.

Jody looked sheepish but vaguely proud as he removed the six-gun from his belt and bent down to kiss her. She had planned to scold him for not telling her his plans, but after looking into his open boyish face, she found herself not only too weary but finally resigned to things. She sensed the need of proud young men to show courage before their fellows in this terrible time and place. She lay in bed that night feeling older but realizing, when Jody made clinging love to her, that this man-boy, for all his faint bravado, needed her to look up to him to affirm his manhood. With that she decided to make herself content and dropped off to sleep.

Chapter 9

HAYS WATCHED THE great war party leaving the mission, moving eastward, down the main trail toward Sequin and Gonzales. He was suddenly restless with concern. There were frequent travelers on that road, families with children coming west, teamsters arriving with badly needed supplies, itinerant merchants wandering in from the settlements, all of them alone, defenseless. There were not enough Rangers to take on this horde of warriors, and the soldiers, being infantry, were of little use in a running fight. But warnings had to be dispatched. A young boy was sent to search for Caldwell and Wallace, and to direct any Rangers encountered to join Hays at the public stables. The first Ranger to show up was sent to circle the war party and warn travelers headed that way. This man was then to continue on to Gonzales to alert McCulloch and let him know of the attack on San Antonio. Hays had no doubt the great dying was about to begin, for no power existed in the fledgling republic to stop it.

*　　*　　*

Hears-the-Wolf, his granite face lined with wrath, led his warriors a few miles down the trail, putting the walls and narrow streets of the town behind them. Soon they were lost in low hills of stunted pines and rock outcroppings. This was country they were used to. The warriors spread out as Hears-the-Wolf signaled them to high ground on the left to scout the trail in both directions. Black Tail at his side was assuring him this traditional approach would soon bear fruit. He was more right than he knew. A brave on the height to the left was suddenly signaling that someone was approaching from the east. Though they were still several miles away, the keen-eyed scouts could see a long line of mules pulling heavy wagons, and behind them a remuda of horses being herded by some vaqueros. It would be a while before this party reached the stretch where Hears-the-Wolf had his braves hidden along the trail. Deciding there were too many to conceal in this one short stretch, he sent more than fifty to the south to circle around behind this doomed party and cut off any attempt to turn back and escape. Finally he and Black Tail sat their horses behind a massive boulder and grunted to each other in satisfaction. Their scalping knives would soon be out and glistening with *tejano* blood.

Ironically, there wasn't a single *tejano* in this ill-fated party; they were Mexicans hauling goods from Seguin for the merchants of San Antonio. They were laboring to reach town by sundown, where the willing arms of their women and the soothing warmth of wine was awaiting them. One sitting on the back of the last wagon had a guitar; he strummed it as vaqueros riding near called for their favorite tunes. They were a people given readily to song and romance; in turns they sang of their love for Juanita, Maria, or Elena with equal gusto and feeling. Such merriment shortened the road, and the few pesos they were earning would buy tomorrow's wine and tortillas.

The wagon master was a gristly old man with white hair and the sorry eyes of a lonely dog. He was sitting in the first wagon, which his grandson was driving, beginning to nod as he wearied of the young man's senseless remarks on the future of this gringo state called Texas. The old man had been born in San Antonio long before the gringos came; he was born a Mexican and he intended to stay Mexican. If his grandson thought he had a future with these *norteamericanos,* that only showed how foolish the young could be. It was clear his countrymen were considered ignorant, devious, and shiftless by these swaggering newcomers, and even though his people vastly outnumbered the Anglos in southwestern Texas, not a single Mexican held public office. He was glad this shipment was nearly over. His right arm was nearly crippled with rheumatism, and his teeth, those that were left, always pained him till he had his evening shot of tequila.

In spite of the soft soothing melodies coming from the rear, some sixth sense he had developed in his lifetime of traveling this risky country made him uneasy. Perhaps it was the sight of prairie chickens running across the trail and taking noisy flight that triggered his senses, but suddenly he knew something was wrong. The lead mule was trying to pull to the left, and failing that, was backing against its traces. There was a weird moment of stillness, then an arrow whirled out of the foliage on his right and sank with a thud into his grandson's side. A deafening roar of savage voices opened up on all sides, and grotesquely painted faces and frightful horned headdresses were around him in a ghastly nightmare that he knew was an ugly screeching curtain of death descending on his whole train.

"*Jesucristo* Comanches!" was all he had time to gasp before a barbed lance entered his side and pierced his heart. His last thoughts were for the vaqueros. They were mounted; perhaps they had a chance. But they were trapped by the warriors coming behind, and those not

quickly killed were seized, stripped, and tied spread-
eagle over the rear wagon wheels. The wagons themselves were looted of flour, molasses, bolts of cloth, and
cheap crockery. The warriors stuck their hands into the
molasses and licked their fingers, but other than the
horses and mules, they found little of interest to loot.
With night coming on, they pulled the wagons together,
cut off many of the captives' tongues and genitals,
ripped scalps from both the living and the dead, and set
the whole train on fire. This quick, easy success convinced Hears-the-Wolf that Black Tail was right; they
would go back to guerrilla warfare. Somehow he sensed
any struggle with the whites in San Antonio, with its
walls and treacherous winding streets, would prove too
costly. The great strength of Comanche war parties had
always been their mobility. As long as they could attack
remote, unsuspecting homes and farms, they had proven
deadly. He would make the soldiers and the killer ones
search him out on the open plain where Comanche warriors fought best. But from now on, he swore, the land
of the Nerm would be a graveyard for every *tejano*
caught upon it. The spirits, to avenge the murdered
chiefs, would visit them in dreams and bring strong medicine to the war leaders of the Penateka.

By sundown nearly forty Rangers had been gathered,
and Caldwell, noticing smoke rising down the trail, declared it was time to follow the war party and discover
what deviltry they had been up to. With night rolling in
from the east, they could see the flare against the sky,
but by the time they drew close, they had to shorten
their breaths against the smell of burnt flesh. Still, knowing Comanches, they approached it warily; it could still
have been a trap. But they found only the carnage of the
ill-starred wagon train and the charred bodies of its pathetic hardworking, song-loving crew. The dead were
gathered and quietly buried in a single grave as Hays
and Caldwell climbed the same high ground from which

Hears-the-Wolf's warriors spotted the train.

"They're gone for sure," allowed Caldwell, moving his chaw of tobacco from one cheek to the other, "but fired up as they be, we ain't heard the last of 'em."

Hays was studying the now moonlit horizon to the north. There were small lonely settlements up there, many of them populated with women and small children. As the miles stretched out to Cibolo Creek and beyond to the Pedernales, he knew there were far too many for his Rangers to protect. But he was certain now the waiting was over. The Texans had to go back on the attack, there were no longer captives to be recovered or fading hopes of peace to be preserved. Now it was destroy or be destroyed. A resolve that Hears-the-Wolf had long since hit upon was now accepted by this most formidable of all Ranger captains. Between the two, death was sure to reap a rich harvest.

The problem of distance was one with the West. It took many days for word to reach the settlements that Comanche war parties might appear on their horizon at any moment. McCulloch was still trying to call in his troop when a desperate boy, on a blown and dying horse, raced in from the north. Libby was already asleep when the eerie sound of the mission bells started tolling like faint chimes in the distance. Jody, awaking with a start, jumped up quickly and hurriedly dressed. With Libby sitting up in bed, pleading with him to be careful, he raced to the barn, never knowing she was biting her lip as she heard Blackie's hoofbeats dying out in the night. After a few minutes she brought Lance into bed with her and spent the long hours till dawn sleepless and apprehensive, listening to her baby gurgling in the dark.

But in San Antonio the first reports of raiding came late the following day. A farm family only ten miles to the northeast had been wiped out. The young female neighbor reporting it was hysterical. The mutilated body of the young man she had been planning to marry had been tied over the well, his body torn open and fouling the water.

Leaving others to comfort the distraught woman, the Ranger captains, Hays, Caldwell, joined by Big Foot Wallace, met quietly. "We'll have to go after them," said Hays. "It's the only way."

"Reckon that's true," allowed Caldwell. "Going to be touchy, though; we ain't hardly enough come a fix."

Hays rubbed his chin for a moment. "We'll get out there and trail them. They'll split up sooner or later. We'll follow a party we can handle . . . We'll just have to start there."

The others nodded in agreement. Caldwell and Wallace were left to see about arms and ammunition for the troop, while Hays went off to organize civilian volunteers for rescue work. To these willing but worried faces his orders were explicit. At any report of a raid, the San Fernando church bells were to be rung, and every man hearing them was to assemble. They were to go where the raid took place, take care of survivors and any burials, then dispatch a rider to him with word of the direction the raiders left in.

It was all he could do. Three hours before sundown he led the troop of Rangers out of town, heading toward the northeast. There were forty-six of them. They were going after hundreds of warriors who were gathered beyond the horizon, painted for war and wanting nothing better than to find a troop of killer ones seeking them out for a fight.

For hit-and-run guerrilla warfare, Black Tail knew at once the war party was too big. Before dawn, urging Hears-the-Wolf to do the same, he left for the eastern settlements with over thirty braves. Hears-the-Wolf, reluctant to give up such a large following, realized with their first victory, as he watched the farmhouse burn, that Black Tail was right. The whites were all dead, their screaming ended, their scalps taken, but it was too quick. It had been a large family, with four grown women, three men, and sprawled about the bloodstained yard were the bodies of eight children. This war party was too unwieldy; everyone wanted a coup, a scalp for his war belt. In the rush there had been no time to sort out these *tejanos* to see which could be taken back as slaves, no time for judging the children, picking those who might be raised as Comanche and swell the ranks of the Penateka. This was not warfare as the Nerm had to wage it. Ten warriors could have surprised and seized this farm, and here they were still numbering over two hundred—another troublesome result of their lost leadership. Some of the braves, still venting their rage over the murdered chiefs, had taken the youngest male, cut open his stomach and abdomen, and hung him over the well. The women and young girls had been impaled on stakes, and the squalling children brutally silenced with war clubs. But destroying this single farm would not drive the *tejanos* from their country. A hundred dwellings of the whites must lie in ashes, a thousand scalps must adorn the lodges of the Penateka. Only then would the whites know death awaited those who challenged Comanche command of their buffalo range.

With the sun ready to set again, he knew this night he must impress on the braves a promising plan or his chance for great power would slip away. Tragic as it was, he knew in such tribal upheavals new leaders quickly rose by attracting a fresh following. Secretly he was hopeful. After the loss of so many headmen, war leaders like himself had risen in prominence. If his medicine proved strong, his following might soon exceed all others. He ordered the two cows and a calf that had been found in the stable be butchered for a feast. Immediately great fires were started on the field beside the farm, horses were taken off to graze, and medicine pipes were removed from their beaded cases. Hears-the-Wolf grunted quietly to himself. The signs were good; the hearts of warriors were always easier to command on a full stomach.

Back in the Comanche camp, a strange event was taking place. A figure rode in from the north. He dismounted and walked to a lodge where a young man, his face blackened in grief, came out to embrace him. The people saw this and held their hands to their mouths in awe. This man, they had thought to be dead. He had gone to visit the Kiowas, a tribe the Comanches were forming an alliance with. He had joined his hosts in a fight against Arapahos on the banks of the Kaw, was seriously wounded and left by his party on the Kansas plains to die. But his wounds, which miraculously healed, proved to be his salvation, for surely had he returned earlier, because of his high rank, he would have journeyed with the other chiefs to San Antonio. His name was Buffalo Hump.

Blue Hawk, alerted by the low roar of startled murmurs spreading throughout the camp, saw him coming through the lodge flap. She wondered if this boded good or evil. Since the death of Rising Buffalo, his brothers had been gone with the great war party, but the remaining squaws were watching her closely. She prayed daily that Hears-the-Wolf would return before the brothers, for every night she heard whispers that a squaw without a single scar to show she mourned her famous husband should be made to join him in spirit land.

The following day it began to seem her prayers were being answered, for Buffalo Hump shook his head gravely when he heard the braves were out on murder raids, stalking the country, destroying isolated farms and small hamlets caught unawares. In half anger he sent messengers, including his own son, in all directions to recall the warriors. He also had special instructions for individual war leaders, the first mentioned being Hears-the-Wolf. ''Come quickly! Buffalo Hump now holds the red pipe.''

Blue Hawk hugged her children in silence as the hooves of the couriers' horses pounded the earth outside her lodge, then slowly died away beyond the camp.

Far to the east an old farmer had found a young deer with a Comanche arrow in its side. The deer, being wounded, had probably come a distance, but it had not been dead long. They had to be dangerously close. He put his young son on a horse and sent him racing to Gonzales. The rest of his large family huddled in the house. This farmer was an old Indian fighter. He didn't panic; he had always figured they'd be coming someday. He was ready.

Black Tail's warriors were approaching the house in a great circle. They no longer worried about being seen; it was too late for anyone to escape. They saw a tethered bull, two cows, and a bawling calf in a small field next to the barn. Beyond, the house lay silent, waiting. Black Tail's instincts told him this isolated family was alerted and going to fight. It made little difference. Others had tried; their scalps hung at his side. But as they closed in, shots began to ring out and a brave far to his left shouted in pain. Black Tail signaled the warriors to hold back. There was no need for a frontal assault; fire could do their work for them. As fire arrows were prepared, Black Tail glanced at the sky. It was late in the day; the braves had been scouring the country since dawn. Perhaps it was time for the badly needed feast his sighting those cattle brought to mind. They could eat while they waited for this low squat house to burn. He sent some nearby warriors into the field, where, using their long deadly lances, they killed the animals within minutes. Only the bull roared as he was dying; the calf's thin bawl was abruptly cut off, leaving an unexpectedly eerie silence behind.

But they soon discovered this house was not the simple rude structure they thought. This farmer had slate on his roof and green wood covering much of the outer walls. The man had obviously thought ahead, for when finally an arrow stuck and continued to burn, there was a space under the eaves to spill over dousing water. The braves growled with impatience; they were angered by this stubborn resistance and wanted to take the house with their war clubs. But Black Tail was too wily and experienced a fighter to let momentary setbacks lead him into foolish moves. The few impulsive forays they attempted proved the house was being defended on all four sides. He was sure he had this farm cut off; he had not seen another for many miles. They would have their feast now; it would quiet the braves. And in the darkness before dawn they would storm and break into the weakest side of the house.

Within the farmhouse the old farmer, his three grown sons, two daughters, and his feisty wife were relieved the attack was being put off, the old man guessed till dawn. By then help should have arrived. But no one could be sure. Perhaps Roy, their youngest, had not gotten through. Perhaps the Comanches had been watching the house longer than they suspected and had seen Roy leave. Perhaps the boy's horse had stepped in a gopher hole and poor Roy was lying somewhere injured or afoot. Anxiety called forth all possible calamities. Only the old lady was confident. "Pshaw! He's my son. He'll sure as hell get to Gonzales; quit yer worryin'."

"Ma," said Caroline, the oldest girl, "you can't really know! All we can do is pray!"

The men were covering the four sides of the building, the women behind them ready to reload their guns. The old man had fought Indians before in his time. He knew their situation was serious, but he also knew Indians were often quickly discouraged, particularly if they began to suffer casualties. He admonished his family over and over again. "Don't shoot too fast; make sure you hit something when you do. It doesn't matter where you catch them; a foot is as good as the belly. It will take them out of the fight and convince them they got bad medicine.''

The youngest girl had her hands clasped in front of her. ''What will they do to us?'' she murmured tightly.

''Nothing!'' said her oldest brother too quickly. ''They ain't getting the chance. You stop fussing.''

They all looked at each other, their eyes reflecting various depths of doubt, and then they settled down to enter the longest night they had ever known.

Another head was facing an uneasy night at that moment, confronted with a different, yet by no means innocuous, threat. Mexican spies in San Antonio had sped word of the courthouse massacre to President Santa Anna, who had returned from exile and was once more in the National Palace. A congenital opportunist, within minutes he had sent General Adrian Woll, a Swiss mercenary, whose military skills were badly needed by the large but ineffectual Mexican Army, with a dispatch to General Canalizo. Canalizo had been sent north to keep an eye on recently rebelling border provinces fighting to break free of the central government and becoming independent as the Republic of the Rio Grande.

Mexico's many attempts to enlist the aid of Indian tribes to reconquer Texas, a province they still regarded as their own, had failed, but they had never been able to enlist the powerful, hostile Comanches, who commanded vast stretches west and north of San Antonio. The murdering of their chiefs would surely make an alliance with Mexico appealing, particularly if the latter could supply guns and even armed support. His dispatch to Canalizo made it clear the general was to bring such a desirable arrangement about.

Canalizo, swearing under his breath and frowning irritably at the dispatch, drummed white knuckles against his desk. Santa Anna, like every bureaucrat in the capital, far away from border villages, where scalp-laden Comanches left bodies of women or heads of men strewn about the burnt-out dwellings, always blithely assumed these savages were easy to approach and simple to deal with. Canalizo knew better. Comanches were a touchy and imperious bunch, accustomed to bribes and tribute. It would be foolish, perhaps even dangerous, to approach them boldly or even empty-handed. Asking Woll to be seated, he called in a Captain Armonte, whom he instructed to seek out the Penateka and promise them rifles and other support if they would follow his guidelines when attacking the *tejanos*.

Armonte smiled nervously; this did not sound like an assignment for a subordinate with a future. How many rifles?

The number, Canalizo wisely decided to leave open. He knew Comanches would prefer to determine it themselves, making the request seem more like a demand. But the army had plenty of old, practically useless rifles they would be happy to discard. Secretly he did not envy Captain Armonte his assignment, but his orders had been explicit, and Armonte's could not be otherwise. Assuming the Comanches would cooperate, and attack as he advised, when the Texans were fully engaged, he would have Woll march on San Antonio. The long-awaited reconquering of "errant" Texas would begin.

As an outsider, Adrian Woll, always slightly amused by the Mexican mentality, made a disturbing yet discerning remark. "General, since these Comanches have been killing and abducting your people for generations, aren't you marrying the devil to get back at a handful of sinners?"

Canalizo looked uncomfortable. "My dear friend, this decision was made in the South. From down there the Texans look like giants and the Comanches like fleas. Santa Anna's pride is involved. Remember, he lost Texas. Some have not forgotten he deserted his army at San Jacinto, running off in his underwear, shaming our colors. He is not a man who likes to live with his sins.

Retaking Texas would restore his pride, not to mention his political fortunes.''

"But, General, what about your people?"

Canalizo smiled bitterly. "My friend, Santa Anna's dreams are spun of privilege and power, not patriotism. Surely you have noticed he has very expensive and lusty tastes. He dresses like an emperor and has deflowered enough women to fill the nunneries of Europe. His energies go into swelling his pride and his penis; there is little left for the people."

"I see," said Woll laconically, turning to stare out the window. "No doubt, one day his people will also see."

Canalizo crumpled the paper in his hand and tossed it into the wastebasket. "No doubt, my dear General, one day they *must* also see."

Chapter 10

NO WORDS COULD describe the scene when Hays reached the devastated farm. The carnage was sickening, and some of the younger Rangers turned ill as they collected the children's bodies and lifted the impaled women from the posts to be settled in hastily dug graves. The man's body was taken from the well, and other signs of Comanche savagery removed. Kinfolk who would one day be coming for the claim would have only a peaceful row of crosses to greet them. Yet the loss in human terms was enormous. Fifteen people had died here, along with the hopes and dreams of the young girl who had reported the raid. Jack Hays was thinking of the military force that should have been but wasn't available. Yet his prediction was right; they followed the great war party's tracks till they saw it was splitting up. Hays and Caldwell decided to stay with the groups heading north and east till they found themselves on the trail of some thirty or forty braves. These they followed northeast till they saw smoke on the horizon. Scouts sent forward reported another farm had been attacked. Hays remembered there was a lonely settlement built near a

creek some miles to the north of this spot. Instinct told
him the Comanches would head there next. He moved
his troop around and, while the war party put the hapless
farmer to death, found a suitable site for an ambush. The
Comanches, flush with victory, were not long in coming.
Their scalp-waving war leader rode in front, the rest
coming behind with a wild abandon that betrayed their
confidence that the country was theirs and the whites in
the lonely settlement ahead helpless.

The suddenness of it added to its horror. After the
first volley, the war leader and eighteen of his braves
were dead or writhing on the ground. The Rangers
wasted no time; they rose from their hiding places to
close with the now-screaming warriors. More deadly
gunmen did not exist, and the Comanches' numbers
were cut down till only a handful remained. It was well
Comanche culture did not include notions of mercy; they
got none. Those attempting to escape were hunted down.
Fresh from the burden of burying hideously tortured
bodies at the farmhouse, the Rangers fought with a cold
fury. They had no need for or interest in prisoners; they
took none. They had no bullets to waste on the wounded;
they smashed heads in with rifle butts. Cattle would have
been shown more respect. Only three Rangers were injured, only one seriously. Hays and Caldwell, always
mindful of their men, sent the two lesser wounded back
with the crippled one, telling them to make for San Antonio.

After they collected the horses, they left the Indian
bodies for the buzzards. The Rangers had won a sweeping victory, but Hays did not delude himself. There were
many other war parties attacking settlers that day, and
he had no way to stop them. He looked at Old Paint,
thoughtfully gripping his chin with one hand. "Well,
partner, mebbe we've made a start."

"Mebbe," answered Caldwell, looking at the sky.
"Weather is making up. Could be a norther coming."

The men looked at each other. A bad storm might

drive the Penateka into camp. Still, such a camp would
be a risky business; the Rangers would be seriously outnumbered. But the Rangers followed a peculiar code.
They did not consider their dangerous life heroic or even
laudable. They were volunteers protecting society
against a public menace. Wherever that menace appeared, it had to be attacked. If they were outnumbered,
aggressiveness or strategy had to equalize their chances.
If they were cornered and facing death, they took as
many Comanches with them as possible. It was a brutal
code and ensured the pitiless nature of the fight, for the
Comanches were discovering these Rangers, like themselves, driven by social imperatives, would not and
could not accept defeat, and that no matter the odds in
any encounter, no quarter could now be expected or
given.

A half-breed scout, slipping across country from cover
to cover like a worried weasel, led Captain Armonte and
his young duty sergeant to the big Comanche camp on
the Nueces. Upon sighting it, the scout turned about
without ceremony and hurriedly retraced his steps, leaving them to enter it alone.

The Mexicans, after a scary welcome by an enormous
brave with a limp and a badly scarred face, found themselves waiting outside Buffalo Hump's lodge, with Captain Armonte looking pale and anxiously chewing a
cigar. He was nervous and had trouble maintaining a
brave front before his duty sergeant. Armonte did not
like Comanches; they had done terrible things to his
countrymen. He considered them wicked, remorseless
killers. In truth he was secretly afraid of them. He had
come only because of Canalizo's orders, but he couldn't
shake off the feeling there was something ridiculous
about Mexicans giving military advice to these ferocious
horse warriors, who routinely raided Mexican territory
and easily routed all attempts at reprisals.

He caught sight of many terrifying things about this

war camp, and not having been invited there, was all too wary. The sergeant, who had noticed some Mexican captives, glancing at the two soldiers with expressions that said they were now more Comanche than Mexican, could not help praying under his breath. "Why do they keep us waiting?" he muttered to his superior.

"They're Comanches. Comanches keep everyone waiting, even Saint Peter." He bent a little closer to his aide. "Don't look nervous; it gives a bad impression."

The sergeant watched Armonte twitching his mustache, wetting his lips, tapping his foot on the ground, and repeatedly clearing his throat. The captain surely couldn't be nervous; he had just advised against it. Perhaps it was a full bladder.

The giant brave was suddenly before them again, this time with a second brave who spoke a rude Spanish. "What does the unbidden visitor want with our chief?"

Armonte snapped his heels together and saluted. "General Canalizo sends good wishes to his friends, the Comanches. He also wishes to help them against the *tejanos*." He deliberately used their own disparaging term.

The two warriors stared at him. Both their faces were garishly painted and looked threatening in the dim light.

A thin smile flickered across the great brave's lips as his companion translated this pompous-sounding Mexican's words about helping the Penateka to fight. It was well he was amused, for it made him decide to take this visibly shaking man into Buffalo Hump's tepee. After a long day of serious talk, the old chief might enjoy the blustering words of this loud-talking yet pale and jittery emissary. He turned and lifted the flap of the lodge, and Armonte found himself in the presence of Buffalo Hump, the cruel despoiler of Mexico's northern villages and enslaver of her people, and a man who now held the fate of West Texas in his hands. Desperately trying to control his fear, the good captain forced his features

into a wide if waxen smile, and in a halting voice began
to speak.

It was long after dawn when McCulloch's troop came
over a rise and the young boy, Roy, pointing to a distant
scrub- and rock-strewn hillside, said the farm was just
beyond its crest. McCulloch called up Tomcah, his Lipan scout, and told him to move up and sight on the
farm. Tomcah, deliberately hesitating and rising up in
the saddle, made the sign for vultures and pointed to the
sky ahead. Quickly searching the sky beyond, Mc-
Culloch spotted black dots slowly circling, banking in
ever-narrowing circles and drifting downward. "Could
be too late," he said, a choke of resignation edging his
voice.

Young Roy turned pale, realizing what these men
were reading from the scene. But suddenly Tomcah was
pushing forward, and McCulloch, with his arm in the
air, was bringing his troop quietly behind. Cautiously
they moved up the slope of the hill, guns ready, senses
alert, but there was no sign of Indians and no shots rang
out. Jody and Dale at the back of the troop were holding
their breaths. Each kept a hand on his six-gun and licked
dryness from his lips. They were sure any minute howling redskins would come pouring over that ridge and
they would be desperately fighting, back to back, to the
death.

Near the top Tomcah dismounted and crawled to the
spine of the last rise. Quietly he swept the terrain before
him, then quickly signaled McCulloch to come up.

McCulloch dropped to the ground and, squirming forward, joined him. Behind them the troop watched their
leader rise on one knee, then, shading his eyes, peer into
the distance while they waited and wondered in silence.

In the false dawn the farmer had quietly roused his
family, whispering hoarsely, "Keep a sharp lookout.
Figure they be coming soon."

With ears straining, they began to hear noises in all directions; some were only the normal noises of night distorted in their minds by fear. But some could well be harbingers of death. The tension began to mount. "Fetch the dog!" whispered the farmer to his oldest son.

The dog was kept in the root cellar at night to keep him from barking at coons, armadillos, rattlesnakes, and other denizens of the dark with which the area abounded. It was a hound dog with drooping ears and deep yellow eyes. It came up panting and rushing about, looking for an exit to get at the intruders who took advantage of its confinement.

The dog's name was Bart. The farmer pointed him at the front door, hissing, "Sic 'em, Bart." The dog sniffed at the front door but then came back looking up, confused, hoping for more reliable guidance.

The old woman snorted. "Leave the dog alone. If there be critters jigging around out there, he'll be heard on the moon."

Caroline, trying to deal with her anxiety, began to hug the dog. It was an affectionate animal and particularly liked Caroline. Normally it stood still and allowed her to embrace its silky neck and rub its flabby ears, but suddenly it pulled away from her and made a beeline for the kitchen. The family, led by the farmer, followed it. The kitchen had a door whose top half could be opened, being held only by a latch, but it also had a low-slung window to siphon heat from the stove. The dog, now barking in excited yips, jumped against the door and forced its way behind the stove to snarl along the window ledge. The farmer knew at once the attack was coming where he least expected it. Forsaking the other sides of the house, he lined his family up with guns pointing at the outer kitchen wall. Only a few had time to pull a piece of furniture in front of them, but the dog's warning had meant their salvation. The assault came with war clubs splintering the door and shattering the window. War cries rose from the warriors bunched

together and ready to force their way in. The dim outlines of some could already be seen working through the
holes they were slashing open when the farmer gave the
order to fire. The blast was deafening, but the shock to
the warriors could be heard in the grunts and screams
of those who, within feet of the gun muzzles, had chests
or stomachs blown open and faces painfully burned by
exploding powder. The women hurriedly passed up the
extra loaded guns, and a second volley sent the braves
scampering back in the still thick darkness.

Now the farmer ordered them to guard the other sides
of the house. "They won't come back this way again,"
he said with a faint hint of confidence. "We've given
them something to think about!" His children listened
to him, hiding the fact they, too, were in shock; never
had any of them been so close to the dreaded Comanches
before. Caroline hugged her younger sister and kept her
from crying by urging her to help reload all the guns.

Black Tail was furious. A successful attack would
have increased his prestige as a war leader. Now the
braves were mumbling to each other, some tending to
the wounded or trying to recover the bodies of the few
dead, but none shouted to him to continue the attack. A
bad sign. It was almost a hour later and dawn was flushing the eastern sky when the braves decided they would
keep the house surrounded and snipe at it, hoping to find
a way to set it afire or force this stubborn farmer to run
out of ammunition. None wanted to leave with the taste
of defeat in their mouths. Black Tail did not need to be
told they were comparing him to Hears-the-Wolf, and
his power over them was waning. But he was both mad-
dened and sorely distressed. His instincts told him be-
sieging this house was a mistake. There were too many
guns being wisely used, and there were no signs of panic
or desperation, which always marked whites feeling
hopelessly trapped. The fact that the body of a deer had
been found near the farm bothered him. It had been

killed by an arrow with the shaft pulled out. To him it meant their presence might have been known or suspected, and help for the farm might be on its way. Deep intuition told him to start these braves back to the Nueces, for bad medicine hung over this venture, but by now the braves were pointedly turning their faces away from him, clearly stating if there was any bad medicine about, it was surely his.

McCulloch was relieved to see the vultures were feeding on the remains of dead cattle that had been butchered near the house. The sight of several Indian ponies being held in a brush corral a short distance from the farm told him the Indians were still about. But it was some time before he spotted them crouching in the undergrowth or behind stumps and barrels that surrounded the outhouse and barn. The firing was sporadic, with little coming from the house. He wasn't surprised. By now the defenders might well be counting each shell.

He estimated there might be some twenty-odd braves, a surmise that had him thinking his troop could make "good Indians" of them all. But first they would have to take the horses. He had long ago learned a Comanche deprived of his horse is a tornado reduced to a zephyr. Not exactly true but close. By scratching on the ground, he showed Tomcah how he wanted him to take two men and, by moving in a big circle, avoid being seen until they could rush in and stampede the horses. He himself would lead the rest of the troop on a stealthy approach that would cut the Indians off from their brush corral. The rest of the orders were always the same; kill as many redskins as you can. Every one throwing up his life's blood on the prairie today was one less to worry about tomorrow.

It was the courier, coming in the midmorning, who saved Black Tail's life. Hearing Buffalo Hump's message, he ordered the war party to call off the attack and return to camp. But the braves were reluctant to give up this victim, who they felt could not last much longer. They needed scalps and trophies to take back to camp. They had lost some men, and the failure of their attack, without trophies to prove otherwise, would be apparent. So either luck or fate had Black Tail at the brush corral when Tomcah and the two young Rangers rushed up, firing their guns to stampede the horses. The horses began to bolt, but not before Black Tail had mounted his painted mustang and had turned back screaming to the braves to save their mounts. But McCulloch was already between them and their brush corral, and the braves had to seek cover as a hail of lead started whining about them.

The Comanches, if nothing else, were brave men. They fought, ducking through the sparse foliage, trying to make their way to their horses, but the advantage was all with the Rangers. One by one the warriors were shot or ridden down by McCulloch's men, who were riding everywhere, six-guns blazing. Only one managed to jump up behind Black Tail, who had his mount at a gallop trying to escape, but he was riding directly into Jody and Dale. Dale opened fire, but it seemed to have little effect. The mounted Indians raced by as Jody, who hadn't gotten off a shot, belatedly spurred Blackie in pursuit. Though the mustang was carrying double, the fleet Blackie was hard-pressed to gain any ground. Jody was amazed at the way the horse ahead was bounding and jumping over the rugged land. Had it not been for a wide gully no horse could clear, he might never have gotten close enough to shoot.

As it was, he was shocked to find the horse had been turned and was now coming directly at him. It was clear the Comanche behind the rider was going to leap at him, try to unseat him, and seize his horse. It was too late to do more than blaze away blindly, as he felt himself suddenly hit and gripped by a desperate Indian who clung to him, struggling to unseat him and knock him to the ground. But the Indian must have been wounded, for Jody almost immediately overpowered him and thrust him from the horse. The Indian fell to the earth, where he lay on his side glancing in cringing pain toward Black Tail, who had started to return. But then the hoofbeats of Rangers following Dale began to thunder toward them. Jody, still stunned by the encounter and seeing the wounded Indian reaching for his knife, fired at him point-blank. The Indian's body seemed to convulse, then spun till his face was pressed against the earth. With the strangest sensation, like something pressing against his heart, Jody knew he was dead. He hardly remembered Black Tail speeding away, he simply sat looking at the Indian's body as Dale and some of the Rangers came up. "That finishes 'em," shouted a Ranger, taking in the dead brave's body.

"No, truth is one got away," muttered Dale, his eyes fixed on Jody's face.

"Damn!" uttered one of the Rangers under his breath.

There was little more said; Rangers were used to death scenes. As more rode up, Jody heard them talking about finding something to eat at the farm.

Jody rode back beside a subdued Dale, glad the other didn't try to talk. He had some thinking to do. He had just killed his first Indian. Emotions he never felt before were touching something in the deep of him. Somehow it didn't help that they called them redskins; he had just killed another man, another human being.

Chapter 11

IN SAN ANTONIO the bells of San Fernando were tolling two and three times a day. Word kept coming in of raids in the upper river valleys and from the few settlements along the Medina. No trail was safe; mail carriers worked at the risk of their lives. Wagon masters refused to travel even to Austin without an escort, and a few small settlements that had sent desperate messengers for help were found overrun and annihilated by the time it arrived. The known dead toll was close to a hundred, and the government was posting warnings to keep settlers well east of the Comanche raiding range.

After several days, the Rangers were exhausted, and though they hung on doggedly, their horses began to give out. "A Ranger is only as good as his horse" was a famous Jack Hays adage, and horses after days of grinding pursuit could no longer keep up and stay together. When the first horse died of overexertion, Jack order the troops to return to their stations. Caldwell, who had taken a troop up to the San Saba, came in two days after Hays, some of his men riding captured Comanche horses after their own had expired. All encounters were not as successful as the first. Now there were dead Rangers lying in lonely graves and critically wounded ones being carried home to die.

The carnage seemed to have no end. Volunteers, facing scene after scene of shocking butchery, had to fight against physical and nervous exhaustion. Some experienced moments, when informing people of loved ones lost in distant massacres, as upsetting as finding bodies mutilated and ravaged by scavengers. Frontier families were often large and spread out, the lure of open land pulling them toward every horizon.

The army, having only infantry available, hopefully stationed troops in several outposts, but war parties rode around them as if they were harmless stands of cactus.

It seemed endless. The heat of summer was beginning to grasp the land. Dry winds raised dust, tormenting the handful of travelers forced to ride the open plains between the rivers. Tracks of war parties crossed every trail, and talk of death and devastation rose from every lip. But then suddenly, without warning, without visible reason, without any discernible clue the hard-pressed Rangers or the harried and terrified settlers could detect—it stopped!

A strange peace, disquieting as it was mystifying, in only a day or two had settled over the Texas frontier. Many settlements, having long pleaded for divine intervention, quietly offered prayers for deliverance. A sense of relief, like awakening from a hideous dream, struck many lonely farms, which had fearfully watched smoke climb distant horizons at dawn. Yet the toll had been appalling and it would leave its legacy. Blood seeping into the Texas soil was soon feeding the roots of fear, hatred, and vengeance. Together with a fury brought on by years of exhaustive effort left in ashes, they promised a cruel harvest.

"Jody, what's a-troubling you?"

"You got to keep asking that?"

"Heaven knows, you've been quiet as a grave for a spell."

He turned away; it was daylight and he wanted to clear bramble and weeds from a far section of the corn lot before the day got too warm. Libby was fussing with the baby, laying out its clothes and feeding it. She continued to talk, watching him, her face faintly taut with concern. "Becky is putting up preserves today; I'm fixing to help her. You be all right alone?"

"I'll make do."

She picked up Lance and went to stand over him. "Dale told his sister, Kate, they had to shoot a passel of Indians to rescue that farm. Lord, I don't hope to ever hear those mission bells ring again."

Jody stomped into his boots, finishing his mug of coffee and slice of honeyed corn bread. He kept staring outside and studying the sky to the west, where clouds, catching the first rays of the sun, were turning pink and pale gold. They seemed to hold him for a few moments.

Libby, still watching him, kept talking, not knowing what to say but wanting him to respond. "You reckon those Injun women fuss like we do when their men traipse off? . . . Reckon they get themselves all stirred up and weepy like us when they don't get back?"

Jody stood outside the door, still looking at the sky, but it was clear his mind was elsewhere as he muttered back, "Reckon they do, Libby . . . reckon they do."

Jack Hays could only admire the grim tenacity of many downcast and bereaved settlers. Always there were a few who gave up, turning back east, deciding the road ahead was too hard, too lonely, too hopeless. The frontier winnowed out all but the hardiest, the most resilient, the most doggedly determined. But courage and perseverance aside, he knew there were tragedies beyond the capacity of the human heart to endure. One such was Clint Bishop, Jess Bishop's brother and Becky's youngest brother-in-law. He had lost his budding family and his best friend in a scene almost too terrible to relate. Yet Clint insisted on talking about it. It seemed some demon within kept him going, as though the whole world had to bear witness to an ordeal too monstrous to rest sanely in any man's mind.

He had traveled half a day from his claim on the Perdenales to where that river joined the Colorado. There was a trading post there with a few but vital supplies. Isolated, he had not known about the raids, but communications on the Colorado were far better than they were to the west. The startling news left his pulse pounding and brought a lightness to his head. With an eerie sensation something frightening was happening to his wife, Anne, and their baby, he quickly turned his weary horse around and started back. He tried to take comfort from the knowledge that Prent Silby and his beautiful wife, Cora, were staying with them till they built on their own claim. Prent was new to the frontier, but he was a plucky young man and Clint's best friend. The Silbys also had a baby, only three months old. The two women, sharing the endless farmhouse work in this very lonely land, were a great comfort to each other.

His trip back seemed to take an eternity. He had lost patience with his near-exhausted mount and drove it forward, pushing it beyond its limits, knowing it might not survive. But it was to no avail. When he reached his claim, the house and barn were in ashes. Anne's body lay sprawled on the ground; she had been stripped and raped. The two babies had been impaled on lances that were stuck into the ground beside the burning house, their bodies charred. He found poor Prent staked to the ground, facing the sun, his eyelids cut away and what had been hot coals stacked against his armpits and scrotum. There was no sign of the beautiful Cora. He found her clothes on the ground, so she had been stripped like Anne and probably raped, but then carried off to be a plaything for the braves before her enslavement by vermin-ridden squaws.

His horse foundered and died within five minutes of his arrival. Some neighbors, straying far and wide on a hunt, found him demented and ranting to the skies as he attempted to follow the departing tracks on foot.

They took him to San Antonio, where the only doctor in town, an immigrant German, shook his head and tapped it with his forefinger. "*Ja,* lots of rest. Dot's all ve can do. Lots of rest, *ja.* Maybe he comes all right."

Within a week he was at least rational but had taken to drink, a development that had Jack Hays biting his lip and confiding to Matt Caldwell, "Reckon we got us another crazy brewing. I do believe it for a fact."

Caldwell nodded.

Crazies were white men driven to near lunacy by the obscene and degrading murders of their loved ones. Many ended up as Comanche killers, taking to the buffalo range to live like animals and prey on isolated Comanche men, women, and children. Sooner or later they were caught and suffered agonizing deaths. Even the well-known Indian reverence for insanity failed to save them. But deranged, they were no longer fit for civilization, and in the end it mattered little.

But Clint Bishop just drank till he reached a stupor, repeatedly and morbidly describing to himself, or others he could get to listen, that nightmarish scene of rape and murder that seemed emblazoned on his brain. Locals were secretly glad to hear that, after selling his abandoned claim for liquor money, he was finally destitute. The sheriff, noticing that once deprived of whiskey, he tended to get violent, advised him to leave town before he got into trouble. A few days later he was observed leaving San Antonio to visit with his older brother and sister-in-law, Jess and Becky Bishop of Gonzales.

That the Comanches had unaccountably disappeared did not sit well in all minds. After a few weeks of quietude, Jack Hays grew worried. He didn't believe the widespread rumor that the Penateka had gone south to raid deep in Mexico. There were suspiciously few reports of movement on the trace that spring. Something was happening, something being carefully hidden and therefore, in frontier terms, ominous. Hays enlisted two Lipan scouts, and knowing Big Foot Wallace was familiar with the far reaches of the Comanche buffalo range, asked him to find the Penateka and discover where they were and why. Wallace, always joking, said he was being picked because Injun squaws were hungry for him, he being the only lover who ever satisfied twenty of them "all t'once." In answer to the ready smirks of skepticism, he added, "They mostly keeps the back of the tepee pinned up so I can slip in and out." This spoofery always came with a straight face that broke listeners into waves of laughter.

"Best you don't get to messing with them at all," counseled Hays seriously. "Just find out where they are and what they're likely up to."

"And don't take any long chances," added Caldwell. "When Comanches look like they're asleep, that's when they're watching the hardest."

"All that good advice has got to be worth a heap of drinks," answered Wallace, looking appraisingly at the two Apache scouts. "Tell them two bucks we leave tomorrow before dawn. We'll talk by sign, and Comanche scalps are off limits till I say so."

"Don't worry," said Hays, "they aren't getting any closer to Comanches then they have to. Their whole tribe was nigh wiped out by the Penateka. These two are just throwing in with us for a little revenge."

June 6 was Libby's eighteenth birthday, and Kate and Becky both thought it a fine excuse for a celebration. They decided to have it at Becky's, whose barn was not as large as Kate's but big enough for the number of guests expected.

Libby left all the inviting to them, but she noticed the Munsters were never mentioned, and Buck and Maude

Chauncy were left out on Pete Spevy's opinion that
Maude was in a bad way and not capable of setting up
for a party. Libby felt she should be doing more around
the settlement, but until now the baby and fixing up her
home had kept her days full. Her concerns about Jody
had lessened as he seemed to have resolved some inner
conflict and started talking again. More significant, his
lovemaking had resumed some of its boyish abandon;
sometimes between sessions he would tickle her and
they would laugh together. Yet, for all that, he appeared
a little more reflective, a little older, a little more a man
aware of another side of life.

One day, using the one-horse rig borrowed from the
Sutters, who had several, she visited the Chauncys. It
proved a difficult ordeal. Maude could not stop weeping,
and Buck, who came in from the field when he saw her
arrive, was clearly concerned for his wife's mind. Lucas,
the young boy, stood in the corner bewildered by his
mother's state. His eyes seemed to plead for the love
and care she could not give him, though Buck made him
attend her constantly, never letting her out of sight. The
boy was to run for Buck if she turned violent, talked
strangely, or tried to hurt herself. Buck looked like a
man whose soul had been tried beyond the breaking
point. Libby wondered how long he could go on. Pete
Spevy had also reported Buck wasn't keeping up with
his farmwork and their crops would be poor. She made
Maude some tea and sat comforting her, but an hour or
two was as much as she could stand. She hugged Maude
and Buck and little Lucas and left. On her way home
she ran into Pete Spevy looking at some hatchet marks
on a cottonwood that stood along the trail.

"What do you suppose those are?" he asked after
removing his hat and greeting her.

"I really can't imagine," said Libby, trying to pull
herself out of the mood the Chauncys had put her in.

"Them's Comanche markings. Put there a while ago.
Came by on a raid once, and the story is, two were shot

from cover under this tree. Tomcah, McCulloch's scout, says them markings mean they'll be back to even the score. Mighty strange doings, but that's the way those critters think.''

''Have they come back?''

''They've been back twice since. Don't need to tell you how much more than even those devils made the score.''

Pete kept his horse beside her for a while. He was a strange but gentle man who had no family. Libby suspected he was secretly lonely and grateful for her company. She tried to think of things to say. Before she knew it, she was saying, ''How are the Munsters these days?''

Spevy looked at her peculiarly. ''Reckon they're fixin' to leave. Didn't you hear?''

''No, I haven't heard a thing.''

''No room around here for folks takin' the redskin side . . . Too much blood has gone into the ground.''

Libby felt a strange emotion running up through her chest to her head. She could still see Nat Munster's eyes quietly and painfully questioning hers at the prayer meeting. It had flashed through her mind that she should visit them on the morrow, but Pete's expression was now warning her it might not be the wisest thing to do.

Spevy must have sensed his remarks had disturbed her, for he began explaining away the new awkwardness between them. ''Folks is funny,'' he said, looking down. He gestured as if he wanted to say more, but when he tried, the geniality had dropped from his voice. Shortly thereafter he tipped his hat and cantered away.

Blue Hawk saw Hears-the-Wolf coming into camp and, knowing the brothers would not be far behind, quickly sent Bright Arrow to summon him. Though trail-weary, he came at once, and his expression at seeing her lifted her heart. ''You will come to my lodge,'' he said, coming up and taking one of her braids in his hand.

Blue Hawk managed a tense smile. "My children and I now belong to the brothers . . . You must give them many horses so there will be no trouble."

Hears-the-Wolf looked as though he were on the verge of laughing. "Does the wolf give presents to cowardly coyotes when it takes a fawn they have trapped by luck?"

"It is our custom . . . I want to come to you with honor."

Hears-the-Wolf studied her for a moment. "Woman, speak the truth! It's the young ones, isn't it?"

She grasped his hand that had pointedly released the braid. "Yes . . . but the brothers are angry . . . They will look for ways to punish me."

The war leader snorted, "They will look for places to hide when—"

Blue Hawk saw the hulking form of the lame warrior with the scarred face coming up. He had been Buffalo Hump's chosen lieutenant until leg wounds kept him from mounting a horse. The limping giant ignored Blue Hawk and spoke gruffly to Hears-the-Wolf. "You have been called to the lodge of Buffalo Hump. He does not wait while warriors make idle words with squaws."

Hears-the-Wolf threw him a defiant look, but only nodded reassuringly to Blue Hawk as he turned away. Irritated as he was and wishing to say more, he knew all too well Buffalo Hump was not a man to trifle with. Hears-the-Wolf entered the spacious lodge and was soon settled across the fire from the legendary chief. Within minutes he discovered why the lame giant was in such a foul mood.

"*Isi-man-ica,*" began the old chief, "the Penateka must make all its warriors' hands into one mighty fist, to strike the *tejanos* and drive them from our lands. We will go north to seek help from the Kotsoteka and other bands of the Nerm; perhaps even the Kiowas will ride with us. A great war party must be formed, greater than any here can remember. I have taken sacred oaths to avenge the murder of our chiefs. Their spirits will not rest until the blood of *tejanos* makes our rivers run red.''

Sensing the chief had more on his mind, Hears-the-Wolf replied quietly, ''Your words are good,'' then watched the chief reach for his pipe before quietly adding, ''Does Buffalo Hump wish something of me?''

The chief packed the pipe and put a burning twig to it before answering. ''My favorite war leader is badly wounded and can no longer lead warriors into battle.'' He leaned across the fire, extending the pipe. ''I have chosen you to replace him.''

Hears-the-Wolf, weighing these words, took the pipe and sat silent for a moment. This was more than just an honor; Buffalo Hump's great following would now also be his. This was one step away from being a chief, a tribal leader of high rank. Buffalo Hump was not only an outstanding commander, but one who rarely thought small. He had led raids into Mexico lasting over a year, enriching the tribe with untold loot and hundreds of captives. He had raided as far south as Durango and even Zacatecas. For successful war parties, his record had few equals, and now he was planning the most deadly and destructive raid in the tribe's history, an all-out assault on the hated *tejanos,* a bloody, relentless onslaught to drive them from the land of the Nerm forever. His plans for calling on the powerful northern Comanche bands and the Kiowas for assistance made it clear Buffalo Hump was taking no risk of defeat. Though it would surely take time to assemble such a force, what it promised would keep the warriors content until the time to strike came.

After Hears-the-Wolf accepted this honor, saying solemnly he stood ready to do anything requested to avenge the chiefs, he discovered his first task was to assemble a band of experienced scouts. Then Buffalo Hump threw some medicine grass on the fire and it appeared the meeting was over. But the old chief, raising his eagle fan to cover half his face, motioned for Hears-the-Wolf, who was rising, to settle again. *"Isi-man-ica,"* he said stoically, "great warriors must obey the customs handed down by our fathers. In war it is dangerous to allow the spirits to dwell on bad medicine. All affairs for those who lead the people in times of trouble must be settled with honor."

Hears-the-Wolf knew at once Buffalo Hump was speaking about Blue Hawk. It was an issue, in the excitement of the moment, he had forgotten. For a long while he stared back at Buffalo Hump, finally sensing the wisdom of the old chief's words. "Put your mind at ease," he half whispered. *"Isi-man-ica* and our great leader, *Pohchanah-kwoheep*, will ride proudly together when they go against the *tejanos*."

The old man smiled and slowly lowered the fan.

Chapter 12

JODY ENJOYED WATCHING his pretty wife get dressed. She had gotten a light green gown with tiny gold frills from Kate, and after taking it in to fit her rounding form, she was preparing to don it for her birthday party. He was amazed at how her figure had blossomed at the birth of Lance; her bustline was fuller and her hips more rounded. There was a little less of the girl and a little more of the woman. She still had a certain shyness, evidenced by how she slipped one piece of clothing on as she removed another, never appearing nude, but it made her seem more sensuous than ever. Something else had happened. He sensed she was questioning much about herself. Often he would see her gazing toward the river as though some dissident feeling for this country wouldn't settle in her heart. There were nights when she gasped with passion as he made love to her and nights when she seemed remote, unable to cross some field of doubt growing in her mind.

Jody had his own reckoning with this land to deal with. He hadn't told her about the Indian he had killed, knowing it would disturb her, however presented. He himself went through a few days when he kept telling himself they had killed his father, his uncle, and poor harmless old Josiah. It was only his duty to avenge those murders. At first it didn't help, but finally his strange moods lessened as he fell back on his grandfather's stories about fighting Shawnees in Kentucky and later in the Creek and Choctaw wars. They had always seemed like romantic adventures, tamed by distance and teeming with colorful Indians who fought fiercely but died easily. He never heard his grandfather talk about Indians the way Rangers spoke about Comanches. He remembered McCulloch coming back to ride beside him on their way home, obviously noticing Jody's reaction to the killing. He reached over to pat him on the back. "Just wait till you see some of their handiwork, fellow . . . It gets easier to pull the trigger then."

Libby looked beautiful in her dress. She had braided her dark hair carefully in the style of the day, and her green eyes, matching her dress, seemed exotic, transforming her for the moment from a naive little farm girl to a seductive-looking female. He smiled to himself and went over to kiss her. She kissed him back and let him settle her on the bed, but when he put his hand under her dress, reaching her bare thigh, she gave him one last kiss and pushed herself up again. "Don't go getting me all mussed! Lord knows it's taken me a heap of fussin' to look party-like." She straightened her dress and turned to wake the baby. "Why aren't you dressed?"

"Been busy looking at you."

"Well, just keep a-lookin' at me tonight and don't go getting any notions I'm flirting."

"Well, tonight, now that you're a big old eighteen, you can flirt. Just be mighty, mighty certain it's with me!"

She looked at him, a teasing smile flickering over her lips. "We'll see."

*   *   *

Hays, never one to depend on rumors, had to know whether the Penateka had gone south to raid in Mexico or not. Caldwell, growing equally concerned, pointed out it might not even be wise to wait for Wallace's return. If he failed to find them, the vital question still remained unanswered. Finally the two captains, made impatient by suspicion and restless by worry, mounted and headed west.

For as long as any Texan could recall, Comanches, even those from northern tribes, had ridden down the great trace to raid and plunder south of the Rio Grande. If they had traveled that way this year, their tracks should still be visible. Even though it was a torturous season for riding, the ovenlike plain making them stop frequently to pull at their canteens and swear at the broiling sun, they kept doggedly on.

Arriving at the trace before sundown, they looked around for a few minutes and then, spitting dust from their mouths, grunted to one another. Not more than a handful of horses had past there in weeks. Neither had to say what it meant. Curiously, a few of the tracks left resembled the heavily shod hooves of Mexican cavalry horses, revealing two had recently traveled north and then hurriedly returned.

Caldwell let out a low whistle. "What do you make of that?"

Hays looked up at the sky like a man adjusting to a new and troublesome thought. He finally glanced over at his companion. "What I make of it puts me in mind of a drink, but I got a feeling we just got us a piece of the answer."

Jess and Becky Bishop argued over the punch bowl before any of their guests arrived. "You can't deprive the lot of us because poor Clint is grieving and a bit out of his head." Jess held the bottle of mash whiskey over the punch bowl containing a mixture of fruit juices and sliced apples.

" 'The lot of us,' is it!" she screamed back at him. "You mean yerself and a few other drunkards! You know what Clint is like when he takes liquor."

"Stop making such a fuss. I'll speak to him. There'll be no trouble."

"That poor man is daft and we both know it . . . Ach, you never listen until it's too late, do you!" She watched him pour the powerful spirit into her punch bowl and, storming out of the room, went to rinse her best dishes in such fury she broke a plate.

When Jody and Libby arrived with little Lance, the party was well under way. Unexpectedly there were quite a few birthday gifts for Libby, which Jody, seeing some piglets and a matching rooster and hen, enjoyed, but there were also a few single men who insisted on kissing Libby, which he sourly declined to watch. But lively Kate, with her blond curls filling the air, soon had Pete Spevy playing and a dance going, which warmed people up and increased activity around the punch bowl.

Becky had been keeping a sharp eye on her brother-in-law, sure he would spoil her party if allowed to drink. Jess had apparently decided to warn him, but now Jess was drinking himself and she couldn't hover near the punch bowl all night. Sitting in a corner brooding, Clint had said practically nothing. If he talked at all, it was only to himself. Word of his tragedy had circulated among the guests, and with a ready understanding, no one bothered him with questions that might prove painful.

Libby only sipped at her glass of punch; she did not like the taste of liquor and was glad Jody was only nursing his. Becky finally whispered there was some plain fruit juice out in the kitchen, explaining why many of the women were trooping that way. But inevitably, with midnight approaching, the party began to break up. Not that people left—parties were too few and far between to cut short—but with food being laid out, those with similar interests began to settle together; men discussed crops, politics, or new models of firearms, while women covered children or fancy clothing that could be ordered from New Orleans or from a new supplier in Houston.

No one noticed how Clint got started, though someone said later he picked up a nearly full glass Libby had put down and forgot. Perhaps he had managed to find others, but before anyone was aware, Clint was becoming inebriated and Becky was at her wits' end. She demanded Jess take him out to the barn and douse his head with water from the livestock trough, but Jess, while not yet drunk, had had enough to be quarrelsome and display that irate stubbornness liquor brings with insensitivity to others. The two, to keep from being heard, although it was clearly too late for that, stepped outside the back door, Becky hoping her neighbors would grasp the situation and understand.

But no one knew quite what to do. Clint had taken the floor and had started ranting to any and all who turned toward him. "I was just trying to get back . . . It was a long trip . . . My horse was dying . . . dying, I tell you . . . Why didn't I die too! I could smell the dead fires and then I saw my Anne . . . Her legs were sprawled . . . They didn't leave her any dignity in death . . . Those bastards . . . those filthy miserable bastards . . . they defile and destroy everything in a man's life!"

Libby had retreated behind Jody, not knowing what to expect and hearing a rising hysteria in Clint's voice. It was his mention of babies that froze her mind, and then with his terrible description of their deaths on lances, she almost screamed. "Babies! They kill babies?!"

Clint swung on her, his eyes suddenly darting about in what could have been an onset of madness. "Kill babies!" he shouted. "Kill babies! They'd kill Christ Himself in the manger and burn the stable down around Him! These are Comanches, lady! Stinking wicked Comanches . . . How long have you been—" Fortunately

Jess appeared to seize him by the arms, trying to subdue him. Libby was holding her breath; she was frightened beyond belief. For a moment she thought he was going to rush at her. Never had she seen a man so distraught, so crazed with hate, so unhinged from sanity by unbearable memories.

Jody, taking her by the arm, helped her out to the rig, where she lifted and hugged Lance. The teenaged girls, who were tending several sleeping infants, gathered around her with looks of curiosity or concern. Was something wrong?

Libby shook her head, no, she just wanted her husband to take her home. Becky, who had followed them out, covered her embarrassment by embracing Libby, but was relieved to hear Jody saying, "We understand, Becky; that poor fellow has been through a lot. Don't let this bother you; it was a wonderful party."

Becky hugged him warmly, giving him a motherly kiss on the cheek. "Thank you; you're a good boy, Jody. You won't forget Libby's gifts, will you?"

"I'll pick them up in a day or so."

They rode several miles with Libby holding Lance to her bosom and staring into the night. For all the warnings Kate and others had given her, not until tonight did she realize she could lose her baby in this country where infants were coldly murdered. The thought seemed to paralyze the lifeblood coming from her heart, and for a time it had to beat furiously to keep going. Jody glanced at her several times and even put his arm around her, but he sensed she wasn't ready for words. They were home and in bed before she finally turned to him. "Jody." Her voice was a whisper made almost brittle with fear. "Why do we stay here?"

"It's our home; we haven't got another."

"I'm frightened, terribly frightened. I don't want to live if anything happens to our baby."

"Nothing is going to happen."

"You say that, Jody, but how do you know? Look at

that poor man . . . What will become of him?''

''That's up to God.''

''No, it's up to us. We have to make peace with these wild people; this horrible fighting has got to stop.''

''Libby, there will be no peace.''

''Why?''

''Because nobody wants it . . . What they want is the land.''

Libby was silent for a moment. She had snuggled into Jody's arms, wanting the protective feeling of having him close. She looked up to watch his face. ''Jody, do you love me?''

''Of course I love you.''

''Then take me home.''

''You are home.''

There was a curious bated moment. ''No, I mean to Missouri.''

Jody looked at her in the darkness; she could just see the growing anguish on his face. She had thought he was trying to answer her, but as the minutes passed she realized his silence was his answer. When she awoke the next morning, still wrapped in his arms, both suddenly felt the need for oneness and they made love. But Libby knew in her heart her only line of retreat had been cut off. Missouri was never mentioned again.

General Canalizo dismissed Captain Armonte with a look of satisfaction edged with faint traces of irritation. The captain had done well; the Comanches were going to cooperate. President Santa Anna would be pleased they had succeeded in secretly enlisting this formidable ally. Canalizo's irritation had only arisen at the price, two hundred rifles! That was more than he had bargained for. Nevertheless, he dispatched a rider to Monteray to see what was available there, suspecting he would, in the end, have to send to Mexico City for the balance. This meant the rifles would not be delivered in less than three weeks. But no time limit had been set, and for his purposes he judged the Penateka already adequately armed. Surely they would serve his objective; they would open the door to the reconquest of Texas.

General Woll, summoned to the commandant's office and offered a cigar, crossed his legs and sat back to watch Canalizo gesture before a giant map that still showed Texas as a province of Mexico. "The idea, my friend," began Canalizo, "is to draw their strength away from San Antonio. That is our . . . I mean that will be your first target. The Penateka have agreed to bypass San Antonio, turning south at Gonzales and raiding down the valley of the Guadalupe, attacking and, if possible, torching Victoria and Linnville. When we hear Linnville is in flames, it will be your signal to march on San Antonio."

Woll drew quietly on his cigar and mused for several seconds before clearing his throat to say, "I fail to see how destroying Victoria or Linnville serves any military purpose. If the objective is to draw fighting forces from San Antonio, wouldn't just establishing the Indians' presence that far east serve as well?"

"You don't understand, General, those traitorous Federalists I have just driven across the border are regrouping in Victoria; they are receiving supplies through the port of Linnville. Both those treasonable centers must be destroyed."

Woll responded with a wry smile. "Then you've made a political decision."

Canalizo looked vaguely annoyed. "Whether it's a political or military decision? Does it matter?"

"In war, everything matters."

Canalizo, secretly irate but aware of Woll's reputation in military circles, went and settled in his chair. "I am prepared to be enlightened."

"It's really quite simple. Political decisions lead to military ones, but military ones, once required, should not be compromised by political ones. To be more explicit, the decision to reconquer Texas was a political decision, but reconquering it is best left to military decisions alone.''

Canalizo looked down at his desktop in silence for a moment. ''Perhaps I'm a poor strategist, General Woll, but I know that decisions made with savages a hundred miles away cannot be easily changed. We shall have to hope those decisions were right.''

Woll clicked his tongue as he arose. ''General Canalizo, perhaps you recall Napoleon's listing of things he regarded important in battle. If my memory serves me right, he made no mention of hope.''

Chapter 13

In SPITE OF the excitement that ran through the camp, once word spread of a trip north for a great council of Nerm tribes, Hears-the-Wolf gathered a string of prime horses and several guns he had looted from burnt-out farms, and sent them with the tall Elk Slayer to the brothers. The brawny warrior was to tell them these presents were in exchange for Blue Hawk and her children, making it clear the gifts were not an offer, open to refusal, but a settlement honoring tribal custom.

The brothers were incensed. This proof that Blue Hawk had surely cuckolded their brother led to threats to disfigure her or strip her and force her to walk humiliated through the camp. But Elk Slayer's words had carried an unmistakable ring of warning. Hears-the-Wolf was a dangerous man, and there were rumors Buffalo Hump had just that day bestowed great honor upon him.

The older brother, stroking his chin, finally counseled acceptance, arguing that Blue Hawk was too hard to manage and had kept the lodge upset with her strange ways and subtle defiance of their authority. Better they trade her off for these valuable presents. But the younger one, chagrined at losing this toothsome and lusty female, who had no match in the robe, argued bitterly against it. It was only after the older one repeated Elk Slayer's words—that Hears-the-Wolf was confident the brothers, wishing to live in peace, would accept the offering—that he sullenly agreed.

Yet it was hard to suppress his craving to somehow strike back at Hears-the-Wolf for his act. The younger one, still smarting at his loss, boldly appeared in Hears-the-Wolf's lodge. "Your presents are not enough," he said arrogantly. "There is a spotted colt in your herd and two decorated knives among your weapons that must be added."

Hears-the-Wolf knew the brothers neither needed nor wanted the colt or the knives. It was an attempt to embarrass him, to show others he wasn't able or willing to pay an adequate price for the woman he wanted. But he said nothing and sent them the colt and the knives. Yet, having done it, the brothers looked nervously at one another. Hears-the-Wolf was not only a dangerous but a fiercely proud man. Such a slight was not likely to be forgotten.

Within a week a great gathering high on the Palo Duro had begun. Not only the Kotsoteka but the Yamparika and Kwahadi, along with many others, answered Buffalo Hump's call for a mighty war council. It was a stirring sight. As dusk approached and fires were lighted, drums began to sound and warriors brandishing scalp sticks, many with hawk bells tied to their elbows and ankles, began to stomp the earth. They came with buffalo-horned headpieces or those of the great mountain elk, whirling about, shouting and grunting like animals, for it was animals they were emulating. Their vital spirit helpers lived in animals, and it was from their mysterious power that strong medicine came.

Like the experienced campaigner he was, Buffalo Hump allowed word of his great raid to spread, and soon fiery young warriors from other tribes began to hang about the Penateka camp. The war honors and booty possible in such an overwhelming assault could bring quick riches and a new importance among one's own people. For a time Hears-the-Wolf worried at the number of chiefs who might also join, for each might dilute Buffalo Hump's power, each another voice in council. But his worries were pointless. After the dancing and the long talking were over, the solemn chiefs put down the pipe, one by one, saying their own raiding season was here; the whites were also threatening their hunting grounds; they, too, had many scores to settle and important deaths to avenge. Even the Kiowas, who came belatedly, offered only a token number of warriors, some so young, they were clearly sent for seasoning.

Buffalo Hump showed little concern. Whatever the chiefs decided, an impressive number of fired-up young braves saw in his great raid opportunities that did not exist at home. Hears-the-Wolf even suspected Buffalo Hump foresaw this happening from the beginning. He shook his head in admiration. Here was truly a great war chief. Without making any enemies, while smoking with chiefs politely declining to help him, he had succeeded in mustering a war party greater than any in the memory of the Nerm.

But young braves are impatient; the lust for battle must not be allowed to slip away. Overnight the tepees were struck and a great force headed south.

A contented Blue Hawk, watching Liza and Tad Chauncy, brought by the Tenawas to the meeting, come to her lodge, had been quietly wondering at the wisdom of all this. Surely the Penateka did not hope to kill all the *tejanos*, who rose from the east like endless winds sweeping in from far mountains to the west. Yet being a woman, she could say nothing. Liza and Tad came before her quietly. They did not look badly treated, though the girl's hands looked roughened by work. Still she could read in their strained faces and silence they were living in fear. Was Hears-the-Wolf going to adopt these children? The boy looked sturdy and the girl could one day bear him children. Many Comanche men were beginning to think it desirable to have white blood in their offspring. These two were slightly older than her own children but still needed caring for. She decided she would not mind their presence in the lodge. She liked children, and the girl, who would surely not object to her own strain of white blood, might be a good companion.

It was Hears-the-Wolf who sent them back with the Tenawas, giving Blue Hawk her first hint of where the attack would take place. Comanches never allowed captives near areas from which they had been abducted. Their familiarity with the land and knowledge of places of concealment or support made escape too easy. She looked at her slim hands clasped together before her and sighed deeply. The thirst for revenge was leading her people into a daring and dangerous adventure; she could only hope the spirits were watching.

Big Foot Wallace and his Lipan scouts had also been on the Palo Duro. They had followed the tracks of the Penateka until they spotted the loom of the camp's many fires against a darkly clouded night sky. The following morning Wallace, even from a distance, could see the immense size of the Comanche gathering and the telltale circle of Kiowa lodges. The scouts would go no closer; war parties came out of a camp that size like bees from a jarred hive. But Wallace had no need to go closer; he had been asked to find them, not join them.

With his typical sense of humor, he found Hays and Caldwell in the Silver Dollar Saloon, where he went to settle trail dust gathered on his trip back, a bitter chalky taste that could hang in the mouth for days. Horsemen on the Texas plains soon learned no amount of spitting could match the curative powers of whiskey.

Hays was relieved as he watched Wallace settling confidently at the bar. "Figure you found 'em."

"Reckon I did."

"Where?"

"They bunching up on the Palo Duro, like hogs smellin' slop buckets. More redskins churning around up there than burning in hell."

Hays waited till Wallace downed his first drink. "What you figure it's about?"

Wallace rubbed the back of his hand across his mouth. "Likely a prayer meetin' . . . likely they praying for our souls."

Caldwell, used to his banter, chucked him in the ribs. "Nothing gonna save your soul, Big Foot; it's already been decided. Even forgettin' yer real sins, folks figure you deserve damnation!"

They all laughed, but Hays wasn't fooled. Wallace was worried. "How many you figure there were?"

"A heap. And not only a sight of Comanches either . . . Them Penatekas has got more relatives than a fellow striking gold . . . But they was buying drinks for Kiowas, too; figure they hatching a mess of trouble, but didn't get no chance to ask them what they had in mind."

"Too many to take on," murmured Hays almost to himself.

"Damn right!" said Caldwell. "All the Rangers who ever rode would be like piss on a prairie fire if we rile up a crowd that big. Figure we ought to sit tight, let 'em show their hand."

"That's a mighty easy choice," Hays said, smiling, "seeing as how we ain't got any other." Wallace and Caldwell grunted their agreement as Hays nodded genially at the bartender and ordered another round.

But before the drink was finished, a second dust-laden Ranger, this one worried and grim-faced, strode into the bar. He had been desperately searching for Hays. He had come from the Rio Grande with a report that made Hays grip his glass tightly before emptying it. Heavy formations of Mexican soldiers had appeared at Laredo. High-ranking officers had been spotted, and patrols were slipping across the river by night, secretly scouting the San Antonio road.

In the blazing heat of summer Jody began to get in his crops. It was backbreaking labor, and the torrid days saw him coming sweating from the fields, drinking the cool well water and spending his short breaks helping Libby make soap and candles. Both knew there would be some rest in the fall, but the easier days of autumn seemed far away. Busy as she was, Libby now had to tend to chickens and swine, a chore that had her spreading kernels of corn twice a day or emptying slops and rough feed into the pig trough. Exhausting as each day was, it kept her thoughts from other concerns that still simmered in the back of her mind. Thanking God the mission bells had not rung in weeks, she began to hope, as Jody continually muttered, the Indians had gone westward to a far country, there to feed on the buffalo, paint their tepees, and make medicine to protect them during the coming winter. He had never told her what he'd heard about Ranger attacks on Penaketa winter camps—he thought it best not to—but the day might come when he would find himself leaving to join one.

Because of the work, Libby saw less of Kate and Becky, but Pete Spevy came by often enough to keep her up on events that troubled her mind. She felt a strange cringing feeling upon hearing the Munsters were gone. They had not even bothered to sell their claim but simply abandoned it. She wished she had visited them just once, but now she had to live with a secret admission she lacked the moral courage. Maude Chauncy was reported doing poorly, with Buck feeling he might have to take her back east for confinement and constant care. Poor as he was, he couldn't afford to leave his claim; it was all he had. The poor showing of his crops was made up for by his neighbors, but for his real problem, Maude, there was no way to help.

Calm as the country was Ben McCulloch, when he came by, looked troubled. He spoke to Jody and occasionally to Libby, but like many confirmed bachelors, put uncomfortable stress on proper manners when addressing women. "Yes, Mrs. Holister, seems to be pretty quiet. July is usually troublesome, but don't get to worrying . . .'Magine they're off making meat somewheres."

Not only McCulloch but the Rangers themselves puzzled Libby. She was surprised to hear Jody telling her they weren't all illiterate farm boys or border types accustomed to fighting. Many were professional men, some simply adventurers from good families back east. Most amazing of all, a few were highly educated and had traveled abroad. If many of the Rangers had trouble expressing themselves in proper English, there were a few who could do it in Latin and Greek. The Texas Rangers were a magnet for young men who loved the saddle and the challenge of wide-open spaces. If it was a nasty job that many approached with misgivings, it was also an outlet for young men wanting to experience, in dangerous but often exciting trials, a rite of manhood Comanche warriors would have been the first to understand.

No matter the conversation, one subject no one wanted to raise again was Clint Bishop. He had gone into the wilderness, where Jess, forced to get in his crops, could not take time to follow him. Becky was secretly relieved, even though every time Jess drank, he threatened to go off and not return until he found his brother. But sober again, he would realize the futility, not to mention the dangers, of such an effort.

Ben McCulloch shrugged helplessly when asked for advice. "Where he's gone, I'm afraid only God can fetch him back." People watching Ben's eyes searching the sky above the far horizon knew he was talking about Clint's mind, not his body.

Hears-the-Wolf had listened in disbelief when he first heard Buffalo Hump's plan to take his enormous war party almost a hundred miles east of San Antonio before launching an attack. Surely they could not do this undetected: surprise would be lost. It was only when he heard the Mexicans would attack from the south, once they had swept down the valley of the Guadalupe and destroyed Linnville, that he listened with growing interest to Buffalo Hump's scheme to travel at night, stay clear of all settlements, turn at Plum Creek, and, striking Gonzales, sweep forward in a great assault on unsuspecting Victoria and Linnville.

This was the stuff of greatness. Such an undertaking would exceed Buffalo Hump's greatest forays into Mexico. And so propitious were the signs that, as on his lengthy campaigns south of the border, the warriors of the Penateka were to travel with their squaws and even some of their children.

But Buffalo Hump left little doubt about their aims. They were to kill *tejanos*, to burn and scalp and destroy as much of the white man's property as possible. Hears-the-Wolf, who was to command the scouts, was cautioned against braves slipping off for sneak attacks before reaching Plum Creek. The least warning to any settlement would cost Comanche lives. At Gonzales the need for concealment would end, for there destruction was to begin.

Hears-the-Wolf smiled. He knew the valley of the Guadalupe well, and the settlement at Gonzales, he had raided many times. "There is a walled mission there," he remarked to Buffalo Hump. "The *tejanos* rush to it and fight to save themselves." A strange light seemed to flicker across his eyes. "This time we will seize that mission first."

*   *   *

August came in with scorching weather and the sun keeping air boiling in rippling waves over the plain. Occasional winds that rose above the *despoblado* to the south and west were like puffs from a roaring furnace sitting beyond the horizon. Domestic stock and wild game moved slowly and lingered in meager slivers of shade near the waterways.

The old man and a weary squaw led the crippled brave along Sandy Creek near where it joined the Colorado. His leg had been broken in a final raid before the tribe left for the Northwest. The old man had killed a deer and he was leading the woman and her disabled warrior to the kill so that they could eat. The land seemed empty, and the vultures wheeling overhead merely told them they were nearing the carcass of the deer.

The carrion birds had been seen from a distance. Though exhausted and suffering from the unrelenting sun, a man with wildness in his eyes and covered with dirt he had shoveled with his hands back on the Perdenales saw them. It was Clint Bishop, traveling north from his abandoned homestead, where he had found his wife's shallow grave had been torn open by wolves, and had been forced to cover her decaying remains again with his bare hands. He had a gun, a hatchet, and a knife, but he hadn't eaten for days and was not sure of his direction. He knew only he was moving into Comanche country, although the plains seemed peculiarly quiet and the game wary.

Staying behind a rocky ridge, he crept forward slowly till he saw the three Indians, the woman cutting up the deer and the old man building a fire. He studied them for a while till he became aware the young man was crippled and the others preparing a meal for him. They were clearly not expecting trouble, for they rarely looked about. Comanches, watchful as preying owls on the warpath, could be indolent and careless on their own range. He did not wait too long; these three might not be alone. His first shot killed the old man. The young warrior, though disabled, swiftly reached for the bow on his back with its handy quiver of arrows. Clint shot him in the stomach, and the brave grunted and collapsed.

As he came from under cover, the woman stood with the skinning knife in her hand, her face a mask of hatred striated with fear. Clint approached her slowly, her body tightening as she saw his smile, a smile that left his eyes fixed and lusterless. He knocked the knife from her hand with the barrel of his gun and ordered her on the ground. She went down reluctantly, trying to reach out for the wounded brave. Clint saw the brave was trying to recover, but a rage that had been simmering since the Perdenales now seized him. In a frenzy he grabbed the brave by his hair lock, and before the squaw's eyes, using his hatchet in several savage blows, he lopped off the man's head. The squaw threw herself on her knife and with a scream, tried to claw his face as she struggled to rise. He killed her with two swings of the hatchet and sat back to stare at the bodies strewn around him. After a long silence he began to talk. Just who he was talking to, even he didn't know, but there was another person inside him, and that person was in command. That person could even talk to Anne; that person told him he had done right.

An hour later he had cooked and eaten some of the deer. He had to start moving; there was still much to do. The person inside told him so. Methodically he chopped the woman's and the old man's heads off, cut three stakes, and impaled each with their blank eyes staring into the northwest. He wanted the Comanches to know he had come into their land, had come to tell them something. Somehow they had to know there was a grief so great, it was beyond sanity's power to contain.

Libby's days had finally worked into a routine. She did chores in the morning, and after that, her mounting housework. There were many days she had to help Jody with the crops before repeating the chores in the afternoon. But early evenings were saved to take Lance down by the river and watch the quiet green water flow by. She had cleared out a little bower where they were comfortable, and where, by standing, she could see Jody working in the fields or moving between the house and barn. This was her golden hour that made the rest of the long drudging day bearable.

Libby secretly realized how much she was given to daydreaming, and her dreams, as she held her baby and sang softly, always included a glorious future for Lance. She had him as a man too handsome and charming for anyone to resist. She had him upright, modest, fearless, but never violent. She had him successful, with glory crowning all his efforts. Once she even had him president, living in a magnificent mansion he insisted she share. But she decided her dreaming was harmless and it was easier to face the drab present by borrowing a little excitement from the future.

Though the heat was still stifling, she could tell by the sky it was going to be a beautiful sunset. Somehow this land had a beauty of its own that could only be caught in rare moments. For all its frightening threats, it was a land that inspired men to fight for it and struggle to enjoy its bounty. But suddenly a new quietude and a subtle reaching of shadows said it was sundown. Orange streamers began to branch out in the western sky, and the blue dome above began to shift through a kaleidoscope of colors. She had to stand to gaze at it, for there was something stark and dramatic about the burst of carmine gold that started welling up from the sun's burnished if slowly sinking disk. But it was then, in that moment of near rapture, that she first heard it; heard it and, grasping her baby, felt a weakness claiming her body and sapping strength from her knees.

It was the mission bells. They were ringing.

Chapter 14

MIRACULOUSLY, THE STEALTHY approach of the greatest war party ever to descend on the Texas frontier went unnoticed until the morning it reached Plum Creek. That morning, at a brook crossing Buffalo Hump's painted mustang had swept by a few hours before, fate played a critical hand. A courier delivering dispatches from Austin to Gonzales had entered the loneliest part of his journey, a dry level stretch crossed by a shallow stream where he halted to water his mount.

This was dangerous territory, and he considered himself lucky the land seemed empty with no sign of Indians. Gonzales, his first stop, was still several hours away, but after that he would turn east, leaving danger behind him. But as he looked across the small stream, his expression froze, his face paled, and his eyes widened with shock. Before him lay a broad band of tracks, made by thousands of unshod pony hooves moving toward the southeast. For a moment he had trouble breathing, but after dismounting and studying the tracks closely, he realized they were at least several hours old. Perhaps he could get away unnoticed.

Though alarmed, his breathing tight with anxiety, he
started pressing his horse forward, trying to stay among
the random clumps of trees and chance foliage as he
rode desperately for Gonzales. He was an experienced
horseman and knew when his mount began tiring, he
should have stopped to rest it. But visions of Comanche
hordes nearby was distorting his judgment. It was almost
a costly distraction, for suddenly his horse began to stagger and threaten to founder just as riders appeared on
the horizon.

Fortunately for him, Ben McCulloch, responding to
an uneasy premonition that things weren't right, had
been making a brief scout north of Gonzales with Tomcah and a handful of his troop. Calmly he listened to the
badly shaken courier, whose excited outbursts were so
chilling, he had to see for himself. Advising the courier
to rest his mount before continuing to Gonzales, Ben
quickly backtracked over the courier's trail until he
reached the brook. There he stared in icy astonishment
at the tracks of an army of unshod ponies, leaving a trail
over a hundred feet wide. In spite of the courier's warning, it took a moment or two before the enormity of this
sight settled in his mind.

But if Ben was momentarily shocked into silence, he
was also a seasoned fighter, a Ranger captain with blood
on his buckskins. He knew at once the Indians' greatest
advantage was the frontier's baffling ignorance of their
presence. Incredibly, they had slipped by San Antonio
and the outer settlements and were now poised to strike
where defenses were weak and enough manpower to
make a stand would require days to assemble. But here
every moment counted. Signaling some men up beside
him, he ordered one rider to race for San Antonio, another to Bastrop, reporting the size of the attacking force
and requesting all help possible. If he did not know
where the massive war party would strike first, he knew
the vulnerable settlement of Gonzales lay right in its
path. Within moments he was leading his troop at a wild

gallop across country, knowing that death was hovering over his friends and neighbors, and grimly praying he could sound an alarm in time.

Blue Hawk had long wondered at the wisdom of this restless and unwieldy force. Two days and two nights of enforced silence and stealthy traveling had left many young braves chafing for action, secretly wanting the first scalp, eager for the honors it carried. With their party's strength, they saw no need of caution. Hears-the-Wolf, concerned that a rash move by some reckless youth would alert Gonzales and spoil his chances of taking the mission, could not contain his anger when Black Tail reported that a handful of braves had slipped away during the night. Upon hearing this, the grimly furious Buffalo Hump shook his fist and stamped the ground. Could any war chief succeed if plagued with these stupid glory seekers! Were all his efforts to be in vain?

Knowing that time was now running out, he agreed Hears-the-Wolf should take twenty picked warriors and try to seize the mission before an alert was sounded. "But we cannot delay there," he ranted. "We must destroy Victoria and Linnville before the Mexicans will march on San Antonio." The old chief's voice was dejected and bitter. "Surprise, our great ally, will soon be gone. When it is, more of our people will lay down their lives."

The handful of young braves who recklessly deserted the war party by night traveled hurriedly to the southeast, finally reaching the crude and ungraded Columbus-Gonzales road by morning. They were intent on drawing first blood, seizing the first scalp and the honors that went with it. But they were in too big a hurry, and their approach to the road was anything but stealthy. As a result, two whites traveling west saw them first. Dr. Joel Ponton and Tucker Foley needed no warning of their peril. They turned about and raced for cover, the warriors howling and streaming after them.

Dr. Ponton's horse was a poor runner and he was soon overtaken. They swung their war clubs at him, and a lance sent him wounded to the ground. But they wanted the faster horse Foley was riding, and left the doctor to be finished later.

Foley made it to a small creek where he attempted to hide but was finally discovered. He was taken back to where the doctor had fallen. By now the doctor, in spite of his wounds, had crawled away to hide. He could hear poor Foley being forced by the warriors to shout for him, but he didn't dare answer. In the end Tucker Foley was to die a terrible death. The soles of his feet were cut off and he was made to run behind a horse that dragged him when he faltered. Finally, and mercifully, he was slain and scalped.

The Comanches had drawn first blood. The screeching braves, brandishing his scalp, had their honors.

Though painfully wounded, Dr. Ponton, a man well respected for his courage and fortitude, forced himself to make his way to Lavaca Flats, the nearest farms east of Gonzales, for he knew, with Comanches this deep in the settlements, many lives besides his own were at stake. His first words on arriving, even before accepting any aid, were, "Hurry! Fetch someone to warn McCulloch!"

Pete Spevy had had a bad day. Apart from the heat, the wood he was trying to haul and stack for winter would not stay on his wagon. Twice he piled it up, and twice, because the trail had ruts over a foot deep, it toppled over. He was about to give up when he saw a rider coming lickety-split in his direction. It was a grim-looking farm boy from Lavaca Flats. "Where's McCulloch?" shouted the youth.

"Out on patrol," Pete yelled back. "Why?"

"Injuns out our way ... nobody knows how many

... Damn! ... We got to find McCulloch!''

It was growing late in the day, and Pete remembered Ben had been planning a short scout to the north. Perhaps he'd be back before dark. To ring the mission bells now would only bring everyone running before it was clear Gonzales itself was under attack. "No way I can fetch him," allowed Pete, turning to his barn for a saddle horse, "but he may be along before sundown.''

"Where'd he go?" shouted the youth, desperation edging his voice. "Mister, we got to find him!''

Pete was far more alarmed than he let on. Indians appearing to the east could mean real trouble; perhaps he should ring the bells anyway in warning. He saddled and mounted a horse, planning to ride to the west side of the settlement to see if McCulloch's patrol could be sighted. The youth, still breathing hard and looking on the edge of panic, rode along beside him. From a rise on the western edge of Gonzales they saw no sign of McCulloch, but they spotted a lone figure riding slowly toward them. He was carrying a bag of dispatches, and deep lines of fear and exhaustion were trenched in his face.

Pete did not wait beyond the courier's mention of heavy hostile tracks headed their way. Leaving the youth to help the pale, dust-laden figure, he raced to the mission. It was nearly sundown, and though Indians almost never attacked at dark, he jumped from his saddle, grabbed the little steeple rope, and pulled it for all he was worth.

With the distant bells still sounding, Jody raced for the house, his eye catching Libby rushing up from the river with Lance. He had been perspiring all day and had been looking forward to a dip in the water before his evening meal. He had his six-gun on and was clutching his rifle when Libby entered. "Good heavens," she began, "what can it be?''

"Trouble!" was all he could answer as he ran to the

barn for a horse. Dread swept over her like a high fever
as she watched him galloping off. With so many weeks
of peace, she had forgotten the threat this land faced with
every dawning. For the first time in her life, she wanted
a weapon. There was only an old Kentucky long rifle
left by Jody's father or uncle. She loaded it with trembling hands, wondering if she was doing right. She had
only fired a gun a few times in her life, and then only
at Jody's insistence. But now she was all alone with
Lance, and aghast at how defenseless they were, she felt
the first dizzying sensation of panic. It was several
minutes before she realized, as the bells continued ringing like a sinister dirge, that in their excitement they had
forgotten the rough code the settlement followed. Bells
at night was a call for men, bells by daylight was a call
for everyone. She and her baby should have left with
Jody and by now be approaching the safety of the mission.

Hears-the-Wolf had started too late. He might have
reached the mission before the alarm sounded, but Elk
Slayer, riding scout on his right flank, spotted Mc-
Culloch's patrol also racing for Gonzales. They had to
circle away to avoid an encounter, which would only
have delayed them more. When Hears-the-Wolf cautiously mounted a rise a little over a mile from the mission, the bells were already silent. Again figures could
be seen near the walls, and a handful of wagons was
already in sight approaching in the distance.

Such was the price of the young warriors' pride.

Ben McCulloch had raced into Gonzales to find the
settlement frantic with activity; the faces rushing past
him were strained and feverish with anxiety. Panicky
reports of hostiles nearby had spread. There were already
twelve men at the mission, and a sizable group, following in the wake of the farm boy from Lavaca Flats, rode
in to report a mass of Indians had been sighted coming

down from the north. McCulloch, though now with over fifty men on hand, knew he could not defend against such numbers. The entire valley was helpless; there was no way murder and rapine could be avoided. God only knew if some weren't already dead, some taken. He could only dispatch warnings to all settler families to flee; if possible, to the east.

Having assigned as many men as he could to spreading the alarm, he then did what duty told him had to be done. He had to find and track this dangerous band, hanging back and keeping them under surveillance, rescuing its victims when possible, burying them when not. As night fell, a pall of terror rose with moonglow throwing an eerie light, casting menacing shadows along the valley of the Guadalupe.

Chapter 15

THE SCOURGE OF Comanche vengeance, so long hovering over the Texan frontier, was now descending. Hatred had clawed away all other emotions, and the trail of blood, once started, could not be stopped. The war party, in spite of Buffalo Hump's efforts, saw more and more warriors slipping off for scalps and loot. Unsuspecting settlers and travelers began to die along the valley of the Guadalupe. With agonizing slowness word of the massive raid spread southward, creating a wave of terror that flowed from settlement to settlement. But there was no defense against such numbers. The few who courageously ran for their guns, trying to make a stand, died gallantly, but they died. Never before had such a bloodletting rampage struck the frontier; never before had men known they could do nothing but bury their friends and neighbors, while desperately trying to summon enough manpower to ward off their own massacre. Penateka warriors, drunk with the frenzy that came with the spilling of enemy blood, were running wild, striking out miles beyond the main body. There was no way to tell where they would attack next, no direction in which safety lay. Only terrified settlers, grasping loved ones in lonely cabins at such moments, really knew how hideous the face of a warring frontier can be. Only they experienced the paralyzing vision of their own slaughter, the scraping pain of the scalping knife, the scorching tongue of the fire.

Fortunately for Gonzales, Buffalo Hump's eyes were on Victoria, but the confusion brought by knowledge of the great party close by turned a night of community dread into a thousand private nightmares.

Libby could hear hoofbeats approaching in the darkness. She held her breath, and the long gun against her chest, till, in relief, she heard Pete Spevy calling to her. "Libby! It's me! You got to get shut of this place. Take your child and head for the mission; there be other women there you can join up with."

Libby came out onto the porch in the darkness, clutching Lance to her. "Where's Jody?"

"Gone with McCulloch. Every man in the settlement has got to muster; Ben needs 'em all. Better get moving."

"When will he be back?"

"Jody? No telling . . . Valley is swarming with Injuns; only Jehovah knows how many." He swung his horse around. "Got to get to the Sutters. Best hurry!" He galloped away, heading downriver.

Libby hitched a horse to the rig, wrapped a little food and water in a blanket for Lance, and leaving everything, including the long gun, behind, made her way through the inky darkness to the mission. The moon was a dimly lit mask behind low clouds. Never had a night seemed so haunted, never had her lips trembled so as she tried to pray. The dark limbs of trees overhead were spidery arms reaching for her; dark patches she passed, darker than the night, were menacing lairs from which screeching savages would leap at any moment. She wanted to stop and cry but didn't dare.

She found the mission lit with only one low lantern but crowded with women and children. They were forming little trains and leaving, most of them escorted by older men McCulloch left behind. She found Becky Bishop readying a mount and preparing to go. "Jess had to muster," Becky grunted, checking the cinches on the horse. "Reckon it's pretty bad."

"God!" gasped Libby, looking about her at the nervous confusion. "What will we do?"

"What everyone else is doing . . . clear out!"

"What about our things . . . ?" She found it hard to say it. "Our homes?"

Becky sighed. "Libby, when you haven't got a choice, 'taint no point in even thinking. Where's Kate?"

Libby had remained in the rig holding Lance; she noticed Becky was armed with a pistol, and a rifle showed in her saddle scabbard. She suspected Kate would be armed too; maybe she should have brought the long rifle. But her thoughts were interrupted by raucous sounds on the other side of the yard. An old man was trying to get Maude Chauncy into a wagon as she cried hysterically for Buck. Two women already in the wagon were trying to tell her Buck, like the other men, had to muster, but she kept screaming he was never coming back. Young Lucas gripped her arm and, pleading the danger they were in, begged her to get in. Maude's screams had everyone on edge; it was not a sound to comfort distressed people trying to keep their nerve.

Finally Becky strode over to her, taking her by the folds of her cloak. "Maude, shut up and get in that wagon!" she said firmly. Maude looked at her, her eyes losing focus as she tried to slip to the ground. But Becky with her strength pulled her up, and as the old man quickly lifted her legs, they settled her in the wagon. Lucas climbed in and put both arms around her. The old man signaled the woman who was handling the reins to move ahead. Becky came back mumbling under her breath. "Heavens to Bessie, never seen the likes . . ."

Kate was suddenly there, coming up on a big roan and leaping to the ground. She and Becky hugged each other, and Kate leaned in to peck Libby on the cheek. It was an unexpected gesture but so like Kate. Strangely, Libby felt it helped.

The yard was emptying out. "We'd best get moving," said Becky. "We'll ride ahead; you keep up behind, Libby."

"Where are we going?" asked Libby, somehow feeling it was a silly question, making her seem green, untested.

"Jess said go east," Becky responded thoughtfully, and mounted.

Kate looked about; the mission yard would soon be empty. "Nobody knows where those Injuns are headed," she said, glancing up at the sky. "But wherever we decide to hole up, we better get there before dawn." To Libby, neither betrayed the numbing dread she herself was fighting to hide.

It was late that night when Buffalo Hump ordered fires built to signal in the many warriors still foraging through the valley. He was sitting with his unlit pipe, deep anger sewn into his heavily creased face. Hears-the-Wolf, striding about trying to determine how many warriors were still out, finally realized only a few were missing. He raised his arm in a prearranged sign to the old chief. Buffalo Hump rose and pulled his painted antelope skin about him, tying it at his waste. His bare chest showed his medicine sign, its colors dim in the weak firelight. Silence swept the camp as the warriors turned to him.

"We have come to avenge the Penateka!" he shouted. "We have come to kill *tejanos* and teach them the Nerm punishes those who speak falsely, those who raise the pipe with treachery in their hearts. This we can do only if our warriors fight like wise wolves, running together and deadly in the hunt, not like young cubs romping in spring grass. There is a great gathering place of *tejanos* ahead. Save your arrows and shot for the moment we surround it; save your war cries to chill their hearts as our knives and hatchets bring them their deaths.''

Buffalo Hump spoke for many minutes and finished with a warning that their medicine might prove weak if they did not stay together and strike like the hawk that had appeared in his dream the night before. This brought a stirring. Warriors gripped their medicine bags as Buffalo Hump described a great red hawk that had swooped down in his dream to hit a settlement the *tejanos* call Victoria. It was the dramatic kind of revelation that moved and swayed warriors. Dreams were powerful things. Hears-the-Wolf grunted to himself. He must remember to relate that dream to the missing warriors when they arrived, though for the first time, it struck him as strange Buffalo Hump had such handy dreams whenever great actions had to be taken. Perhaps he was learning something about the skills of a chief.

Blue Hawk, standing back with the squaws, heard the dream, too, but she was secretly uneasy. By now the whites knew they were there. Though they were meeting little resistance, surprise was gone, and in the darkness beyond, surely the whites were gathering. All her life she had seen her people attack *tejanos* and quickly disappear. There had been many victories, scalps taken and plunder and captives seized, but Buffalo Hump's words told her many days would now be spent striking the big villages of these armed, stubborn people. They were not the defenseless *ranchos* of Mexico, and Buffalo Hump's brave talk could not make them so. She would have worried less had her children been safe on the Nueces, and she might have found some solace in old Hump's words had she shared the faith in dreams many warriors did. But Blue Hawk had long suspected her intuition fitted reality better than the dreams of a fretful and demanding chief. Yet she could only stare at him and

Hears-the-Wolf in silence. She had learned a woman had no right to speak such thoughts.

In San Antonio, Hays, his suspicions mounting daily, sent only a single Ranger with some Lipan scouts to watch the vulnerable bank of the Rio Grande. He could send no more, for his entire troop had been rushed east. Gonzales was under attack by a war party whose reported size defied belief. But he knew McCulloch wasn't a man who saw danger where it didn't exist. Something terrible and disastrous was taking place. Indians had moved a powerful force deeply into the settlements, skillfully avoiding detection to take the unprepared settlers by surprise. The whole valley was now at their mercy. To him it seemed a strategy alien to the Indian mind. To Hays, who knew the cruel abandonment that typified most Comanche attacks, more sinister forces were at work. He picked up a crude map of the Lone Star state; with several territorial issues unsettled, it was the only one issued. His eye ran along the rough course of the Rio Grande. He grunted as it stopped at Laredo.

Chapter 16

THE FIRST HOUR they moved along in silence, the low hoofbeats of their mounts or the occasional creak of the rig seeming lost in the vast sultry cavern of an August night. They knew others were sharing this desperate scattering, seeking sanctuary with some distant friend or relative or, like themselves, a remote spot promising safety. But to poor Libby they were alone, isolated, groping across a murky plain where her mind saw weird shapes, rising on both sides, stalking, crouching, even gloating. Finally the women before her suddenly slowed their mounts and stopped. Becky had one hand in the air as a signal to pull up and remain quiet. It was a frightening moment, for both women had heard something strange, something they had to hear again before daring to move on.

Libby, anxious to know why the halt, did not wish, even in a whisper, to ask. Finally Kate pulled her horse about, as though ready to continue, but Becky's hand was back in the air. After a long breathless moment all three heard it; it was a distant scream, just audible, just identifiable as a woman crying out. They hung there in dreadful silence, the appalling choices before them robbing them of speech. Someone was in trouble. But what kind of trouble? Had they broken down? Were they under attack? Should the three ride forward to help? Should they, knowing the fearful possibility of Indians, race the other way or hide? Kate finally broke the icy spell gripping them with her tight half-whispered words. "We've got to get closer."

"What are we getting close to?" responded Becky, her brusque voice now carefully measured in warning.

Libby said nothing. Glad that Lance was asleep beside her in the rig, she was beginning to sense, whatever that distant cry, it was enough to alarm and finally scare Becky and Kate. It was the first time they had shown fear. Ironically, if it made her feel closer to them, it also attested to the menace they suspected lay ahead.

After long moments of delay, just standing there, undecided in the dark, began to tax the nerves. The stress of not knowing what lay beyond or perhaps around them was more than Kate was willing to bear. "Let's move up slowly," she muttered across to the others. "We could be worrying about nothing . . . Could be a woman thrown from a horse."

Without answering, Becky and Libby started after her, all three with their ears alert to any sound arising in the pitch-dark reaches of the night. They had gone almost a quarter of a mile when, some fifty yards to their left, the scream broke out again. But this time, in spite of the shock, they knew what it was. It was Maude Chauncy, giving forth hysterical shrieks as others fought to keep her quiet. Those struggling with her could be heard straining and pleading. Becky was the first to recognize the danger; there could only be one reason why Maude was being throttled into silence. "Their wagon must be right over there," she cried excitedly. "Hurry, let's get to it!" They hurried forward and soon saw the dim shape of a wagon looming up in the dark. A few feet away, Becky dismounted. She had seen this wagon leaving the mission and knew the old man guarding it. "Walt!" she hissed through the darkness.

In a moment an old man holding a rifle appeared before them. "Shush," he began. "That you, Becky?"

"Yes, we heard Maude."

"What's wrong with her?" asked Kate, joining them. All three spoke in whispers so that Libby could barely hear.

"Damn woman is out of her mind," said Walt, peering about nervously. "By Jesus, there's Injuns close . . . Don't just stand there."

Walt was an old Indian fighter, well past his useful years but possessing that savvy that, once gained, was never lost. He had heard a coyote howling far to his left and wondered if it was really a coyote, but then heard it answered to the right and knew it wasn't. Indians didn't like to fight at night. If they were killed, their spirits, unable to see, might wander forever. This had to be a small war party after easy kills; a large one would have circled in close and attacked at once. But he and one of the women were armed, and by quickly halting the wagon and sitting silently in the dark, he left the redskins for the moment unsure of where they were. That was, until Maude, upset by the swift rise of tension in the wagon, began to scream they were coming to kill Lucas. Desperate hands pressed her to the wagon floor and covered her mouth, but it only made her more frantic. Walt was about to knock her out with the butt of his rifle when Lucas, who was helping to hold his mother, gasped that someone was beside the wagon hissing his name.

There was no time for explanations; Walt knew an attack was only minutes away. He got Libby and Lance into the wagon, tied the two mounts and the rig to its rear, and told Becky and Kate to take their guns and post themselves beneath the wagon. They were not a second too soon; the first arrow struck the wagon as Kate settled her rifle barrel between the stout wooden spokes of the rear wheel.

Walt was right. It was a small party, nine warriors and a young war chief. It was the party that failed to return to Buffalo Hump's camp, a party that had been suspecting all day they carried weak medicine. They had left early that morning, working east toward the Lavaca River, but the one group of settlers they encountered were well armed and managed to get to a rocky place with heavy foliage from which they couldn't be dislodged. Another rider they struck late in the day, when their ponies were worn down and his fresh, outran them and disappeared. At nightfall they were making their way back to camp, chagrined they carried not a single scalp to show the waiting squaws. Their young war leader was bitter, knowing his reputation would suffer, knowing powerful men like Hears-the-Wolf would not think of him for important tasks. The one scout they had out must have heard a wagon in the distance, for in this darkness he could see little, but he gave the coyote sound, which meant travelers coming their way. They answered him and then deployed to surprise and assault this unexpected prey. Perhaps they would not have to return in shame after all.

The warriors, having tethered their horses behind them, were crawling up to get close enough for a charge. They had quickly formed a dangerous half circle, planning to strike the wagon on three sides. The young war leader wanted them to assault the wagon together, but there were always a few, lured by that warrior passion to make the first kill, who raced ahead. The war leader who had fired the arrow followed it with a great war cry as a signal for the braves to press the attack together. But one was already on his way; he came up to the rear of the wagon, where Kate caught his shadowy figure rising against the dim night sky. Her rifle blast drove him back and he disappeared. But others had reached the wagon, and guns began to roar. There was no time to aim; the darkness was full of lunging figures wielding hatchets or war clubs. Walt killed the warrior who was slashing with his hatchet the mortally wounded woman who had been fighting at his side. But the firing was too wild for killing shots; two warriors were dead, but three others were only slightly wounded. It was Becky and Kate firing from under the wagon that drove the warriors back. Coming up in the darkness, it was not something they expected. The other woman in the wagon was busy reloading guns as Walt, shouting the Indians weren't finished, turned to pull the now dead woman's body back in the wagon. Lucas, stretched on the floor, was desperately holding his mother, not knowing blood from the dead body had started seeping toward them.

The Indians settled down to firing from forty or fifty feet. Arrows thudded into the wagon's sides or tore through the canvas. The raiders had one gun but apparently few bullets; after two shots, one of which killed Becky's horse, it fell silent. Walt cautioned them to stay ready, though secretly he was beginning to hope. This war party seemed less determined, less riled up to fight than many he had faced, yet the danger was far from over. Finally, as Walt called out hoarsely, "Save yer shot," and the Comanches saw their arrows were having little effect, the firing stopped. In the silence that followed, because of an incident no one foresaw, a veritable nightmare began.

Lucas was holding his mother, whom the deafening roar of guns had somehow silenced, but her arms were flailed out along the floor of the wagon. Blood streaming down from the dead woman's body finally reached her hand. At first, in her confused mind, she thought it was water, but then realized it was too sticky for that. Without thinking, she raised her fingers to her mouth and knew at once it was blood. Overwrought as she was, her hysteria returned and she started screaming again and pulling herself up. Young Lucas was unable to hold her and she lunged to the rear of the wagon screeching, ''There's death in this wagon! Death! Don't you hear! We're all going to die!'' And before anyone could stop her, she had torn open the rear canvas flaps and jumped down, racing off into the night.

Lucas, crying for help, jumped behind her and started running, shouting for her to stop, but she flew into the darkness still screaming and adding a macabre quality to this already terror-filled night. Kate, shouting up, wanted to know if she should go after her, but Walt roared angrily back, ''Hell no! Stay where you are! Getting yourself killed won't save her!''

Libby went to the rear of the wagon where the canvas flaps lay ajar. She could still hear Maude and Lucas running into the night till finally, somewhere in that ghastly darkness beyond, they must have come to earth, for after that she could only hear that distant dismal sound of poor Lucas crying.

The Indians had gathered together close to their tethered horses. Two of their number were dead, one the brother of the young war leader. There was no longer any doubt; their medicine was bad. The remaining braves were glancing in disgust at the leader. Weak *puha* was never forgiven among the Penateka; he who claimed to lead in war must have the spirits on his side. Comanches, for all their arrogance, were still barbaric nomads, sullen and suspicious, their loyalty to any leader swiftly dissolved by defeat. Also, embittered warriors could be dangerous for a failed chieftain; the ones with flesh wounds had started grunting ominously together. Their wounds were not serious, but they were noticeable. The camp would see they had been struck and proved unable to strike back. It was a tense moment, and fortunately for the leader, it was broken by the weird sound of a woman screaming in the night and running off on the far side of the wagon.

The young leader, thinking the *tejanos* were abandoning the wagon and trying to escape, seized this opportunity to retain command. "The *tejanos* are trying to escape," he shouted. "Let us whip our horses forward and bring them down as the great mountain cougar does the frightened deer."

But the warriors were no longer jumping at his commands. The oldest among them said, "I heard but one woman, making the loud cowardly sounds of a white squaw facing death." In the darkness he rose to stare at the wagon. "Where are the others?"

"They are crawling away in silence," declared the leader.

The older warrior took his bow and fired an arrow toward the wagon, then struck the earth twice with his empty bow. Immediately a shot sounded and a slug whined over their heads. The warrior knelt down again. "You see, my brothers," he said, glancing grimly at the leader, "it is a trap . . . a trap our leader would have us fall into."

Inside the wagon there was deathly silence. Everyone was listening. No one had an answer to the tragedy besetting them. In spite of Walt's commonsense order that no one leave the wagon, nothing could stop a feeling of guilt from spreading to all, for they could just hear Lucas crying for help in this pitiless night.

Old Walt was suffering as much as anyone; he could not restrain a painful sense of futility that rose in his words. "Not one of us could carry her back alone," he called out loud enough for all to hear. "If two go, we lose this wagon and every damn one of our scalps."

Minutes droned by; everyone was listening for some key to what the next moment might bring. Walt, who would have given his left arm to know what the Comanches were doing, heard an arrow in flight and an unidentifiable tapping in the darkness beyond. He fired a shot at it. Kate and Becky heard the night noises that rose from the dark plain around them, though nothing could have drowned out the furious beat of their hearts. But poor Libby, at the rear of the wagon, staring into the fearful darkness, heard only a frightened child crying for help in the night.

She wasn't sure what moved her so deliberately or gave her such strength to act, but she wrapped Lance in his blanket and reached over to untie the reins of her rig from the tailgate. She was on the ground and stepping around Becky's dead mount before anyone realized what she was doing, and had reached the rig and was already clucking to the horse when Kate started shouting wildly. "Libby! Come back! That's insane!"

Becky's voice joined hers, but Libby kept moving in the direction she had fixed in her mind as leading to the crying boy. When the cries grew suddenly clearer, she knew she was right. Two hundred yards from the wagon she pulled up beside Lucas, who rose and ran into her arms. Quickly hugging the boy, she rushed him to help get his mother into the rig, and soon, with her knuckles white around the reins, she was retracing her tracks to the wagon. Only later did she realize that she had overcome her fear of Indians by refusing to think of them. One vision of them pouncing on her or carving off her scalp might have broken her resolve.

At the wagon, Walt, hearing her coming, was on the ground, unable to keep himself from saying, "Damn, if that wasn't the pluckiest and goldarnest foolishest thing I ever saw a critter do!"

When all were back in the wagon, Walt began to realize the attack was over. The fact that Libby had come back without a sound being raised meant the Comanches had quit. Though later, thinking back, it wasn't so surprising. Maude running into the night screaming like a banshee might have seemed to their crafty but suspicious minds a devilish trap. He sighed with that grim and grisly view of things that only old-timers who have dodged their share of scalping knives can mount. "Wal, got to remember those damn Injuns outfox themselves sometimes too!"

The following morning they buried the woman's body, and Becky, now without a horse, climbed into the wagon. It was a strange day, with Maude not seeming to remember everything that happened the night before, and no one choosing to remind her. Walt, now driving the wagon, allowed they were heading east without any fixed notion on where they ought to go. But Kate said she knew a place they could hole up for a spell and thought it would accommodate them all. Becky, with a questioning glance at Maude, said nothing.

But there was a moment that day that Libby would always remember. It came when Becky turned to her and said openly, "Libby, what you did last night was the bravest thing I ever heard tell of; makes me proud to know you."

Kate, who was riding alongside and heard the remark, looked in at Libby and nodded agreement. "I've been thinking, Libby, it took a real Texian to do that. You got no need to walk small around here anymore." She clicked her tongue as though resigning herself to a troublesome thought. "I only wish I'd had your guts!"

Chapter 17

THE TOWN OF Victoria, sixty miles below Gonzales, was the largest settlement on the Guadalupe. It had a main street, a few stores, a restaurant, and several boardinghouses. It was an active trading center. Not only Mexicans but Lipan Apaches and other pacified tribes came there to trade. It was deep enough in the coastal range and far enough from buffalo country to keep concern about Comanche war parties to a minimum. Though word of the holocaust sweeping down from the north had reached posts nearby, Buffalo Hump was now moving too swiftly for every community in that barren country to be alerted. So it happened that on the afternoon of August 6, while citizens of Victoria were going about their business, the largest war party in the history of the frontier descended upon them.

The traditional faith of Indians in the deadly surround brought them into the outskirts first. The townspeople, catching sight of them, thought they were friendly till they realized these figures were painted, coming from all sides, howling and brandishing weapons as they fell upon those unable to escape to the center of town.

Women, gathering up their skirts, ran screaming; men finding themselves separated from wives and children swore profanely before begging God for help. But all knew they had to make a stand or they and all in their town were lost. Fortunately the middle of Victoria contained a few stone and brick buildings where they could take cover, and here men who habitually went armed began to gather and resist. But the slaughter had started, particularly in the outskirts. Had it been the Indian way to storm the settlement, forcing their way into the built-up area, their numbers would have ensured the massacre of every soul in Victoria. But Indians instinctively shied away from the confines of streets and were leery of defenders firing from rooftops or elevated windows.

Where the people fought from cover; they survived; where they tried to drive the Indians back, they died. A doctor and his friend rallied several men to counterattack and retake the town stable with its many valuable mounts, but they paid for it with their lives. Every one of the participants died or lay seriously wounded. The only thing that kept the desperately besieged townspeople from being overrun and the carnage made complete was the loot being seized on all sides. Horses and mules by the hundreds were rounded up; deserted homes were emptied of guns, knives, and whatever caught the warriors' fancy, then burned. Where stragglers or unwary workers were caught in the outlying fields, they were brutally murdered, their scalps taken. In one barbaric scene after the other, sections of the town were terrorized, plundered, and destroyed.

But finally the day began to wane and other forces, rooted in the arcane past and preying heavily on primitive minds, intervened. With sundown and the threat of darkness, the Indians, with victory almost in their grasp, abruptly withdrew and retreated to Spring Creek a few miles away. Buffalo Hump knew his people's taboo against fighting at night made total annihilation of the town near impossible, for those trapped *tejanos* suffered no such handicap. By morning they would have re-grouped, set up defenses, even received help from other settlements. Also, the enormous amount of loot taken now required many braves to guard it. Over fifteen hundred horses and mules had been seized, and an enormous amount of booty. That huge herd would have to be driven south, for he was beginning to count on the Mexican promise to attack San Antonio when he appeared on the coast. He would need those invading Mexicans to distract the aroused *tejanos* while he and his braves, holding fast to their spoils of war, rode triumphantly home.

But Hears-the-Wolf, sitting in council and drawing on his pipe, was in high spirits that evening. He reported only a few braves lost in the attack, and though several others were wounded, they had taken many scalps. The warriors were grunting with pleasure at the great numbers of horses and mules captured; it was wealth soon to be divided among them. Elk Slayer and other warriors came by to sit and smoke while their squaws filled the night air with an aroma of boiled meat flavored with wild herbs. Only Black Tail, arriving late, came in looking pensive and preoccupied. Yet he offered no words till called upon by the chief. "Black Tail does not wear a face of victory," chided Buffalo Hump, his statement after a pause becoming a question.

Black Tail grunted before looking up to answer. "There is much excitement in our camp, Buffalo Hump, and our warriors are preparing to dance. Soon drums will be drawing spirits to the fires of the Penateka and they will see our people drinking the white man's whiskey, seized today from lodges of many fleeing *tejanos*."

Buffalo Hump frowned, then turned to stare hard at Hears-the-Wolf. "Is this not the growing shadow of some hidden evil, my brother?"

Hears-the-Wolf looked down, his eyes fixed on the pipe. He knew this was but another sign of a problem slowly mounting in both his and the old chief's mind.

Blue Hawk was right; this war party was too big to control. Many of these young braves had come from northern tribes and were here only to find daring exploits to swell their reputations as warriors. Ever since Plum Creek, they had been boldly slipping off, returning either in anger or with fresh scalps hanging from their belts. And now it was whiskey, the firewater that made fighting men of the Penateka careless and even crazy. Yet there was little that could be done. Every brave was his own master; liquor he looted, unlike horses captured with others, was his. To demand it be given up could mean desertions or perhaps even dangerous revolt. "It is a thing that will pass with the next sun," muttered Hears-the-Wolf, hoping he sounded convincing. The chief closed his eyes; such answers meant hope was being offered in place of reason, but he said no more.

Yet he was to discover the troubled warrior wasn't finished. "There are new eyes in the camp," said Black Tail in measured tones as though to prepare the chief for his next words. "They say they are half-Comanche and they speak our language, but I know they are from lands to the south. Why they have come puzzles me, but they joined in the attack today, claiming they have killed many *tejanos*."

A dead silence fell upon the circle for a moment. The old chief took the pipe from his mouth, his eyes searching Black Tail's face. "How many?"

"Six. Two of our squaws say they recognized their leader. He has but one eye and is badly scarred. He came once to our hunting grounds with the Comancheros."

There was silence again. Old Buffalo Hump shook his head. In truth, he knew who they were, or surely had to be. The border was filled with escaped or abandoned Mexican women who had found their way back to Chihuahua or Coahuila with their half-breed Comanche children. Often these offspring spoke Comanche as fluently as Spanish. As bastard half-breeds, they were neither wanted nor trusted by either camp, but their language skills made them valuable to the Comancheros, New Mexicans who traded with the tribes that refused to deal with *tejanos*.

Since it was strange, even dangerous, for dubious outsiders to approach, let alone enter, a war party, Hears-the-Wolf looked at Buffalo Hump, half expecting to be told to kill them or drive them away. But Buffalo Hump was quietly musing on why they had come. He decided he knew. The Mexican government had used such people in the past to travel through Comanche lands, picking up information or seeking out and bringing ransom for important captives. They played an obscure, sometimes devious, but often important role. He decided they were playing one now. They were there to report the success of his raid. He lit the pipe again and sat back, secretly hoping they would report this great victory soon.

Blue Hawk had fretted much of the day. There was always tension among the squaws when their warriors were off fighting, but today early rumors of victory, and large amounts of loot taken, brought excitement too. To distract her children as well as teach them, she had them help build a shelter. After an hour's work they had arranged more comfort than they had known in weeks. But the long trek had been hard on the little ones; the strain of being silent and days without the freedom to play had made them listless and fidgety in their sleep. She prayed Buffalo Hump would leave soon for the buffalo range, for surely somewhere the *tejanos* were gathering, waiting, preparing to strike this great war party, powerful as it was. She could hear the braves nearby laughing and boasting about their successes that day, those with scalps even acting out kills and often ending with war cries. It was a night when the fires of the Penaketa leaped high and their men shouted out boldly in the land of their enemies.

When Hears-the-Wolf came in, she prepared him some food. Though he ate heartily, he seemed only partially caught up in the fervor sweeping the camp. In time she settled the children on their robes and stood before him. "Is it not time to seek the safety of the Nueces?"

He slapped his stomach in appreciation of the meal but looked annoyed. "There is no danger here, woman. The *tejanos* have scattered like antelopes before the swift howling wolf."

"The *tejanos* are not antelopes."

"Woman, leave the fighting to our warriors; we are already rich in horses and have many things of the whites. Soon we will have avenged our chiefs, and Buffalo Hump will lead us home with many honors. Such a victory will be spoken of long after our spirits journey to the stars."

"It will be a victory only when we are home; now we are many sleeps from the hills that shelter us and the buffalo that bring us life."

Hears-the-Wolf rose almost angrily; he was about to caution her against always speaking thoughts that burdened his mind and hung in it like recurring dreams said to be spirit warnings. But at that moment the sound of drums, beating loudly in unison, resounded through the night, and the wild shouts of warriors entering the dance pierced their shelter. Hears-the-Wolf shrugged at the futility of reasoning with this vexing woman, who always provoked him with her quiet searching eyes that were impossible to ignore.

The dance is mankind's instinctive way of expressing exuberance, anger, or those sinister emotions fomenting the primordial urge to hunt and kill. Why the drum has been chosen to express man's exhilaration and bent for violence can be seen in the way it commands the rhythms of his body, raises and matches the pounding of his heart. It is the instrument of all warlike peoples, for it articulates emotions and expresses incomprehensible but compelling drives that often exceed one's powers of speech.

Keeping time with their hide drums, the Comanches stomped the earth and howled like animals as they joined the dance. Though they all moved together, each danced and leaped to his own boasts or secret medicine chant. Headpieces and weapons were boldly carried, and bloody scalps decorated lances and shields. The squaws stood about, bodies vibrating with the drums, watching their braves gyrate and scream as their grease-laden bodies shined in the flickering light of the flames. The entire camp had flocked to the wide circle with its great roaring fire. But few could stand watching for long. The scene was too intoxicating. Many coming up hesitated only a moment before tapping with one foot and starting to circle, then, already chanting or gesturing wildly, moved out to join the throng. It was a ritual that transcended man's mind to find rapture in his animal spirit. The memory of the dead chiefs still invoked secret pledges or solemn pleas to the spirits, but only in the dance did the venting of one's consuming rage seem like ecstasy, only in the dance could the euphoric frenzy of a vengeful slaying be savored.

Hears-the-Wolf knew this dance would last for many hours; often his people danced and chanted till dawn. Like the others; he felt the hypnotic spell the incessant thump of drums had on the mind, but unlike the others, he was also troubled by Black Tail's words and the disturbing eyes of Blue Hawk. This night began to weigh on his mind; it did not have the feel of a tribe turning to pleasure after a daring foray against the enemy, celebrating brave deeds from the sanctity of a camp deep in buffalo range. He sensed something forced in the abandon of the dancers, something frenetic in the screams that rose above the drums. Because of his long attraction to women, there were secretly growing tensions he also detected. Many of these young warriors were long away from the women of their tribes. Promiscuity for young men and unmarried females was allowed, even encouraged, among the Nerm, but here there were only squaws of Penaketa warriors painted for war and constantly in sight. He had seen more than one warrior running sensual eyes down the enticing body of Blue Hawk, but few would dare do more to the squaw of Hears-the-Wolf, a notorious war leader long regarded as a formidable fighter.

Black Tail and Elk Slayer were suddenly by his side. "It starts," whispered Black Tail, nodding to the far end of the circle.

Turning, Hears-the-Wolf could see warriors ducking out of a wickiup near the dance circle and rejoining the dance. He had to watch for a few moments before he noticed one or two were moving with a slight stagger and beginning to dance weirdly.

Black Tail looked at him, expecting some action to be taken, but Hears-the-Wolf knew once braves started drinking, they were truculent, even openly defiant. The camp was heavily armed, and violence, once begun, would be difficult to stop. This was not the white man's army; a chief could lead but couldn't command. Only in battle did warriors respond to orders, and then only until they suspected defeat. Reluctantly he shook his head. "Leave them alone," he said resignedly. "Perhaps the spirit water will put them to sleep." But his voice lacked conviction and his two friends watched him return to his shelter, all wishing this foreboding night would soon be over.

It happened as Black Tail feared it would. The drinking soon spread, the dancing grew wilder, half-inebriated braves let trifling incidents and harmless jests assume ridiculous levels of importance. Strangely enough, it was not the newcomers who ignited trouble but the Penaketa themselves. With that age-old witchery of alcohol, the inhibitions that restrain aggression and homicidal bents in warlike people quickly dissolved. Old scores, imagined debts, or suspected disloyalties, sometimes dating back for many snows, were suddenly raised and, as whiskey eroded the last vestiges of dignity, shameless scenes of drunken accusations began to multiply. Insults were hurled back and forth. Men started reaching for clubs or threatened each other with knives. Often, squaws getting in the way were injured, some seriously.

But the worse was yet to come. The loot of whiskey was larger than any suspected, for the braves, once fired up by the first swallows, kept hunting through the shelters and finding more. But if great numbers were now getting drunk, others were beginning to pass out. Two braves from the Kotsoteka seized a young squaw, and her man, though half-drunk, put an arrow in the arm of one and chased the other with a war club until, exhausted and robbed of his balance by booze, he crashed into a tree. This started a lethal squabble between the different tribesmen, which providentially was settled by the grim figure of Buffalo Hump coming into the firelight and standing before them till silence swept the crowd. "If the great hawks fight each other, can they rule the sky?" he asked in his sonorous voice. "If the lordly wolves fight each other, can they rule the prairies? The *tejanos* have nothing to fear from us; we lack even the wisdom of hawks or wolves. We are like two rutting deer, our horns fatally locked, waiting to die and present our enemies with a feast."

Buffalo Hump was too wise to remain there. He did not want to exchange words with them, he wanted only to shock them to near sobriety, hoping after they'd weighed this stern admonition, the spirit and energy for trouble would drain away. For many this fortunately worked, but, as Hears-the-Wolf was soon to learn, prophetically, for others it did not.

The two burly Yamparika youths, tired of the trek and lusting for a woman, lurked in the dark, shaping their bold plan. They had cut out the horses packed with the booty they wanted, and tethered them in a hidden ravine. They were not drunk but had drunk enough to feel daring and heedless of consequences. They had been watching two squaws, not because they were desirable but because their men had drunk themselves into a helpless stupor. An hour after the camp had quieted down, they crept forward stealthily and found the two squaws still leaning over the prostrate men. They seized them, muffled their cries, and hurried them off to an isolated stretch of scrub pines. There they raped them repeatedly, then tied them up and made their escape. They were the first deserters from the war party, but their going was to have serious effects. For Buffalo Hump saw it as a signal. He was running out of time.

Chapter 18

BEN MCCULLOCH WAS gathering men from all directions, but as yet had nothing like the force needed to challenge the Comanche horde. Riders had been sent in every direction, even to Houston, seeking help, while the war party was closely tracked. The swath of murder and rapine the warriors cut as they drove south horrified those in pursuit, but they had little choice except to watch and wait. But anger and outrage were mounting. McCulloch was worried the gathering force would break loose and attack the Comanches before reaching sufficient strength. But sufficient strength to attack and repulse a thousand mounted warriors was a tall order on this thinly populated plain. Luckily, if all recruits were not trained as Rangers, neither were they tea-drinking missionaries, storekeepers, or bank clerks. There was a heavy salting of rough-hewn settlers from Tennessee and Kentucky, whose fathers had fought the powerful Shawnees and who had been raised in an atmosphere of violence and crisis. McCulloch knew he could count on these men when the showdown came, and in spite of the odds, a showdown was coming. To allow these savages to ride off unscathed was unthinkable. Jody, riding behind him, knew more and more of the men coming up were spoiling for a fight. Those who had seen massacred bodies often arrived with tears of fury in their eyes. McCulloch, thin-lipped and quietly determined, broke his grim silence only to assure them one was coming.

By starts the force was growing. Caldwell had led a troop from San Antonio, and Wallace was scouring the countryside, visiting hamlets and small settlements to gather men. One or two army officers, stationed or patrolling near the frontier, were doing the same. No one needed orders; the disaster blazed forth its own imperatives. A force strong enough to fight this gigantic war party had to be raised to bring this seizing and murdering of helpless settlers to an end.

Through the sweltering daily summer heat of the gulf plain and into the draining humidity of its August nights, the slowly mounting force moved south along the Guadalupe. Before them the destruction continued. Behind them the country lay empty, for its people, like Libby, had scattered, seeing in flight their only hope of salvation.

Jody kept thinking of Libby and little Lance. Many men thought of their families as they rode through the darkness, for though they were determined to fight, God alone knew how it would end. At each burnt-out home with charred bodies, or scalped and mutilated corpse found along the trail, they stared for a moment at this cold, sobering, yet possible end for their loved ones.

In San Antonio, Hays listened to a solitary Ranger, whose weathered face was parched and whose body was gray with dust from his long ride up from the Rio Grande. Three thousand Mexican troops were camped at Laredo. High officers had been spotted by border scouts, and most of these military units were mounted and appeared ready for action.

Hays had sent every man he could to join McCulloch and was about to leave himself. But even the shock of hearing a monstrous war party was attacking sixty miles to his rear did not shake his feeling there was something incredibly strange about this sudden awesome raid. The massive party of Comanches was reported sweeping down the Guadalupe, heading for the large settlement of Victoria. But as he grappled with this fact, others started coming together in his mind. Like most folks in San Antonio, he had many friends in Victoria. He had heard Mexican Federalists, the faction rebelling against Mexico's centralist government, had been feted in that settlement in April of that year—not only feted but supplied with money and arms by Texans who were firmly on the side of freedom and independence. It would have been far more comfortable for Texas to have the fledgling Republic of the Rio Grande as a neighbor rather than still heavily armed, embittered, and vengeful Mexico. The tracks he and Caldwell had seen on the trace swept through his mind. Though it was still a suspicion, Mexico's ill-concealed desire to reconquer Texas was never far from Hays's thoughts. Could the Mexicans have had a hand in this raid? It would not be the first time they used the belligerent Indian tribes of Texas against white settlements. He knew the war party headed for Victoria was the largest and most immediate threat, but he stood now, staring curiously to the south. Watchful eyes would also have to be kept on that far valley of the Rio Grande.

The Comanche camp was astir early the following morning. Many woke up sick; others were so wretched in mood and foul of language, their squaws and children shied away from them. But when the two raped women, after working themselves free, returned with their wildly screamed stories, rage replaced the agonizing effects of alcohol for their many related males. Pursuit of the Yamparikas was openly shouted for, but Buffalo Hump wouldn't hear of it. "They will be found in time," he counseled. "The arm of the Nerm is long; let them live knowing the spirits are watching. Who breaks our people's laws must live like the night-crawling rat, for he will find no place in our great buffalo range where he can stand in the sun.''

This was true, and the braves grumpily agreed to bide their time. Unlike the whites, for whom such crimes led to ropes over handy trees, these youths might well escape all punishment with a sufficiently large gift of horses, which openly acknowledged they had wronged these women's husbands and were making amends. The women, rubbing their many bruises and thereafter covering their faces to seethe at their violation in silence, received nothing.

Blue Hawk was appalled to discover they were continuing to drive south. Her eyes were alive with anger as she saw only a momentary renewal of the attack on Victoria while the braves worked the immense herd of captured animals, many strapped high with loot, around the besieged settlement to resume their march to the coast.

"How far does the brave Buffalo Hump put his gray head into this trap?" she snapped at Hears-the-Wolf.

"Hush, woman! Those are not words fitting for your tongue!" He looked out at the stream of armed warriors filing by. "Can't you see, we are too strong for the cowardly *tejanos*; they cannot trap what they cannot fight. Even their vaunted killer ones do not show their faces. Come, put the children on this white pony I have captured for them; today we must travel fast."

Buffalo Hump was indeed a great war chief. He had not forgotten that mobility was what made Comanche war parties so deadly. They could strike at points and moments of their own choosing, they could retreat at speeds impossible for dazed and disorganized whites to match. Comanches had won thousands of small battles with the whites, but they rarely won big ones.

In his heart he sensed the biggest one of all might be coming, and he was too experienced a warrior not to suspect the enemy was cagily avoiding his war party till it could deal with its strength. But how long would that last? He had been carefully counting the days. He had long calculated he would have a certain number of days to reap the spoils of this surprise raid, as many days as there were fingers on one hand. After that, these *tejanos*, no matter their strength, would surely be striking back. Before then he had to reach the coast, kill as many enemies as possible, and start back for the buffalo plains. He was not blind to the price being paid for this vast number of horses laboring under their plunder. Mobility, long the touchstone of Comanche strategy and battle tactics, was slipping away. But there was no alternative. Many of these braves had come with their minds eager for such loot; they would defy any order to abandon it. To be war chief of these fiercely independent warriors, whose loyalty depended on a steady stream of trophies as well as constant victories, was not an easy task.

Yet, for all his virtues, Buffalo Hump also had a weakness, one shared by almost all Comanche leaders. It was vanity. It stood out on most chiefs like the vivid lines of war paint that added ferocity to their faces. Remarks about their prowess in battle or virility in mating brought grunts of satisfaction and glances of appreciation for recognized merit. Hears-the-Wolf was never given to flattery and he was only stating simple truth when commenting on the more than one hundred miles they had invaded *tejano* territory without a defending shot being fired. They had collected scalps, plundered great wealth, and burned down hundreds of dwellings without meeting any serious resistance. Buffalo Hump could already claim his mantle as the most successful Penateka war chief in tribal history.

But Buffalo Hump wanted this feat to be as visible and memorable a victory as possible. For that he needed captives, many captives, particularly women. Below

Victoria he spread his warriors out in a great semicircle, telling them to advance quickly on the coast, combing the land and taking as many prisoners as possible. At the water they were to surround and take the tiny port of Linnville. It was the port through which San Antonio received its supplies. It was also the port through which arms for the rebellious Mexican Federalists were being secretly shipped.

In a villa outside of Laredo, General Canalizo was tapping his fingers irritably on his desk. He finally stopped and rapped its hard surface with his knuckles, swearing under his breath. "*Carajo! Indios!* They will be the death of me!"

General Woll, seated across the room, settled back to regard him philosophically. "They are savages; they fight like savages. What did you expect, something Napoleonic?"

"You're missing my point! We have information that this renegade Cardenas and his band of traitors are there. They could have wiped out the whole town! The messenger said they stopped fighting at sundown. It sounds like they only killed a handful of gringos."

Woll sighed to cover his unease. "Any word of the Texas military?"

"No, but they must be gathering. A Ranger troop has gone east from San Antonio. However, when they attack the Comanches, they will still be seriously outnumbered; losses will be inevitable. Please remember, that is the moment you cross the Bravo."

"Not before?"

"I cannot risk failure. Santa Anna has been quite specific! We dare not invade unless success is assured."

There was an awkward silence as Woll uncrossed his legs and leaned forward. "What of the Comanches? Shouldn't we be offering them some support?"

"General, if they cannot defeat those *norteamerica-*

nos, I owe them nothing. Remember, we have sent them two hundred rifles for their troubles.''

Woll's smile was oddly strained. "I saw those rifles being loaded on pack mules. Perhaps you should send them to the Texans; a man is safer being shot at by one than firing it. They are dangerous and hardly serviceable relics. In the name of sanity, if not decency, they should be destroyed.''

"Ha! They will do well enough for those savages. They have never learned to repair guns and are accustomed to faulty weapons. Believe me, those bloodthirsty devils will never notice the difference.''

Woll looked down to smile again. Fortunately Canalizo did not see this smile barely concealed a glint of contempt. "What if the Texans decide not to attack?''

Canalizo sat back, his expression a mixture of unease and concern. "The *indios* are heading for Linnville; we believe the Federalists are being supplied through there. It's also San Antonio's only port. *Madre de Dios!* Sooner or later they must fight!''

Woll cleared his throat, preparing to rise. "General Canalizo, if you wish to reconquer Texas, sooner or later you must fight too.''

Chapter 19

ON THE FLATS well east of the Lavaca River sat the Burnside ranch and its already thriving stud farm. Kate had heard of the Burnsides through a distant relative and now frequently did business with them. Race and Dale had been driving Kate's best mustang mares there to be serviced by blooded Tennessee and Kentucky stallions for over a year.

The Burnsides were a hearty couple, and in spite of a heavy workload, spared no pains to make the refugees welcome. Half of a newly finished bunkhouse was turned over to the women, and Walt was given a comfortable loft in the stable. The newcomers ate with this large family, two sons, three daughters, and several hired hands. But hospitality, which the crisis did not diminish, followed a rigorous code. Nobody remained idle for long; the tasks on this busy spread were too many and too demanding. Kate, because of her experience with horses, worked alongside the men; Libby helped the women with cooking, laundry, and other household chores. The woman who came with Walt, a widow called Sadie, stayed with Maude and Lucas, for Maude still had spells when she became so distraught, she sobbed and wept for hours. At night she often called out for her children, and Kate or Becky had to settle beside her and sooth her back to sleep. No one acknowledged she was a drain on them all.

To Libby, because the setting seemed strange, everything seemed strange. The sky appeared jaundiced behind the bleaching sun, hot dust-laden winds seemed forever in one's face. But gurgling little Lance grew more alert with each passing day. Libby, in spite of her stress, marveled at his robust color, his good appetite, and his apparent indifference to their ordeal. She tried soothing her mind by visualizing herself telling him one day how his mother had boldly rescued Maude Chauncy and her young son. She could see his big blue eyes swelling with excitement. She wasn't sure she'd admit she dealt with the Indian threat and the fearful darkness by simply not thinking about them; it was a thing she could decide later.

Word of the war party ravishing the countryside was continually arriving from the west; stragglers reported rumors of deaths all along the valley and a disastrous assault on unsuspecting Victoria. Some isolated settlements were said to have been wiped out. No one knew the truth, and imaginations feeding on anxieties brought on visions of loved ones dying in a pall of despair. Kate, though struggling to hide it, could not conceal her dread of losing her brothers. "I just couldn't go on without them," she breathed heavily one night, and Libby had never heard her sound so human nor felt so close to her. Becky rarely spoke of Jess, and when she did it was with an offhandedness that only revealed her problem with emotion. "That husband of mine best get his butt back and help with chores . . . Damn men grab any excuse to get quit of work."

It was a strange life, but Libby, when not fighting her fears about Jody, which burdened every waking hour, was impressing Kate and Becky with her spunky insis-

tence they not lose hope, that they refuse to believe the
worst. "God has protected us coming here," she said
one morning, "surely He'll hears our prayers for our
menfolk. Like the rest of you, I'm terribly . . . terribly
frightened, but isn't this the time to put trust in our
Maker . . . test our faith?"

Kate sighed. "It's hard, Libby."

"Most tests are hard, Kate, and maybe this one is
hardest because it's His test."

Jody felt a ripple of uncertainty creeping over the
slowly swelling party of men. They were coming now
from all sides, some being led by Ranger captains or
army officers, some just riding up to join. But he sensed
a persistent confusion that grew worse at night. There
was no attempt to keep arriving units together. Riders
just became part of the mounting force. He caught many
glimpses of Race and Dale Sutter, even once spotted
Pete Spevy racing off with a message. Jess Bishop had
earlier ridden by him as he was watering his horse, but
though Jess waved in recognition, he didn't stop. Jody
belatedly waved back. He hadn't seen Buck Chauncy.

McCulloch's expression was the only key to the confusion. Army officers rarely had the field training and
experience with warring Indians that Rangers, by virtue
of their appointed role, simply could not avoid. Jody
heard an army captain telling McCulloch and Caldwell
they should overtake the Comanches and attack in the
hopes of drawing the warriors away from the settlements. Caldwell brusquely replied they had to wait for
better ground; a frontal assault on this flat plain would
not only cost dearly but reduce the strength needed to
eventually defeat and drive the raiders off. McCulloch,
impatience wreathing his face in a web of lines, bluntly
concurred.

But there were several formidable figures arriving
whom Jody knew only by reputation. As they approached Victoria, the Ranger captain and renowned In-

dian fighter John Tumlinson showed up with a contingent of men from Cuero, a settlement in the neighboring county. At McCulloch's or Caldwell's suggestion, Tumlinson began to lead the way and some of the confusion disappeared. By then they numbered a hundred twenty-five men, but were still seriously outnumbered if aligned against the hostiles.

It was in heavily damaged Victoria, relieved as the warriors withdrew to continue on south, that the troop knew fighting could not long be delayed. Several men from the shaken settlement itself joined the force, and the desire for revenge was running high. Added to this was word filtering back of depredations committed as the hostiles drove toward Linnville, for now the Indians were busily taking captives, making any attack on them more difficult. But the tracking Rangers could see the tribesmen were driving a tremendous herd of horses and mules, and it was evident from the many empty and burnt-out farms and ranches they were collecting more. Caldwell, riding next to McCulloch, realized Tumlinson was going to be forced to attack without the numbers needed to turn back this enormous war party. He also knew by now Big Foot Wallace would have ready the men he had been rounding up and directing to muster at Gonzales. Caldwell decided to race back and hurry them down. McCulloch, who elected to stay behind to help Tumlinson, agreed. But those cool Ranger heads, including Tumlinson's, were all too aware of the risks attending a premature attack, and in spite of pressure from the ranks, moved with caution. That night there were more hurried councils held and messengers continually sent off for reinforcements, but by the following morning, when word arrived that Linnville was in flames and the Comanches were returning north, coming directly toward them, it put an end to all hesitation. The long-delayed but unavoidable and critical battle to save the valley of the Guadalupe was about to be joined.

*   *   *

As the great crescent of armed and painted Indians made its way downcountry, striking ranch after ranch, killing the people and looting their livestock, settlers on the coastal strip started to share the fate of their northern neighbors. Men died in the fields, and family members were shot as they stepped, often in baffled confusion, onto their front porches. Incredibly, word of the marauding war party had still not reached this last strip of gulf plain. At the nine-mile point they captured a Mrs. Cyrus Crosby and her young child, taking them and many others that evening to their rough camp on Placedo Creek. It had been a good day for plunder and the camp was jubilant; a feast of roasted meat from slaughtered cattle was being prepared. As sundown came, there were fresh scalps in evidence, and clothes and trinkets stripped from the dead bodies of settlers were being proudly worn by strutting braves. By dark the warriors had settled around their fires to smoke, convinced the lack of resistance proved their strength was too great for these craven *tejanos*, now suspected of slinking about somewhere in their rear, to challenge.

As the fierce August sun sank like a great fiery red shield in a wine-stained sky, Buffalo Hump asked the medicine men to drum their secret chants to the watching spirits, for tomorrow he wanted the Penaketa medicine to be strong. They were now only a half day's ride from the busy and unsuspecting port of Linnville. His five days were almost up, but his great raid was ending in success. He had reached his goal; the murdered chiefs had been avenged, and the tribe's newfound wealth in horses, mules, and countless packs of loot was staggering. He signaled the passing Hears-the-Wolf to join him for a pipe.

Back in her shelter, Blue Hawk watched her children sleep as she tried to deal with the many anxieties that nagged at her, kept her growing ever more restless, denied her even momentary peace of mind. Why weren't her people breaking up into small elusive groups, each taking its share of booty and stealthily fleeing westward across the barren plains for home? That had always been their way, that had spelled their many successes, that alone was sanity. To delay here any longer would surely anger the spirits. Strong medicine held too long often turned weak. But she knew her brave but arrogant husband, and his aging chief, were being lured by the ease with which they had swept down this undefended valley. The absence of any resisting *tejanos*, even Rangers, those killer ones who always stood and fought, had not, as it should have, raised their suspicions but only made them bolder. To her they were riding into this deep and unfamiliar heart of *tejano* land like youths in the entrancement of a dream. Yet the reasons for this alarming mixture of nonchalance and brashness were all about her. Never had the tribe amassed such riches, never had they seized such numbers of horses and mules. What they had captured here exceeded the bounty of many years in Mexico. But such a mass of wealth could not be moved quickly, such an endless train of animals would have to be herded, guarded. Secretly she knew what was troubling her spirit. Should the need to retreat speedily to their buffalo range arise, this mountain of spoils would act as fetters to their hands, hobbles to their feet. But these were not matters for a woman to remark on, these were thoughts to be buried deep, for they would only anger Penaketa men.

She lay down beside her children and closed her eyes, but Blue Hawk's mind found no peace and she did not sleep.

The cruel incident that started that eventful day could have been a harbinger for what followed. As the line of prancing warriors drew nearer to Linnville, Mrs. Crosby's child, hungry and exhausted from rough handling in captivity, began to cry. Its mother, who had been stripped and tormented during the night, could not silence it. After a few minutes, without warning, a warrior snatched the child from her, threw it to the ground, and speared it to death before her eyes. The war party, once again forming its deadly crescent to surround the now visible seaport, callously moved on.

Few could remember when a war party had been last seen near the coast, so when people looked up the Victoria road and saw horsemen approaching, they assumed they were Mexican traders bringing a *caballada* for sale or trade. It was only when the warriors whipped their mounts into a furious gallop and started screaming war cries that the warning shouts of "Indians!" went up from startled citizens and people began to rush down to the water.

The first charge killed three white men and two Negro slaves. One of the whites was Major Watts, customs collector for the port. He and his handsome wife, whom he had just married, might have made it to the boats had they not hesitated to retrieve his gold watch. Mrs. Watts, appalled at her husband's death, tried to lock herself in the customs house, but they broke in and seized her. The warriors immediately tried to strip the buxom woman but couldn't remove her heavy whalebone corset. She was thrown over a pony in her underclothes to be dealt with later.

The death toll would have risen far higher had they not found on every side warehouses surrounded by packing cases, many opened with goods stacked at loading sites. Avarice had replaced anger in a growing number of braves. In Indian terms this was incredible wealth. While the people jumped in boats and rowed offshore, the half moon of screeching warriors closed around the stricken town, and all remaining stragglers were ridden down and dispatched.

With the port in their hands and the people lying in boats offshore, many having reached the steamer *Mustang* anchored in the bay, the warriors began their orgy of destruction. Before the eyes of its citizens, Linnville was pillaged and set afire. Its many horses were collected and added to the already gigantic herd, its cattle were driven into pens and killed with lances and arrows by howling braves delirious at their own destructive power. The squaws coming up and seeing the colorful goods, particularly bolts of cloth and heavily decorated glassware and pots, hurriedly started tying packs on horses and mules to carry off this miraculous windfall.

In anguish the stranded people watched wildly painted figures going from house to house, pulling out and smashing their belongings, cutting the ticking on featherbeds and roaring with laughter to see the feathers flying as the warriors dragged them behind their horses. Always they ended by setting the dwellings on fire. Many people saw the efforts and sacrifices of years going up in smoke. Judge John Hays became so exasperated, he took a gun and, rowing close to land, jumped out and waded to shore. He was going to have one shot at these "damn red devils" anyway. The Indians, seeing him crazily shaking his fist and ranting at them, even putting himself in reach of certain death, decided he had been struck with insanity. Madness, in their minds, meant the presence of disgruntled, even dangerous, spirits. They paid no attention to his dares to come within range of his gun. Acting as though he didn't exist, they cautiously steered a wide berth around him. Later when some friends finally coaxed him back to safety, it was found his gun wasn't loaded.

All day the devastation continued until not a building or warehouse was left standing in Linnville. Even the docks had been set afire. From one burning warehouse they belatedly pulled crates of umbrellas and fancy hats. These they wore till they tired of racing about the ash-lined streets, and finally the approach of sundown brought Buffalo Hump's signal to withdraw. Following the cornucopia of loot raised during the devastation of Linnville, they crossed to a nearby bayou and camped for the night.

Standing outside their new campsite, Buffalo Hump and Hears-the-Wolf looked to the north. "It is well," said Buffalo Hump, "we ride now to the buffalo plains. The Mexicans will know we have kept our word; I saw one of their spies leaving camp. He will report our victory." He grunted with satisfaction. "The *tejanos* have not shown their faces; the might of the Penateka has shrunken their hearts."

Hears-the-Wolf nodded toward the great mass of animals, many of them strapped with packs of loot. "The braves are taking great wealth back to their tepees; they will be eager to fight with Buffalo Hump again." He paused and looked at the sky. Lightning was leaping along the horizon, and a low rumble of thunder came faintly against the ear. "The rain spirit is speaking. We go north tomorrow. Has Buffalo Hump chosen a trail?"

Buffalo Hump stared at the flashing horizon. "We have marched proudly through the land of the treacherous *tejanos*; they have hidden from us like rabbits in a hutch. Let our people see the Penateka warrior still rules wherever his lance reaches. We return by the trail that led us here. It is the shortest way to our buffalo range . . . It is the shortest way to the honors that await us."

Chapter 20

THE DUST AND clamor of over two thousand animals, being hurried northward by the circling and howling braves, made it difficult to hear that morning as Blue Hawk, her children mounted on their white pony, watched the long string of captives tied to their horses and made to ride in the center of the moving camp. At the realization that they were heading back over their own trail, she was too alarmed to keep her fears to herself. She turned to Hears-the-Wolf, who had ridden up beside her. "Buffalo Hump has painted a trail of blood through this country. Will not the smell of that blood draw the killer ones toward this trail, as prairie wolves are drawn to the blood of slain buffalos?"

Openly irritated, Hears-the-Wolf made the sign for silence as he waved her forward. "The *tejanos* have fled like deer frightened from a salt lick at the snarl of a mountain lion. The Penateka now rule this land. The false-hearted *tejanos* have no courage for war. Soon our warriors will be dancing and chanting their victory by the Nueces." His fist pounded the thick leather pommel of his saddle. "Let there be an end to this squaw talk!"

He pulled away abruptly, but not before she caught a vague uneasiness in his eyes. It hardly diminished her worries. In a moment she was soberly fretting again, wondering if pride, his or Buffalo Hump's, wasn't driving them forward, contemptuous of *tejano* strength, boldly, even heedlessly, riding into this now-alerted enemy. But she was only a woman, and her man was growing impatient, even angry with her. She must stop voicing her fears. Mutely, holding a halter on her children's pony, she rode along, trying to console herself with a few comforting thoughts. They had come well over a hundred miles through *tejano* territory without an attack. Perhaps they could do it again. Perhaps. But that morning as they moved along the west bank of Garcitas Creek, the heat and confusion making her look longingly at the still, cool reaches of sky, she heard scouts racing along the outskirts of the vast Comanche train, making those low but piercing cries of warning that from time immemorial meant "Enemies sighted!"

Tumlinson and McCulloch, rising before dawn to carefully scout to the south, finally, an hour after sunrise, spotted the great mass of Comanches moving northward near the juncture of Garcitas and Arenosa creeks. It was an awesome sight. Already a dust cloud rising to several hundred feet hung over the hostile procession, and noises that always mark great herds of moving animals could be heard in the distance. But now the time for cautious scouting and trailing was over. The men spread out in two parallel lines and advanced against the Indians' right flank. Within minutes groups of warriors began to break away from the train and gallop furiously toward the oncoming Texans. As they rapidly closed the ground, heavy gunfire broke out and a swarm of screeching Comanches swept up to surround the smaller force. The suddenly besieged men started dismounting and firing from a crouched position. Though heavily outnumbered, some of the best shots on the frontier were now zeroing in on red flesh over bare gunsights. Though the Indians fired back, amazingly they did not charge and overrun, as they clearly could have, this inferior force. Instead they seemed content to contain the Texans while in the distance the train continued northward. Within half an hour the moving mass had filed behind a distant outcropping of rock and disappeared.

It was McCulloch who first saw the Indians were less intent on fighting than getting away with their loot. Though the warriors were skillfully dodging in and out, their many wild feints and maneuvers plainly lacked the ferocious death-defying quality that made Comanche warfare so terrifying to endure. "We've got to break out of here!" shouted McCulloch. "They're holding us here to let the main party get away!"

Tumlinson, smiling grimly at their predicament, agreed. But the disparity in numbers couldn't be ignored. It would have been suicidal to give up the defensive formation that was keeping these howling Comanches at bay. It wasn't until much later that, in spite of stunning feats of Indian horsemanship, sharp-eyed Texans began to hit their marks and Comanches were tumbling to the ground. Then without warning the warriors suddenly broke off the attack, threw the bodies of their five or six dead on spare ponies, and raced off in pursuit of the train.

Within minutes the Texans were mounted and, though still confused as to how to match the forbidding power of the train, quickly jammed their rifles in scabbards at Tumlinson's command and rode determinedly after them.

It wasn't until evening, because of intermittent skirmishing with a shifty and stubborn Indian rear guard, that they overtook the swiftly moving train, but by then another problem was making itself felt. Tumlinson and McCulloch realized their horses, after the long pursuit, were tiring. The Indians with their large supply of mounts were changing animals repeatedly to keep up the grueling pace. Some twenty rough miles had been covered by nightfall, and it was clear the Texans could still not maneuver into a promising position to attack. Some would have thought it ridiculous their small force wanted to engage the massive train, knowing they were outnumbered eight or ten to one. But the ranks were now filled with men livid with rage at the deaths and destruction these savages had wrought upon their homes and loved ones. Also, experienced Indian fighters among them sensed the redskins were beginning to run, a sign they had their fill of killing and now wanted to escape with their spoils, wanted the boasting and glory of the inevitable scalp dance among the richly scented cooking fires of their home range.

But for tired Texans, nightfall only saw their quandary mount. Before any talk of inflicting defeat on the warriors, they had first to bring this formidable force to bay. There was much excited discussion, but few ideas emerged that could be safely translated into action. Many of the hurried suggestions, Tumlinson dismissed out of hand. But this persistent lack of a plan was having other effects. Secretly McCulloch was beginning to lose patience with the indecisiveness he now sensed in Tumlinson and others. As he saw it, this was not a moment for hesitation. It was time to strike the Indians and strike them hard. Darkness or not, he wanted to attack. But Tumlinson repeatedly shook his head. He was convinced such an attempt, before they received reinforcements, would fail. The argument between these two blunt and forceful men continued into the night, with both sides getting frequent support from followers. But by dawn the Comanche train was moving again and McCulloch was still kneeling down beside Tumlinson, trying one more time to convince him to attack. He was sure if this unwieldy hostile formation was broken up, they could rout the entire force. Tumlinson, looking at the dark mass moving along the horizon, continued to shake his head. "If we fail, there's no way left to stop 'em. We need more guns . . . Be tarnation foolish to move before we git 'em!"

But McCulloch was through talking. He couldn't see the sense of stalking this train like a lone wolf, waiting for its pack to gather to attack. His mind had already moved ahead. These hostiles were not, as suspected, breaking up into small evasive groups to disappear into the arid wastes south of San Antonio. To him it was clear they were driving for the safety of the hills to the northwest, counting on their strength to fight their way through and sensibly taking the shortest route, the one by which they had come. That meant they would be turning westward somewhere above Gonzales and most likely near Plum Creek. He called some of the men from his home troop together, among them Jody, Dale, Jess Bishop, and Buck Chauncy. There were others, but they all had lasting faith in Ben McCulloch. At his quiet command they mounted and, ranging behind him at a brisk pace, speedily followed him up the now-abandoned and devastated valley of the Guadalupe.

The two half-breeds had finally reached the waters of the Rio Grande. They were now nearing Laredo, and as they and their thirsty mounts gulped down the cool river water, they failed to notice a Ranger lying in wait for them along the river trail. It had been a long, exhausting ride in the mid-August heat, and they were anxious to report to General Canalizo, after which they would be dismissed from duty and could drink some wine.

This close to Mexican soil, they did not expect trouble, so when they rounded a bend in the trail and found the Ranger's gun trained on them, they froze in their tracks.

"Señor, qué pasa?"

The Ranger's expression failed to change. "Get off those horses!"

As they started to comply, a shot rang out. A Mexican

army patrol had appeared across the river. It diverted the Ranger enough to tempt one of the half-breeds to use his spurs and quirt to drive his horse forward to freedom. The Ranger coolly fired at him and hit him in the shoulder, but immediately turned to making sure the second one didn't get away. Across the river the patrol had dismounted and its men were firing carefully, trying to hit the Ranger but not his prisoner.

The Ranger pulled the half-breed behind a boulder and, disarming him, used a short piece of rope he had carried from his horse to tie his hands. The Ranger was under no illusions. That patrol would sooner or later cross the river and try to trap him; a border established by treaty meant nothing in this violent and lawless valley. Calculating every move and using the man's horse as a shield, he backed them away from the exposed river's edge and finally, finding some brush for cover, reached his own mount, which, on seeing the half-breeds, he had cautiously concealed. Within minutes they were traveling northward toward San Antonio and the Ranger captain Jack Hays.

The wounded man was taken before General Canalizo. The general anxiously searched his face, paying little attention to his wound. "Quickly! What is happening?" he demanded.

"General, they have burned the place call Linnville and killed many people, but now they go home."

"Go home? Haven't they started fighting the *Rinches* or even some soldiers yet?"

"General, the *tejanos* do not fight."

"What! Are you telling me they are not resisting those murderous savages? That's ridiculous!"

"General, it is true."

General Woll had entered the room; his questioning look to Canalizo brought only an exasperated gasp. "*Jesucristo*, can you believe it, there's been no fighting?!"

Woll studied him for a moment. "Valentin, you must never count on the enemy helping your cause."

"But certainly they should help themselves! The Comanches have inflicted tremendous damage." In frustration he slapped his desk. "Why are these damned gringos always so anxious to fight us? . . . I just can't understand it."

Woll was studying a map that Canalizo had placed on his wall; it was one of the largest ever made of Texas, the onetime Mexican province. Woll started marking with his finger a line from the gulf coast up the valley of the Guadalupe. For a few moments he seemed to be reflecting on distances to be covered. Unable to bear his silence, the still-fuming Canalizo turned on him. "Well, what do you make of it, eh?"

Woll raised a hand to stroke his chin. "I think they're still going to fight, but not just yet."

"Not just yet? But the Comanches are going home!"

"I understand. But the Texans apparently aren't ready yet . . ." A wisp of smile touched the corner of his mouth. "But then again, those Comanches, the ones you say have done so much damage, they aren't home yet either."

In his excitement Canalizo had almost forgotten this wounded man's companion had been captured. His overriding concern had been the Comanches inflicting a defeat on the sparse military forces of Texas and making its western regions ripe for invasion. Now, with no talk of fighting, he was beginning to despair of his cautiously prepared campaign. He stared coldly at the wounded messenger, locking him in eye contact till the poor man began to shake. "And just how did this stupid companion of yours get himself captured?"

"Excellency, this *Rinche*, he surprised us. Poor Miguel, he had no chance. Could I have a little wine?"

Canalizo turned to his attendant. "Get this blubbering idiot out of my sight! I want that *Rinche* trailed. Find out where he is going. Send a patrol of six men. If they are overtaken, I want the *Rinche* shot and his prisoner returned!"

Woll, standing across the room, smiled wistfully at
him. "Valentin, that will not recover Texas for you. History is never written in such simple terms. You're shooting at the spirit of a young defiant nation, and all you're
going to hit is a man."

Canalizo looked at him, irritation twisting his mouth.
"And what, may I asked, would you do?"

"I would march. We agreed to invade when Linnville
was taken. I would think it wise, not to mention honorable, to keep our word."

"One has no obligation to keep one's word with savages wearing dung in their hair."

"No?"

"No. They are not our comrades-in-arms. Accepting
that shipment of guns makes them mercenaries. They
were suppose to attack and weaken the Texans!"

"So were we."

"General, you don't understand. I cannot take a
chance as long as victory is in doubt. There is no room
at Santa Anna's table for defeated generals."

"Ah, but was he not himself defeated several times?"

"You see. Clearly you don't understand. That, my
friend, is different!"

Chapter 21

IN THE WAKE of solitary riders racing desperately for reinforcements, word of the assaults on Victoria and Linnville spread outward from the valley of the Guadalupe. The fearful news traveled like floodwaters over a plain, rushing forward in rivulets, then eddying back to touch isolated and less accessible spots. And just as water rushing over earth becomes muddy, so did distance distort the stories springing up around the war party's exploits. Many reasoned the Indians had disappeared to the south, till McCulloch, reaching Gonzales after an exhausting run, reported the redskins were now returning north. Ben's mind was still fixed on Plum Creek. He was relieved to see some familiar faces at Gonzales, and before dismounting, was shouting for Caldwell. When his brother Henry rushed up to greet him, he sent him off to watch for Indians coming up their downward track. Excitement mounted again and word of the returning menace was on everyone's lips. Caldwell, upon hearing the Comanches were driving north toward the hill country, agreed with Ben's guess about Plum Creek. But time was already working against them. Tumlinson's troop was still far to the south; other forces would have to be mustered. Everyone knew the many couriers immediately sent out could not all reach their destinations in time, but if a few succeeded, they could prove crucial. When Colonel Burleson, a veteran Indian fighter on the Colorado, was finally and fortunately reached, he wasted no time raising a force in the region of Bastrop and heading for Plum Creek. When word reached Austin, that still hardly inhabited capital in the wilderness, Major General Felix Huston, though without troops, was dispatched at once to form a command.

Slowly the remaining forces of the wracked and bleeding frontier were gathered, but they were far from sufficient to allow hope for a successful encounter with a thousand well-armed and mounted marauders. As always, the frontier would have to make up with mettle and raw guts what it lacked in manpower. Yet there were few signs of despair; if anything, one heard murmurs of relief that some offensive action was finally being planned. Hazardous and hotly contested borders attract a salty stubborn breed. No one suggested the war party be allowed to travel home in peace and thus be removed from their lives. Survival here had always carried its pall of uncertainty, and no one needed to be told how uncertain were their prospects at Plum Creek.

In their sanctuary well east of the Lavaca, the women listened to sparse reports sifting back with an occasional refugee, or those who passed to the west on the Columbus road but quickly swung their wagons around at the first reports of trouble. The frontier wasn't for everyone. Yet lack of word about their menfolk was beginning to depress and distress the women. Arguments for discovering what was happening, or even attempting to return home, were being raised with more force every day. It was Walt who gave them their final encouragement, but he was only exercising a conventional wisdom shared by veteran Indian fighters. ''If they've gone that far south,'' he allowed, ''chances are they'll split up and start slipping away to the west. Injuns don't hang about much once't they've carved a few scalps and rounded up a fair passel of loot.''

''Think it might be safe then?'' asked Becky.

''More'n likely . . . especially if you stay well to the north . . . give 'em plenty of room.''

Two days later Kate, Becky, and Libby decided to chance it. There seemed no point in taking the wagon, which would only make travel more difficult. After an hour's discussion they decided to leave Maude, Lucas, Sadie, and Walt behind. They could follow later when the trails were known to be safe. Becky borrowed a horse from the Burnsides, and Libby bundled Lance up in her rig. In a slightly emotional scene the Burnsides gave them some rations and wished them well. These harried women had earned their keep, and some of the younger members of the family were clearly going to miss their company, worried and unsettled as they were.

With Becky and Kate leading the way, Libby followed at a good clip. The heat was stifling, but within an hour she noticed storm clouds gathering before them as they moved steadily onto the slowly rising plain that stretched to the northwest. How far northward the others had decided to swing, she didn't know, but Libby hoped they would be turning for home before dark. She didn't want to spend another frightening night on the prairie.

The long procession of warriors, trotting and snorting animals, squabbling squaws, stark-eyed children, and mute doleful captives made its way up-country under a towering cloud of dust. Almost gratefully Blue Hawk watched the storm clouds gathering ahead, knowing the rain would be heavy but brief, a typical summer downpour, but it would settle this dust that was hanging over them like a banner, helping enemies mark their progress. She looked at her children, shy pensive Blossom and faintly smiling Bright Arrow, sitting astride their white pony, their eyes clinging to hers in a search for assurance. For some time they had sensed her growing anxiety, noticed her continually scanning the horizon, watched her bite her lip and remain silent when Hears-the-Wolf came by, his face seeming more and more trenched with concern.

Blue Hawk was not a warrior and knew little of war, but she saw her tribesmen spread out along the long line of horses and mules and knew they were poorly arranged for a fight. She could not believe they would make it to the hill country without a challenge from the *tejanos*. Once when she glanced at the prisoners she was seized with a queer premonition she might soon be one herself. The woman whose baby they had killed and the one whose corset they couldn't remove had been tied over horses, the one stripped to her underclothes suffering as her smooth white limbs were exposed to the broiling sun. The inflamed scarlet flush of her skin signaled the pain she must have been enduring. But Blue Hawk was mainly nervous and distracted out of fear for her children. Nor could her fright be dismissed as imaginary. The *tejanos* would find the dead child the warriors had killed, and though the killer ones needed no encouragement, now perhaps all *tejanos* would be seeking to avenge that child. She wondered what plans Buffalo Hump and Hears-the-Wolf had for the squaws and children if the train was attacked.

They plodded along for an hour, then with a long crackling thunder, the storm started to break. She looked up at the sky to see the first sheet of rain sweeping over the procession like a cool hand coming to lessen the fever of the day.

Hears-the-Wolf and Buffalo Hump were riding far forward in the procession. They, too, were glad of the rain. It would swell little streams they were passing and help water their hard-driven herd. Neither had to be told they were still a day or two's march from safety. Neither had to be told this herd with its endless packs of loot would be a problem in a fight. But the die was cast now; there was only one direction left to go, ahead. Scouts sent out had not sighted any enemies, but the train was moving so rapidly now, proper scouting of the land before them had been difficult at best.

Buffalo Hump was grunting to himself. The fact that the *tejanos* had not appeared in force was to him a promising sign. Secretly he felt news of his taking and burning Linnville had reached the Mexicans, and their promised invasion was taking place. He decided the *tejanos* had failed to attack him because they had been drawn off to defend San Antonio. He spoke of this to Hears-the-Wolf and the morose Black Tail, who had come up to join them, but their responses were hardly assuring. Comanches did not hold Mexican fighting ability in much esteem; after all, a handful of *tejanos* in a single battle had seized Texas from them. Could not these same *tejanos*, skilled gunmen and unrelenting killers that they were known to be, keep the Mexicans from taking it back?

Hears-the-Wolf listened to Buffalo Hump's words, but his thoughts were with their straggling lines of warriors. A sudden attack would be hard to repulse, and the problem of dealing with this enormous herd, if serious fighting broke out, began to gnaw at him. They came out on Big Prairie as the cooling rain stopped. Welcome as the rain was, their relief didn't last long. Gradually the sun reappeared and its scorching heat swiftly returned. Finally the wind rose sluggishly like puffs from a broken bellows, drying the land and feeling gritty against the face. After an hour's trek, and the raising of another telltale dust cloud, they began to approach Plum Creek.

McCulloch and Caldwell arrived first, leading a force that had slowly risen to over ninety men. They camped at a spot called Good's Crossing, behind dense foliage running along the now almost dry Plum Creek. Scouts

reported the Indians were rapidly approaching and were
now only a few miles away. The great dust cloud marking their progress had been visible for almost an hour.
At first it was thought Caldwell or McCulloch would
direct the attack, but with the arrival of General Huston,
Caldwell, deferring to the general's rank, asked the men
to vote Huston their leader. Texans, and particularly
Rangers, put little store in ranks that came with epaulets.
A man's courage and character were his rank. Not a few
volunteers remarked openly they preferred Caldwell or
McCulloch, figures known for their savvy in Indian
fighting. But Caldwell persuaded them to support the
general, and Huston started to prepare a plan of attack.

Jody and the men from Gonzales, who had come
north with McCulloch, watched all this with increasing
excitement. By now they had lost much of their unease
about engaging such a formidable mass. All signs said
the redskins were no longer on the offensive and were
withdrawing with their scalps and spoils to fight another
day. But the moment saw strange if unseen alliances
springing up. Everyone knew McCulloch was determined these marauders would not slip away without a
fight. Since this suited the temper of more and more of
the volunteers, Ben found an increasing number of eyes
following him about. "If we stick with him, we're sure
of getting to kill a couple of those murdering bastards,"
said Jess Bishop. Everyone knew he was thinking of his
brother's fate. Others like Jody, worn by his worries
about Libby and Lance, and remembering his father and
uncle, joined the group in mumbled agreement. It would
have been hard to find a face in that gathering without
a grievance.

Only Buck Chauncy remained quiet, but some noticed
his eyes never left that spectral dust cloud drawing near.
By now he had accepted the deaths of his children and
the dementia of his wife. Secretly his mind had closed
on any further hopes for life. He had a blood score to
settle with these human hyenas. If his chance didn't

come today, he might consider the way taken by Jess Bishop's brother. Pete Spevy, regarding him, shook his head and quietly winced. One could almost smell the hatred that now exuded from this aggrieved man. But he was not the only one; vengence beamed hard in the eyes of many.

Huston, looking about uncertainly, had to reckon they were still outnumbered eight or ten to one, but runners were now reporting Colonel Burleson was on his way and drawing near. Word was sent to him to come at a gallop, for the Indians were now visibly marching diagonally across the plain toward the Clear Fork, a small stream lying just beyond Plum Creek. The moment to attack was almost upon them.

Burleson was making what haste he could, though at Cedar Creek he collected a strange addition to his force. Of all the Indian tribes history has recorded on the Texas coastal range, none quite won the reputation accorded the Tonkawas. They were few but dangerous; they were often feared but always hated; they had no friends, let alone allies. They were crafty killers, and most startling of all, they were cannibals. But they hated Comanches, as they were hated in return, and offered to scout for the Texans, a job Burleson knew they would likely do well. They had no horses, and so had to run behind the mounted volunteers, but though Burleson galloped the last three or four miles to get there on time, the thirteen Tonkawas sped into camp right on his heels and immediately started their scout. They were told, like Tomcah, to tie a white rag on their arms to distinguish them from Comanches, for they were going to be working close to the enemy and mistakes could be made. Their chief, Placido, his wiry body covered with tattoos, went boldly forward with his men.

Huston decided to attack with a hollow square open in front. Burleson would command the right wing, and Caldwell the left. Other men coming up would serve the rear line or reserve, which he placed under one of his staff, Major Thomas Hardeman. There were now over two hundred men in the attacking force, yet incredibly, the great Comanche war party, slowly stretching out across the prairie, was unaware of their presence. But the Indians made a stirring sight marching along. The warriors, some in full regalia with bright ribbons tied to their horses' tails or manes, raced about. The great herd of over three thousand animals steadily moved forward, led by a medicine man with a drum on each side of his mount, chanting and drumming a secret message to the great spirit that lived in all things and could grant strong medicine. The squaws and the young ones rode together, and the captives could be seen tied to their horses and surrounded by young laughing braves. The train extended for almost two miles, and when Huston gave the order to advance, the Texans emerged from the heavy brush to strike it just above its center. It was a moment many would remember, for it was the start of a battle that would determine the history of a nation.

Chapter 22

WHEN THE INDIANS saw mounted Texans, suddenly appearing and coming across the prairie toward them, an audible shock, like the sonic convulsions of a whip, went through the crawling train. Warriors began to rush up from all directions; a wall of mounted braves quickly formed between the approaching Texans and the great strung-out herd of horses and pack mules. As the two forces approached each other, distant shots broke out. From time to time warriors raced forward and fired arrows toward the volunteers, but as the ground closed between them, it was clear every Comanche not preparing to fight was busy hustling the train of spoils into a heavy stand of oaks on a prominent rise to the northwest. The Texans advanced steadily, but the numbers before them continued to mount, and though the warriors were mostly riding up and down and wildly crying out threats, their numbers swelled ominously. Yet, in response to this, Huston's order to dismount and form a defensive formation brought only shouts of anger from the men. Many were bristling for a fight; most could see, in spite of their numbers, the Comanche attempt to protect the train was making them vulnerable to a direct assault.

McCulloch, not wanting to see the check to Tumlinson repeated here, galloped over and shouted at Huston. "General, this is no way to fight Indians. Can't you see they're fooling with us! They don't intend to fight; they're trying to get away with their captives and plunder. Order a charge; we'll kill a mess of them and get those captives back!"

Just at that moment a towering warrior in war regalia rode out before the Texans and raised his war hatchet and shield high in the air. It was the age-old challenge to single combat, a tradition long enshrined in the fighting code of Plains tribes. Its purpose was to determine whose medicine was strongest when neither side wanted costly or prolonged combat. But the Texans had little appreciation of Plains culture; they saw this as only another delaying tactic. When the warrior, seeing his challenge going unanswered, spit at them in the standard insult meant to provoke the enemy by implying cowardice, Caldwell shouted, "Shoot the bastard!"

A half dozen rifles roared and the warrior was lifted from his saddle and sent sprawling to the ground. From the mass of braves came a deep moaning sound, for many perceived in this warrior's death the bane of bad medicine. But this bizarre scene was enough to galvanize Huston into action. Suddenly he was shouting, "All right, boys! Charge the devils! Give 'em hell! Get those captives back!"

With wild yells, not unlike charging Comanches, the Texans galloped forward. The plain was suddenly a maelstrom of combat and confusion as fury and outrage, fueled by vengeance and hate, drove the Texans into the Indian ranks and red men and white men began to die.

Blue Hawk, kept alert by her fears, spotted the Texans first, though her screams of alarm were quickly drowned as the sudden awareness of the *tejano* threat swept through the train. She saw Hears-the-Wolf signaling warriors at the rear to press the animals faster and come forward. Everywhere people were rushing toward the great stand of oaks looming ahead. Shots were ringing out like a drum beaten faster and faster, and war cries of both Comanches and Texans mingled in a hellish chorus that made hearing impossible. She raced toward the cover of the oaks, shouting to her children to hold fast to their white pony, which was beginning to pull and buck against its halter as its fright at the uproar mounted. Already the horses and mules ahead were creating a barrier as they began to congest at the edge of the oaks. More coming up only increased the confusion, and everywhere fractious animals began to rear up, threatening to bolt, ready to ignite a stampede. Blue Hawk knew they had to abandon the herd and start an all-out attack on the Texans or they were lost. Still many braves stubbornly refused to believe their superior numbers could not carry the day. But the fog of battle had already descended on the plain. Numbers began to lose their importance. The battle line had lost all coherence. The wave of Texans had broken through the cordon of braves separating them from the massive herd, and now they were deliberately riding into the frenzied animals, firing and dangerously spooking this remuda of over three thousand head, creating a murderous wave of plunging hoofs that menaced riders on every side. The exploding chaos soon challenged belief. Animals, racing through the oaks, piled up in ravines along the Clear Fork or the soggy ground beyond. Some warriors, trying to control them, were caught between the panicking animals and crushed to death. Others saved themselves by jumping from their own mounts and running across the backs of terrorized animals to reach safety. But Texan rifles were now spitting flames, and Comanches on all sides were paying a heavy price.

Buffalo Hump and Hears-the-Wolf, seeing the mounting danger, were furiously signaling the warriors to abandon the rampaging animals and defend a corridor through which the squaws and children could escape. The squaws, many having been under fire before, were already hurrying ahead, using hastily seized switches to drive the animals bearing the captives before them. Here and there warriors were gathering to make a stand, but now the deadly role of the Tonkawas made itself felt. Racing about, they kept the Texans informed about pockets of resistance trying to form, allowing the volunteers to wipe out these desperate attempts before they could take hold. Some warriors, cut off by the charging Texans, fought till they faced death, a few managing to slash tree trunks and mark spots where tribesmen would take revenge.

The deafening turmoil began to follow the track of escaping women and children. The battle stretched out into dozens of little pitched battles. Everywhere there were animals galloping to exhaustion or finally being slowed by heavy underbrush or wide ravines. The Indians could still have made a determined stand, but something had arisen to match their hatred of *tejanos*. It was the Achilles' heel of the primitive mind, superstition. It was his friend Elk Slayer whom Hears-the-Wolf had called upon to delay the enemy. It was that towering warrior who had challenged the enemy to single combat. The Comanches believed a warrior performing this time-honored act of bravery was protected by strong tribal spirits. But now his body lay riddled on the prairie floor. To them it meant one thing. The faces of guardian spirits were turned away.

Valiant if futile rallies were attempted by Buffalo Hump, Hears-the-Wolf, and even Black Tail, but the fighting heart of the Comanches had lost its fire. With their failure to save the valuable loot and their loss of control of the scattered herd, the great war party seemed helpless to resist the bloodlusting Texans, who were driving forward like demons, spreading death everywhere. The Penateka leaders, still brave in the face of disaster, turned like wounded animals to salvaging what was vital to their tribal life. The squaws and young ones had to escape, and the captives slowing their retreat had to be dispatched. By now the fighting stretched out for three or four miles, but the squaws, though still urging forth the captives, were finally overtaken and the infuriated warriors hurriedly turned to their grim task. Captives were pulled from their mounts and tied to trees. There they were cut up and stabbed with knives or pierced with lances. Some were shot through with arrows. In such a way did Mrs. Crosby meet her death. It was only discovered later she was the granddaughter of Daniel Boone, the great Kentucky frontiersman. Mrs. Watts, still in her corset, was also tied to a tree, but the one arrow fired at her struck whalebone in the corset, saving her life. She, suffering only a painful sunburn, was the sole survivor.

But the time taken for this massacre proved critical. The Texans, like baying hounds on a ripening scent, swept into the clearing where many of the captives were slain. Some, with only a look, pressed on; they knew there were squaws and young ones ahead. To enraged men, only blood absolves blood. The flint eyes of these pursuers carried their own prophecy. Foremost amongst them was Buck Chauncy, his stark face tight with anger and pale with hate.

As the shouting Texans thundered up behind her, Blue Hawk was almost yanked from her own mount by the wild-eyed white pony, for the young horse was panicked by the screeches of women suddenly filling the air. It was only her mastery of horseflesh that kept both mounts from bolting. But the cries of squaws and children, as the Texans bore down on them, were too much for animals already badly spooked to remain under control. Squaws and young ones were thrown from their mounts; others were shot or knocked to the ground. In scenes that would never be recorded, Indian women and children died as Texans, caught up in the white heat of vengeance, expressions hinting at madness, brutally destroyed the families of men whose tribesmen had destroyed theirs. In one scene a squaw and her child were thrown from their horse; a Texan, dismounting, took a discarded lance and pinned them both to the ground, repeatedly running them through till both were dead. If many Texans riding up ultimately balked at the act of killing a woman or a child, the bloodlust of others, suffering unforgettable memories of loved ones obscenely outraged or callously butchered, was insatiable. A hideous and macabre slaughter reigned, and had not the squaws been such skillful riders, and wise enough to attempt escapes in all directions, thereby momentarily rattling the Texans, the carnage would have reached ghastly proportions. As it was, a string of bodies spotted both sides of the trail, and those desperate to kill more began firing at horses on which terrified Indians were seeking to escape.

Blue Hawk thought she was in the clear. She didn't see the horseman who had circled the fight and posted himself ahead to ambush those trying to escape in that direction. When she did, it was too late; he was on the ground firing from only thirty feet. The white pony, catching the bullet high in its withers, reared up and tore the halter from her hand. Stunned, she spun her own mount around and headed directly for their assailant, hoping to run him down as he struggled to reloaded. It was all her dazed mind could think to do. From the corner of her eye she caught the pony wheeling about and starting into the trees that formed a barrier on her right. She could feel death hovering over her and her children, now desperately holding to the wounded pony's back. The gunman never expected her to race toward him; he was sure she would try to get away or at least run with her children. With startled eyes on the flaying hoofs of her onrushing mount, he swore to himself and excitedly started to reload. He had just succeeded when the horse crashed into him and sent him reeling, the loaded gun flying from his hand. Blue Hawk was on the ground in a flash; she seized the gun as the dazed man tried to clear his head and come at her. He managed only a step or two before his own gun sent a slug through his chest and left him slumped in death seconds later.

Hears-the-Wolf knew they had lost their gamble. The brave attempt to ride proudly back to the buffalo plains, bringing spoils that meant riches for all, had failed. Hardest of all was the sight of warriors fleeing the fight, convinced Buffalo Hump's medicine had weakened, wanting only to escape the Texans who only hours before they regarded with contempt. But now he was racing along the lengthening trail of retreat, marked with bodies and the remnants of violence. Word had reached him that the squaws and children had been caught by the *tejanos*, and his fears for Blue Hawk and her children had him driving his horse into a lather as he galloped ahead to where he thought she might be. It was only the incredible confusion that enabled him to stay clear of the victorious Texans, but he knew that couldn't last. Buffalo Hump and Black Tail had already agreed to meet him on the Blanco many miles to the west, but he could not leave without Blue Hawk. He cursed himself for not keeping her with him, even though her children had made that impossible. He vowed if he found her dead, he would kill a hundred *tejanos* before he died. But in spite of his fury, his plight was fast becoming hopeless. Texans were now scouting everywhere, hunting down Comanches who had taken cover in ravines or heavy brush, flushing them out methodically, often, ignoring age or sex, slaying them with relish.

Then miraculously he caught sight of Blue Hawk. Against what were surely incredible odds, he spotted her riding alone behind a distant line of trees. But she was heading for a gaggle of Texans who were coming together after exploring a nearby wooded area. He had to get to her in time. Riding low on his mustang, he circled a small hill, to keep his racing figure off the skyline, and came up behind her. Her face was a mixture of agony and hysteria. She glared at him with tearing but enraged eyes. "They are gone!" she openly screamed. Hears-the-Wolf quickly gestured for silence and pointed to where the Texans were gathering. She didn't seem to care. Between sobs and broken breaths, Hears-the-Wolf learned the white pony had been wounded and saw at once she was following a trail of blood made through this heavy stretch of woods. He knew at once the pony had been badly hit and would not last long, but they could not pursue these tracks any farther; they would have led them into clear sight of the Texans. Blue Hawk was so distraught, her eyes started taking on a deranged glaze. "You lost them! You must bring them back!" she half screamed. Hears-the-Wolf reached over to cover her mouth with his hand. "Woman! If we live, I will bring your children back! Now we must run; the *tejanos* are coming!"

Hears-the-Wolf was more right than he knew. One of the Texans had heard Blue Hawk's anguished voice and immediately signaled the others to spread out and approach the nearby woods. Hears-the-Wolf saw them coming and, grabbing Blue Hawk's reins, turned and drove his horse at a breakneck pace through the trees and out the other side of the grove. It was a close call. The Texans were a while getting through the heavy growth, and when they did, word suddenly arrived from Huston to return and muster at their starting point, left so many hours ago, Plum Creek.

Chapter 23

THE STRICKEN PONY ran gamely on. The bullet had not struck a vital spot, but blood from its gaping wound gushed forth at each stride, streaking down six-year-old Blossom's leg and dropping to the ground. Her brother, Bright Arrow, a year younger, was clasping her about the waist, screaming in her ear. "Stop him! We must go back!" Had he dared, he would have jumped down, but knowing the *tejanos* were pursuing them, wanting to kill him, he was terrified of being alone. Poor Blossom could not reach the halter being dragged along the ground and was desperately pulling on the pony's mane in an attempt to slow it down. Only after several minutes did the animal's loss of blood begin to sap its strength. They had galloped through a heavily wooded area and then found themselves stumbling along a wide gully lined with brush. It was while trying to climb out of this gully that the frightening end came. Suddenly shuddering and twisting its foam-covered head from side to side, as though struggling for a final glimpse at the sky, the pony collapsed. The children, agilely leaping to the ground, immediately hunkered down to look about. There was no one in sight, but hoofbeats and an echo of shots rose from beyond a low-lying ridge. After a few breathless moments, Blossom grabbed her brother's hand and together they ran to hide in a nearby thicket.

Because of the fierce and relentless Comanche rout, Texan losses were mercifully low, though a sizable number were wounded, many seriously. Since the fighting had continued for over fifteen miles, it was several hours before the volunteers could gather again at Plum Creek. Many didn't arrive until after dark; others only appeared the following morning. But the mood was both grim and joyous. A great victory had been won, the valley had been saved, the savages sent reeling back to their far country. But their painful legacy of blood and wanton destruction remained. Even though over a hundred Indian bodies had been counted, and many more would be found in the long grass and heavy foliage in the weeks and months to come, no Texan felt their punishment was enough.

That evening they sat around campfires, talking about the fight, passing bottles of whiskey that suddenly appeared, and sharing experiences wherein lives were either lost or saved. Among the wounded were Jess Bishop and Race Sutter. Jess had taken an arrow in his shoulder, and Race a lance wound in his leg. Both had been bandaged up by a German immigrant doctor who came hurriedly from Lavaca Flats at word of the battle. Straight whiskey was the only anesthesia or antiseptic available, but the young doctor made it do. As full darkness set in, the night took on a strange quality. Heat lightning streaking the sky, and the haunting drums of the nearby Tonkawas, seemed to make it a fitting setting for eruptions of anger that still smoldered like lava in the depths of these men. The relief brought on by the victory also released the pent-up hatred days of anguish, impotence, and outrage had been brewing in their minds. Cries to wipe all Comanches from the face of the earth were on every lip. There were constant demands that this war party continue to be tracked down and every male over twelve hung. No measures were too drastic, no thoughts too satanic or genocidal, to voice. It was a hate reserved for those threatening one's racial seed, a hate that flowed like acid through the thin veneer of culture the frontier strove to maintain. It revealed men covertly retained emotions bred in their primordial past, that their nature still included vestiges of a world of tooth and fang. Man had always destroyed what he couldn't conquer or convert, and like all tyrants, annihilated what he feared.

But a few were rendered pensive, darkly wondering. One of the wounded, a man named Robert Hall, sat on the side watching the Tonkawas, all of whom were now mounted on captured horses, bringing the bodies of two Comanche braves to their fire. One they chopped up and put in a large pot to make a kind of stew. The other they sliced into large pieces resembling steaks. These the "Tonks" impaled on sticks and roasted over their fire. The hatred this tribe held for Comanches, those mounted death-dealing scourges who had decimated their people until only a remnant remained, found no equal in words. Hatred so possessed them, they became delirious as they bit into Comanche flesh. Nor could they sit still; they began to dance awkwardly about the fire, groaning in orgasmic delight, clearly intoxicated as though some overpowering spiritual need was finally being met. Like animals they growled as their teeth tore at the charred flesh; like men they wiped grease from lips curled in vengeful smiles. Hall, in great pain and forced to tend his wound, could not sleep. During that night he started to wonder who hated these Comanches the most, Texans or Tonks, but by dawn, as fires were dying in both camps, he decided the rivalry was too close to call.

It was the day after the big fight that the three women were attempting to make their way back to Gonzales. They had been circling to the north for some time, and the increasingly worried Libby had began hinting they should be turning southward before the day grew any older. The others were finally ready to agree when suddenly a rider was spotted on the horizon. They were all armed, though this rider was clearly a Texan, and when he drew closer, at Kate's waving, he signaled with his hat and turned directly toward them. While he was still a hundred yards away, they could see it was Pete Spevy. He was taking word of the victory to Gonzales, from where it would travel quickly down the valley.

In great excitement they heard about the Indian rout and the capture of the great train of spoils. It was only when they heard that Becky's husband and Kate's brother had been wounded that a tense dread spread over them. Libby asked eagerly about Jody, but Pete could only add that Jody had not been among the wounded he saw. However, since all the men had not come in, it was hard to say.

Libby sensed at once Kate and Becky would be heading for Plum Creek. She listened to them draw from Spevy exactly where the camp lay. With the Indians gone, the danger would be considered over and they would feel she could make it to Gonzales on her own. But Libby was now thinking of Jody. What if he, too, was hurt? What if he needed her? She bent over to make Lance, who was gurgling and squirming beside her, more comfortable. When she looked up, Kate was bending from the saddle, her eyes searched Libby's. "Lib, Race is going to need nursing. I'm going with Becky; she's real upset about Jess. If you can keep up with us in the rig, fine; if you can't, follow our tracks. It shouldn't take more than a few hours . . . Ought to be there before dark."

Libby knew she couldn't keep up with them, and it was clear Kate knew it too. As Pete rode away, Becky came over, her troubled face striving to look reassuring. "Pete says we're bound to run into men returning from Plum Creek; there'll be plenty to help point the way."

"Don't fret yourselves none 'bout me," Libby answered matter-of-factly. "I'll be fine." She waved them on ahead. "You two get a-goin' and take care of your men. If you see Jody, tell him I'll be by shortly."

The two galloped away and Libby started up the rig, clucking to the horse and bravely eyeing the strange horizon, now rising in dusky contours formed by low-lying hills beyond.

In the great chaos of the retreat, the Comanches still struggled to preserve themselves. Buffalo Hump kept exhorting his braves to make a stand, which, if failing to turn back Texans, at least enabled more and more squaws and children to escape. The old chief knew it wasn't the *tejanos* but fear of evil spirits that had turned his magnificent war party into a panicky throng of terrified faces racing for life. Even now, if only his warriors were capable of the discipline that made even small numbers of whites formidable in a fight, they could have rallied and turned this disastrous defeat into a partial victory. But the old chief knew his people too well. They would run much like stampeded animals, run till they were exhausted, run till their sense of distance told them they were safe. Then, and only then, would they stop and rest, slowly coming together again, keening over their losses, making offerings and chanting prayers to the spirits, begging for stronger medicine in the future.

Ah, was not his own reputation now lost, and with it his power? No chief could survive such an ill-fated venture. The warriors would turn their faces away from him; he would die abandoned by his people, an old man disgraced by defeat, no longer permitted the council pipe. He knew many of his people were dead, and all about him he saw wounded braves riding double to escape the oncoming *tejanos*. They who had just commanded thousands of horses now had to share a single mount to survive. It was truly a dark day. He saw a squaw riding by, a badly wounded child holding weakly to her robe. It brought anger to his eyes. Why had their scouts not seen the *tejanos* gathering at that creek? Why had they not quickly abandoned the captured animals with those weighty spoils? The tribe's fate was at stake! Had their warriors attacked immediately en masse, surely they would have won. But this was wisdom given belatedly to fools to measure their stupidity. Pained as he was, he sensed something wrong, something about the way these *tejanos* had shown up in greater and greater numbers that didn't fit the scheme of things. Something was missing! Suddenly, realizing he had caught sight of the last of the half-breeds fleeing camp just before the Texan onslaught, he knew what it was: the Mexicans! Where were they? Why weren't they attacking? Surely if they were striking at San Antonio, so many *tejanos* could not be here! Black Tail coming by and reminding him of their meeting with Hears-the-Wolf on the Blanco cut into his thoughts. Spitting in the dust to register his feelings for *Mexicanos*, he put his quirt to his horse and rode off in a gallop.

Libby was finding it harder and harder to follow the trail left by the others. There were more and more rock-strewn stretches where their hoofprints disappeared, or heavy growths of foliage that they had ridden through but she was forced to go around. Finally she lost it and spent many minutes finding it again. When she did she could see they had ridden into a heavy grove of trees and for some reason dismounted. Perhaps they were resting their horses or had met someone; she couldn't tell. But their trail had become mixed with others running south, and after circling the spot for half an hour, she started growing confused. Warily she was watching the sky. It was late in the afternoon; in a few hours it would be turning dark. She did not want to be out here alone at night. Trying to think ahead, she removed the bridle from the horse so it could graze. Quickly she nibbled on some bread she had brought along while opening her blouse to feed Lance. There was little she could do now but try to reach the campsite on her own. She knew the direction she had to go in, and surely she would soon be meeting some of the men returning from the battle. Setting her mouth determinedly, she replaced the bridle and, clucking to the horse, started toward the still distant but now darkening slopes to the northwest.

Jody had never drunk as much as he had the night after the battle. He had been following McCulloch all day and had done his share of fighting, killing two braves before pulling away as they began overtaking the squaws and children. He had long since lost his fear of howling Indians and had found that opening charge into their panicking ranks almost exhilarating. He knew Race had been wounded, but Dale, as flushed with excitement as himself, was still with him. Both Buck Chauncy and Jess Bishop had swung to the right when it was known that the squaws and young ones were escaping in that direction. Jody, momentarily startled, watched them in disbelief, but they were not alone.

All along the way men had dropped off to round up loose horses and mules, many still carrying their packs. Not a few animals were seriously injured in the stampede and had to be humanely shot. It was an ordeal that forged strange emotions, emotions that turned either frightening or farcical when fueled and heightened by whiskey. Jody felt himself caught up in the furor for revenge expressed that night, sharing scenes that this morning hardly seemed real. But the light of day did not change one sober immutable fact. Innocent blood shed by the Comanches had to be atoned for, and few felt this score was settled.

That morning he had awakened with a terrible headache, but after a cup of coffee and some words with McCulloch and Caldwell, who he noticed now addressed him as an equal, it began to feel good to be alive. He felt close to these men about him, sensing the camaraderie that springs up between those risking death together.

Later, as he was gathering his gear, preparing to return home, he saw two women riding into camp, and recognized them as Becky and Kate. He watched them hurrying to Race and Jess, who were settled among the wounded. Within minutes he was beside them wanting to know about Libby. Kate, relieved to find Race's wound wasn't fatal, tried to smile as she said, ''Oh, Libby is coming right behind us. She has the baby with her . . . The rig will be here before you know it.''

Libby didn't think she was lost, but for some reason the land seemed deserted, as though no one had passed through it for a millennium. There was no sign of game, and the only birds visible were vultures circling at a great distance. Shadows were beginning to gather and the sky was taking on a faint purple hue. She knew she had been going in the right direction, but as she drove forward, the land continued to stretch around her in empty wastes, broken occasionally by stands of trees or a single lonely hill. Twice she left the rig and climbed to a high point to study the land, but saw no signs of riders or even smoke that might have marked a campsite. She realized now she might have drifted too far north, believing the others' tracks had been tending that way. But the more she tried to reason things out, the more confused she became. She studied the almost level terrain that lacked even a single prominent landmark to fix her mind on. Evening was approaching and she could feel anxiety gathering at the edge of her mind. She had to do something before darkness settled. She decided to drive forward a few more miles and, if she found nothing, stop and build a fire. Surely by now Kate and Becky would know something was wrong, something was delaying her; surely others would be out searching for her.

Twenty minutes later she did see movement, two coyotes scurrying away from something they had been feeding on in the grass. Taking her rifle and approaching it warily, she felt her breath stop in her throat when she saw it was a squaw sprawled across a baby. They were both dead. Ugly bullet wounds, rimmed with congealed blood, appeared on both bodies. Fighting to contain her gorge, she hurried away, but after a few hundred yards, stopped again. A shocking realization brought her hands up to cover her face, leaving only her eyes to stare about her, confirming what a creeping dread now whispered to her. Not more than a quarter mile before her, and to her right, she saw the buzzards she had noticed circling earlier dropping to earth to feed. Somehow she had stumbled onto the bloodstained battleground. In fear she clung desperately to silence, but in the depths of her soul she wanted to scream.

Jody didn't need to be told something was wrong. The women's assurances had kept him waiting until the day began to wane, but with the threat of darkness, he had quickly ridden several miles back over Kate and Becky's trail, hoping to pick up the tracks of Libby's rig and to follow them till he found her. He had to travel much farther than he thought, but as night closed about him, he came at last to where Libby had circled her rig many times before driving off on what she thought was the right direction. Actually she was not far wrong but had succumbed to the tendency of lost persons to be guided by a subtle sloping of the land. It had carried her several miles to the north. In the darkness he could no longer follow her tracks, but he now had a fair idea of where she might be. Surely Libby would be smart enough to build a fire; a fire could be seen for six or eight miles in this kind of country. With the Indians gone, he decided not to worry and to scout the range above Plum Creek where his wife was almost sure to be.

Distressed as she was, Libby realized she had to stop. Her horse was backing as though needing rest, and now

Lance, as his feeding time drew near again, was growing restless and emitting small sucking noises. Besides, she could not bring herself to go forward another step. She turned to her right and drove the rig into a small grove surrounded by thickets. Here she removed the bridle and fed her horse the few mouthfuls of corn she had brought along. When leaving that morning, she had only taken supplies for what she thought would be a day's journey.

But it was getting dusky already, and suddenly she thought she could hear wolves in the distance, snarling as they fed. It was probably only coyotes or smaller predators, but she could not believe the dead bodies she sensed lying beyond would not draw prowling wolf packs during the night. She placed the rifle against the whip socket where it would be handy and set about feeding Lance. Peculiarly, what she found most disturbing was the complete lack of evening noises, birds giving a last closing chirp, insects beginning to drone as they rose to mate or feed in the humid night air. The quiet was chilling, filling her with imagined forms of evil hanging over this place, this satanic scene where mothers and babies died to be eaten by animals because men destroyed each other for power. She thought of building a fire; it would certainly attract any out searching for her. But what if the savages had not all gone, what if they were still hovering about this stretch of earth, which Pete Spevy had described as an unending trail of unburied corpses?

For Lance's sake she had to keep her nerve. She finished feeding him and gently laid him back in the rig. Then, while she was turning forward again, with a stab of fear she heard it. A noise that could not be fitted into this setting and that she knew at once was very close. She picked up the rifle, her mind fighting to identity the sound. Probably it was a small animal, a groundhog coming to life in the thicket or a jackrabbit startled by a casual pound of her horse's hoof. But silence set in again and she sat there knowing whatever had made that noise was still close. Now it was almost dark; only the faintest blush of light from a darkening western sky was left to mark the outlines of the grove's interior. And then she saw it. At first she thought it was only a tiny pale spot deep in the thicket, but then she knew it was an eye. As she stared at it, it became two eyes, and then just below it she saw two more. She raised the rifle, but something told her these eyes weren't hostile; nothing about them seemed threatening. In fact, they looked wide with fear. They were looking at her as though she were something to escape, and as though they had been there for some time hoping she wouldn't discover them. Above all, the outlines she made out around the eyes told her they were very small, told her, as her breath settled and she almost smiled to herself, they were children. After a moment she beckoned them out with her rifle barrel. Dropping down, but holding fast to each other, they started to crawl forth. When they stood up again, their faces were rigid with fear. Libby sighed in amazement but also relief as her eyes for the first time fell upon the lonely terrified expressions of little Blossom and Bright Arrow.

Chapter 24

THE LAST OF the half-breeds had been lucky to get away. Once alone, he had secretly decided to ignore Canalizo's spy work and boldly rejoin his father's people. Their victorious march through enemy country seemed a far better life than that of an outcast, living in poverty in ravaged and repeatedly raided Coahuila. Riding deep in the train, urging pack animals forward when the Texans appeared, he took far too long to decide to flee. It was only with a chancy and conspicuous dashing to the rear, and a desperate circling of the swampy ground beyond Clear Fork, that he managed to escape the charging Texans. But with his last look back he knew that the great war party and its train of spoils were being routed.

Racing southward, and finally reaching the Rio Grande, he avoided his predecessor's fate by hearing from a passing herder that *Rinches* had been seen along the river opposite Laredo. Wisely he crossed the river farther east and arrived at General Canalizo's headquarters undetected.

But his greeting there was anything but cordial.

"What!" screamed Canalizo, bringing a fist down on his desk and coming to his feet. "What do you mean . . . running away?"

"Excellency, I tell the truth. *Los indios*, they ran from the *tejanos*. It was very bad; I think many died."

Canalizo swore and turned to his attendant. "Get Woll! This is a crazy country, full of crazy people! *Carajo!* A man only escapes insanity here by dying!"

The half-breed stood, turning his hat in trembling hands, until Woll finally strode into the room.

Canalizo slammed the desk again. "Those ugly painted devils have run away!" he began. "The one chance they have to fight and they take to their heels!" Woll looked like he was going to respond, but Canalizo wasn't finished. "Of course, you know what this means!"

Woll, now noticing the trembling half-breed, lifted a hand to his chin and studied Canalizo for a moment. "No, General, I don't. What does it mean?"

"It means our plans to march on San Antonio are no longer expedient, politically or militarily. Santa Anna will not be pleased. Our report will have to be carefully worded."

"Our report?" A half smile rose and faded on Woll's face, but he remained silent.

Canalizo dismissed the half-breed and ordered the room cleared. Within moments only he and Woll remained. Canalizo came from behind his desk and, taking one of the large armchairs that rimmed two sides of his office, waved Woll into an adjoining one. "General," he began gravely, "you will, of course, confirm my explanation of this disturbing and, need I add, most inconvenient development." There was a silence as he carefully steepled his fingers before him. "Explanations will surely be expected, and we will have to supply them."

"Indeed." Woll settled back in his chair.

"I intend to establish that the Comanche failure to

cooperate was the main reason for our decision not to carry out a march on San Antonio at this time. I will remind Santa Anna of his specific instruction that we move only in keeping with the strongest prospects of success.''

Woll looked at him quizzically. "General, forgive my curiosity, but where and when did the Comanches fail to cooperate?"

Canalizo weighed Woll's question for a moment, seeming vaguely annoyed. "When they did not persistently force the Texans into combat. When they spent their time looting instead of fighting.''

Woll looked like a man treading uncertain ground and choosing his words carefully. "My understanding, and I must assumed theirs, was that when they reached and attacked Linnville, we would march on San Antonio to distract the Texans and draw some of their forces away from the Guadalupe. By now the natives must know we have not kept our end of the bargain."

"General Woll, you are not following me. Please remember the president is not a reasonable man. Only *he* is allowed to be wrong, make mistakes, or misjudge a situation, and believe me, such occasions one might wisely ignore. Faulty judgment from those serving him is not permitted. One could safely say it's forbidden. Now, do I make myself clear?"

Woll smiled awkwardly. "What is clear is that the Comanches have suffered a defeat, but they were not wiped out. I understand whole tribes did not join in this raid. Aren't you concerned about your people?"

Canalizo got up and paced across the room. He took a cigar from a silver humidor on his desk. Failing to offer Woll one, he lit it and drew on it heavily. He returned to stand behind his chair. "General Woll, in Mexico convenient myths must often serve as reality. It is not something your Teutonic mentality will readily grasp. The Latin mind is given to courtly gestures, romantic postures, and above all, proud and honorable endings. The facts of life must often be tinted slightly to fit more smoothly into a desirable view of things. If those savages feel we haven't kept faith, what does it matter? In Mexico City it will not appear that way. Political as well as pious minds never grant ethical standards to their opposition. The president will be persuaded to think that because of unbridled greed, they failed to carry out their assignment. As I've told you, at the *Palacio Nacional* it's appearances that count. We need not be concerned if savages hundreds of miles away are outraged! Who will know? If the filthy heathens end up smoldering with anger and resentment, that's their problem.''

Woll remained silent, but he could not help reflecting, *My friend, one day you may discover, with regret, that this self-delusion is Mexico's problem, and it could prove fatal.*

With darkness Libby knew she had to build a fire. While the two children, stiff with fear, watched her, she gathered some dry leaves, and by striking her flints on a stone, soon had a little blaze going. She took a dry piece of pine branch and, pointing to it, gestured around her. Both children were tensely holding a hand up to their mouths, telling Libby they were bravely trying not to cry. Speaking softly to them, she kept pointing to the stick till Bright Arrow bent down and picked up a large twig and offered it to her. She smiled and nodded. Then Blossom did the same. Her smiles seemed to reassure them, and each time they brought her a small stick, they waited till she grinned and nodded before they sought another. Soon she had a good fire going, and the children, now holding hands, stood beside it watching her eyes as though the warmth or lack of it in her glance offered some inkling to their fate. She sensed they were as wary and frightened of the darkness as she was, and though confused as to what to do next, she was strangely glad of their company.

More than anything else she wished they would stop looking so scared; it pained her to think that these two little ones, hardly more than babies, should be so terrified of her. As she thought of things to do, she decided they must surely be hungry, and reached into the rig for the bread she had brought along. Tearing off two chunks, she offered one to Blossom. At first the child didn't respond, but after Libby held it to her mouth and made a chewing motion, she let it be placed in her hand. After a moment she tasted it and, realizing it was food, hurriedly broke the piece in two and gave one half to Bright Arrow. The children quickly finished both chunks of bread, and before long their expressions turned more hopeful. She also found she had two strips of dried meat along, which they quickly downed, and a little sugar, which disappeared moments after it appeared.

Libby had a mounting desire to talk to them, but neither she nor they knew a word of each other's language. She tried hand signals, but in response to every gesture, Blossom mumbled words that meant nothing to her. She gave up trying to get their names and decided for convenience' sake to give them ones. After some thought she pointed to Blossom and said, "Sarah." She said this several times, until Blossom began to repeat it. Then she pointed to Bright Arrow. "Sam," she said over and over again. Bright Arrow, looking down and bashful at having to speak at all, finally mumbled something that sounded like "Sim." When she went to tend to Lance, both children came over to stare at the baby. They seemed fascinated by Lance's big eyes and soft white skin. Libby had the feeling they were delighted to discover someone on hand more helpless than themselves. After she cleaned her baby and settled him in her arms, she noticed, when sitting by the fire to rest, the children now sat surprisingly close to her, and from time to time Blossom's hand touched her arm. Though she couldn't talk to the children, she now heard them beginning to talk to each other. On one occasion Sarah muttered something to Sam, and Sam jumped up to fetch more wood for the fire. After that he kept a healthy blaze going and seemed to be proud of it.

That healthy blaze had another effect that Libby would have appreciated even more; at a distance of three miles it caught the eye of a worried Jody, who started to gallop toward it with vocal relief. "Thank God!" he shouted as he spurred his horse into a run toward it.

Many miles to the northwest a weeping, wretched, embittered Blue Hawk followed Hears-the-Wolf's bounding figure through the night. Had he been close enough to look into her eyes, he would have seen not only the pain and grief she was suffering but the hatred she was directing toward him. As it was, he was bent on saving the two of them and getting his people back to the buffalo range, where their safety, and with it their confidence, would return. Concern for Blossom and Bright Arrow was swept from his mind by his distress at the staggering losses they had suffered in the running fight, and an awareness of the reckoning he and Buffalo Hump had to face when a tribal council demanded punishment for this calamity wrought upon the people. There was no hope of avoiding guilt for the disaster; Comanches considered leadership the measure of favor a chief enjoyed with the spirits. Defeat meant disfavor, a refusal of the spirits to work their magic. Defeat revealed a leader was powerless, fallible, guilty of false claims to strong medicine.

The old chief, Buffalo Hump, might well not return to their camp at all. He could scarcely be blamed if he decided to spend the remainder of his life far above the Canadian with his friends the Kiowas. As for Hears-the-Wolf? Well, Black Tail would tell him what whisperings were spreading among the braves when they gathered again, then he could decide.

But Blue Hawk had already decided. She would never open her legs again for this man she rode behind if her

children were not returned. It was his stubborn pride and
that of their arrogant chief, Buffalo Hump, that had kept
them in this land of their enemies long after they could
have slipped away in small groups, spiriting their weak
ones and much of the spoils beyond the reach of these
tejanos. She knew many killer ones were in that fight
and that her children would not be spared. She galloped
through the night, feeling a desperate sense of loss lodging like an icy arrow in her breast. From time to time
she could only moan when a swelling loneliness, painful
and near paralyzing, assailed her. Thoughts of her children being killed, their tiny bodies left on the prairie for
scavengers and vermin, brought a clawlike chill around
her heart. And all this because of vainglorious men
whose foolish pride produced this tragedy for their people. Under her light deerskin robe she gripped her skinning knife. If the *tejanos* did indeed kill her children,
their deaths began here with Comanche stupidity.

As the night ran on, Blue Hawk became enraged as
well as despondent. She was deathly sick of these tribal
customs that denied her a voice and restricted her life.
She was aggravated to the last foothold of sanity by
boastful talk about defeating the whites. The whites, particularly these *tejanos*, showed a deadliness with guns
Indian bravery could not match. The whites were persistent; they fought in every season by night and by day.
At any threat, they gathered quickly and fought together,
unlike Indians, who failed to grasp the mortal need for
unity and left troubled war parties at a whim. She sensed
the whites, now rolling across the prairies toward Penateka hunting grounds, were as unstoppable as the wind.
In her heart she knew the whites would one day win and
the Penateka would have to flee beyond their reach.

As they worked their way toward the Blanco, heat
lightning crackled above them and illuminated the far
horizon. It was a night when Blue Hawk felt the ghosts
of old warriors were watching them as they fled west-

ward, shaking their heads in shame, making the hopeless sign.

Hears-the-Wolf was aware that Blue Hawk was coming behind him. From time to time his thoughts turned to her, hoping she would soon recover from the shock of losing her children. Women, instead of seeking revenge, lamented loudly and grieved at the loss of near ones. It was a thing that lasted for a week; a man learned to live with it. He would be patient with her, for if he had to leave the tribe, Blue Hawk must go with him. She was the only woman he would never tired of. In time she would have other children, fathered by him, and be happy again.

But in spite of his confident feelings about Blue Hawk, he was wrong. Yes, she was grieving, but not loudly, and the emotions welling up in her would last far longer than a week. She was still grasping her knife under her robe and watching his back as he galloped before her. He might think she was just another squaw venting her misery, bemoaning her loss and slashing her breasts or limbs in nights of keening. But that was only because she hung behind him in the night, and when she came up beside him, her face stayed back in the darkness where he couldn't see and read her eyes.

Chapter 25

As Jody came galloping up, Libby, her face registering relief, rose to meet him. She still had the baby in her arms, and his eager embrace enfolded them both. It was only the sudden stiffening of his body and a quick lifting of his head that told her his eyes had fallen on the Indian children. "What in the devil . . ." was out of his mouth before she could explain.

"They were hiding in the brush. They're frightened to death. Don't stare at them like that . . . They're only babies."

"Babies?"

"Yes."

Jody released her and stood back. "Libby, they're Comanches; you've got to get rid of them. Keeping them here is dangerous. God only knows who might show up!"

"Dangerous? Why dangerous?"

"Libby, there's just been a god-awful fight! We think the Indians are gone, but who knows? Worse, some of our own fellows have gotten a little out of hand."

"I know. Ugh, I saw a dead child and its mother.

Jody, my God! That's sinful! How could they?"

"Libby, you've got to remember those devils killed white children. It's not something you or I can do anything about. Now, send these two on their way—don't worry, they'll survive—and let's get home."

Libby looked at the two children, now holding each other's hand again. Their widening eyes were fixed on Jody, their expressions again stiff with fear. As she watched, Sam put his free hand to his mouth; she knew he was trying not to cry. No words were spoken, but when they turned to her again, their faces openly pleaded for help.

Jody gestured to the rig. "Come on, let's get started."

Libby didn't move, and as he began to step away, she stopped him by handing him Lance. Then she rubbed her hands together for a moment, as though this motion helped her mind clear some hurdle, dissolve some troubling mist. Finally, with a sigh, her hands dropped to her hips and her green eyes came up to hold his. "I can't," she said in a half whisper.

"Can't what?" muttered Jody.

"Can't leave them."

"Libby, don't talk nonsense! What the hell will we do with them?"

"Keep them until we find someplace safe."

"For Christ's sake, Libby, they're Comanches!"

"They're babies!"

Jody placed Lance in the rig and came back. "Libby, are you out of your mind or something? How are we going to explain taking in two Comanche brats? Have you any idea what people are saying and thinking around here?"

"That's why I'm keeping them!"

Jody looked stunned. "That's why you're keeping them?"

"Yes, I saw what they do to children . . . might do to these two if given a chance. Jody . . ." She turned to him, her expression suddenly flushed but firm. "I'd never forgive myself!"

"Libby, you can't do this . . . you'll cause all kinds of trouble. For Christ's sake, come to your senses!"

"Jody, you don't have to understand, but please don't try to stop me. My mind's made up."

Even though they had been married for over a year and their love was quietly deepening, paradoxically drawing strength from the trials of this harsh land, they had not yet reached the stage when one another's inner world was easily shared with the other. Libby had never told him the quiet regrets she suffered at not visiting the Munsters, the troubled moments her lack of moral courage brought her, the lingering regrets at failing to live up to what her conscience and her Christian training told her was right. They were simply not ready for that level of intimacy wherein couples live humbly and openly together, facing life's trials, knowing no admissions of weakness can imperil a bonding caulked by many seasons of love. But for the young Holisters, the willful passions of youth, the sense of losing sovereignty over self, still flared up. Jody made no pretense to understanding her feelings. He was angered to the point of forcing his will upon her, and only the sound of distant hoofbeats stopped him. "Quick," he said. "It must be some of the men out searching. We've got to put this fire out!"

As he kicked dirt on the burning wood, the fire sputtered, smoked in noisy puffs, and finally went out. But it was too late; the approaching riders came on, knowing a fire had been burning in that spot but moments before. Jody walked forward to meet them. It was, as he had thought, Rangers out scouting for Libby. "Howdy!" he shouted. "I found her, fellows. We're just about to leave for home. Mighty obliged to you gents for lending a hand."

Gruff voices came out of the darkness, congratulating him on finding his wife. One added a menacing note.

"Keep an eye out for redskins. We've already found a few that must have been overlooked." Another voice joined in. "Yeah, we've been giving 'em a boost up to that big tepee in the sky."

Jody was reasonably sure the mounted men could not see the Indian children sitting ten yards behind him in the darkness, but he was more than relieved when, with a few more comments, they rode off.

He turned back to the campsite to find the Indian children clinging together on the floor of the rig, with Libby throwing a blanket over them.

Dawn found the Comanches gathering on the banks of the Blanco. Buffalo Hump, sitting quietly beside a fire Black Tail had built for him, turned vacant eyes on Hears-the-Wolf and Blue Hawk as they came up. The old chief seemed to have grown smaller and more wizened during the night. His high cheeks, which once shined with a ruddy sheen, now appeared ashen. All about him braves were arriving, dropping to earth, building fires of their own, avoiding each other's eyes, and many, if not searching for squaws or young ones who had survived the rout, simply mumbling chants to the rising sun. There were dark looks being cast toward the fire where Buffalo Hump and Hears-the-Wolf sat studying the coals and waiting for one another to speak. Many minutes went by before Black Tail broke the silence.

"The people's hearts are down; good words are needed to lift them."

The old chief's eyes stayed fixed on the fire. "There are no good words in Buffalo Hump's heart. He wishes to join his fathers; his eyes are turned toward the lodge of the great spirit."

Hears-the-Wolf drew a small pipe from his saddlebag and gave it to Black Tail to light. His voice fought against a druglike exhaustion. "The people must be told the Penateka will fight again; they must not believe the *tejanos* have defeated us. Our hunting grounds will be taken from us if we lose our will to fight."

"Hears-the-Wolf is right," added Black Tail, taking a stick from the fire to light the pipe. "If the heart is weak, can the arm be strong?"

Buffalo Hump was offered the pipe, but puffed on it only once before passing it to Hears-the-Wolf. "You must lead the people, *Isi-man-ica.* My medicine is bad; their faces are turned away from me."

"You must tell the people there will still be great victories," urged Hears-the-Wolf, struggling to sound convincing as he bent over the fire, keeping his voice low. "We must put hope into their minds before suffering from this defeat destroys their spirit."

Or the witless arrogance of foolish leaders destroys their loyalty, thought Blue Hawk, sitting behind him.

"Will they think it the truth?" murmured Buffalo Hump, looking down.

"You must make it the truth!" gritted Hears-the-Wolf. "Our power to lead depends upon it."

There was a long silence, strangely broken by Blue Hawk as she rose and hurled her skinning knife, which landed in the earth between Hears-the-Wolf and Buffalo Hump. "While you are deciding on the truth," she spit at them, startling them with the acid in her voice, "be sure to remember the real truth—far more than power depends on that!"

As the men who fought at Plum Creek returned home, many felt that as great as their victory was, it fell short of meting out the punishment the Penateka so richly deserved. Horrible tales were still being reported on the misery and tragedy the raid had spread throughout the valley. Bodies continued to be found around isolated farms and ranches, and travelers who had disappeared from the lonesome trails were discovered when vultures were spotted flocking around stretches of tangled undergrowth or nearby gullies. The task of returning the spoils rounded up to their rightful owners was deemed impossible. Lacking the means to judge the value of individual items, a rough sharing took place, though many refused to take anything. The long-celebrating Tonks were well rewarded and promised to serve again if another chance to kill the despised Comanches came up.

Jess Bishop and Race Sutter slowly recovered from their wounds, but their hatred for Comanches now colored every remark, and mention of redskins sparked violent emotions more readily than ever. Some men came back with scalps, others with medicine bags or primitive pieces of jewelry cut from dead bodies. If some women were horrified, others smiled grimly and spit at the trophies. There were men who came back under a cloud; Buck Chauncy was one. There were rumors of his joining assaults on women and children, though specific acts were left obscure. But folks were inclined to dismiss such talk as the moralizing of those whose families had escaped the Comanche scalping knife. But Buck was a changed man, dangerously moody and unaccountably resentful of others. People now tended to avoid him.

On making a trip for Maude and Lucas, he returned to find his harvest finished by his neighbors, who wanted to lighten his burden in the only way they knew how. But they got scant thanks, and Becky Bishop, hearing of a coming prayer meeting, allowed if he didn't thank them, he should at least thank God. But Buck was grateful for nothing. Maude, emotionally unstable and prone at any moment to imaginary frights and spells of hysteria, had his nerves frayed and his temper on the quick. Secretly he had moments when he questioned his own sanity. When he was alone, Tad and Liza still called out to him from horrible scenes his mind kept inventing. At night, when Maude ranted she could hear her lost children, he would pound the floor in frustration until finally he had to scream at her to shut up. Only Lucas was able to remain calm around her. Though Buck had tried to slake his thirst for vengeance during the battle, he had come away feeling worse than ever. The woman and child he had pursued and killed were still looking back at him in terror, terror that became the terror of his children, terror that said the world was hopeless, godless, left to madness. There was nothing to ease his tormented mind or salve his frayed nerves, there was only Maude, in agony, calling out in the night for her lost ones.

A deep and restless feeling, running through the valley, that the Comanches needed a more severe reprimand than they had received at Plum Creek was galvanized by the appearance of Colonel John H. Moore. Colonel Moore had brought a group of men from Fayette County to fight at Plum Creek but had arrived too late. However, after reviewing the devastation the lower settlements had suffered at their hands, he was grimly determined to punish the Indians severely enough to discourage any such bloodstained adventures again. Among the valley settlers he found plenty of agreement and, more important, support. On August 28 he advertised for all volunteers, ready for a punitive strike against the Indians, to meet him at La Granger on the twentieth of September. One of the first enlisting to go was a worried and strangely disturbed Jody Holister. Some wondered at this, for his wife, Libby, to the amazement of many, had suddenly become the center of a seething cauldron of trouble.

In San Antonio Jack Hays had the half-breed prisoner brought before him again. He was slowly putting together Mexico's part in this Indian trouble. That there were three thousand troops assembled in Laredo, he already knew. That Canalizo was carefully studying the progress of the raid, he surmised from what the half-breed, terrified at finding himself in *tejano* hands, tremblingly told him. Of more interest to him was what was in the burro train that had been reported traveling up the trace. The half-breed in badly broken English pleaded ignorance, but as desperation sharpened his memory, he offered, in exchange for his freedom, to try and find out. Hays wanted information, not this sweating, shaking wretch before him. The half-breed claimed he had a friend from his village whom, because he was partially blind, Canalizo had sent with the burros instead of the scouts. His friend was to be in Laredo again in a few days, and they were to return to their village together. His friend would surely know what those burros were carrying. Hays felt the man's proposal sounded promising, but he was not about to send him to Laredo to await his friend. After some thought, and a warning to the half-breed about Texas's well-known treatment of spies, he and the Ranger who had brought in the prisoner headed for the trace.

Fortunately they arrived early the following morning. No longer burdened by the rifles, the burros made far better time returning than they had on the journey out. Hays spotted them far to the north, but had they been an hour later, they would have missed the empty train entirely. As it was, they had plenty of time to arrange an ambush. The five men accompanying five burros, aware they were nearing the Mexico line, were singing. It was a song that praised women and wine, inspired no doubt by thoughts of dark young girls who flirted as they served in the shadowy catinas of Laredo.

There was almost no resistance; none of these poor *campesinos* wanted to die. Readily they told of the rifles and the sour reception they had received from a handful of old Comanche men waiting for them on the San Saba. No, they were carrying back no messages, they were just poor herders anxious to return to their families in Mexico.

Hays knew, just as they openly admitted their mission to him, they would reveal this encounter to Canalizo. But what did it matter? The deed was done; it was only after some thought that he found a virtue in it. This was information that might convince Houston a Mexican threat hung over them, convince President Lamar a dark-

ening storm was gathering across the Rio Grande.
Someone had to persuade those tea-drinking, peace-
minded bureaucrats safe in East Texas that the inevitable
attempt to reconquer their fledgling country was coming.

Seeing no point in holding the herders, he sent them,
including the desperate-looking half-breed, on their way.
They were a simple people, peaceable and wanting only
bread and the gift of life. For a moment they had faced
his threat, but now he was gone. Even from a mile away
he could hear them breaking into song again.

Chapter 26

AT FIRST JODY refused to believe it. Libby was surely looking for a place to set them free and allow them to disappear in the dark. But the rig continued to move on and on, and as late evening turned to late night, Libby was still holding the reins, grim-lipped and silent, urging the horse pulling the rig forward. Finally Jody signaled her to stop. "We're getting too close to the settlement," he said, a plaintive ring of command edging his voice. "Better get rid of them while we can."

Libby did not answer at once. She turned to stare at him in the darkness, allowing a long tense moment to pass before replying, "You mean leave them out here . . . alone?"

"Of course! They'll find their way back to where they belong. We can't take them any further!"

Libby sat in the darkness, allowing another long moment to pass. "Jody, they have no food. They belong over a hundred miles from here. Is leaving them out here to die any different from killing them?"

"It's not our concern!"

"It may not be your concern, but if there's a God in Heaven, Jody, it's mine!"

"That's nonsense!"

"No it isn't. But it's why everyone here lives in mortal fear of their lives . . . The answer to everything is killing!"

"Libby, you're dealing with a bunch of murdering heathens!"

"And you're talking like one! Killing children . . . my God! . . . The thought of little Lance . . ."

"Libby, it's not you I'm talking about! It's our neighbors, the people around here; they've suffered too much. They'll never understand."

"Then let them deal with their conscience. Libby Holister was raised a Christian; she'll deal with hers!"

As they continued in silence, Jody dropped back. Though now aggravated, angered, and struggling for control, he was anything but sulking. He was deeply alarmed and gravely worried about what lay ahead. He had heard the volunteers obscenely thirsting for greater revenge the night of the battle. He knew Libby's sheltering of Indian children could not be kept a secret. Feelings were now at a feverish pitch in the settlements; no sentiment favoring Comanches could be safely expressed. He rode in the darkness wondering at their plight, his love for Libby confused by a hovering fear for her sanity. To his amazement, he suddenly realized he was powerless to stop her. He had uncovered a side to her more resolute and defiant than any he could have imagined. But this silence also concealed a frightening awakening for young Jody. In the darkness he sensed some strange spirit had entered into Libby. He rode behind her sensing the soft, tender, fantasizing girl he had married had inexplicably disappeared, and a woman asserting the strength to stand alone against an armed community was now his wife.

*   *   *

On the distant banks of the Colorado, the Penateka, hungry, wearied, and dejected, began to put their camp together. They were short of everything, particularly food and, ironically, horses. If the keening for their terrible losses was over, the pall that followed their defeat was not. Had there been other chiefs to turn to, Buffalo Hump, and Hears-the-Wolf with him, would have been deposed, but the San Antonio massacre had left their tribal council lodge vacant, where in the past many proven leaders had gathered to smoke. And all knew the crisis was far from over. Measures had to be taken to feed the people, more horses had to be secured. It was decided to send emissaries to the Tenawas and the Kotsoteka to request buffalo meat and more mounts. There was no danger of being refused. The Nerm traditionally helped each other in times of stress. But it was at this point that trouble started.

Two members of the camp who were bent on seeing Buffalo Hump, and with him Hears-the-Wolf, removed from power in disgrace were the dead Rising Buffalo's two brothers, whose lodge Blue Hawk once shared. They insisted on being the emissaries to the powerful Kotsoteka. They demanded, when they brought back the means for their tribe's survival, other chiefs would be chosen. Few were fooled that they were hoping a grateful people would choose one or both of them. Hears-the-Wolf could only smile grimly. He should have settled his score with those two many moons ago; now it would not be easy.

But he had grievances greater than that. Blue Hawk had become a surly hellion. She kept a knife in her sleeping robes, warning him she would use it if he tried to force himself between her legs. Bitter as that was, the lashings of her tongue were worse. She screamed at him that his cherished pride was rank stupidity, that his and Buffalo Hump's arrogance caused tragedy to fall upon the people. Above all, she berated him for the loss of her children. At times, driven to near madness by her

endless screeching, he was tempted to roughly silence
her. But that move was fraught with danger, for she was
not alone. Whenever he walked through camp, he had
to listen to braves, looking the other way but making
sure he heard their words. "A chief who leads his people
to death should die with them." "A wolf that cannot
safely lead the pack is driven out."

When he gave up trying to make love to her and
moved across the tepee to sleep, she sat up and wailed
for her children far into the night. Hears-the-Wolf, not
wanting the camp to see him driven from his lodge, lay
wretched, fuming with frustration and tossing in his
blanket, until dawn.

It was with great relief that he listened to Black Tail,
who had come to him one morning, reporting a strange
mystery and asking him to join in an extended scout.
Knowing few warriors were now likely to follow Hears-
the-Wolf, they left quietly, not waiting for the shipment
of arms that was expected to arrive from the San Saba
that day.

Black Tail had been out on a local hunt, having spotted some antelope on the plain to the north. A few hours'
travel from camp, he came across a bolt of bright cloth
lying partially unraveled on the prairie. The only tracks
around it disappeared in a rocky place, but these tracks
were not made by a horse, they were made by a man
afoot.

When they arrived at the spot, both men looked at
each other, sharing the same thought. That bolt of cloth
looked strangely like part of the loot lost at Plum Creek.
But what was it doing here? How did it get here? The
faded condition of the cloth said it had been there for
many days, too many to have come directly from the
battlefield. They decided to spread out in slowly enlarging circles to see if they could pick up any clues to this
puzzle. Almost an hour later they were rewarded. They
came across two heads mounted on stakes, the eyes and
most of the flesh eaten away by buzzards and other scav-

engers. Black Tail dismounted and examined the bits of clothing left, along with a badly chewed headband. He stood up and stared about him. "Yamparikas," he said quietly, still shocked at the sight. "Surely these were the two who had left after raping those squaws. That bolt of cloth was part of what they decided was their share of the loot."

Hears-the-Wolf joined him on the ground and both men stood together in silence, looking cautiously about them. Hears-the-Wolf finally gave a grunt of understanding, mixed with revulsion and decision. "This is the work of a crazy white . . . a *tejano* full of evil spirits. We will find him and cut his eyelids off, then his man parts, so he can face the sun in pain and know the wrath of the Nerm. With night and blindness he will scream to the moon for death, and by dawn his black heart will be crushed by the jaws of hungry wolves!"

Black Tail looked at him peculiarly, sensing Hears-the-Wolf's anger was greater than the death of these two—who had, after all, deserted their war party— warranted. But he had seen Blue Hawk's face and suspected the answer to the war leader's foul disposition was there. "This we will do," he said in measured tones, "but we must be careful; madness is the work of spirits . . . We must not anger them."

Again they picked up the tracks that now meandered like the trail of some sly, furtive animal, drifting northward and cagily following the few concealments the land offered as it rolled toward the distant horizon.

Clint Bishop peered across the empty plain. He saw only dust devils the hot wind raised in spurts, and heat waves that made the earth seem to ripple along the horizon. His madness could now be marked from his attire. Hair from his face and head hung down in long filthy strands, his skin erupted with untreated sores, many covered by patches of caked dirt. His body emitted odors like putrid meat. His clothes were stained and encrusted with both blood and dung, and his eyes glowed dully like lingering red coals in a pale bed of ashes.

For a time he found no Comanches, but several days ago he had caught up with two sleeping in a gully just before dawn. They had many possessions and three good horses. His first shot killed one and awoke the other. The one still alive tried to reach for his bow, but Clint's next shot hit him high on the spine and he lay back helpless and paralyzed. Clint let him watch as he beheaded the dead brave and arranged his head on a stake. Then he pulled him up so he could see appendages being cut from his own body until Clint's knife reached his throat. With the two heads mounted, he freed the horses and turned them loose. Horses were too easy to track; even madness did not keep him from realizing he would only last in this country as long as his whereabouts were unknown. Once the Indians picked up a trail, his days were numbered.

Among their possessions he found a bolt of bright red cloth. Why he took it, he didn't know, but he soon realized its brightness was a hazard. Vivid colors did not blend in with the drab brown and grayish landscape of the arid plains. He threw it away, deciding only later, as he stopped to wolf down some of the dead braves' food, that this might have been a mistake. His half-crazed but still wily mind told him he should have buried it.

By nightfall he had crawled into a small ravine. He could hear owls hooting above him and coyotes howling in the distance. He liked these moments when nocturnal predators came out to hunt, for like him, their only way of life was stalking and killing unsuspecting prey.

Hears-the-Wolf and Black Tail continued tracking through the day. The desultory trail led them across an almost treeless plain and into some low-lying hills. It was clear this elusive figure had no destination in mind but was wandering about as though hoping to chance upon something. With darkness his light tracks could no

longer be followed. Had he been going in a determined
direction, they might still have followed, but his uncertain trail kept swinging off unexpectedly and for no apparent reason, so resignedly they settled down in a dry
camp to wait for dawn. Hears-the-Wolf was not overly
annoyed by this. He had no desire to return to camp, to
Blue Hawk's ravings, nor did he wish to see Rising Buffalo's brothers, flaunting their new importance, departing
for the Kotsoteka. A little solitude, crowned by this *tejano*'s scalp, better suited his mood. Black Tail, lying
back and watching an early spray of stars, as though they
were suspicious campfires just visible in the distance,
kept his uneasy thoughts to himself.

Rising Buffalo's two brothers, though only a few
hours from camp, were already quarreling. Which of
them was the real leader? Who was to speak for the
people, the proud Penateka? The Kotsoteka by custom
would want to know. The older one maintained his sen-
iority entitled him to that honor. The incident with Blue
Hawk and Hears-the-Wolf was brought up, proving the
younger one had unnecessarily created a dangerous ad-
versary by needlessly humiliating Hears-the-Wolf. That
bold warrior's stares made it clear he had not forgotten.
The younger one shouted that Hears-the-Wolf was now
of no consequence; they would shortly have the power
to force him from the camp. Their heated argument
lasted throughout the whole first day, until finally they
made camp and both, withdrawing into bitter silence,
sulkily mouthed some food and fell asleep.

Had there been any hint of danger, they might have
taken some precautions, but they had made camp assured they had left the *tejanos* far to the east. They settled down to sleep thinking the buffalo plains were again
a Nerm sanctuary no enemy dare enter. They had spent
the day in futile argument, one that would soon have no

meaning. For as their fire died out, a pair of demented
eyes rose from behind a nearby mound to stare at them.

It was Black Tail who got them up in the false dawn;
he had not slept well and was anxious to finish this hunt
and return to camp. He reasoned the figure they were
tracking must have slept, too, and if they moved now,
they might happen on him while he was still asleep.
There really wasn't much light, but Black Tail now
knew what to look for. He stayed in low spots and circled around rather than climb over rock outcroppings.
He hurried across open spaces, and though he had to
retrace his own tracks once or twice, he spotted enough
footprints to tell him he had not lost the trail.

Finally dawn dabbed a pink brush across the eastern
sky and thin probing fingers of light began to spirit
across the land. Black Tail soon spotted a clear row of
tracks leading to a field of boulders strewn like medicine
mounds over the now visible prairie to the west. He
motioned to Hears-the-Wolf to hurry the pace; this was
the ideal time to overtake their quarry. But they had not
gone more than a hundred yards before a shot rang out,
and both knew it was not more than a quarter of a mile
away.

Clint was too cunning to approach the camp in the
dark. If they both awoke at once, one might get off a
shot. He wanted enough light to make killing at least
one at thirty feet a simple task. Then, with the advantage
of cover, he could deal with the other, who would be
out in the open. This had succeeded for him twice already; he decided it would succeed again. Besides, it had
another advantage; it saved cartridges. He had only six
left.

Knowing he had to strike before they awoke, he was
ready long before dawn. As the first gleam of light swept
gloom from the campsite, he leveled his rifle and fired.
The older brother sighed audibly, rose up, his back des-

perately trying to arch, then dropped back, his eyes open in death.

The younger one twisted out of his blanket and, as though instinctively grasping his plight, tried to run. But it was no use; Clint's bullet caught him in the back and he sank to earth, blood suddenly appearing around his mouth, his head going down as he gripped his throat like a man choking.

Clint did not wait for the younger one to die. He was over them, hacking at their necks with his hatchet, chortling to himself, when a strange chill suddenly gripped the top of his spine. Like an animal hearing a sound that doesn't belong, he sensed he was not alone. His eyes went up to the line of boulders he had just left, somehow knowing the danger was there. He jammed the hatchet under his belt and slipped another cartridge into his gun. He looked around for a place to hide. There was no place near except back among the boulders; perhaps he could reach one lying a few yards to the south. He decided to try. But then from within the boulders a prairie grouse took wing, thundering into flight, betraying something had frightened it from its nesting place.

A single vulture, a speck in the early morning sky, appeared as if by magic, as if some macabre homing instinct had led it to the dead bodies of the brothers who only moments before were alive. The bird was still very high but turning with that rare dihedral of grace as it circled the campsite. It was an eerie moment; Clint was caught between a decision to run or remain stock-still. He wasn't sure which was right, he only knew that death, like that buzzard, was in the air. His quandary deepened and the tension grew unbearable; he had to choose. He decided to run; it was the wrong choice. As he approached the boulder, an arrow struck him in the chest and he stumbled to the ground. He tried to bring the gun around, but another arrow lodged in his gut, making him double over with a sickening groan. It would have been easier on him if the arrow had entered his heart or brain, for now two fiercely shouting warriors were over him, slashing at his body with knives. His last sensation was a sharp blow that cut deeply into the nape of his neck. He never knew it was caused by his own hatchet and its next blow would hack off his head.

It did not take long. Black Tail took his scalp and they placed his head upon a stake looking to the southeast. They only half covered the two dead brothers, leaving it to their many wives to come and place them on burial scaffolds. Then they turned back to camp, leaving behind them this remnant of horror. Clint Bishop's empty skull would whiten in the sun, scavengers and vermin would return his flesh to the great cycle of existence, but surely those who had loved him in life would have found even this ending to his odyssey of hate a blessing.

Chapter 27

A HANDFUL OF captives had been rounded up after Plum Creek, mostly squaws along with two badly wounded young braves. There had been many attempts to make house servants of captured natives, but they always escaped, usually taking with them whatever they fancied, including an unwary owner's scalp. Secretly Ben McCulloch wanted to get rid of them; they were a useless embarrassment and, particularly the young males, a threat that had to be continually watched. There were those who wanted to dispose of them in a way that would have avoided the need to feed them or worry about the trouble they might cause. But McCulloch knew better. What you could do in the heat of battle could not be done when the moralizing eyes of eastern newspapers, safely removed from these warlike nomads, were fixed on you. For their own protection he kept the captives away from the settlement and loosely guarded. Within a day or two they predictably disappeared. That is, all but one. An old squaw, who had been shot in both legs and could neither walk nor sit a horse, was left behind. McCulloch put her in a shed in back of his quarters until he could find some way to transport her back to her people.

No one suspected Libby Holister had brought two Indian children to her home that night, though Jody kept insisting it was only a matter of time before word spread about the community. He had pleaded with her for hours, offering to take them many miles to the west and set them off in the right direction to travel. They could easily carry enough food to last for days. But Libby was too tired to consider things that night and argued they should wait until morning. She sensed how desperately Jody wanted the children out of their home, but he seemed unable to grasp that would not get them out of her mind or conscience. Sam and Sarah stood together, their eyes on her, their hands clasping. For some reason they would not look at Jody, as though his expressions filled them with an alarm they dared not let themselves feel. Libby bedded them down before the fireplace, and taking Lance with her, to keep beside her in bed, she worked out of her clothes and finally laid her weary, worried head against the soft down of her pillow.

Jody, left alone, disturbed and sorely bewildered, went out to tend the horses and, sensing the trouble that was coming, stared nervously into the night.

The guns Canalizo sent the Penateka might still have been valuable had the Indians known how guns were put together or how to repair them. But beyond fitting bullets into breeches and pulling triggers, they had neither the skills nor tools to keep firearms functioning. Some of the barrels contained pieces of dirt, causing the gun to blow up when fired. Several bystanders were hurt. The springs and firing pins of others were rusted away and rendered useless. Though a few still worked, Hears-the-Wolf and Black Tail knew they had been sent a pile of dangerous and, for the most part, worthless junk for their tribe's costly agreement to strike deeply into the heart of *tejano* land. Now, despondent as the Penateka were, a tiny flame of anger began to lick at their thoughts. It would grow with time.

As food and horses began to arrive from surrounding tribes, the mood of the camp began to improve. Group hunts were started and horse-stealing raids into New Mexico were organized. Buffalo Hump, weary of sitting alone in his lodge, left for the Llano Estacado and the distant Kwahadi; it was a real enough if subtly disguised form of exile. With the camp largely leaderless, Hears-the-Wolf secretly began to hope, but knew he had to bide his time. Black Tail, seeing the chance the guns offered, was smart enough to turn the warriors' remaining wrath against the Mexicans, against those defenseless rural communities the Comanches had so long despoiled and punished at will. Still, it was a strange and vexing time for the Penateka, with many sensing big and perhaps frightening changes hovering over them.

Blue Hawk remained adamant; she would not allow the man whose doltish pride had deprived her of her children to embrace her. Hears-the-Wolf stewed about it. Now, with the many tensions he had to endure daily, he wanted, no, needed her. Though the knife she kept hidden in her blanket was a problem, it was hardly an insurmountable one. He could surely have taken her by force, had he dared. But something told him such an act would lose her forever. Doubtless she would find some way to kill him, and at the moment, many in the tribe would side with her. Black Tail, knowing that the loss of Hears-the-Wolf might well seal his own fate, kept cautioning restraint as he continually whispered advice. "Why do you not offer her the white children? They could fill her tepee and perhaps, in time, her heart."

For the first few days, as the settlement returned to its abandoned livestock and chores, no one came by. Jody started work again in the fields, but his mood, if not sullen, stayed grim with concern. Libby kept searching

her mind for ways to get Sarah and Sam safely back to
their people, but nothing she thought of held much
promise. With Jody outdoors, she taught them to do little
things around the house, keeping them occupied. By
continually smiling at them, she finally got them to smile
timidly back. If they weren't happy, they were at least
feeling a little more secure. Whenever she tended to
Lance, they liked to stand and watch. Once, when he
gurgled, she heard them giggling as she picked the baby
up and patted him on the back. On the second day she
saw Sarah, who had watched her placing Lance in a
rocking chair, where she often rocked him to sleep, slip
over at a cry from the baby and rock the chair gently
till he fell asleep again. Sam willingly brought in wood
for her stove, and she couldn't help feeling relieved
when she heard them chatting together in their language.
The words meant nothing to her, but the tone did not
seem stressed and at times sounded playful. As with
children the world over, their fears were dissolving under her soft gentle ways. She started to feed them before
Jody returned in the evening; his presence seemed to
make a difference to them. But still they sat quietly,
looking down, as he gestured toward them while making
points to his wife. There was no letup in his demand
that one way or the other, they be removed from the
house. Libby stared back at him impatiently, her face
tightening with growing aggravation. "What kind of
community is it that resents people feeding and sheltering children?"

"They're not just children, they're Comanches!"

"You saying Comanches are never children?"

"You know damn good and well what I'm saying!
No one around here is going to think of them as children!"

"Jody, stop shouting, you're frightening them."

Refusing to conceal his frustration, he bolted his dinner and stormed out to work in the barn. But the follow-

ing day the fears that had kept his anxieties at such a
stressful pitch began to become reality.

Pete Spevy had fallen into the job of spreading news
throughout the settlement. Between odd jobs he fitted it
into the only social life possible for an aging bachelor
on the frontier. He managed to visit a little on his
rounds, talking about crops or the latest mail from Houston. Where good cooks resided, he tended to arrive
around mealtime, and where jugs of good corn liquor
lay cooling in the well, he was likely to dismount with
a hearty handshake at sundown. No one objected; any
kind of news was a welcome break from the oppressive
silence hanging over the lonesome plain.

This time he was advising people of an important
prayer meeting to be held in ten days. It was to be led
by the Reverend Bumeister, who, assured the Indians
had departed, had promised to return. It was a service
for the poor souls lost in the recent Comanche raid. All
good Christians were invited to attend. Gifts of food or
money for survivors of the deceased were welcome.

Pete didn't expect much from the Holisters, although
Libby's cooking wasn't bad. He decided to arrive there
at midday, assuring himself of a reasonably good lunch.
Unlike the Sutters or Bishops or even the Chauncys, the
Holisters did not keep liquor. He wasn't surprised to spot
Jody just visible in a distant field, but when he dismounted and caught sight of a small Indian boy carrying
wood into the house, he grunted. "Well, jus' look at
that!"

Libby was glad to see him, but catching his expression
when he entered the house and saw Sarah, who was
taking the wood from Sam, she completely forgot a
greeting. "I found them in the brush on my way home,"
she began quickly. "They're just babies . . .'Pears
somehow they got lost."

Pete rubbed his chin for a moment, his eyes turning
from hers and fixing on the young ones. "You bringing
'em in to McCulloch?"

"Might." Libby was visibly holding her breath. "Would Ben get them back to their people?"

Pete seemed to think for a moment. "Reckon he would. In any case, I'd get shut of 'em myself, was I you."

"They're not doing any harm."

Pete stared at her for a moment, clearly trying to adjust to the protective tone in her voice. "Libby, listen to me; you can near get shot for not spitting after the word 'Comanche' down this whole valley. You get rid of them . . . take 'em into town, then if anything happens to them, it won't be your fault."

"That's dreadful," she gasped back. "Why would anyone hurt little children?"

"Most people won't," replied Spevey, but his aging eyes held hers steadily, "but there are white children this young and younger lying scalped or impaled on fence posts all the way to Linnville. Their kinfolk might not see things same as you."

After telling her about the prayer meeting, Pete didn't stay to eat. He left looking at her as though the mulishness of some people confounded him. But he had at least started to convince her that the course she was following was fraught with trouble.

It took a few days for the word to spread. Pete hadn't meant to start it, but two evenings later, sipping a bourbon and hearing the comment "When that old squaw McCulloch keeps in his shed is gone, we gonna be shut of Comanches for good," without thinking, he shook his head. This led to a few curious inquiries and an accidental leak was opened in the dike. Oddly enough, it moved very slowly; it was two days before it reached the Sutters and three before it reach Becky Bishop.

Kate arrived first. Libby watched her ride up to the front of the house, talking before she was fully dismounted. "What's this I hear about two Comanche young 'uns you've taken in?"

"Babies, really," answered Libby, surprised to hear her voice sounding defensive.

"Babies?" Kate came up to the edge of the porch where Libby was standing. "Hear tell they're fetching wood and doing chores for you."

"Kate, I just want to get them back to their people."

"Well, you'd best be quick about it. You know how people feel around here. Folks is already beginning to talk."

Libby glanced back at the house, where she knew Sarah and Sam were probably listening. Though they couldn't understand what was being said, she had discovered with Pete Spevy they were wary of newcomers. "I've been thinking of taking them to Ben McCulloch; do you think they'd be safe with him?"

"Safe? Libby, no one is safe in this country as long as we got those red devils around. Race is still laid up with his wound; he ain't hardly able to work yet. He near split a gut when he heard you was sheltering Injuns!"

"I'm only trying to get them back to their people. Surely at their age they're not dangerous."

"Well, take 'em in to Ben . . . Come to think of it, he's not here. Had to leave for San Antonio, some trouble with the Mexicans. But take them in anyway. There's an old squaw there; Marylou is feeding her. Stick them in with her. Reckon Ben will handle it when he gets back."

"Are you sure it's all right?"

"All right? I'm sure it isn't if you go to pampering them any longer. Folks is still grieving for their kinfolk, children included, murdered by those hellions. Libby, wake up; this ain't the time to be coddling Comanche brats!" Libby put one hand over her mouth and sighed. Grateful for some company, she was going to suggest they have tea. But Kate was turning to her mount again. "Got to get back. Dale is going to sign up with Colonel Moore; he's planning to follow them damn Comanches up-country and teach them a badly needed lesson.''

Libby, distressed at seeing her leaving, looked at her hopefully. "Kate, you going to be at that prayer meeting?"

"Sure thing. Dale will be away, but Race, though he's still hurtin', and myself 'spect to be there.'' Kate turned her mount around and looked back at Libby. "You do like I say with them young 'uns . . . and be quick about it, hear!"

Jody, riding through the settlement, was already beginning to encounter what he had secretly feared: poorly concealed surly looks and callous remarks that ignored the charity in Libby's act, implying it to be traitorous "Injun loving." He was getting a taste of what life in this community was to be like if his neighbors decided the Holisters were no longer fitting company for right-thinking people. A chance meeting with Dale was most trying of all. Dale seemed embarrassed to be standing talking to him, making a lot of his brother's Comanche-inflicted wound. It was clear he wanted Jody to say something to disclaim any part in sheltering the Indian children, but Jody couldn't think of a thing that didn't sound like disloyalty to Libby. She had taken those children in, and right or wrong, she was his wife. On the face of it, it seemed ridiculous that such a fuss was being made over two harmless children, but wisdom was coming to Jody. He was beginning to realize what was happening had nothing to do with children, it was people's emotions he was confronting here, and he was confronting that most intransigent emotion of all, hate. Dale's parting remark stayed with him that day, for it both hurt and helped in different ways. "I'm signing up with Moore,'' muttered Dale, looking away. "The Sutters may not be much to brag on, but they sure ain't Indian lovers.''

That night, after dinner, he told Libby he was joining

Moore's punitive expedition. She looked at him aghast.
"You're what?"

"I'm joining up."

"Jody, you just got back from fighting; you can't
mean it."

"I mean it, all right."

"Why?"

"Because people have got to know where we stand."

"What does that mean?"

"It means if we want to live here, we've got to show
our neighbors we're one of them, that we belong. We've
got to heed what they think."

"And what do they think?"

"That we're cottoning to Comanches."

"That's ridiculous!"

"Of course it is ... to you. You haven't seen the
bloody corpses I have, and you didn't lose Lance or me
in that raid. Butchered bodies of a person's loved ones
do strange things to the mind."

She came to him, grasping him by the shoulders and
looking into his eyes. "I still don't think more killing
can end it."

"Of course it can't, but if I do my share, it will keep
us out of trouble and allow us to go on making a home
here."

She fell into his arms, almost moaning, "Jody, that
can't be right."

He hugged her but was silent for several heartbeats
before whispering, "Blood has been shed, Libby; we
can't go on living in fear. You've got to understand
when people fight to avenge the death of those they
loved, being right doesn't matter."

Her sobbing was muffled as she buried her face in his
shoulder.

Chapter 28

ONE COULD SENSE Becky Bishop's anger was being fueled by some hidden alarm. She looked at Sarah and Sam and shook her head. "Land sakes, Libby, what's gotten into you? . . . How could you ever manage to do such a thing?"

Libby was more disturbed by her tone than her words. She put down the teapot and came over to the table. "Becky, I'm taking them in to Ben McCulloch as soon as he returns. No one needs to worry; I'm not keeping them."

"It's the way it looks," added Becky, making a fist and faintly hammering the air. "Folks are praying these Goddamned Comanches be swept from the earth and roasted in hell, and here you are a-nursin' some of their young 'uns."

"Becky, for heaven's sake! Why are you so upset? Surely two children are not that important. Is something else wrong?"

Becky rose and moved to the door, standing with her back to Libby. "Libby, try to remember my Jess was wounded. The pain of it keeps him awake at night,

250

swearing himself into damnation. Now because of it, and his brother, Clint, he can't keep a Christian tongue in his head when it comes to Comanches." She paused and glanced back nervously at Libby. "He didn't want me to come here today."

"Becky!"

"I'm sorry. He's been drinking again and taking up with two troublemakers, saddle tramps hanging around the settlement after Colonel Moore, hearing something about their past, refused to let 'em sign up. It's enough to drive a saint out of mind."

Libby came up and put an arm around her. "Becky, try to understand. Can't you see they're harmless?"

"Today they are . . . but tomorrow they'll be growed up and ready to murder folks who ain't never done them harm."

"Do you really believe we've never done them harm?"

Becky shrugged away and stamped her foot. "Libby, that kind of talk has got to stop. What you're doing, girl, is God Almighty dangerous. Buck Chauncy was over the other day, shouting and raging, his face enough to frighten the devil. Everyone knows Maude ain't no better, and he was taking oaths to Lucifer, Satan, or whoever to avenge the stealing of his children."

"My God!" breathed Libby, her voice muted by concern. "That poor man."

"You won't be saying 'poor man' if he comes to your door . . . Believe me, he's half-mad."

Taking a step back, Libby looked long and hard at her friend. "Becky, just what is it you're trying to tell me?"

"I'm trying to tell you there's some mighty nasty talk starting up, and before it goes any further, I'd get shut of these two, particularly since Jody and the few you can trust around here are leaving in a day or two."

Libby, feeling something inside her beginning to tighten, folded her arms in front of her. "Becky, I don't dare bring them in till McCulloch gets back.''

"Why not?"

She firmed her mouth, wanting to keep her voice steady. "You have to ask me that after what you've just said about Buck and the others?"

"They've got reasons for the way they feel."

Libby drew herself up; she knew she had come to a precipice. But it was not a thing she could stop and reason out. Her heart made a stand, and an urge to express her thoughts simply followed. "And I've got reasons for the way I feel."

Becky's expression lost some of its vexatious quality, but collapsed into one of grim resignation, her broad face creasing with lines of futility and disgust. "I'd best be going," she said dryly. "No use trying to talk sense here."

Libby extended a consoling hand. "Oh, Becky, try to understand, please. Don't be so annoyed with me. It's just that I'm sick of this fighting, this killing, and above all, this endless hating. My God, are we animals?"

In shock and surprise Libby was forced to step back as Becky turned and almost screamed at her. "No! We're not animals! We're Texians! We're what that murdering scum has made us! We'll become human again when we send all their filthy souls to hell, where they belong." She was moving forward, passing through the door, slapping her jeans with her riding crop and throwing her voice behind her. "Anyone siding with that vermin had best clear out before . . ."

Libby, appalled and shocked into silence, no longer heard her. Rushing up and clinging to the doorframe for support, she watched, in swelling confusion and despair, as the second of her two closest friends rode away.

Hears-the-Wolf, hoping Black Tail was right, returned from the Tenawas with Liza and Tad Chauncy. The children were now deeply tanned, and while Liza showed signs of being hard-worked, they appeared healthy and even somewhat adjusted to the strange nomadic ways of the roaming Nerm. It was their good fortune that, since they were the property of a famous war leader, the tribe in whose custody they had been placed treated them far better than *tejano* children could normally expect. Even so, they entered Blue Hawk's tepee with an apprehension that had been growing since being ordered to follow Hears-the-Wolf to the camp on the Colorado.

Blue Hawk did not greet them in anger, but she knew what Hears-the-Wolf was hoping their presence would accomplish. For hours she simply sat and looked at them, smiling at their awkward attempts to use the Comanche tongue, although secretly surprised at how well they could express themselves in so short a time. She was particularly impressed with Liza, who knew all the workings of the lodge and quickly offered to do much of the work. But Blue Hawk was not ready to give herself to Hears-the-Wolf. His bringing her these two white children showed he wanted her badly enough to make great efforts to reclaim her. That, she wanted time to ponder. She was grateful for the company of these captive children, especially Liza, who seemed anxious to please and was patient with Blue Hawk's many moods. Though she still cried, sometimes wretchedly, over Blossom and Bright Arrow, in the back of her mind the realization that they might be dead was beginning to grow. She was still young enough to have more children. It was a thing Hears-the-Wolf kept hinting at, but she was not ready. Besides, if she did take him back, she did not intend to let him, with his stubborn pride, rule over her tepee as he had before. He came over to her on the second night and put his hand on her robe. Without looking at him, she gripped, almost beneath his touch, the hidden knife, but with the other hand she pulled the robe fringe up over her face. She was not ready. He would have to wait.

*   *   *

Libby never understood why she didn't tell Jody
about Becky's visit. Perhaps it was because her mention
of Kate's coming by had brought only a quick lowering
of his eyes and a knowing grunt, implying it was little
more than could be expected. The next day he was traveling to the Waterloo settlement, which people were beginning to call Austin, for the final mustering of Moore's
expedition. She didn't want him to leave, sensing he
didn't really want to go, but a troubled if not bitter look
greeted every effort on her part to dissuade him. "Libby,
think about it; we no longer have a choice. Listen to
people talk. Rightly or wrongly, folks figure they're under siege. It don't rightly make sense, but any suspected
of favoring redskins is going to find it a hellish business
living here." He sighed, rubbing his forehead. "We've
just got too much to lose."

Yet, in spite of Jody's cautions, strange things were
happening to Libby. She knew she had brought it on
herself, but the waves of guilt that arose kept dissipating
in a new awareness that was entering and subtly
strengthening her tenuous grasp on things. Whatever the
consequences of sheltering Sarah and Sam, after searching her heart, she realized Libby Holister could have
done no other. It was a liberating if anxious realization.
But insights were coming at a deeper and even more
frightening level than that. The people were not wrong;
something within her was fighting this settlement, fighting its fatal convictions, its flawed vision, its venomous
emotions. Something within her told her these settlers
were blind, they were groping through their own fears
for a haven hatred would always deny them. For a moment a chill seized her. She was sure if her real feelings
were discovered, she would be rejected, scorned, perhaps worse. Even poor loyal Jody would think her mad.
Yet in the keep of her heart she was finally grasping
what her real transgression was. She had dared to think
alone, to break with this community's bloodstained legacy of answering death with death. Because of this she

was now truly and perilously alone, with no way back, at least in her mind, to the prejudices, or that ready sanctuary of self-righteousness, that had for so long sustained her neighbors even while it eroded or warped their humanity.

She lay awake that night before Jody left, searching for some way to reconcile her fears, fear for Jody and his hopes for a decent, hardworking but happy life, and fear for herself and thoughts that, even when inviting tragedy, she wasn't sure she could suppress.

In Ben McCulloch's absence the widow Marylou took care of the old squaw. She fed her twice a day and read to her from her prayer book for many hours each afternoon. That the old squaw didn't understand a word being read to her didn't discourage Marylou. She felt the spirit of Jesus would manage to get through any linguistic barriers and inspire this old woman to surrender her savage ways and seek salvation in the Christian faith. Most passing folks smiled. A long line of dead missionaries had proven the hard way Comanches weren't convertible.

It was generally assumed the old woman was crippled and therefore harmless, but the truth was, the old squaw was no longer as crippled as she looked, and had been working at night to get back the use of her legs. She sat under her blanket studying the goings-on around her, spotting where people left their horses, where food was kept, noticing what time of night the settlement seemed most asleep. She considered this chatty white woman who fed her something of a nuisance and likely a little insane, but she would also be an easy guard to slip away from.

Marylou, daughter of a preacher and long addicted to religion, had an evangelical streak that reveled in saving souls. She secretly adored the stern pageantry of frontier religion, the thunderous hymns, the simplicity yet severity and power of primitive crosses, the quietude that

followed inspirational sermons that transported her to the
train of her Savior on the shores of the Galilee. She for
one thought Reverend Bumeister was the spiritual de-
scendant of Saint Paul, the man chosen to carry the
Word throughout the hinterland, the modern-day
prophet, heralding the coming of the kingdom of
Heaven.

The old squaw was unaware Marylou had decided
Reverend Bumeister's sonorous voice would reach into
her soul and uplift it until divine power made it yearn
for the blessings of baptism. Hunched in her blanket, the
old woman was preoccupied with her plans for departing. She realized she could have simply walked away;
it had been clear for some time the *tejanos* wanted to be
rid of her. But it was a long way to the buffalo range;
she would need a horse. That was not likely to be presented as a gift. She would have to find one whose
owner was too engaged in something else to be on
guard. That wouldn't be easy, for the horse with sufficient speed and stamina to carry her to safety would be
too valuable an animal to be left unguarded. She would
have to bide her time. But she couldn't wait too long.
Among other things, a handful of men, some of whom
smelled of whiskey, were coming by lately to stare at
her, one even brandishing a gun.

Instinct, nature's secret of survival, decreed it was
time to go.

Because Libby had been alone for two or three days,
she was glad to see someone riding up from the river.
At first she didn't recognize him. He was coming slowly
and looked strangely stiff in the saddle. But out on the
porch she discovered it was Race Sutter.

"Hello there!" she caroled.

"Howdy," he responded. She noticed he didn't tip
his hat, a frontier custom men rigorously observed when
meeting a lady.

"Good to see you," she continued, giving him a

warm smile in spite of the fixed expression on his face.

He looked about as though his mind were on something he hadn't intended to discuss. "You finished with the rig?" he asked.

"The rig? Well, of course, if you need it."

"We need it . . . my wound and all. Where is it?"

"In the barn. You'll find it with no trouble. How is Kate?"

He didn't answer her. Dismounting and moving awkwardly, he made his way to the barn. A few minutes later he emerged with his horse drawing the rig.

Still on the porch, she called out a little anxiously, "You want to come in for coffee?"

"Don't have time . . . Be seeing yuh." It was half mumbled. She watched the rig as it made its way into the foliage along the river and disappeared. A deep pain began high in her chest and descended around her heart. She knew the Sutters had three rigs and a stable full of carriages and wagons. Race coming for that one was a sign their friendship was over. The blunt rudeness of it shocked her. No matter how she tried to bite her lip, pretending it didn't matter, the hurt kept spreading until tears began to well up and she fell across her bed and wept. She had lost gay exciting Kate, the kindly girl who had helped her deliver Lance, the ready hand that had soothed the way when she, young and frightened as a fawn, came to the frontier. She thought quickly about Becky; she mustn't lose Becky. Tomorrow morning she would get their old wagon out and make the trip to visit her. Somehow Becky would help get Kate back. It would all work out in the end. She fed the children and the baby and went to bed early; one couldn't see much when the sun went down, and she didn't like wasting candles. They were getting low and she was always afraid a lone light in the night might attract drifters. Jody had left her two guns, a pistol and a rifle, but she hated to think about what might cause either of them to be used.

Morning found her feeding the children and nervously pondering what to do with Sarah and Sam. She was afraid to take them with her and equally afraid of leaving them behind. They would be alone here for hours; anyone might show up. Somehow a disturbing caricature of Buck Chauncy kept flashing across her brain. With every glance at the horizon she prayed silently for Ben McCulloch to return.

Tired of her quandary, she finally decided she had no choice but to take them along. They could stay in the back of the wagon, out of sight and instructed by signs to be quiet. She would keep Lance in the seat beside her.

The sun was already well up when she reached down to release the wagon brake, the distant sound of hoofbeats suddenly making her straighten again and glance toward the river.

It was Pete Spevy. He rode up, looking about the place as though expecting to see something that didn't appear. As he drew near she noticed he was making an open effort to smile. "Morning," he said casually. "You fixin' to go somewheres?"

"Just about to visit the Bishops."

Pete looked away awkwardly, coming back and tightening his face before saying, "Sure you want to?"

Libby stared back at him. "What do you mean?"

"Maybe I could save you a trip."

Libby squared her body to face him directly. "Pete Spevy, what are you talking about?"

Pete looked like a sick man bravely forcing down bitter medicine. "Happens I just left there. Didn't seem like the time to visit. Jess, hearing I was coming by, asked me to fetch their candle mold back."

Libby drew her breath in quickly. "Becky wants it back! She said they had a new one!"

Pete nodded in pointless agreement but sucked a tooth twice before saying, "More'n likely it's Jess. Been some riled up, folks hereabouts, lately." He looked behind him, his expression growing boldly curious. "Where are those Injuns?"

"The children are in the wagon," answered Libby, struggling to hold herself together in front of Pete. "When is McCulloch coming back?"

"Shouldn't be more 'n a week or two." He sat studying her for a moment. She felt he could see her insides trembling as she tried to deal with his remarks about the Bishops. A long silence hung between them before he finally said, "Let me take them, Libby; it's getting dangerous . . . Time to think of Jody and yerself."

Libby held her breath. "And just where would you be taking them?"

"Libby, you got to stop a-worryin' about them. This ain't a very respectable fight, but remember they made the rules."

Libby, trying to deal with the tension, shaped two fists and for a moment held them against her chest. The pressure seemed to help her settle something in her mind. She jumped down from the wagon. "If you'll wait a moment, Pete, I'll fetch that candle mold."

It was bad timing; she was low on candles and had no oil for the lamps. But she managed to hold herself together until she handed him the mold and watched him ride away. Then it descended on her. The morning sky seemed to darken. Her mouth felt dry and an icy rivulet started down her spine. The thought of going into that empty house again was agony, for she had never in her life imagined a person could feel so terribly lost, so terribly alone.

Chapter 29

COLONEL MOORE'S FORCE was gathered along Walnut Creek. There were ninety in all, almost every man now an experienced Indian fighter. The value of the Tonkawas at Plum Creek was not wasted on the Texans; when it came to scouting, Indians could only be matched by Indians. But this time, instead of weirdly tattooed cannibals, fifteen Lipan Apache scouts were taken on to guide the expedition. Their leader was Chief Castro, a man familiar with the country and burning with his people's legendary hatred for Comanches.

Jody was impressed with the confidence of these men; unlike the wary pursuit of the great war party, this force was unabashedly spoiling for a fight. There was something bold, even predatory, about the camp's attitude. They had come for one reason only, to destroy Comanches and stamp the fear of white power into the hearts of these fiendish barbarians who swept in like a pestilence from the buffalo plains.

Jody was glad Dale was along; the young man now seemed more congenial, even sharing some food and coffee beans he had in his pack. Nothing was said about

Libby and the Indian children, both sensing in this setting it was not a subject discretion encouraged. But Jody
couldn't help thinking of Libby, and wondering how she
was faring alone. Now, with the harvest mostly in, there
would be food enough to last for months, and if other
needs came up, some of her friends or neighbors would
surely help. He mentioned this to Dale, but Dale, busy
checking his gun, only cast a strained expression his
way, saying nothing.

Far up the Colorado, the Comanche camp was bristling
with activity. Hunters were bringing in large cuts of buffalo meat, and several deer had been taken in the brakes
along nearby streams that flowed into the river. It was
time to prepare some meat for the coming winter. Although buffalo were usually available, there had been
times when they seemed to vanish from the prairie.
Weapons, particularly bows, were repaired or strength-
ened, and trips to the mountains to search for fresh lodge-
poles needed for the heavy hide-covered tepees were
planned and carried out. The few guns from Mexico that
worked were distributed among the warriors, but the
handful of cartridges sent along made even these near
useless. Several warriors stood up in the first council and
cried the Penateka should not forget this treachery of the
Mexicanos, and Hears-the-Wolf, seeing his chance,
quickly urged a winter raid south of the Rio Grande. It
was almost certain to be a success and would help restore
the hearts of the people. A few warriors, noticing who
spoke, grunted suspiciously, but when the pipe reached
Hears-the-Wolf, he deliberately held it for several
minutes and heard no comments. Seeing this, Black Tail
looked down at his upturned palms and smiled.

Blue Hawk, Liza, and Tad were getting on well. Blue
Hawk still cried off and on for her children, but Liza
comforted her and, with Tad now eagerly helping, did
most of the work. Their command of the Comanche
tongue was continually improving, particularly as Blue

Hawk had started patiently teaching them. Liza was old
enough and wise enough to know this woman, who
seemed to have such a hold over Hears-the-Wolf, their
fierce and moody captor, was their only chance of ever
reaching home. The young girl understood life in the
camp well enough now to know what was in store for
them if they were forced to remain. Tad still talked of
wanting to get away, but he also took spells when he
enjoyed riding wildly around the camp with other Indian
boys, and she had seen him watching hunters going off
as though he saw himself one day going too. Her own
lot was not only clear but more than a little frightening.
She saw girls only a year or two older than herself being
taken under blankets by full-grown braves. She was a
sensible child who had watched farm animals mating
and giving birth; she knew how the male and female
organs were used, but she also knew that this particular
act would cut her off from her people like no other. An
added dread was sown into her fears when she discovered from Blue Hawk that the man most likely to take
her first under his blanket was the grim, fierce-looking
Hears-the-Wolf. ''You belong to him; he will do as he
chooses,'' said Blue Hawk coldly. This prospect, she
realized, even adoption into the tribe, that traditional
hope for captives, would not spare her.

Throughout the Gonzales settlement, people were
packing food and counting out small sums of money to
take to the campgrounds. Word was Reverend Bumeister
had prepared a sermon that might last through the morning. In the afternoon there was to be general hymn singing, followed by an outdoor feast and a chance to visit
with one's neighbors. Much of the farmwork had been
done, and the settlement was ready for a break from its
difficult and danger-ridden summer. It was a marvelous
day, cooler than usual with the sky a deep blue except
on the southern horizon, where cottony wisps of clouds
were slipping by.

The widow Marylou had gotten the old squaw ensconced in the back of a small buckboard, and with her prayer book and shawl on the seat beside her, was urging an old and badly spavined horse to the campgrounds. Like a child looking forward to a holiday from school, she had excitedly awaited this day. Now it was here and she was exalted by the sight of the great gathering, proving the need of human hearts for the nourishment of prayer and communion with the divine. To the rear of the field that led to the rise, where Bumeister was already raising his arms in supplication, and people were building a small mound of gifts and dropping donations into a hanging pot, empty carriages and wagons were lined up in orderly rows. Marylou was glad she had arrived early enough to secure a space for her buckboard far enough forward so that Bumeister's voice would reach and inspire the old squaw. She had no doubt the power of this man's elevating and exhilarating rhetoric would penetrate the sullen temperament of her charge, not only communicating the inner fire she herself felt, but the ecstatic trembling the joy of redemption brings to the heart. She herself was going forward to sit at Bumeister's feet, not wanting to risk missing any of his cherished words, when the congregation released gasps or sighs of revelation, or the air was rent by vocal outbursts as the settlement's few remaining sinners experienced the miracle of spiritual rebirth.

The old squaw was a little confused by the sight of so many *tejanos* thronging toward a little hill, where a large man stood in a red and gold cape, throwing his arms in the air like someone surprised he couldn't fly. But she studied with great interest the number of mounts she saw tied to the rear of wagons, or the trunks and low branches of trees. Some animals were merely hobbled and allowed to graze. This endless array of available horseflesh had her grunting to herself in anticipation. She was not sure why this queer white woman had brought her to this strange place, but what-

ever the reason, she saw in it a miraculous opportunity
for herself to be "saved."

Loneliness had been added to worry and confusion in
Libby's mind. She had tried to deny how dejected and
alone Pete's last visit had left her, filling her days and
keeping the children busy by teaching them to do minor
chores. But even as she watched them dutifully carrying
out these tasks, she knew she was really waiting and,
after a few days, secretly praying for someone to come
by and tell her McCulloch or Jody would soon return.
Yet as day followed day, the waiting became nerve-
racking, and her heart more and more drained of hope.
She knew she was hiding, waiting for others to come
forward and assure her this loss of human contact was
only incidental and certainly temporary, but as often as
she heard horses traveling along the river, none turned
in to her fields or even paused, as though the rider were
considering approaching the house.

Sarah and Sam, unaware of Libby's silent anguish,
seemed to enjoy being alone with her. For a time she
entertained them by teaching them English names for
things about the house. Soon they could say "chair,"
"table," "door," and "water." They giggled when they
learned to say baby, repeating it many times and pointing to Lance, as though they had broken through some
mystery about him. In spite of herself, she began to wonder what would happen to them after being turned over
to McCulloch. Would they be treated well? How long
before they would be delivered to their people? In some
obscure way she was aware this concern for them was
only inflaming an already threatening situation. In her
sober moments she realized the more protective she allowed herself to feel about them, the more she was setting herself apart from the community.

One night she awoke from a terrifying dream. It had
no beginning, but she was suddenly and helplessly spin-
ning through space, approaching a dark void she was

sure was death. She awoke with a start, rising from her bed in the darkness and calling upon God to protect her. It was a night of dread. Feeling abandoned by her neighbors, she turned to her religion, spending many hours in desperate prayer. It was while praying that she remembered the great meeting planned for the campgrounds. By dawn, tears misting her sight, she was clenching her calendar, realizing it was to be held that very day.

Had the morning been wet or overcast, a different feeling might have seized her, but it broke beautifully, the sky a satiny blue and the breeze a gentle caress. Even in the early hours she could hear people moving up the river trail, clearly heading for the campgrounds. It was not something she could reason out, but she knew at once she needed the presence of others, needed an uplifting voice of compassion, needed the comfort she remembered coming from the pulpits of her youth. She wanted and needed a sanctified setting of grace, charity, forgiveness, and love. Her thirst for some spiritual reassurance kept rising like a fever as she visualized flocks of people kneeling in prayer or roaring out hymns to the glory of their Savior. She could no more resist wanting to go than keeping her mind from churning over the problems it would present. Without the rig, she would have to again hitch a team to the old wagon that had brought them from Missouri. It would be slow, but it would carry her and Lance to the campgrounds. But what to do about the children? She would be gone most of the day, perhaps even until after dark. Could she dare leave them behind?

As she quickly fed them and nursed Lance, she decided she could not. But she could again have them hide in back of the wagon, remaining there under some blankets she could hang about like a tent. She would leave them some food. With so many people about, they would be scared to be seen. Perhaps because of their fears, they were surprisingly obedient children, anxious to obey every wish she could express to them. Surely they would be safe at the campgrounds, particularly with the word of God ringing through the air, moving and softening people's hearts.

Chapter 30

As THE MOORE expedition moved slowly onto the arid plains to the northwest, they found the land empty, with little sign of Comanches. They passed the headwaters of the San Gabriel River and moved toward the San Saba. As they approached the Conchos, they began to reach country almost no one was familiar with, and even their Apache scouts had to cautiously explore. The fair weather held for several days, but one agonizing night a series of storms brought torrential rains that raised the streams and carpeted the prairie with mud. Soaked, and realizing their horses were tiring in the heavy going, they stopped for two days to let their gear and the land dry out. When they continued on, Moore, keeping track of his expedition's progress, repeatedly commented, "Damn if this isn't God Almighty big country!"

Jody began to count the days, for he could not get Libby and Lance off his mind. After a week he knew he was getting farther and farther from home, with no talk of the expedition turning back. Moore, a man sworn to his mission, was determined to find the Penateka and

267

punish them. But the lonely plains continued to stretch
out before him, and the Comanches were nowhere to be
found. After two weeks a less resolute troop might have
been discouraged, but Jody saw in this grisly column
only grim avenging faces, bent on a swift deadly reckoning, one that would only be settled in blood. After
what seemed weeks of futile searching, they finally
struck the Red Fork of the Colorado. It was there, as the
bearded, trail-worn men were brewing their morning
coffee, that the Apache scouts came rushing in.

Libby, pressing the team as hard as she could, at last
reached the campgrounds, but arriving late, she had to
leave her wagon far in back. With a few gestures of
warning to the children, she slipped down and made her
way forward to where the multitude of settlers were
kneeling in prayer. For a moment she hesitated at the
rear of the crowd, not knowing where she herself might
kneel, but it was enough to catch the eye of a few who
looked up at her askance. It led to a faint murmuring
that Libby in her nervousness missed. It was only when
she settled to her knees in the nearest open spot that she
realized people were raising their heads to look at her.
It was a queer sensation, for the looks were a combi-
nation of irritation and surprise. She bent her head, not
wanting to confront them, feeling a woman bent in
prayer gave little reason to stare, but she was wrong.
When she looked up again, several were glaring at her,
and she began to feel the skin at the back of her neck
stiffening as though some insect had crawled under her
dress.

As the prayer ended there was a clearing of throats
and a heavy shuffling as people shifted their bodies to
sitting positions, preparing to hear Bumeister, now
standing before them with his arms raised. Then
something happened that made Libby clench her fists
until her fingernails dug into the heels of her hands. A
couple who had suddenly found themselves beside her

stood up and moved away. On her other side the same thing happened. This time it was a woman with two children. The empty spaces on both sides made her stand out, exposed her to the glare of gathering eyes, made her want the earth to open up and swallow her.

Though Bumeister's resounding voice slowly pulled more and more eyes away, Libby now felt her heart hurrying its beat and her cheeks beginning to burn. As painfully alone as she had felt at home, this public shunning hurt far more. She tried to pretend it wasn't happening, which only made it worse, for she knew her cheeks were turning a dull scarlet and her hands were tightly gripped before her as tension stiffened her body. Why had she come? She sat looking up at Bumeister, not seeing him, not hearing him, desperately focusing her eyes on the sky behind him, trying to pretend she didn't see the vacant spaces about her, acting unaware of the glances still coming her way. After a minute or two she could not resist quick peeks at stretches of the crowd, secretly hoping to spot Becky or Kate. She failed and then, half closing her eyes, she tried to settle herself in silent prayer.

The Reverend Bumeister, in full voice, was exhorting the power of Heaven to deliver earth's bounty to the devout, to bring faith and peace of mind to the bereaved, to smite the wicked and reward the holy. In nearly three exhausting hours he toured the biblical pages, extracting passages that assured the defeat of evil and the saving graces of charity and love. Only at the closing did he warn against the sin of vengeance, calling it a soul-demeaning emotion prudently reserved for the Lord. By then most people had stopped listening and were glad to rise and stretch their legs. But Libby, who hadn't heard a word, stayed on the ground. She was lost in her own communion with something emerging within her, something that had kept her there when she wanted, like the Munsters, to leave and turn her back on this settlement callously rejecting her. In these hours of silence and suffering she had gone from why she had been foolish enough to come here to exactly what were her sins? She had sheltered two lost children. She had stood between them and fear and hunger. Had she been listening to Bumeister, she would have heard him extolling these very acts as virtues. But she no longer needed Bumeister; she didn't even need approval from this community of sudden strangers, from this gathering of censorious faces, these embittered bigots who hid their vengeance in a cry for justice. She no longer needed any of that; she had found new strength in spiritual convictions of her own. But she did not mistake this new strength for victory; she was as deeply sobered by it as she was mysteriously assured. She knew it for what it was, a weapon, a weapon she was going to need as soon as she rose from this lonely spot of ground.

The old squaw waited patiently until she saw the great flock of *tejanos* watching the man on the little hill, apparently enthralled by the power of his medicine words. She, too, was praying; she wanted the spirits that watched over the Penateka to help her escape, to lead her quickly to a sturdy mount, to make those noisy children playing close by move away. Under her breath she chanted some sacred words she had heard warriors use when asking for strong medicine. Almost at once a late-arriving farmer and his wife appeared and sent the children to an open spot farther down the river. As they romped away, she knew the spirits were with her. Cautiously she lay on her stomach and started pushing herself backward until her legs cleared the tailgate and swung down. Aware of the danger of quick movements, she stayed bent over and slowly withdrew into the rows of carriages and wagons until she found herself alone. The horses she passed were mostly eastern breeds, farm horses with little speed and, for the long run to the buffalo plains, of doubtful stamina. But at the very back beside a few carriages and one lonely wagon she caught

sight of a rugged buckskin, whose lines spoke of hardy
mustang blood. The rider must have been in a hurry, for
the reins were simply looped about a discarded wagon
wheel and the bridle was still on. Now she was sure the
spirits were guiding her. It was time to offer them
thanks.

She put her hand on the upraised tailgate of the wagon
and chanted a few words of gratitude for the strong medicine granted her. She was already starting to turn for
the horse when suddenly two small heads, one above the
other, pressed through the slit in the rear canvas and
stared at her with wide curious eyes. Startled enough to
scream, she would have, had not the sight taken her
breath away. She was an old woman and had to squint
to see them clearly. Had they been any other children
from her tribe, she might well not have recognized them.
But Blue Hawk's were too well known, their mother was
too notorious, the sole wife of a famous war leader, en-
vied for her beauty, hated for her white blood. The old
squaw recognized them at once, but the sight of them
left her frightened and confused. What could she do? At
any moment someone might come by, and her chance
to take this buckskin lost. She couldn't take them with
her, and delaying any longer was foolhardy.

"Are you well?" she asked hurriedly in Comanche.

"Yes," they answered together.

Shaking her head but glancing furtively about her, she
moved to the buckskin; seizing the reins and steadying
the pony skillfully, she mounted. Forced to hurry away,
she turned to the children. "Be brave, our warriors will
soon come to rescue you!"

Seeing her go, they called to her a strange word she
had never heard before, "Good-bye." It rang peculiarly
against her ear, but they seemed to enjoy saying it, for
they said it many times.

As she galloped into the nearby woods, the children
drew back into the wagon. "Perhaps we should not have
been seen," murmured Sarah.

"She was one of our people . . . We heard her thanking our spirits," Sam said, pouting. "Besides, it's only bad *tejanos* we must hide from."

They followed the Indian trail the Apaches found on the Red Fork for many miles, finally reaching a wide-open space where they discovered a grove of pecan trees had been cut down for their fruit. Moore now decided the Indian village could not be far away; still, hours of scouting turned up nothing. The colonel threw a worried look at the sky; the weather was turning foul again. In the evening they moved back to the Colorado and made cold camp. With this new promising sign, security had to be tightened. The men were beginning to look scruffy and played out, the horses trail-worn. But there was little talk of quitting.

Low and menacing clouds started gathering after dark, and long before dawn, bolts of lightning lighted up the sky and rain came down in buckets. Dale and Jody sat up to share a slicker, hoping to keep their soaking to a minimum. Dale was trying to keep their spirits up with conversation, but Jody, finding himself weighted down by concerns about Libby and Lance, had to struggle to respond.

"Think we're finally getting close to those rascals?" muttered Dale.

Jody's voice was distant, half a whisper. "Seems we've been getting close to them for weeks."

"Maybe so . . . but that trail was only a few days old." He rubbed his mouth like a man trying to remove the taste of sleep. "You reckon Moore is fixing to keep going?"

"Reckon."

"Ever think of what folks at home might be doing?"

"Yeah."

"Betcha they're hoping we do those redskins in real good."

"Reckon they are."

"Jody, this might be our last chance to get a lick at these bastards; ever think of that?"

"All the time."

"Betcha when we catch 'em, Moore don't leave 'em much to celebrate."

"Reckon he won't."

"I always figure if you kill enough of 'em, the rest is bound to squat down and listen. That makes sense, don't it?"

"Reckon."

Dale stopped speaking and sat staring out at the darkness and rain. Jody had been doing that for some time.

Libby had to rise and make her way to the wagon. By now the crowd had pointedly withdrawn from her, but even standing back, there were gruff remarks she was clearly meant to hear. "Injun lover" and "Why ain't you wearing dabs of paint on yer face?" Libby held her head up and refused to hurry her step. Suddenly there were children there, picking up their parents' remarks. They began to trail her, the older ones giggling and repeating, "Injun lover" over and over again. Behind them were many adults, probably coming for their own carriages and wagons but stopping to point at her, their faces scowling or drawn up in repulsion. She couldn't wait to climb to her wagon seat, and once there, she quickly roused the team to pull the wagon away. She had to turn around to leave the campgrounds, and as she did, some of the bigger boys picked up stones and rocks. They began to pelt the wagon. There was little she could do even as a dangerously large rock struck the rear, breaking through the split in the canvas and landing inside. In a moment two frightened Indian children looked out and a roar of disapproval erupted from the crowd. "What d'yuh know," shouted one man, "she's bringing 'em to church...Likely wants 'em baptized...Figuring maybe to adopt 'em!"

Shouts and insults that were clearly little more than

threats surrounded her; with the wagon turned about, she could see the aroused crowd gathering before her. For an instant she caught sight of Kate and Becky standing together, looking toward her, their faces a mixture of pity and regret. She didn't care, she didn't need their pity. Behind the women, with their arms akimbo, were Jess and Race, along with Buck Chauncy, staring at her in visceral disgust. She rapped the team as hard as she could with the reins and worked them into a trot. As she drew away, she closed her ears to the clamor that followed her, but in her mind she knew her predicament had just taken a serious and even sinister turn.

Chapter 31

THE OLD SQUAW moved across the country, guided only by an instinctual knowledge of where she should head and where her people might be. Like all Comanches, she had been raised on horseback and kept the buckskin going without exhausting it or losing its edge for a quick burst of speed. She would stop every afternoon, find a stream bottom or a swale where the grass was deep, and remove the bridle to make a hobble of it, looping it around the pony's neck and tying it high on a foreleg. It allowed the horse to graze while hindering it from running or straying too far. Then she would pick out a concealed spot far enough away so if the horse was discovered, she would not be seen. There she would sleep for several hours before awaking to continue traveling the remainder of the night. At dawn, after surveying the land, she would rest for a few more hours.

She saw no one, although she crossed the tracks of some riders moving to the northwest. But during the first night after reaching the San Saba, she came close to disaster. She awoke with a start and a strange premonition that something was wrong. At first she glanced toward where her horse was feeding, but saw nothing. Though it was still dark, a full moon bathed the landscape in an eerie light. Knowing her eyes were no longer reliable, she decided to wait, hoping whatever awakened her had not yet discovered her hiding place. She stayed alert until dawn, but by then she realized there was a game trail a few feet to her right, leading down to the water. Someone had walked down it in the dark, and though certainly moving stealthily, had allowed the light snap of a twig or a slight shifting of gravel to reach her senses and wake her.

Wanting to be sure she was alone, she descended the trail a few steps herself. But as soon as the stream came in view, she saw a lone figure working along the opposite bank, his head down as though searching for tracks.

Her first hope was that it was a Comanche, but she knew at once it wasn't. Comanches didn't dress that way, nor did Kiowas or Wichitas. This figure was wearing a cloth turban. This was an Apache! Slipping back to her horse, she made a wide tour to the north to avoid any possible encounter and continued on her way. But now she was sorely puzzled. A single Apache, alone in the land of the powerful Nerm? The warriors would greet such an old woman's fantasy with laughter. Yet two days later, following signs only tribal members could read, she topped a rise to find her people had set up their village in a small bend of the Colorado. Though the sight made her heart sing, that lone Apache who had passed her in the night still lingered at the far edge of her mind.

Blue Hawk sat over her cooking fire thinking of Hears-the-Wolf. She realized he was getting exasperated with her and incensed at her thwarting his desires. Whenever they were together, his eyes roved over her body, and his manner became testy and ill tempered. She was truly not ready for him, but in her feminine wisdom she realized a man growing more and more desperate for a woman sooner or later became dangerous. Perhaps she could forgive him his pride, and let him back between her legs, but the pain of losing Blossom and Bright Arrow would not go away. She kept waking up thinking they were still in the lodge, and then lie for hours crying because they were not. She knew Hears-the-Wolf was growing weary of her grieving; only Liza would awake to hold her hand, using the few words of Comanche she knew to try to comfort her.

As the days passed, she could see Hears-the-Wolf was slowly getting back his high standing in the tribe. Many still disapproved of him, but fewer and fewer were willing to reveal it. Black Tail predicted in two or three moons Hears-the-Wolf would be accepted as a chief. Although such a move would honor her, she wasn't looking forward to it; yet, like her fellow tribesmen, she didn't reveal that either.

Stragglers from the great defeat had long been coming into camp, many deliberately arriving at night to avoid the shame of saying they had run from the Texans; others, wounded and often crippled, were found a few miles away, unable to cover the final leg home. The half-eaten bones of a handful who had succumbed for one reason or another were found scattered on the lonely plains.

On the day the old squaw rode in, little was said. Squaws were not warriors; they didn't hunt yet had to be fed. Young ones could produce future warriors, but old ones could only complain, and feed and scold the camp's dogs. Some became community charges, fit only for keeping fires or scraping flesh from fresh skins. Little attention was paid to her until she approached Blue Hawk's tepee. There she settled down as Liza, thinking she was an invited guest, offered her some food. Blue Hawk coming back from the stream with a parfleche of water found the squaw gazing into the fire.

"What do you want, Grandmother?" asked Blue

Hawk, using an appellation commonly applied to old squaws.

"Your grateful ears," responded the woman.

Blue Hawk looked at her steadily for a moment. "You have words that would gladden my ears?"

The old squaw savored the coming revelation, rubbing her hands on her upturned knees before she voiced it. "I have seen your children."

"You have what?! Where? Tell me! Tell me, quickly! Where are they? Are they well?"

"They seemed well enough and did not look ill used."

Blue Hawk settled down beside her. "Grandmother, you must tell me . . . please . . . tell me everything you know. Where they are? What did they say? I must get them back!"

"They are with *tejanos* who might send them back, but I do not know. Some *tejanos* want only to get rid of us . . . Others, well, you know as well as I."

Blue Hawk looked about her in nervous excitement, her eyes falling on Tad. "Go, quickly," she ordered. "Bring Hears-the-Wolf!"

When Hears-the-Wolf reluctantly entered the lodge, his expression was dour, his mood almost truculent. He rarely came around during daylight now, spending his time taking on camp duties he was carefully and cleverly assuming. He stood before them, his dark eyes, with their now increasingly angry and possessive look, fixed on Blue Hawk. "What does the woman of *Isi-man-ica* want?" It was his way of reminding her of her status, and perhaps his growing power.

"This woman has found my children," answered Blue Hawk. "You must get them back!"

Looking unmoved, Hears-the-Wolf turned to the old squaw. They exchanged several words, then he grunted and turned to gaze through the lodge flap at the far horizon. So, they were in the settlement that held the old mission he had failed to take. It was a long trip, and he had other concerns plaguing him. Now, with all that was happening, he had many, too many, things to ponder. He turned back to Blue Hawk. "We will speak of this when the sun rests; send this old woman on her way."

The old squaw, hearing herself being dismissed, spoke up. "There is an Apache in our land. He walks about studying the ground. Is this not a thing for our warriors' ears?"

Hears-the-Wolf stared at her. "One Apache, no more?"

"I saw but one."

Hears-the-Wolf smiled harshly. "Then he has come to die. His bones will feed the wolves that sweep our plains."

Blue Hawk quickly intruded. "She saw but one." A trace of alarm was tightening her voice. "Who's to say there weren't more?"

Hears-the-Wolf turned his harsh glance on her. "All the Apaches hiding in the western mountains could not threaten the Nerm. We sharpen our arrows for Utes or the skulking Osage, but not for Apaches. We have driven them from these lands as the spring sun whisks away final specks of snow."

In the silence that followed his leaving, the old squaw hurriedly ate some food, then quietly slipped away. Blue Hawk watched her go, knowing Hears-the-Wolf would be returning at dark. After a time she slipped into her best deerskin dress and dabbed a touch of red paint on her cheeks and the center of her forehead. At sundown she sent Liza and Tad to Black Tail's lodge, asking them to remain there till she sent for them.

Hears-the-Wolf was a man beset by mounting problems. He was slowly improving his status, but it called for constant effort, with the risk of overreaching for power, and thereby losing it, being run at every turn. The people were still wary of a defeated war leader with an itch in his palm for a chief's rank. They eyed him as

he strode about the camp, wondering at his qualities of
leadership, but cautiously treating him with a distant respect. The lack of competition made his position promising, and he sensed the people would prefer someone
familiar, whose faults were known, rather than one
whose faults might emerge when the power invested in
him would only serve to multiply their effects. Yet success was far from an accomplished fact. And now there
was this thing with Blue Hawk. He had almost run out
of patience with her, and now he sensed she was going
to match sharing her robe with the rescue of her children. Normally he would have been glad to go; this
chance to strike another blow at the hated *tejanos*, and
recover two Comanche children, fed his undying thirst
for revenge. The sight of his family being butchered by
a Ranger onslaught had never left him. But this was a
bad time to leave; the people were beginning to accept
him, and he had to remain prominent in their eyes. Black
Tail, also personally concerned, urged trying to reason
with Blue Hawk, and as usual, Hears-the-Wolf, caught
up in a nettlesome quandary and afraid anger and resentment might affect his judgment, decided to follow
his friend's advice.

It was cooler that evening, and the threat of rain was
in the air. It has been a wet season and the stream was
high, but the hunting had been good and the smell of
roasting meat repeatedly scented the air. After dark a
thin musk, raised by dung fires, would add spice to the
breeze about the camp. There was a welcome sense of
peace among the Penateka, and the camp caller was going about asking for prayers to thank the spirits.

Hears-the-Wolf came into the tepee and glanced at the
low fire that was throwing some light but little heat. He
had eaten with some of the warriors and heard remarks
that helped reduce his anxieties. Several voiced the feeling that the tribe now needed a fighting man to preserve
it until it got back some of its strength. No one was

named, but such a qualification surely enhanced his prospects. He saw Blue Hawk lying on a robe; she was uncovered with no sign of a knife. He felt a stirring in his loins but settled across from her with his features determinedly cast. "*Isi-man-ica* will listen to the thoughts of his woman."

"You know her thoughts; she wishes her children back."

Hears-the-Wolf grunted impatiently. "The old squaw says they are alive; they will be sent back. The *tejanos* do not wish to raise our young."

"The *tejanos* try to make slaves of those they take and do not kill. My children will not be slaves; they must be brought back."

Blue Hawk was lying in a position that stirred Hears-the-Wolf's desire; in spite of himself, he began to feel aroused. By shifting and turning, he moved a fraction closer to her. "When the frost giant paints the western mountaintops white, *Isi-man-ica* will smoke on this thing."

Blue Hawk, watching him draw closer, drew her feet under her. "There is danger in waiting . . . *Isi-man-ica* knows that . . . Can you not feel the pain that has come to freeze your woman's heart?"

Hears-the-Wolf stared at her for a long moment. "And there are things that lie like ice on a man's heart . . . Can Blue Hawk feel those too?"

Blue Hawk sensed the moment she expected was coming. She opened herself up a trifle more. "A woman feels for a man who feels for her." Considering Hears-the-Wolf's ego and temperament, it was a brave statement, one few squaws would have dared, but Blue Hawk knew his breath was picking up the tension that precedes lust, and when he put his hand on her calf, she did not pull away.

"You are a strange woman," he said almost resignedly, for he knew now she was boldly but subtly inviting him to take her.

Blue Hawk watched him yielding to his fast-mounting lust and managed a fetching smile. "All important things are strange in some way," she murmured, "even the moods of a mighty warrior."

In the silence that followed, an unbearable tension swept over them and then broke as he moved beside her and tore at her dress. Blue Hawk did not resist. She had never been shy about her own lust. She knew how to make love and she adroitly massaged him with skilled hands. When he mounted her, she kept her legs in the air so she could answer his body with her own. It was a wild session; his pent-up passion and her desire to please came together to make this tryst the most memorable in their long, steamy relationship. It left Hears-the-Wolf drowsing in the after moments, knowing the druglike effect this woman had over him had dissolved any resistance he could even pretend to have to her will. They did not speak for some time, but both knew on the morrow he would leave to rescue her children.

C h a p t e r   3 2

A LONELY RED sky paled and faded as the sun dipped below the horizon, signaling with a final faint flourish the end of day. Somehow the approach of darkness chilled Libby; the coming night seemed a shroud of hidden eyes, concealing morbid, even malignant, intent. Knowing she was being silly, she tried to concentrate on the children, on Lance, on a thousand little distractions offering temporary haven to her mind, but at every attempt to escape her anxiety, it deepened.

As unnerving as her experience at the campground had been, she was hoping that once home, she could blot out those vindictive, spiteful faces that momentarily terrorized her, made her body, especially her hands gripping the reins, shake, but she was wrong. They followed her, glared at her from every shadow, stared back at her from her mirror and hovered behind her, sinister, waiting, just out of sight. This time the children sensed her fear. They had seen the angry crowd, were frightened by the rocks and stones hurled at the wagon, and now somehow perceived she was in danger because of them. Sarah came over and put both arms around her as Sam stood behind, his eyes wide with trepidation. She attempted to bustle about, putting water on the stove and setting the table, hoping the sight of her at normal tasks would ease their minds. She could only risk one candle and kept it burning for only half an hour. They ate nervously and went to bed early, but only Lance fell asleep. The others lay staring into darkness as endless hours stretched into the night. Sometime before dawn, Sam and Sarah dozed off, but Libby, her eyes vacant and rimmed with shadows, greeted the sun with tearful relief, even though she knew daylight could not dispel the simmering hostility she sensed had mounted to a dangerous pitch in this settlement, where hate turned cherished friends into callous strangers.

Yet the morning proved quiet, with birds feeding in the harvested fields and cranes or loons crying out along the river. As the day wore on, she could hear the children laughing at play and began to take heart. She couldn't believe rational, Christian-minded people would not regret, as much as she, yesterday's tragic happening. Surely the world could not have changed that much; charity and forgiveness were still mankind's sanctuary from a world of evil missteps. Surely sensible minds would shrug off these children as unimportant in an issue that involved two conflicting races. Above all, Jody and Ben McCulloch would soon be returning, and the tenor of normal living would certainly return. But before sundown, poor Libby, trying to find the strength to see her through the day, would realize once again, this time in terror, that she was grievously wrong.

Hears-the-Wolf's leaving was not attended by much ceremony, but he had not forgotten his goal. He advised Black Tail that the camp should not be moved until his return. His old friend was to go to the Tenawas and the Tahneemas, and other closely related tribes, saying he was bringing an invitation from Hears-the-Wolf for a great hunt. It was a gesture that would put his name on the tongues of many. To Blue Hawk he said only that he would return and bring her the scalp of the *tejano* who held her children captive.

Blue Hawk watched him go, her heart at last at peace. She had missed much while grief assailed her, thinking of little but her loss, but now she began to grasp there were other things to raise concern. For one, she noticed that Liza rarely left the lodge, and when Tad did, he often came back looking pensive, if not ill at ease. This puzzled her until the day she took a small beaded belt to the old squaw as a gift for her gratifying news. The old woman thanked her and looked at her inquiringly. "Does *Isi-man-ica* wish to adopt the young *tejanos* into our tribe?"

Blue Hawk looked at her, made curious by the question. "It is not a thing that has been spoken about."

The old woman sighed. "We have many here whose children have been slain by the whites. Would it not be wise?"

Blue Hawk remembered the white captives, children among them, being tortured to death in revenge for the murder of the chiefs. Only those adopted into the tribe were spared. She found herself trying to discount such a possibility, but suddenly realized, even as she spoke, it was she who needed reassuring. "In that sad moon our people were enraged at their great loss." Her voice was carrying more conviction than she felt. "Now the *tejanos* are far away and our people are learning to forget."

The old squaw managed a smile, but it was clear her mind still struggled with some hidden burden. "Who forgets the death of their young?" she said quietly.

There was a long silence.

Then Blue Hawk settled slowly beside her. "Grandmother, something troubles your heart. Does your spirit wish you to share it with a friend?"

The old woman looked up, almost startled. "Friend?"

"Your eyes have given me back my children. I can

only offer you friendship, but Blue Hawk could be a worthy friend.''

The old squaw looked down at her hands; they were rough and gnarled from years of labor. She had never been important in the tribe; all but a few of her relatives were dead. Now this woman, who rumor said might soon be the wife of a chief, was offering her friendship. It brought tears to her eyes. She looked up at Blue Hawk, her words rising with the anguish of sobs. ''It's a dream that has frightened me. I have had it twice. No one thinks an old woman can have dreams through which the spirits speak. No one listens.''

Blue Hawk's hand touched her arm. ''I will listen.''

The old woman collected herself. ''It's that Apache I saw. In my dreams he sees me, chases me, follows me to our village. He leaves and returns with many others. They destroy our village. I saw much blood, many on the ground, many fires around me. I scream and wake up. I am too frightened to sleep much anymore.''

Blue Hawk studied the woman for a moment, remembering her remarks of the day before. ''Where did you see this Apache?'' she asked thoughtfully.

''At the San Saba.''

''And he was alone?''

''Yes.''

''Did you see anything else . . . ashes of camp-fires . . . tracks?''

The old squaw thought for a moment. ''Only tracks I had crossed the day before.''

''Tracks of our people?''

''No, tracks made by iron shoes worn by horses of the whites. They were going north.''

Blue Hawk mused for a moment, then grimaced and shook her head. Why was it she, and not the warriors, who was asking these questions? ''I will tell your dream to Hears-the-Wolf when he returns,'' she said, trying to placate the shaken woman. ''Your dream will be known. If it is the spirits speaking, they will be heard.''

The old squaw looked away doubtfully. "The rabbit that waits for the shadow of a hawk to warn of trouble forgets that the snake casts no shadow."

Blue Hawk knew she was being told not to wait. Hears-the-Wolf's return could be many days away. But as she withdrew from the old woman, her mind first fixed on Liza and Tad, and what could be done to ensure their safety while *Isi-man-ica* was away.

It was Buck Chauncy coming to the mission house that started it, though Becky, finding Jess drinking with the two drifters, could see trouble already in the making. By now everyone knew the old squaw was gone, and a young farmer's prize buckskin with her. "Thieving bastards, the lot of them," snarled one of the drifters, turning to spit. "Shootin's too good for 'em," allowed the other. Jess's face was flushed from liquor, but he was far from drunk. Buck Chauncy, coming up, refused a drink, but his expression held a freakish quality that made others look away. Becky thought there was something weird about the way he kept driving the fist of one hand into the palm of the other. His eyes hinted at the thirst for violence that rises in men torn by rage and rancor. All these garrulous men carried side arms; two had knives sticking from their belts. Becky caught sight of Pete Spevy coming, attracted by the group, and beckoned him over. "Help me get Jess home," she whispered hurriedly under her breath. "This is only going to lead to trouble."

Glancing about uncertainly, Pete dismounted, but as he approached Jess, the young farmer and two companions showed up, surrounding Jess and blocking the way. "Just how long we gonna take this?" demanded the young farmer. "That buckskin cost me the price of a claim. God damn redskins! Couldn't catch that old bitch, but if we had, we'd had to let her go." He kicked at the graveled soil beneath him in fury. "A white man stealing horseflesh gets hung!"

"It's these Injun lovers back east that's got our hands tied." It was one of the farmer's companions, a man with a heavy growth of beard and jaws clamped on a chaw of tobacco. "They're all the time makin' out like we're the ones lookin' to murder folks!"

"We got Injun lovers here too," snapped Buck. "It's a disgrace how we let 'em come and go, like they was decent and right-thinking."

"And damn if we haven't got 'em even coming to prayer meetings, listening to Scripture and all!" added the man with the beard. "Ah just had a brother killed and scalped, by Jesus! Ah figure it's time we put an end to this coddling the devil."

Fortunately the jug, now moving through more and more hands, was soon empty, but something more suborning than whiskey was working now. Becky saw it coming. "Jess, you'd best come home!"

"Woman, stay away from me. This community has got to be cleaned up, and it ain't gonna be done sittin' back a-jawin' for sure."

Becky had arranged herself in front of her husband. "Jesse Bishop, you ain't fixin' to take the law into your own hands, are you?"

The young farmer turned on her. " 'Taking the law in yer own hands'? What the hell do you call stealing a man's best horse and ridin' off free as air?"

"No use to keep talking," cried Buck. "This will keep happening until we do something about it!"

One of the drifters slapped a hand against his holster and spit determinedly. "What I wants to know is, what are we waiting for?"

Pete Spevy, at a glance from Becky, shouted out, trying to be heard, "Ain't gonna do no good startin' trouble over them youngsters out to Holisters. They be gone soon as McCulloch gets back."

"That's the kind of talk that keeps those filthy vermin above ground," snarled the man with the beard. "What we need around here is a little action to convince Injun lovers there ain't room enough hereabouts for them and us!''

The sun was beginning to set, and the young farmer eyed it as though the hour demanded a decision. "We gonna stand here breaking wind or we gonna start straightening some folks out?''

There were shouts of agreement as the men started for their horses. "What you fixin' to do?'' demanded Becky, knowing full well what they were about.

If Jess ignored her, Buck, riding by, didn't. "We fixin' to save the souls of two little heathen bastards by putting 'em where Gabriel can't hardly miss them coming by.''

In a thunder of hooves, Becky was left looking at Pete Spevy, resignation and dread fighting to register first in her eyes.

Blue Hawk was confronting Black Tail with questions he was hard-pressed to answer. What were the tribe's feelings about Liza and Tad, two *tejanos* in their midst?

"They belong to *Isi-man-ica;* his name is again respected.''

"Then they are safe?''

"If the *tejanos* do not spill more of our blood, the people will leave them in peace.''

Blue Hawk, who had spent the day in heavy thought, now looked at him, a brooding concern in her eyes. "The old woman dreams of a lone Apache she saw scouting our land; she has seen the tracks of many whites traveling north. Does this not worry the heart of Black Tail?''

"A lone Apache?'' Black Tail's grunt expressed contempt. "He has come to die or prove his manhood by taking home a Comanche scalp. There have been others before him. He will leave his bones for our wolves to gnaw on.''

Blue Hawk's tone sharpened with impatience. She was tired of this arrogance men of the Penateka seemed cursed with. "Those were *Isi-man-ica*'s very words. What if this Apache is serving the whites, the *tejanos*, and is scouting for them as have the Cherokees and Tonkawas?"

Black Tail looked at her peculiarly, as though her tone startled him. But he said nothing.

Blue Hawk lifted a clenching hand to the beads at her throat. "What if the *tejanos* are still angry about our coming into their land? What if running away has made them think we are no longer to be feared? What if they feel it is wisdom for an enemy, wounded but waiting for another day, to be swiftly killed?"

Black Tail took a step back, as though he were too close to this resolute woman for comfort. "Blue Hawk," he said, trying to hold her eyes, "it is not a thing women easily understand. We are deep in our buffalo plains; surely few *tejanos* would dare venture this far. Here the Nerm has always defeated its enemies; here the land is our friend, its wide rivers our shields, its hills and mountains platforms for our warriors' eyes. Put your heart at ease; our people are strong, our tribal spirits are with us. All will be well."

Blue Hawk's glance could have passed for one thrown at a fool. But she kept her expression fixed as she said, "Are our own scouts out in the hills watching for danger?"

Black Tail looked down, but he seemed to be reflecting on the growing strength of her surmises and perhaps the relative lack of substance most of his glib assurances contained. He was not stupid and was beginning to suspect he wasn't giving sufficient heed to Blue Hawk's suspicions because she was a woman. Unlike Hears-the-Wolf, his man-pride did not deafen him to common sense, just because it was a woman's voice crying it out.

He looked up; there was a touch of uneasiness in his eyes. "I will speak to the warriors before I leave. They will send wolves into the nearby hills. All will be well."

Blue Hawk studied him for a moment. "You are leaving?"

"I go to the Tenawas and then the Tahneemas. There is to be a great hunt, with much feasting and dancing. Think, *Isi-man-ica* will be back by then. The spirits will smile on him and our people will be choosing a chief."

Blue Hawk watched him walk away, but the following morning she was on hand to hear him speak to a council of warriors. He gave them her warnings, but only a few seemed impressed. It was enough for her. When Black Tail came out of his tepee, ready to leave camp, he found Blue Hawk, Liza, and Tad waiting for him.

"What is this?" he asked, looking at them in surprise.

Blue Hawk surveyed the sky as though she were judging the weather, then she turned her eyes on him. "We're going with you," she said bluntly.

Black Tail thought for a moment, then, remembering it was Blue Hawk, a woman he was beginning to secretly fear, who addressed him, he simply nodded.

Chapter 33

COLONEL MOORE WAS openly relieved; big as this country was, his weeks of tireless searching were finally rewarded. The remains of a freshly killed deer told the experienced eyes of the Apache chief, Castro, they were getting close. He took the colonel to view the find. Some hunters had killed a buck, skinned it, taken the choice cuts of meat, and left the carcass. Though coyotes and vultures had gotten into it, the chief said the remaining entrails were barely a day old.

Yet the need for secrecy continued. If they could catch the Comanches off guard, Moore was sure they could deal them a blow that might put them on the defensive for years. Accordingly he made the men camp under a bluff along the river and asked Castro to send out only his two best scouts. They were to move in a slowly enlarging circle until they came across the Indian village or firm evidence of where it lay. They were to be given two days, but as the second day ended, the chief began to worry about his men, one of whom was his son. Climbing a hill just before dusk settled, he caught sight of them in the distance and could tell from the way they were hurrying back they had found the Comanche camp.

They told a strange story of futile searching until early that day when they spotted four riders moving to the west. Two seemed to be youngsters and perhaps white; they were traveling with a Comanche brave and what was probably his squaw. Warned not to let themselves be seen, the scouts hid until the party passed, then they came up to the tracks and followed them back in the direction from which the riders had come. After almost an hour, they came to a rocky rise, not far from the Colorado, and from that height they could see lying in a bend of the river a large Comanche village.

It was all Moore needed to know. That night they began to move. By dawn the force that had come with a vengeance to bring these red heathens of the buffalo plains to heel would be ready to strike. The men rode along silently, watching lightning dance along the far horizon, a few wondering if the night winds sighing through the buffalo grass were really spirits settling some warrior's fate as red men facing battle believed.

Libby was sorry to see the day end; in retrospect it had brought moments of peace to her wretched and over-wrought mind. It was only at sundown when Sam came rushing in, one hand to his mouth, a mark of fear, the other pointing toward the river, that it changed. With her heart starting to race, she stepped out onto the porch and glanced toward the grove that lined the stream. With an icy flow of blood starting through her veins, she saw horsemen sitting in the long shadows, gazing toward her. Although she couldn't make out their faces, something told her stark and wrathful eyes were fixed on her. She forced back an urge to scream, realizing that only by keeping her nerve could she possibly handle what her heart said was coming. The rifle was loaded, but it was useless; there were too many of them, and besides, it might give them an excuse to use their own guns. Then she saw them moving out of the grove and coming slowly toward her; desperately she tried not to panic. By now Sarah and Sam were clinging to her, stiff with fear. She got them back into the house, talking to herself to keep her courage up. Soon she could hear men talking gruffly, coming up to the porch. There was an eerie silence, then she heard Jess Bishop's voice. "Libby, send those two Comanche brats out, or we're coming in to get 'em!"

Libby had trouble finding her breath. "Please, go away!" She stopped for another gulp of air. "Why are you here? These children are not your concern!"

Now it was Buck Chauncy's voice, sounding shrill. "We're making it our concern! Blast you for an Injun lover, Libby, you ain't far from being run off yourself. Send the Goddamn bastards out here!"

Libby fought to keep her voice steady. "This is my property; you got no right being here!"

She could hear them mounting the step, coming to the door. The young farmer was now in front. "Ma'am, we want those redskins; better give them to us before something happens."

"No!" she shouted. Sarah and Sam were now behind her, each holding on to a leg.

"You only making it hard on yourself," cautioned the farmer.

The bearded man appeared beside him. "You want us to come in and take 'em?"

"I want you to go away! What kind of men are you anyway? Jesus! You must be brave that so many of you had to come for two little children! Have you no shame?"

The press of their bodies had opened the door, and the men were now filling the room. "We've heard enough," said the bearded man. "Give us the kids."

The breaths of some of the men were reaching her, the sour musk of whiskey tainting the air.

Jess Bishop was now before her. "Libby, you're a damn fool; you've got the whole settlement against you, and what for? . . . For a pair of savages that will pretty soon kill you and Lance before breakfast.''

Libby could feel hands on her; they were trying to reach around her for the children. She began to scream. "Stop! What you're doing is wrong!" She wrenched away, pulling the children with her back against the wall. Her rifle was just above her head.

Now Buck Chauncy was before her with eyes that blazed with near madness. "Stop screaming about what's right or wrong; we're dealing with a race of murderers! When you deal with murderers, there ain't no right or wrong, there's only killing!"

Libby continued to scream, fearlessly pounding Buck back with her fists. "That's where you're wrong! There is a right and wrong!"

"Not with this scum; there's only winning!"

Libby battled back, screaming at the top of her lungs. "Why won't you listen to me? Can't you see? There's *has* to be a right and wrong—or nobody wins!"

The room was suddenly silent, with Libby crushed against the wall, struggling for breath, the children squeezed behind her. It was only with Buck backing away that she saw Becky was standing in the doorway. Suddenly some of the men were looking down, as though so many of them assailing a lone woman was cause for embarrassment. But now Jess and Buck had their guns out, and Libby was mentally measuring the reach for her rifle. Jess was closest to her, but Buck was talking, his rabid eyes on Libby. "We aim to take those kids one way or the other, 'less you want it done right here.''

Jess, suddenly seeing his wife, looked bothered, a little uncertain, but Buck had raised his gun to the level of Sarah's head. Only Becky walking up and turning her back on Libby to confront her husband stopped him. "Jess Bishop, you leave here with blood on your hands and you go home alone,'' she said stolidly.

Buck was suddenly howling, "Becky, you're interfering where you got no right! You're fetching trouble!''

Becky stared at him for a moment. ''Buck, you're half out of your mind. Go home before you do something to disgrace yourself.''

Buck took a menacing step toward her, his gun still in his hand, his body trembling with inchoate rage. ''You telling me that woman is gonna spite us all, and she being nothing but a sonofabitching Indian lover?''

Becky looked at him as though repulsed by his presence and sickened by his words. ''I'm telling you that sonofabitching Indian lover risked her life to save Maude and Lucas when the rest of us Indian haters were scared to leave the wagon. Like I said, Buck, go home!''

The young farmer cleared his throat. ''Ain't saying I'm forgetting, but ain't much point in hanging on here.'' His companions and the two drifters grunted to each other, then, scraping the floor with their feet, reluctantly followed him out.

Libby was holding herself and breathing heavily, trying to get her heartbeat to settle and her mind to clear, before she could offer Becky a grateful look and manage to murmur, ''Thanks.''

Becky had taken Jess's gun and shoved it back into its holster. With one hand she held him by the arm and led him away. As she crossed the room, she seized the now strangely mute Buck with her other hand and wheeled both men through the door. When she turned to Libby, all she said was, ''Don't be thanking me . . . I didn't do it for you.'' She nodded at Sarah and Sam. ''If you keep them any longer, they're going to die for sure.''

Libby, still not completely recovered and not understanding, could only repeat weakly, ''They're going to die?''

Becky glanced at the rifle on the wall. ''Either you keep that gun a hell of a lot handier than you did today, or Buck Chauncy is bound to kill them.''

*   *   *

Colonel Moore kept the men moving toward the Comanche village until 3:00 A.M. Then, with only a mile or two to go, he sent the two Apache scouts ahead for a closer look. He wanted to know the strength of the camp, the location of the horse herd, and any possible avenues of escape. The scouts returned before dawn, saying the number of tepees counted could mean that well over a hundred braves might be on hand. But the horse herd was loosely guarded just outside the camp; stampeding it hardly seemed a problem. They weren't sure, but the only possible escape route appeared to be across the river. This boded both ill and well, depending on how easily the river could be forded. But Moore was taking no chances. He sent for a young cavalry officer, Lieutenant Clark Owen, and ordered him to take fifteen mounted men across the river to serve as a pursuing force if the Indians escaped that way. The colonel had come on a punitive expedition. He hadn't come to engage these savage nomads in battle; he had come to destroy them.

Slowly the men approached the camp. By the time they were two hundred yards from the nearest tepee, it was almost dawn. Then, as Moore checked the attacking line, there was another moment's pause. Suddenly the Apaches were slipping ahead; they were sure surprise was complete and the chance for scalps and honors great. Reacting to the very first blush of light, Castro's shrieking scouts rose and raced into the camp. Behind them came the volunteers, their eruption of shouts adding to the clamor. Shots began to ring out, followed by howls from braves and screams from squaws. Almost at once Comanches began to die as Moore's men, reaching the camp, dismounted and kneeled to level their rifles. Within moments dazed figures were pouring out of tepees to find death was everywhere. Men, women, and children alike began to fall, some lying like heaps of rags on the ground, others wounded and crying out in pain. Here and there warriors, attempting a stand, were overwhelmed by charging Texans. Women fleeing with babies in their arms were caught in a hail of wild firing, and several lay sprawled with their offspring in death.

Arrows and lances were useless. Some braves had guns, but they were far from enough. Escape from the deadly rifle fire seemed impossible this side of the river, and many plunged into the water. As they tried to cross, they were greeted by Lieutenant Owen's men. Picked for their marksmanship, these volunteers zeroed in on the struggling figures as, one by one, the desperate swimmers, striving to escape, began disappearing beneath the Colorado's cold swirling surface. Those who made it across were mercilessly pursued, most dying, gasping for breath, a few yards beyond the opposite bank. Only a small handful who took to the river and quietly flowed down with the current survived.

By sunrise the chaos was ended, the slaughter complete. Moore's official report would appear in the *Telegraph and Texas Register*. "... The bodies of men, women, and children were to be seen on every hand wounded, dying, and dead. The enemy was entirely defeated."

Entirely defeated also meant an orgy of destruction. Only the horses, by now a sizable herd tirelessly gathered by the tribe, were taken. All else was piled in tepees and set afire. Only one large tepee was spared for some fatally wounded whom, with the return of sobriety, no one wanted to dispatch and were to be left behind. Some prisoners were taken, most of whom Moore knew would soon escape, but he didn't care. He had made his point. These Comanches would never again raise their war hatchets and spread death down the valley of the Guadalupe. Yet, for all the frantic fervor of the moment, the Texans had simply proven what both sides saw in the wilderness about them, a truth nature made no attempt to hide. In the struggle for territory, the most persevering and efficient killers win.

With fires burning on all sides, one of the Apache

scouts, collecting scalps, noticed the body of an old squaw. In one hand she was holding an attractive beaded belt. He stooped to pick it up and suddenly decided to add her scalp to his stick. Though dead, she seemed to be looking at him, her glazed eyes fixed on him in dread. Not comfortable beside her body, he rose up and left. By some odd turn of fate, he was the same Apache she had first seen searching for their tracks on the San Saba.

Chapter 34

WHEN LIBBY HEARD their hoofbeats fading away and found herself alone, she sank down with the children and let them clutch her in silence for a few moments, then she began to tremble. Her arms rose to grip herself, but the shaking wouldn't stop. With the danger gone, at least for the moment, something unaccountably kept her shuddering, kept her from grasping that she had come through a terrifying scene unscathed. Sarah and Sam, keeping one hand on her to assure themselves she was not moving away, could feel the quivering. Then, seeing her hugging herself in an effort to steady her limbs, and wanting to help, they began hugging her too. Finally she started to laugh in short broken starts, but it was the laughter of emotional release, the laughter that must come to dissolve that paralyzing grip of sustained fear. After that, tears streamed down her face for a full minute, and then, knowing she was going to be all right, she quietly hugged the children back and went to get the three of them some water. With the children trailing her, she carried her glass into the bedroom and sat down to gaze at the sleeping Lance. He had slept through it all, but a low gurgling signaled he was about to awake. Lifting him up gently, wanting to feel he was secure, she realized for the first time it was almost dark.

That evening a strange spell hung over the house. Again they burnt a candle sparingly and ate quietly, but though Libby could think of nothing else to do, sleep seemed impossible. She tried to teach them a few more words of English, but they were restive and had to struggle to follow. As with her, a vague anxiety had crept into their consciousness, and though the intruders were gone, they left in their wake a fear no mere distraction could dispel. Becky's final words were as unsettling as a recurring nightmare; Libby couldn't drive them from her mind. Buck's seeming madness only lent them a gruesome quality no resort to reason could lessen.

In the end her earlier prediction was borne out. When she was finally bedded down, it was impossible to sleep. She lay in the darkness, listening to the children huddled in blankets before the fireplace. Occasionally she heard whispering, occasionally whimpering, but her own restlessness kept her twisting and turning, kept her mindful of her own childhood and the frightening things that had then denied her sleep. Listening to the children, it dawned on her that there was only one solution to her nighttime fears at their age, the warmth and security of her mother's bed. Though she wrestled with the thought for a while, after a troubled hour the continual sound of distant whimpering forced her to give in. She called to them and within moments they were beside her bed. She patted the blankets and gestured for them to get in. They did with alacrity. Within minutes they were snuggled down beside her, already seeming sleepy. She turned around, feeling now she could sleep herself. But she couldn't help an involuntary smile at the thought of Jody's face were he to know that children of the very Comanches he was out searching for were sleeping in his bed.

*   *   *

The following day passed quietly enough, and though she kept a wary eye on the river trail, it was not until late afternoon that she heard hoofbeats coming up toward the house. Her first thought was that it was Pete Spevy, or someone to report McCulloch was back or that Jody was expected soon. It was neither. It was Kate Sutter, and while her expression wasn't unfriendly, it was clear she was there with knowledge of yesterday's trouble. "How long you fixing to stay here alone?" Kate began, not allowing time for a greeting.

Libby looked at her; it was hard to believe this was the ever-smiling, warmhearted Kate speaking. "I'm not alone," she said as behind her Sarah and Sam slipped out on the porch, "and I reckon I'll be here till Jody gets back." She looked questioningly at Kate, trying to smile. "Just where would I go?"

Kate seemed bothered by the question. "It's just that we don't want any calamities. You've got to know by now Buck is out of hand . . . acting queer and everything."

Libby looked at her, beginning to understand why Kate was there. "I didn't make him that way."

"Isn't the point. Maybe you going back east, or to the Burnsides for a spell, would help."

Libby heaved a short breath of resolve. "Kate, I'm not leaving my home."

"Libby, whatever makes you so damn stubborn?"

"I'm not stubborn."

"Everybody is fighting Comanches but you."

"What makes you think I'm not fighting?"

Kate looked at Sarah and Sam. "You call this fighting?"

"Yes."

"Libby, you're crazy." She turned her mount about as though preparing to leave, then seemed to recall something. "Race just got back from San Antonio . . . Been up there to see a doctor about his wound. He heard there was a big fight up on the Colorado;

Moore's men about cleaned the filthy vermin out. Your own husband is up there! Dale too! Can't you see we're all fighting these bloody heathens except you?''

Libby's eyes held Kate's firmly. "Kate, I ain't asking anyone to understand, but since I've come here, killing has only led to more killing. Can't you see murdering little children makes us all heathens!'' She shook her head as though sick of confronting this blind resort to violence. "You fight your way, I'll fight mine!''

Kate, looking grim but finally resigned, started putting spurs to her mount. "Word is the boys will be back in three or four days,'' she shouted. "If you're too stubborn to do anything else, try to keep a sharp lookout till then!''

On the third day Hears-the-Wolf began approaching the Gonzales settlement. He would have to move more slowly now; there was much to watch for, and any encounter with even solitary *tejanos* had to be avoided. Until he discovered the whereabouts of Blue Hawk's children, he must remain hidden. Even the hint of a Comanche skulking about the settlement would raise an alarm and complicate, if not make impossible, his mission. He stayed in the hills just west of the trail that bent down from the north and led toward the mission.

At night he stalked one lonely farm or ranch house after the other, hoping for a glimpse, or even the telltale sound, of Blossom or Bright Arrow. It was difficult and risky work; watchdogs and night riders were a constant threat. After several fruitless nights, he grew tired of it. He started developing another plan. He would have to seize some local person, force him to reveal where the children were held, kill him quickly, then kill whoever was holding the children and be off. Because he had to be sure the one seized was from this settlement, he decided on a very young person, one too young to have left home. It was not an easy bill to fill. With recent events, people had learned to keep an eye on their young folks. But his diligence paid off, and late the following afternoon he saw a slightly built boy riding along the outskirts of the settlement. The youngster looked troubled, his mind drawn to personal cares, his attention far from the lonely trail he was loping along. Without warning a lariat snaked out from behind a high thicket and young Lucas Chauncy found himself yanked from his saddle and sprawling on the ground. He looked up and saw the darkly painted face of Hears-the-Wolf.

The day following Kate's visit was a strange one for Libby. She spent most of it in thought. She knew when Jody came home he would discover his fear of the settlement turning against them had become a reality. What could she possibly say to him? Could she say no other way was open, that Libby Holister had to be true to Libby Holister? Would he think that a good enough reason to live in isolation here, or give up this claim, on which they had worked so hard, to try another settlement, to start over again? Would he go on loving her now that she had brought this onerous problem, this stigma, into their lives and alienated a community he wanted so much to be a part of?

The hours brought no answers and no relief. Sarah and Sam followed her about as she did the few chores that needed doing. Some they helped with, but mostly they stood looking at her, aware she was deep in thought. Strange how they stayed attuned to her moods, gay when she was and thoughtful at moments like this. She sensed they were getting dangerously attached to her, making her realize with a start that she was also going to miss them when McCulloch took them off. Surely that had to be soon now. Sighing, she realized for her it would be best if they were gone when Jody came home.

At sundown she went out to the barn to throw some hay to the horses, Sarah and Sam tagging along. She pressed the barn door open and stepped inside. The sun's dying rays poured in after her, and at that unsuspected and terrifying moment she saw him, his black-streaked face hideous, his war hatchet already raised and aimed at her. Shocked and staggering backward, she felt herself falling, fainting with fright.

Lucas Chauncy was glad to get away from the house for even a short spell. It wasn't often he was allowed to take a horse and carry a message to someone in the settlement. But strange things had been happening lately; the neighbors had been over to see his father and for some reason were trying to make him stay on his claim. Finally one of the men came out with a message to Pete Spevy. He heard them say it was to tell the next mail courier heading for San Antonio to ask Ben McCulloch to come back to Gonzales, he was needed.

He had already given Pete the message and was heading home. He wasn't hurrying. He no longer liked his grief-ridden, joyless house; it had changed so from what it had been before his older sister and brother had disappeared. He wondered if his mother would ever be right again. He wanted to grow up fast so he could help her and his father, although his father seemed different and remote these days, as though his mind at times had left his body and nothing was in control. The expressions on their neighbors' faces also bothered Lucas. They looked aggravated and even alarmed, as though his father's ways were causing them to worry. Someday soon he hoped they would go away.

Where the rope came from, he would never know, but all of a sudden it was yanking him from his horse and he found himself lying sprawled on the ground. A large, fearsome-looking Indian warrior appeared over him, wielding a war hatchet, and after studying his face, pulled him to his feet. They were in a barren stretch of the settlement; the nearest house was at least two or three miles away. Lucas felt the muscles in his chest beginning to cramp with fear. The warrior drew him back into the brush, into a clearing where lay a small space of open earth. Lucas was sure he was looking at his burial ground and wanted to scream, but the warrior made it clear any noise would bring the hatchet down. But this was hardly necessary; fear had frozen Lucas to where he was not sure he could even draw a breath.

After a few moments the warrior took his hatchet and with its sharp edge drew something on the ground. Lucas looked at it but couldn't make it out. The warrior drew some more lines, then pointed at it with his hatchet and grunted. Lucas studied it, desperately trying to understand. He knew now this Indian wanted to know something; if he could tell him, he might be set free. But the drawings, even when added to, didn't make sense, and the warrior's grunts sounded more and more annoyed and threatening. Poor Lucas, straining his mind to make something of the drawings, could think of nothing they resembled. He was sure the Indian was running out of patience and would shortly kill him.

Then the warrior made a wiggling motion with the hatchet, and left a strange mark above one of the drawings. Lucas couldn't keep it in; it looked like a feather. "Indians!" he blurted. The warrior seemed to recognize that one word, and nodded quickly. "What kind of Indians?"

This was wasted on the grim-looking figure, but after seeing the confusion on the boy's face, he put his hand down to measure the distance of a few feet from the ground. Lucas breathed a sigh of relief. "Little Indians!"

The warrior kept looking at him, for Lucas was now grasping what was being asked. He looked at the figures again; there were two of them. Two Indian children! This awesome-looking figure was looking for two Indian children, and Lucas was suddenly sure the two everyone said were at the Holisters were the ones being sought.

He gestured in every way he could think of that he knew what this menacing figure wanted, and could tell

by the warrior's responses he was being told to lead him
to the children. Lucas was glad to do it; anything to keep
that war hatchet away from his head. But he was to
discover the Indian wanted him to travel from cover to
cover, staying off the main trails and keeping a sharp
eye on the terrain ahead. With such a need for stealth,
it was going to take a while to get to the Holisters', but
Lucas was now clutching to the hope that once there, he
would be set free.

By the time they reached the river trail below the Holister place, it was less than an hour to sundown. From
the heavy growth along the bank, Hears-the-Wolf studied the house and barn. He wanted to strike at dark,
giving himself the best chance of getting away and
avoiding pursuit. But he had been carefully watching
Lucas, his thoughts far from setting the boy free. Though
Lucas was five going on six, he was small for his age
and looked younger. Unfortunately he looked about the
age Comanches liked to abduct children. It was an age
when boys successfully adopted into the tribe often produced valuable warriors. His first plan to kill the local
who led him to the children was abandoned and replaced
by a far more satisfying one, that of taking this young
tejano and raising him to be one of his people's enemies.

Hears-the-Wolf had soon arrived at a sound plan for
his attack, but decided it would take time to carry it out.
First he took the startled and now panicky Lucas and
tied him up, carrying the bound-up boy and hiding him
deep in the brush fifty yards downstream.

Then he took their horses and brought them up as
close to the house as seemed safe. Then, by circling
behind hummocks and low stands of brush, he angled
his way toward the barn. It was almost sundown and he
wanted to be close to the house at dark. There was a
rear portal at the far end of the barn; he crawled along
the adobe base until he reached it. Then, with a quick
glance toward the house, he leaped through its open up-

per half. Now he was ready; he had only to wait until dark.

He was wrong, he had only to wait a few minutes before he heard footsteps coming up to the barn door, and then a low creaking of rusty hinges as someone started pressing it open. Readying himself to attack, he brought his war hatchet to a throwing position and waited tensely.

Chapter 35

I<small>T WASN'T UNTIL</small> Ben McCulloch met the mail courier just west of town that he realized he was needed back at Gonzales. He and Tomcah had left San Antonio the day before, having spent over a week scouting for Hays, trying to determine the imminence of the Mexican threat. A final meeting between Hays, Caldwell, and himself had decided the Mexicans, while their troops were still marshaled at Laredo and probably going to invade, for some reason or other had elected to delay. In the meantime word from the Moore expedition offered some assurance the Comanches, particularly the Peneteka, had gotten their fill of fighting for one season and western Texas might be in for a period of relative peace.

It was late in the day and Ben was hoping to make it home before dark. He couldn't understand why he was needed; in the absence of any Indian threat, it was hard to imagine a problem coming up that couldn't be handled by others. It was after sundown, and the old mission had finally come into view, when suddenly he saw two figures riding hurriedly toward him. It was Pete Spevy and Jess Bishop. When they pulled up, Pete was the first to speak. "Good you're back, Ben; reckon we could use some help."

Ben peered at them through the gathering darkness, taking in Jess's wild and unkempt appearance. "What's happened?"

"Damn if we know," said Pete anxiously, "but young Lucas Chauncy has disappeared! If the redskins got him or we find him kilt, there sure is gonna be some murders round here!"

Libby was certain she was about to know death. The frightening figure before her was hurling a wicked-looking hatchet at her. Had she not sunk back in a half faint, her skull would have been split open. As it was, the warrior had closed the ground between them and, now wielding a knife, was about to grab her. But screams were suddenly filling the air and Sam and Sarah were rushing forward to grapple with this hideous figure in whose eyes lay the glint of death. Paralyzed with dread, she saw the huge warrior thrusting the children from him and coming for her again. But the children held on and kept screaming, the warrior howling back at them, all in Comanche, which she didn't understand. She only knew there was no way two small children could stop this monster who was intent on taking her life.

She was almost right. Hears-the-Wolf was going to use his knife on the *tejano* squaw's throat; he already had one hand in her long dark hair, forcing her head back. But Sarah was clinging to the arm that held the knife, and Sam, clasping a leg and desperately searching for ways to stop him, bit hard into his calf. With a roar Hears-the-Wolf shoved them away again, but it was to no avail. The children wouldn't quit as he shouted in Comanche. "Are you crazy? . . . I've come to rescue you! We must take this *tejano*'s scalp and go!"

"Do not kill her," screamed Blossom. "She saved our lives!"

"She is a brave woman!" added Bright Arrow. "But for her you would have found us dead!"

Hears-the-Wolf looked at them in confusion. "This is the talk of children!" he blurted. "She is an enemy; her people have killed many of ours!"

"*Isi-man-ica*," said Blossom, "this woman has killed no one. Do not harm her; she gave us our life."

"We will tell Blue Hawk if you hurt her," said Bright Arrow. "Without her, Blue Hawk's lodge would be empty."

Such words out of the mouths of children left Hears-the-Wolf speechless. The last thing he ever hoped to hear on this earth was Comanche children pleading for the life of a *tejano*. But his bold audacious mind was soon functioning again. He was only interested in getting Blue Hawk back; if returning these two would do it, then he would seize them and be off. But he was in for another surprise. In the few seconds he took to deliberate, the children had moved closer to Libby, timidly standing before her. At his gesture to come with him, they hardly moved. This was too much! He had come all this distance at great risk, and now they were acting like they wanted to stay with the *tejano*. Roughly he pulled them away, taking one under each arm and starting to make his way out to where he had hidden the horses. The children began to call out to Libby, who rushed to the door of the barn to watch them being carried off. In anger Hears-the-Wolf realized these children of the Nerm were clearly distressed at having to leave this strange *tejano* squaw. Perhaps she had put them under a spell. For surely they now knew strange words, one of which they cried out many times, even whispering it between sobs. He would have to find out what that word meant. It would be easy to recall; its sound was easy to remember. "Gud-bye."

But Hears-the-Wolf was more upset than he knew. He handled them roughly and bid them be silent. His mood grew uglier as he moved into the trees. He was secretly

angered he did not have that *tejano* squaw's scalp,
something he had pledged himself to take. He was even
more annoyed that he could read into these children's
words their awareness of Blue Hawk's hold over him, a
bitter thing for a proud warrior to face. But above all it
galled him to see Comanche children could so quickly
become attached to such a hated enemy. So aggravated
was he that in heaving the children on the second horse
and hurrying away, he completely forgot about little Lucas lying bound and helpless in the brush.

In the dun-colored hills, where a little stream looked
like a necklace of swirling pools looping toward the Colorado, remnants of the tribe began to gather. They came
stark-eyed, stunned, dazed, with expressions of shock
and pain fixed on their faces. They came on foot, without
weapons, without clothing or cover, without food. They
sank to earth and sat speechless, frozen into silence by
a disaster too devastating to fit into words. They sat for
the better part of a day, as stragglers kept appearing to
collapse beside them. There wasn't a family without
members missing, most already known to be dead. But
there was no loud grieving; the catastrophe was too great
for that. There was only a desperate hanging on to that
flicker of energy needed to sustain life. In time, like
animals, they began to nudge each other, needing some
movement, some confirmation that they were still alive,
that somehow life could go on, food and shelter could
be found. But it was not to come quickly. Many had
been wounded during the escape; many were too
stricken with grief to want to go on. There was no leadership, no organized effort to help them reach for survival.

The first night only a low moaning could be heard
rising in the darkness; there were no chants to bring
strong medicine, no low drumming of shamans, reminding the people that tribal spirits watched from the skies,
that they were not abandoned. All such endeavors would

have been in vain. The people, stripped of the trappings of power, fell back to a more primitive stage of tribal existence. By morning, squaws were out digging for roots and wild tubers their grandmothers had disdained in the plethora of buffalo meat won by mastery of the horse, by command of the endless herds that roamed their plains. With great effort a fire was built and the few remaining young men struggled toward it, knowing someone had to make the long trip afoot to the camp of the Tenawas. It was no longer horses and weapons they needed but shelter from the elements and some aid for the still dying and, perhaps, hope for the despondent. Whisperings of suicides, sometimes taking a wounded child or parent with them, were quietly nodded at. People understood.

By the second day two young men had started on their journey of salvation. Without horses they would be days finding the Tenawas, and behind them this dismal camp, with its many sick and stricken, would just have to wait. And wait they did, several days until the many prisoners Moore had allowed to escape began to come in. These were also sobering days as they began to think of why this calamity overtook them. Agonizing days when the few remaining warriors agreed if the guns the Mexicans had given them had been usable, they could have defended themselves better. In the end they were increasingly bitter days, with sorrow finally distilling into the toxin of revenge and a new lust for *tejano* blood. It was then that they thought of Hears-the-Wolf and the two *tejano* captives he had left behind. Someone said Blue Hawk had taken them with Black Tail to the Tenawas. Dire looks were exchanged. It could only be a few more days before they were within reach again, and then . . .

Libby stood watching them disappear. Conflicting emotions had her clutching the thin lace at her throat. Relief at seeing that terrifying Indian leave was lessened by a twinge of sadness that the children were gone. She

stood for several minutes just looking about her,
somehow less shaken by this close encounter with death
than her initial shock promised. It was a moment she
would remember. The sun had gone down behind the
horizon, and streamers of orange and gold were festoon-
ing half a dome of sky. A strange emotion seized her.
It was not in her to accept fatalism, but looking up, she
knew she had come to a crossroad in her life. The awesome indifference the world presented to a feeling heart
had her wondering at those values born in a little church
in the hardscrabble country of Missouri. Was there really
a divine spirit? Did someone really care? For several
minutes she stood there, until finally the wind, sweeping
through trees along the river, seemed to whisper,
"Libby, you care."

Above her she watched the orange and gold merging
together, becoming soft lavender spears that bent and
slipped away in the train of vanishing sun. A young
woman, alone in a country torn by war, clinging to a
faith that seemed too fragile to survive the endless ter-
rors hate spawns among men. She drew herself up and
walked toward her house, knowing her baby would soon
awaken and need her, knowing now she was totally
alone, yet also knowing she could meet whatever tests
those convictions holding out in the lonely outpost of
her heart promised to bring.

The men gathered at the mission were as divided in
their opinions as they were different in temperament.
Buck Chauncy and Jess Bishop wanted a torchlight
search of the entire settlement; even at night they argued
tracks might be picked up, a start on trailing little Lucas
could be made. But Ben McCulloch, and most others,
stated it was pointless to try tracking until dawn. Torches
were poor for studying the earth, they threw too many
shadows, and a lot of people stomping about in the dark
could obscure tracks on which the only hope of a pursuit
might be based. They knew young Lucas had reached

Pete Spevy and were reasonably sure of the trail he would have taken home, but somewhere along that lonely stretch, trouble overtook him. Buck Chauncy, who had already lost two children, was helplessly sputtering and trying to bite back his rage. Everyone knew Maude, who had not been told her young son had disappeared, would soon begin to suspect, and then who could say?

Ben finally settled it. "We'll meet here an hour before dawn. Tomcah and I will start at Pete's and work our way along the trail. The rest of you spread out and circle the whole settlement. It will take hours, but try to stay on hard ground and keep a sharp lookout for tracks—I mean all tracks! We'll eliminate those that don't matter later. If someone has taken Lucas, they're sure not going to stay around the settlement, and they can't leave without leaving tracks. Send a man back here every time you run across hoofprints traveling outward, 'specially to the west."

In spite of grumbling from Jess, and strings of foul profanity from Buck, the men, knowing they were listening to a man who was thinking his way through this crisis, began to mount their horses. There weren't too many hours left for sleep.

Strangely enough, Libby had no trouble falling asleep. With Lance safe beside her, she said a short prayer and then, exhausted from so many tension-ridden days and the strain of contemplating Jody's return, gave herself over to the numbness in her brain and the leaden feel of her limbs, and quietly drifted off. But during the night she awoke with a start. She knew she had been dreaming, and as she lay, her eyes fixed on a beam of moonlight striking the foot of her bed, she realized she had been dreaming of the night on that dark plain, when she and Kate and Becky had been trapped in Walt's wagon, surrounded by Indians.

What had awakened her was a cry, a low indistinct

cry that at first made her think a fox, or some other nocturnal predator, had caught a nesting bird down by the river. Yet as she lay there, it didn't seem right. There was something about that cry that made her think of Lucas crying out in the darkness as he and his mother lay helpless and frightened that night, dangerously far from the wagon. But such a thought was too fantastic to retain; she put it from her mind and turned over, hoping she could quickly lose herself again in sleep.

But it was not to be.

Within moments she heard the cry again. This time she sat up in the bed. Had it been daytime with birds noisily moving about or insects droning over the fields, or even had the dry season not just passed and the river been higher, giving its muted yet soothing hum, she would not have heard it. But it was the dead of night, a time when only owls or the rustle of field mice enable the ear to measure the silence. It was not an animal. There was something in the cry that made it human, hinting at hysteria or muffled terror. She rose and reached for her cloak.

Slipping into her shoes, she took the rifle from the wall. In spite of her conviction that this was a person in trouble, the long shadows cast by the full moon made her see lurking eyes on all sides. Though she was so alone she would have been no safer in her bed, it seemed more secure indoors, and leaving the house and making her way to the river challenged her courage. The ground seemed rough and pitted in a way she did not remember, but as she drew nearer, the cry rang out again, and now she knew it was not only a person but a young person, perhaps even a child. That it was a child didn't frighten her, but that a child was here crying out in the middle of the night did. Cautiously she approached the thicket from which the cries arose, amazed that she had to steel herself to pull the brush aside. In the darkness, but with a modicum of light supplied by the moon, she made out a bound form looking up at her, a gag still partially covering its mouth. She realized at once it was Lucas Chauncy, even before his features became clear and he struggled again his bonds. She pulled the gag from his mouth and started to work the other bindings free. The poor boy could hardly speak for fright, though he kept saying over and over again, "Is he gone? Is he gone?"

Libby, realizing he meant the hideous-looking Indian, untied his hands and then hugged him for several moments before turning to release his feet. She could feel in the boy's clinging grip that he was still in trauma, openly unable to coordinate his feelings. He laughed and cried at the same time. He held her and kissed her. He said he was sorry, but not what for. He let her help him up, but immediately, trying to run, he fell down. Libby knelt beside him and rubbed his limbs where the tight bonds had cut the circulation off. She spoke to him softly and assured him the Indian was gone, feeling somehow a new confidence rising in herself from words directed at him. Several minutes later they were in her kitchen and she was making tea. The boy finally quieted down and told her how he had come to be tied up in the brush, informing her how the menacing Indian had found her. She saw that talking was helping him return to normalcy and listened to him tell the story several times. But it was still many hours till dawn, and her body was aching for more sleep. She asked Lucas if he wanted to rest.

"Where you going?" he asked, looking troubled.

"To bed. It's nighttime and we should be asleep."

Lucas shifted uneasily. "Where you fixin' to sleep?"

"In a bed. Don't you? I'll fix you a place here on the floor."

Lucas looked down. She could see him growing tense again. "Don't leave me," he murmured, staring at the stub of candle she was about to snuff out.

She studied him for a moment, then smiled and, taking him by the hand, led him into the bedroom. It took her a moment to shift Lance around, but then she patted the bed and Lucas jumped in. She crawled in beside him, smiling, not unkindly, at how the innocent hearts of children wanted constant comforting. Deeply she was glad she was there to give it; she liked mothering. Men made such an fuss about being brave, but before she fell asleep she decided this was life's secret reward for being a woman.

Far across the settlement Buck Chauncy was pacing the floor, waiting for dawn. His eyes were bloodshot and his face ravished by emotions too deranged or violent for expression. If Lucas was gone, only the savages could have taken him. For Buck it was the breaking point; living with this unbearable outrage was not worth his final grip on sanity. His mind was made up. He was a man hurtling through space, indifferent to all but his thirst for retribution. He had no way of knowing his son, for whom he would have gladly destroyed the only world he knew if he could get him back, was fast asleep in the bed of the woman he was determined to kill.

C h a p t e r   3 6

BLACK TAIL, LEADING Blue Hawk, Liza, and Tad, finally sighted a Tenawa hunting party that directed them to their tribal village farther north in Mustang River country. They were warmly welcomed in the customary way and given a lodge to settle in, but Black Tail had to wait several days for the council to meet. He wanted the right setting to deliver Hears-the-Wolf's invitation.

Blue Hawk made it clear she did not want to wait too long, for if her children were being returned, she wanted to be there to greet them. The signs looked good, yet when the council was held and the Tenawa chiefs heard the notorious war leader *Isi-man-ica* was soon to be a chief and was issuing an invitation to surrounding tribes for a great hunt, Black Tail received something less than a rousing response. The chiefs looked at him over their pipes, one saying laconically, "And where is *Isi-man-ica* that he sends others with these words?"

"He has gone to the land of the *tejanos* to rescue two of our children."

The chiefs looked at each other. "Two of our children

319

lost when he and Buffalo Hump led our warriors to war?'' asked one.

Black Tail knew he was in trouble; a war leader who shares in a ruinous defeat does not easily regain favor in the minds of the Nerm. ''The spirits were not with us,'' said Black Tail, trying to keep his head high. It was a lame excuse that rang hollow in his mouth, but he could think of nothing else.

There was an embarrassing silence as many eyes lowered to the fire.

''We will smoke on this before the next moon,'' grunted an old man chief. ''Black Tail will have his answer then.''

But Black Tail already had his answer. His only hope now was the Tahneema. But Blue Hawk knew better. ''It is too soon,'' she said. ''Our people are not used to defeat. It has come like a terrible dream that cloaks the heart in fear, but like the spotted sickness that once emptied our lodges, given time, it will be forgotten.''

''Then we return to our people?''

''Yes,'' she said, quietly nodding to Liza and Tad. ''We will return, but we cannot take these two into camp until *Isi-man-ica* is back.''

The following day they started preparing to depart. Black Tail asked the old man chief to send a runner when the council had made its decision. The chief looked at him and smiled. ''Such a long trip for so short a message,'' he quipped, not even trying to conceal his amusement. The remark was more cutting than would have been any insult, but Black Tail now saw the wisdom of Blue Hawk's words. These few days he had spent with her had only left him more and more impressed. This was truly a remarkable woman.

Had the Penateka runners arrived an hour later, he might have missed them, but he saw them straggling into camp and knew they were from his village. By the time he had alerted Blue Hawk and made his way to them, they were surrounded by several chiefs and a crowd of warriors, every face in the startled crowd registering either astonishment or shock at what was being said.

The men were off and riding before sunrise, Pete Spevy staying close to both Jess and Buck. He didn't like the way Buck kept spitting and muttering to himself. He tried to enlist Jess's help in watching Chauncy, but Jess abruptly cursed any concerns about threats to Indian lovers. They saw few tracks, and none that looked suspicious, but in keeping with McCulloch's orders, they sent a man back with each sighting. Trouble was, it was getting close to Buck's turn, and Pete didn't know how to keep him from leaving. Yet Pete was sure Buck Chauncy riding alone was a menace with high potential for tragedy. Still, there was no way to avoid it. Finally, with Jess already gone, Buck looked at the tracks of two horses, one unshod, and pulled his mount quickly about. "Bet this is it!" he shouted. "I'll get Ben to start moving!"

Pete watched him go, then stared down at the tracks again. They were very likely to be the ones, but they were hours old. What chance they had of overtaking these clearly hard-running ponies was slim, but an attempt had to be made. He hoped Buck would wait long enough to make it.

Ben and Tomcah had started from Pete's place at first light. It was difficult trying to do a thorough job at that hour, but Tomcah kept watching the sides of the trail, particularly where they ran along high brush or other places of concealment. In little over a half hour it paid off. Tomcah spotted the strange hoof marks where the boy's mount must have shied and then steadied itself when he was dragged from the saddle. Then he found the tracks just inside the brush. Within moments he was in the little clearing studying the two strange figures scratched on the ground. Tomcah had less trouble reading these markings than did young Lucas. There was

more light now and the tracks left by two horses were
easier to follow. Both Ben and Tomcah had been away
and were not as aware as many others of the two Indian
children lodged at the Holisters'. So they patiently followed the tracks that apparently were made by two riders
moving cautiously, even stealthily, toward the river trail.
In a little under an hour they found themselves approaching the Holister farm. It was then they heard two
shots ringing out, separated by a scream.

Buck Chauncy knew his life was over. His children
were gone, his wife going mad, his farm doing poorly
from neglect. Why did he bother to stay alive? Only one
reason kept coming to him: to strike back, to destroy
what had destroyed him, to cleanse the earth of the evil
filth that had mangled his heart, shattered his dreams,
left him a leper exiled from humanity and incapable of
happiness. A man had the right to avenge, when God
did not, his own flesh and blood, to punish those who
had transgressed against him. Even animals, the dumb
beasts of the field, killed to defend or avenge their
young. Was he expected to do less? He saw those tracks.
Something told him Lucas was gone, he would never
see his little boy again. When Maude realized they had
lost their last child, she would surrender to the insanity
that was already in her eyes, her voice, and her desperately clawing hands.

His mind was suddenly settled. He would seek Ben
out, but first there was something he must do. He must
kill this evil that had destroyed his world, he must help
to do away with this scourge that brought the roaring
fires of hell into his life, he must bring death to those
who had brought death—a living death at that—to him.

By now he had his horse at a gallop and he was riding
into a rising sun that was turning the horizontal clouds
behind him into a scarlet rim of fire.

*   *   *

Libby had awakened at dawn, but still tired and not wanting to disturb the still-sleeping Lucas, she lay in bed thinking. The happenings of the day before must surely have caused troubles she had yet to hear about. A hunt must be on for Lucas; the sooner she got him home, the better. She would feed him, lend him a horse, and send him on his way. It was beginning to occur to her that there might be some danger in keeping him here if Buck was out desperately searching for his son.

The thought of feeding him got her out of bed. She pumped some water in the kitchen and quickly washed. Then she took a bowl and started for the chicken coop, where she had a laying hen. Her mind was on eggs, but at the edge of the porch the bowl seemed to crumble in her hand as a shot rang out and a slug, humming past her breast like a hornet, dug itself into the doorframe, spraying chips of wood in every direction. Though stunned for a moment, she screamed as panic sent her plunging back through the door. Someone had fired at her and had come within centimeters of hitting and likely killing her. Lucas came streaking from the bedroom, his eyes wide in alarm. "They're shooting at us!" he gasped. "Somebody's shooting!"

Libby was frantically searching her mind for who "they" could be. Without thinking, she took the rifle from the wall. Cocking it and forcing herself to stay in control, she edged back toward the door and began to scan the ground beyond the house where the shot must have come from. She could see a figure dismounting from a horse and coming toward her. She opened the door with her foot far enough to get the barrel through. She drew a bead; though she was not ready to kill, fear for Lance, Lucas, and herself had desperation seizing her mind. She fired into the ground before the oncoming figure, then saw a man dropping to one knee and leveling his rifle. A second later a strange thing happened. Her ears picked up hoofbeats coming up from the river, and Lucas, who had raced to the small window opening

on that side, was excitedly shouting, "It's Ben Mc-
Culloch! It's Ben! Ben is here!"

Libby could hear her breath going out and her chest
collapsing in relief. But her mind was still whirling. My
God, my God, was there no end to death and the threat
of death in this land? The arrival of McCulloch brought
the figure to its feet and started it again toward the
house. Now she could see it was Buck Chauncy, now
she knew her narrow scrape with death was no accident.
She was spellbound with horror, her eyes frozen and
focused on her would-be murderer. For all the world she
wanted to break down and cry, but instead she forced
herself to step out onto the porch. McCulloch, seeing
her, removed his hat, but his gaze was fixed on the approaching Buck. While nodding to Libby, he was obviously going to deal with Buck first.

"What you shooting at?" he said to Chauncy, leaning
forward in the saddle, his face at a slight angle like a
man withholding judgment.

Buck had stopped to slam the stock of his rifle against
the ground. "You got no damn right to . . ." Buck's
voice was cut off as Lucas appeared on the porch beside
Libby.

"Dad!" shouted the boy. "Dad, I'm here!"

Obviously dumfounded, Buck at first gaped, then
threw the gun down and rushed to embrace his son.
"Lucas, Lucas, where the hell have you been? Jesus!
Tell me! For Christ's sake, tell me! What happened to
you?"

As Ben, seeing the father and son embracing, turned
to her, Libby began to tell him what had transpired yesterday. Ben took it all in, and as Buck, still holding
Lucas, finally began to listen, too, his reaction went full
circle. Though he had come in a fury, gratitude at getting
his son back seemed for a moment to soften his features.
But as he heard the whole story, his latent rage returned.
"That's what comes from keeping those redskin brats
here!" he yelled. "It brought that Goddamn Comanche

prowling around, seizing my boy, scaring him half to death. Christ only knows why he wasn't killed or carried off.''

Though Ben planned to warn Buck about taking the law into his own hands, secretly he agreed it was a miracle Lucas wasn't killed or carried off. What's more, Ben had trouble understanding why Libby hadn't been killed; this was a strange-acting Comanche brave. Perhaps some riders had come along the river, and mistaking them for an armed patrol, he had decided to seize the children and run. But somehow that didn't quite fit. Later he found Tomcah agreed with him. He would often wonder at this strange happening in the days ahead.

Libby was glad he stayed after the Chauncys left, but she found little comfort when, after seeing she was still shaken by Buck's near fatal attack, he offered some advice. ''When someone's shooting at you, Libby, firing at the ground hardly ever gets them to see your side of the story. If someone comes by, threatening you again, try to remember that.''

Chapter 37

BLUE HAWK CHOSE not to go with the large party bringing food and clothing to her destitute tribe, so Black Tail went alone. Blue Hawk was afraid the terrible losses her people had suffered might incite a killing frenzy at the sight of *tejano* children, particularly these two, captives of a war leader who wasn't there to fight in the camp's defense, and whose own standing was still in doubt. But it was not only for Hears-the-Wolf's sake that she wanted to protect Liza and Tad; she had secretly become attached to them, particularly Liza. Though she tried to keep it from showing, she felt they had brought some of the warmth to her lodge lost when Blossom and Bright Arrow disappeared. With the knowledge that her own children were still alive and healthy, and hopefully soon to be rescued, she began to think of the spirits, and what she owed them for her good fortune. But Blue Hawk was too wise to believe even spirits could have done it all alone. Somewhere a *tejano* had fed her babies, had kept them from harm; there was no other way Comanche children could survive and stay decently nourished in a camp of the whites, especially *tejanos*.

Several days passed before Black Tail returned, and when he did, his face was clouded with foreboding. Blue Hawk's nervous voice started questioning him as he entered the lodge. His only response was to shake his head and settle on the ground. "Then it is bad," she uttered quietly, sitting across from him.

"The sun no longer lights the way for our people; they are lost in a darkness worse than death."

"Many have died?"

"There is not a lodge that is not keening, not a face free of grief, pain, despair."

Blue Hawk gripped her hands and gazed out through the open flaps. "Where will they turn?" she sighed.

Black Tail stared at her, wedges of alarm tightening his brows. "They are coming here, reduced to tears and anger. Their tears are terrible to behold, but their anger is a rising storm. I saw a cruel fire in their eyes that only blood will quench." His gaze flicked to Liza and Tad, sitting tensely at the back of the lodge. "You must leave," he half whispered.

Blue Hawk, knowing the children now understood enough to realize they were in danger, kept her voice steady. "Where would we go?"

"Into the hills . . . at least until *Isi-man-ica* returns."

Blue Hawk looked at him, her eyes searching his. "Is it safe, wandering a strange country?"

"Safer than it will be here. Remember, you are not hiding from enemies." He dropped his head and stared at the ground. "It's your own people who will come painted for death."

Hears-the-Wolf was making good time, but his mood had not improved. It hardly helped, when the children were allowed to speak, that they told him over and over again how Libby had rescued them and protected them, even when it seemed her own life was endangered. This was not the kind of talk he was comfortable with; he refused to believe *tejanos*, after all their crimes, were capable of such a change of heart. He had seen too much not to know the whites, for all their talk of wanting peace, were really after Indian land, deciding long ago that dead Indians best kept the peace.

He was anxious to get back. Not only would Blue Hawk be his again, but there was that clever invitation to a big hunt, and how it fitted into his bid to be a chief. On the third day he arrived at the known campsite only to look in stupefied horror at the carnage and desolation that confronted him. All the tepees had been burned. Though vultures and other scavengers had almost picked their bones clean, he could see the remains of many lying scattered from the first abandoned drying rack to the river's edge. Some were the slight frames of children.

Blossom and Bright Arrow, just able to grasp what they were looking at, and the awesome loss it meant, began to cry. Hears-the-Wolf, though shocked and sickened at the sight, was alert enough to quickly hush them, not knowing if they were alone. But nothing moved, and though he mounted a nearby boulder and peered about, it was clear the eerie silence that attends death was complete.

He pulled away from the campsite, for a vile stench still hung over it, and settled the children in a hiding place while he marshaled his thoughts. But after a few minutes he almost instinctively began to circle, looking for tracks. It was several hours before he decided that tracks he had picked up downstream, and a few from the campsite itself, with perhaps one or two from across the river, were all tending in the same direction. He returned to get the children and commenced to follow the tracks. By sundown he came to another campsite; this one showed signs of desperation. Ashes of small fires were everywhere. The bones of rabbits and even birds littered the ground; here and there bloodstained skins had been thrown away. This campsite had just been vacated. Tracks of many horses coming up were still fresh.

Someone had come to rescue the people, and from the direction the tracks led off in, Hears-the-Wolf guessed it was the Tenawas.

An icy dread stalked his heart that Blue Hawk was dead. Here was more work of those treacherous *tejanos*. Would these children still make such foolish words about the squaw he had taken them from when they discovered their mother's bones had been left for scavengers, her flesh for vermin? He was still having trouble grasping the magnitude of the calamity that had struck his village—and he not on hand to defend it. Ah, would this not look bad to a council drawn up to select a chief? But sighing, he looked about him. Did it really matter anymore? In the morning he would follow these tracks, hoping the spirits were with him, praying, above all, that they had been with Blue Hawk. But that night he could only lie looking up into a canopy of stars, lighting that infinity of space where the brave dead of the Nerm were said to wander. He remembered Blue Hawk's warning about the Apache scout, he remembered the many times her wisdom, had it been heeded, would have spared much agony, if not disaster, for the people. She was truly a remarkable woman, far more than an exciting mate in his robe. What if she had already gone beyond those distant stars? What if he had returned too late? What would he, an aspiring chief growing secretly dubious of his own wisdom, do without her?

While the children slept, he slipped off to a nearby hill, and holding his hands aloft, chanted a prayer to the spirits of the Penateka. If they had saved his woman, he would keep pledges to them he never dreamt he would ever hear a proud warrior make.

When Jody returned, the joy and comfort Libby felt at being in his arms again was soon tempered by a realization that their standing in the settlement was going from bad to worse. The abduction of Lucas Chauncy had every mother and father saying the Comanche brats that

drew that evil-looking warrior into their settlement put
everybody's child in jeopardy. Libby, already living under a cloud, began to discover that once one fell into
disfavor in a frightened community, criticisms came easily. At first Jody advised doing nothing, hoping it would
blow over, that time would slowly heal what was, after
all, more an error in judgment than a crime. But it was
not to be. Libby's one attempt to go in to the opening
of a general store, the first in the settlement, brought a
series of snubs and even a few shamefully vulgar remarks. She stood in the store for a quarter of an hour,
her cheeks burning with humiliation, before the clerk
approached her. Firming up her lip, she ordered some
coffee and sugar, but the man was so long getting it to
the counter, even serving others while she waited, that
she finally stamped her foot and left.

In the end Jody's encounters, because of his initial
reluctance to take offense, were even more bitter. People
mindful of his fighting with Colonel Moore boldly im-
plied their resentment was against Libby, not him. One
even said, "I sure sympathize with you, partner, married
to an ornery little filly like that."

Jody had decided to keep his responses restrained,
even placating, but this was too much. "Nobody asked
for your Goddamn sympathy!" he snapped. "I'm married to exactly who I want to be!"

The man turned away mumbling, "Sorry, reckon you
deserve each other right enough."

But at home their fretful conversations only made
them more and more depressed. They looked for a way
out, things they could do to win approval from their
neighbors. But every idea struck Jody as too debasing,
too much an admission of stupidity if not outright guilt,
too likely to make them appear to be repentants begging
for forgiveness. Libby was secretly thankful he was not
blaming her for their predicament. Surely he was no
longer the boy she had traveled from Missouri with, and
though he had never mentioned what happened on the

Colorado, she sensed something had transpired to change him.

Pete Spevy came riding out one day. He nodded at Libby, but his conversation was directed at Jody. "How you doing out here?" he said, looking at the house and the fields beyond.

"We're doing fair enough," answered Jody. "Got some reason for asking?"

Pete removed his hat and scratched his head. He replaced the hat before saying guardedly, "Thought you might be thinking of moving on. With the Injuns quieted down and everything, figure you might get a pretty good price for this spread."

There was a long silence before Jody said, "We wasn't studying no moving. What made you think we might be?"

Pete shrugged. "Lots of folks would be."

"That all you came out to say?" demanded Jody.

"Not exactly. Likely you won't be interested, but there's to be a prayer meeting Sunday. Going to be some thanks given for young Lucas's safe return." He glanced at Libby. "Reckon Buck and maybe even Maude will be there."

Jody stepped over and put his arm around Libby. "Thanks for telling us. Anything else?"

"Nope," answered Pete, turning his mount about. "Reckon I'd best be on my way."

"Reckon you better," replied Jody.

Late on the second day, Hears-the-Wolf found himself coming into the Mustang River country. From a brush-covered hilltop, carefully chosen to scout the land, he spotted some Tenawa hunters and knew he was getting close. An hour later, with the sun setting, he caught his first glimpse of the camp. He studied it from a ridgetop for a few moments. Typical of Comanches in their own country, there were no sentinels or guards. Squaws and young men were coming and going freely. It surely explained why the *tejanos* were able to surprise and over-run his people.

Allowing Blossom and Bright Arrow to peer at the camp, which all three were praying would hold their mother, he started to descend to a streambed he could see running to and arching about the campsite. At the last moment his eye caught a figure coming from the camp and looking up to the hill line as though seeking signs of approaching riders. There was something familiar about that figure; as he followed it slowly coming along the streambed, he suddenly knew it was Black Tail. There seemed no reason to hesitate; he pressed ahead, knowing within minutes his friend would see him and shout a greeting. But he was wrong. When Black Tail did catch sight of him, he quickly spurred his horse toward him and started signaling wildly with his hand for Hears-the-Wolf to stay back in the brush.

Hears-the-Wolf simply stopped. He did not think he was as yet visible from the camp, but confusion and a new alarm was in his eyes as Black Tail came up. What could possibly be wrong?

"Good you have returned," said Black Tail breathlessly, "but there is much trouble."

"Blue Hawk?" Hears-the-Wolf almost shouted. "Is it Blue Hawk?"

"She is safe, but she is not here."

Hears-the-Wolf gave an audible sigh of relief. He rose in the saddle as though no trouble could seem big after his release from the dread he had been choking back for days. "Tell me, Black Tail, what's wrong? Why are we hiding?"

Black Tail told him of the mood in the camp and the jeopardy his two captives were in. He explained that Blue Hawk had taken them into the hills to await his return. His friend's advice was not to enter the camp until he had seen Blue Hawk. Many strange things were happening; the people resented his disappearing when he was most needed, and the issue of a new chief was in doubt.

Hears-the-Wolf listened to him in grim silence; there seemed no end to bad tidings. But he dearly wanted to see Blue Hawk again, wanted to deliver her children, wanted to know her woman's warmth again, and, though he must keep it from being apparent, wanted her counsel.

Chapter 38

IT SEEMED STRANGE to look up at a broad expanse of sky, with long lines of migrating birds effortlessly winging across the crimson arc of the early sun, knowing they themselves were under siege because of prejudice and hatred, forces fear invests with power in the human mind. For days Libby and Jody watched each other coming and going, often pausing to talk but always drawn to the issue that bound and separated them, the issue they couldn't avoid, even though it left both withdrawn and troubled in spirit. Libby refused to think of another visit to the campgrounds. That outrageous scene of rejection, those nightmarish moments of being surrounded by threatening and repugnant faces, still came back to her, often making her feel faint and collapsing what little confidence she had gathered to go on. But Jody, though patient, was adamant. "We can't go on sitting here feeling mistreated and misunderstood forever," he said. "If we're going to live in this settlement, we've got to be part of it again, we got to have neighbors we can talk to, folks we can count on." He looked at her, his eyes asking for understanding. "Ones we can turn to in times of trouble."

Libby covered her face with her hands. "Jody, you weren't there! You didn't see it! It was terrible! I was so frightened, I thought I'd die."

"This time I'll be with you, and I just can't believe it will happen again."

Libby shook her head. "Jody, please, I simply can't face it. Can't you see I'm still frightened? . . . Must you keep insisting?"

He put an arm around her. "Libby, if we start doing things different from others, pretty soon we *will* be different. Pretty soon they'll start thinking of us as different, and before you know it, they'll be convinced we don't belong here. I don't want to wait for that."

It was in bed that the pressure of this painful dilemma took its most telling toll. Just when Libby began to feel a more mature Jody had returned, one who was suddenly making love with a new relaxed confidence, giving her more time to get aroused, helping her build up greater tensions, to explode in a more fulfilling climax, her foreboding at having to face the hostility around her rose to capture her mind, stiffen her body, keep her from abandoning herself to the excitement of being possessed.

It was Jody who finally forced the decision. Moving a few inches away, he took her hands in his. "Libby, if you can't see what I'm saying is our only hope, then we just got to leave. I can't live in a community that resents me and mine."

"Leave?" Libby sounded uncertain. Though she had considered it a hundred times, the spoken words still came as a shock.

"Yes, leave, sell out and go. If we can't find another settlement that will take us in, we'll just have to head back to Missouri."

Libby was quiet for several moments. Finally she said, "Jody, that would break your heart, wouldn't it?"

Now it was Jody's turn to be silent, but he was weighing much that told of his increased understanding of life, and his increased feel for this unusual girl he had married. "Libby, not being able to make the girl I love happy is the only thing that would break my heart. I'm just thinking ahead. We can't raise Lance in a community that looks down on his family."

Libby's eyes found his in the dark. Her hands squeezed his to warn of the emotion behind her words. "Jody, promise me one thing." He squeezed her back, well aware he was about to hear Libby voicing a conviction even death had not gotten her to abandon. He was about to hear this strangely determined woman, her courage stirred by maternal instincts, announcing her point of no retreat. "Promise me I'll never have to say I'm sorry for sheltering those two Indian children."

Again it was long moments before he answered, but he drew close to her again, embracing her as he murmured, "I promise."

Minutes later their bodies were entwined in a union that made both stronger, closer, and suffused with a warmth that even in the darkness dissolved their many fears.

Hears-the-Wolf was surprised at how well Blue Hawk had managed to hide herself and the two white young ones. But when they finally got to the brush-covered wickiup in the bend of a small stream, his joy at seeing her had to be temporarily suppressed because of the excitement caused by her reunion with Blossom and Bright Arrow. Black Tail, seeing him standing waiting, motioned him aside. "Let us smoke while this storm of grateful cries and words subsides." He cleared his throat. "Your presence brings the need for decisions closer."

Hears-the-Wolf turned to him. "Decisions?"

"The Penateka are a changed people. You may find them lost and leaderless, but not as eager to receive you as you may hope. I'm afraid hard choices lie ahead."

Hears-the-Wolf studied his friend's face for a moment. "Choices? What choices?"

"Yes, choices. The many deaths on the Colorado have filled them with vengeance. They are looking for white blood to spill; with every nightfall they pray to the spirits to bring them *tejano* blood."

Hears-the-Wolf's eyes narrowed with suspicion. "Ah, are you saying they want my captives?"

Black Tail nodded. "Had it not been for Blue Hawk, they would have long since known the fire iron and the scalping knife. They would have joined our many people in death."

Hears-the-Wolf sat for a long while staring at the pipe Black Tail had lit and passed to him, his mind on the fact that Blue Hawk had left the camp to protect these young captives. Surely she would not want them killed. Surely, he sensed, such an act would displease her, even cause her pain. "Killing these two harmless ones will not bring our people back," he muttered at last. "I will refuse."

Black Tail shook his head slowly. "Not if you wish to be a chief."

Hears-the-Wolf's voice carried a faint tinge of alarm. "This they have said?"

"That and more. The people do not know why you left, they know only that you were not there to fight as any war leader, certainly one bidding for greater power, should have been."

Hears-the-Wolf lapsed into silence again and did not stir until Blue Hawk and Liza came out to build a fire and prepare some food. Rising, he stared toward the distant horizon before he said, "If there is great anger in our camp, it cannot be hidden from; I will ride there tomorrow."

"Alone?"

"No. They will not welcome me alone."

"Is *Isi-man-ica*'s heart still yearning to be chief?"

"Yes."

*   *   *

Sunday morning broke clear with a fresh wind from the west. As Jody went to hitch up the wagon, Libby cleared away the breakfast dishes and dressed Lance. Little had been said, but both knew the trip to the campgrounds would be made mostly in silence, not because of anger but because there was nothing left to say. Their reception couldn't be predicted, and the many uncertainties surrounding it wore the mind down with futile guessing.

They had their first warning as they drew near; other wagons heading the same way began to appear, couples on horseback rode stiffly by. Jody tried calling to a few, but the responses were pointedly tardy, and the few that rose, brief. Libby felt this to be a far more dangerous sign than Jody was letting on; she wanted him to turn back but didn't dare ask. At the campgrounds she pleaded to be allowed to stay with Lance, who by now was asleep in the wagon, but Jody said tensely that would defeat their very reason for coming.

As they approached the hill, where Bumeister was already robed and gesticulating to the sky, they noticed the ground was rapidly filling in. Jody, forcing her to move with the crowd, selected the first open spot he saw and settled them both down. In moments, though, Libby could see the spaces closest to them were not being taken. Within minutes after they were seated, there was an empty cordon around them several yards wide. She tried to nudge Jody and whisper in his ear, but he kept his eyes fixed on Bumeister and signaled with his silence for her to do the same.

Libby, glancing nervously around, finally spotted Buck, Maude, and little Lucas sitting up front. It was little Lucas, restlessly moving about, who saw them sitting apart in the crowd. She watched him going over to Buck and pointing in their direction. Buck was quickly up on one knee peering toward them, clearly preparing to rise, when Bumeister's booming voice rang out and pulled all eyes to the hilltop. Maude's drooping head remained down, her eyes fixed on the ground.

Bumeister began his service with a reading of the Twenty-third Psalm and an exhortation to the throne of Heaven to smile upon this congregation with love and charity. This proved only a prelude to a lengthy sermon on the power of faith to perform miracles, and how gifts to those spreading the word of God were the stepping stones to paradise. Libby didn't hear a blessed word.

Though the first hour seemed interminable, nothing happened until well into the second. By then Libby had sorted out the Bishops seated behind the Chauncys, and the Sutters farther to their left. She wondered if Becky and Kate knew she was there, even though it was evident from the glares and the quick furtive looks they were getting, everyone present knew she was there.

What started it was Bumeister rounding into his group prayer. His arms spread to engulf them all, his words addressed to the kingdom of Heaven. "All these souls have gathered here with goodness in their hearts," he boomed. "They have struggled to act in Your name, to defend their homes and deny the savages who would destroy your works and slay your servants . . ." It was Buck jumping up and shouting, his arm stiffly extended, his finger pointing at the Holisters, who touched it off.

"I'll not pray with her!" he screamed. "She's a devil and has no right coming to this place of worship! She and her kind belong with filthy savages, she and her kind are why my children have been taken! Why my wife is losing her mind! Drive her away; she is a disgrace to all Christians and not worthy to stand in the sight of the Lord!" By now everyone was standing staring at the Holisters. Jody tried to answer, but the ominous murmurings beginning to run through the crowd had Libby pulling him toward the wagon. Trouble was about to break out. Jess Bishop was on the move; like many of the men there, he was armed. Becky couldn't keep him

from striding toward the Holisters, with Buck now coming behind him.

"You ought to find somewhere else to squat down
with your redskins," snarled Jess. "We don't cotton to
Injun lovers coming to our meetings, making like they
was decent God-fearing folks."

"Yeah," added Buck. "And you've had enough
warnings! There's no room here for them that can't
make up their minds which side they're on! If you're
not gone by the next Sabbath, we'll help you leave."

Jody was trying to control his anger, but their remarks
had him choking with indignation and he could take no
more. "Don't try threatening me!" he half raged. "I'm
not some lonely woman trying to protect helpless children."

"Damn it all, you're siding with her!" bawled Buck.
"What the hell do you think that makes you?"

"A gent who was killing redskins on the Colorado
while you brave bastards, and other trash like yourselves, were scaring my wife half to death!"

Libby was straining to pull him away, and Bumeister,
finding his voice, was calling for peace in the presence
of the Lord. But the crowd was aroused, and working
toward a dangerous pitch. Religious fervor was being
sublimated into something ugly and evil. Had Jody had
his way, the confrontation would have spun out of control, surely with tragic consequences, but fortunately
Ben McCulloch was suddenly standing between him and
the others. Ben coolly stared Jess and Buck down, but
then turned to speak to Jody and Libby. "Best you folks
go," he said quietly. "Meeting is about over anyway."

Jody and Libby backed away, but Jody couldn't be
restrained. "Anybody thinks he can scare me off my
land knows where to find me!"

Libby continued to pull him and hush him until they
got to their wagon. She was trembling, but he, his jaw
hard set, slapped the team with the reins and, throwing

the crowd a look that was anything but chastened or contrite, drove off.

Blue Hawk knew why Black Tail had taken the young ones along the stream to a high point they used as a lookout. It was to give Hears-the-Wolf a chance to be alone with her. She didn't mind; she was so happy to have her children back, and so grateful to him for returning them, she would refuse him nothing.

But his needs proved to be beyond anything she had expected. First he wanted her, and she entered into his lusty embraces with a willingness that had him mounting her repeatedly until, sighing with relief, he slumped beside her, emotionally satisfied but physically spent. She smiled at him and, rising, pulled her robe about her; it was good to have a man again. But when she moved over to settle down before him, she discovered this man's mind had drifted far beyond her cozy wickiup. As he sat up and pulled his legs beneath him, it was clear he was burdened with thoughts he was reluctant to voice. She watched his face being braced between his hands and his eyes studying her closely. Instinct warned her that whatever he was about to reveal was not going to please her, but she could never have imagined the shock she received when he stated he was taking Liza and Tad into the Tenawa camp.

"What!" she gasped. "That is taking them to their deaths! Has Black Tail not told you?"

"Black Tail has told me our people are thirsty for *tejano* blood."

"Are you saying the blood of two children will satisfy that thirst?"

Hears-the-Wolf looked away from her, uncomfortable with the rising fire in her eyes. "If it does not, I will lead the warriors east again and we will redden our war hatchets and return with bloody scalps to dance around the victory fire."

Blue Hawk threw up her hands, then turned and

hissed furiously at him. "Fool! Are you blind? Has not the death of half our village convinced you the Penateka are no match for the *tejanos*? Surely the youngest child must know we need to disappear into the hills until the spirits smile on us again and our strength returns."

"But a chief must hear the pleas of his people."

"A chief must give them food for their bellies and victories for their hearts. You are a war leader without braves to follow you . . . You have nothing to give!"

Hears-the-Wolf stood up and turned to go. "Blue Hawk does not want her man to be a chief."

"No, she does not want any man to be chief: whose thoughts go only to war."

"It is the way of the Nerm."

"*Isi-man-ica*, the Nerm have known days when their enemies fled before them. Now many of us sit here, helpless and hiding in these hills. Is it not time for wisdom to seek the road to peace?"

"Blue Hawk speaks of peace with an enemy who does not want it, who wants only our land."

"He wants our land, not our lives. With peace we may hold on to much of one and avoid losing the other."

"That is coward's talk. There is no room in our councils for the voice of fear."

"*Isi-man-ica*, when will you learn that fear is the wisdom of survival? Is the wood rat stupid to fear the snake? Is the chipmunk stupid to fear the hawk?"

Hears-the-Wolf sank down again. He did not know why the words of this woman always seemed stronger than his. The qualities that had always served him best in life, boldness and bravery, no longer seemed to count. The world had become confusing, devious, complicated. Something in this woman's eyes told him he was no longer a match for it: the wisdom it required had been denied him. If only he could enlist her aid, induce her to help him achieve the prominence he was sure, with the tribe so reduced by circumstance, was now there for the taking, he would do much in return. "Blue Hawk," he said, looking into her eyes, which seemed to have become cold, distant, looking down on him from some lofty inaccessible height, "is there still a road open for me, a road that makes a brave warrior a chief?"

He thought he saw the whisper of a smile touch the edge of her mouth. "There is always a road for bravery that knows the strongest weapons cannot take the place of the simplest wisdom."

"How does one find this road?"

"It starts with a search for peace."

"Peace? You know I cannot fight! How can I bring about peace?"

"I will show you how to start."

Hears-the-Wolf grumbled, but he wanted to hear her thoughts. Something far back in his mind told him she might bring a glimmer of light to the darkness persistently lying over his hopes. "Well, woman, I am listening."

"Take these two young captives and return them to the *tejanos*."

Hears-the-Wolf's face broke into a scowl. "That's madness! That will not bring peace! And the people will know I denied them a wish I had it in my power to grant."

Blue Hawk sighed and looked away. "*Isi-man-ica*, you will never be a chief. A chief thinks for his people, not they for him! If they must think for you, they do not need you!"

Hears-the-Wolf looked down; he couldn't help a sulky manner claiming him. Why did this woman always sound so right? His mouth tightened as he said, "Words come easily to your tongue, but where would I take them? Do you know how dangerous it would be for me to go back there now? I forgot a captive I had tied up and left in the brush. The *tejanos* will have found him. The place will be like a hornet's nest."

"It's the only way."

They sat for a moment in silence.

"I do not believe it will make me chief," he said at last.

"No, it will not. But if you do this thing, when you return, I will help make you a chief."

He looked at her, his eyes struggling against doubt. "You know how to win the people over?"

"The people are like children; their joy and sadness of the morning become their judgments of the afternoon. We will find a way."

Again they sat for several moments in silence. Hears-the-Wolf finally rose and turned to her. "All right, I will take them to the Guadalupe and turn them free. They will be found and you will have your wish."

"No," replied Blue Hawk, "you will take them to the woman who protected my children; you will leave them with her."

He looked at her in confusion. "Why?"

"Because we are trying for peace."

"Ach, you have been listening to your children. We know nothing about that strange *tejano* squaw!"

"We know what counts. She does not hate us and she is not for killing. She is a brave woman, the kind of bravery that leads to peace."

His shoulders slumped and he looked down, shaking his head. "This will be a very dangerous trip and I have little time to pray for strong medicine. I hope it leads to your peace."

Blue Hawk came over to stand close to him, telling him with her eyes she was again feeling some pride that he was her man. "It will be a start," she whispered. "If the spirits are with us, it will be a start."

Chapter 39

BY THE TIME they reached home, Jody's anger had faded from his face and voice to congeal in a bitter if muted resentment in his mind. No matter which way he turned, the frustrations he encountered left him incensed and too upset to think clearly. What he had seen on the Colorado and what he had just witnessed convinced him a form of madness had settled on the border, a lunacy seizing them all and, in the end, likely destroying them all. Work on the farm now seemed pointless; their labors, their hopes, the few dreams that had kept them striving, were now a waste his heart refused to measure. His resolve to let time repair their estrangement from the community had vanished when he saw armed men demanding he take his little family and depart. Part of him wanted to stay and fight, but secretly he had lost whatever faith he ever had in violence, and such bravado could only endanger his wife and child. As a boy he had always dreamt, as did all boys his age, of brave men settling differences with guns. But the sight of Buck and Jess, ready to reach for their weapons, and the cool manner of McCulloch, using only his eyes to warn them

345

against any gunplay, had him wondering what really constituted bravery. "All angry men are brave," he remembered their town marshal saying when he was a child. "That's because they're too riled up to think straight." That marshal served for over twenty years, always claiming his real claim to fame was never having had to use his gun.

Libby knew how disturbed he was. Her mind could not dismiss what his loyalty to her was costing. Yet she couldn't think of a single thing to end the threats or ease the troubles surrounding them. Had she been able to, she would have thrown herself on the bed and cried, probably for hours, but that would have been a sight too cruel to thrust on him. She was grateful he appeared to be stolidly thinking through their plight. In spite of the rage that occasionally flashed in his eyes, his words at least carried no promise of violence. "We'll give ourselves a week to decide what to do," he said finally. "By then all our prospects should be pretty well talked over."

Nothing more was said. For days, strangely enough, Jody busied himself walking about the property, mending a fence or two and shoring up some beams in the barn. She could see he was just trying to keep himself busy so he could think. She let him be; it was his way. She also kept herself busy, tending Lance, cooking, and mentally evaluating her household goods. She was preparing for the moment he would announce they were leaving, and wanted her mind already set on what to take. Each afternoon she would take Lance down to the river and sit beneath the great trees that rose to form her bower. There she would watch the sun go down, finding some beauty in the day in spite of the mournful emptiness that had descended around them.

It was three days before anyone came by, then McCulloch and Tomcah came riding up from the river. Ben gave no indication his mind was on what happened Sunday, though both Libby and Jody knew he could not possibly have forgotten it. "Seen any tracks hereabouts lately?'' said Ben, tipping his hat to Libby and nodding to Jody.

"Tracks? What kind of tracks?" inquired Jody.

"We're not sure," answered McCulloch. "Just got a report of some strange tracks west of here. Could be nothing, probably is. Best keep an eye out, though; you never can tell."

"Which way were the tracks headed?" asked Jody, his interest growing.

"They were coming this way . . . Why we're here." Ben saw the sawed beams Jody was preparing for the barn. "Fixin' things up, eh?" It was Ben's way of seeking an indication of their plans.

"Just patching a bit," said Jody, his tone noncommittal.

Ben didn't press.

"Can we give you some coffee?" Libby smiled, glad to have this formidable but reassuring man on their property. There was something about Ben's presence that made everything seem more normal.

Ben muttered something to Tomcah, but Tomcah shook his head and gestured downstream. "No, thank you, Libby," said Ben. "Tomcah thinks we better keep moving; we got a ways to go before sundown."

They rode off with Libby and Jody watching them till they disappeared in the heavy foliage along the river-bank.

Hears-the-Wolf never lacked courage, but much about this trip sat uneasily in his mind. First, he knew the last time he had traveled this way, rescuing Blue Hawk's children, the *tejanos* had just driven his people west and were not expecting Comanche warriors to be prowling about their settlement. But now they were alerted; he would need the slyness of a fox to carry out this mission undetected, particularly as he had two *tejano* children to deliver, deliver to the very white squaw he had tried to kill. The children knew they were going home and made

no attempt to escape, but even so, their presence made
concealment a trying task, one laden with risks and often
seeming impossible. His other concern was this *tejano*
squaw. Who was she that Blue Hawk thought so much
of her? What kind of *tejano* protected Comanche children even with their own life at stake? Did saving Blossom and Bright Arrow, two enemy children, make her
more important than others? It was puzzling, but he
knew that among the Nerm, great gifts or sacrifices were
an accepted way of increasing one's prestige. Many
chiefs made themselves poor by generosities carried out
to achieve or confirm a high standing. Did saving those
children so that they could be returned to their people
make this *tejano* squaw powerful, powerful enough to
bring about peace? Was she already some kind of chief?
He knew *tejano* women were often stupidly treasured by
their men, some returning captives reporting seeing
white men near worshiping their wives, others acting
like servants to them. Surely they were a strange people.
For some reason he was not struck by how much he
valued Blue Hawk, or how he allowed himself to be
guided by her counsel.

They had to make haste, but it was causing hazardous
mistakes. They were crossing the tracks of others and
leaving prints on well-traveled trails. Both children were
mounted on one horse, but they were good riders, especially Tad, who sat in front, and they kept up with
ease. But in a land where every rider stopped to study
tracks, this was courting trouble.

The children realized from what they had heard Blossom and Bright Arrow telling Blue Hawk that it was the
Holister farm where Hears-the-Wolf found them, and it
was the young Holister woman who had protected them.
Liza at least suspected it was this woman's defense of
Blue Hawk's children that was partly responsible for her
and her brother being sent back. She was well aware
Blue Hawk had taken them into those lonely hills to
keep them from the angry people all knew were coming

to camp. Liza had a funny feeling Blue Hawk and this Holister woman were a lot alike. It made her glad that she had decided she was going to be just such a woman.

By the night before they expected to reach the Holister farm, they started passing through territory the children recognized. But their excitement was tempered by the realization that the presence of Hears-the-Wolf might bring sudden gunshots from their own people. But hoping they would soon be safe, they decided not to anger their grim-looking captor; his every order was met with a quick response. Tad even helped him by suggesting ways of getting to the river trail while avoiding open country. But the following morning the perils Hears-the-Wolf had foreseen began to cast their shadow. They topped a rise and spotted two men on the horizon riding in the opposite direction. They were not moving fast, and Hears-the-Wolf could tell by their formation and the way they zigzagged they were studying the ground. It called for more speed, but by noon they caught a large party coming behind them and had to hide while they passed. It was late in the afternoon before they had reached a spot along the river just above the Holister farm, and Hears-the-Wolf slipped off to make a quick scout.

To his surprise and relief, he found the *tejano* squaw down by the river, sitting in a clump of large trees. She seemed to have something beside her that she kept looking at. Somewhere he suspected there might be a man, but there was none in sight.

Motioning the children to stay behind him, he began to creep through the foliage along the bank until he was barely fifty feet from the sitting Libby. Now he could see she had a baby beside her. He still didn't know why this squaw was so important, but he must make sure she knew he was important too.

When he stepped out of the screening brush, Libby looked up at him, an expression of shock and fright freezing on her face. Had not Liza and Tad stepped out

behind him, she would have fainted. She had never seen
them but knew immediately who they were. As it was,
she couldn't speak even as the children rushed forward
to embrace her. Her mind was still numb as she started
hugging them back until tears finally rose in her eyes
and began distorting her vision. She didn't see Hears-
the-Wolf slashing at a large tree with his knife; she was
embracing the children when a shot rang out, and only
vaguely heard it hitting the tree the warrior was busily
slashing.

When she looked up, Hears-the-Wolf was down
crouched on the ground, backing away toward where he
had left the horses. But it was too late. Jody, who was
seeking out Libby to tell her of his decision to leave,
had been walking diagonally across the fields to the
river, catching sight of the Indian warrior as he stepped
out from the brush.

Libby came to her feet. She could sense the children's
fright and alarm, but a deep and overwhelming voice
told her this Indian must not die. A force that blotted
out all else had her rushing forward, desperately determined his act of bringing the children here must not be
rewarded with death. She charged over to Hears-the-
Wolf and stood before him. Jody, rushing up, stared at
them in confused shock. Breathless, he took in the
Chauncy children, but was clearly unable to grasp why
Libby was shielding this dangerous-looking Indian.
"What the hell is . . .." He couldn't go on.

"Please don't shoot!" cried Libby. "He brought back
these children! He must go free!"

"Free?"

"Yes, put that gun away. Maybe my prayers are being
answered."

Jody lowered the gun but held it in his hand. Libby
turned to Hears-the-Wolf and pointed upstream. "Go,"
she said. "Tell your people we're thankful." Hears-the-
Wolf looked at her; her words meant nothing to him,
but Liza, who appeared at Libby's side, managed to

translate their meaning. Hears-the-Wolf's only response was to stare back at Libby, thinking this was surely an unusual woman. The man had put the gun down and she was signaling Hears-the-Wolf to escape. She must truly be very powerful.

Turning, he slipped away into the brush, and the children and Libby, and even Jody, fell into each other's arms in embraces of gratitude and joy. Everyone knew something vastly important had happened, but no one could fix a name to it or guess how long it would take to be fully grasped. But their joy was short-lived. Within minutes Hears-the-Wolf was back, hurriedly leading two horses, pointing grimly behind him and holding up two fingers.

Jody and Libby knew at once he was saying two riders were coming, and Jody, slipping close to the water, managed to glimpse at a distant turn in the river Ben McCulloch and Tomcah coming on at a steady pace. He and Libby looked at each other, Libby's eyes pleading. "Jody, you must help. The barn!"

Jody's glanced shifted between the warrior and his wife. He could not serve both imperatives pulling at his mind, but at that moment Libby had an air about her that could not be resisted. Whatever this strange wife of his was doing, two children thought long lost were saved. He jumped on the second horse and motioned Hears-the-Wolf to follow him. Together they went racing up toward the barn.

C h a p t e r 4 0

BEN MCCULLOCH WATCHED Tomcah signaling he had spotted the tracks reported earlier by a passing mail courier. Told the tracks were heading east, they had tried to pick them up along the river, but to no avail. Now they were back searching the area where the tracks were discovered, and as Ben rode up, Tomcah pointed to the clear prints of two fast-moving unshod ponies.

As they followed these tracks, they began to see that as rapidly as these riders were traveling, they were pointedly staying to low ground, and working behind stands of trees or great outcroppings of rock. There was a fugitive air to this trail, and it convinced Ben these riders knew where they were going and were trying to avoid any encounters until they got there.

Finally, striking the river again, they began to move downstream. Two miles above the Holister place, Ben's mind turned to the Comanche who had kidnapped Lucas and left with the two Indian children Libby was sheltering. Was he coming back for some kind of revenge? At the sound of a shot, Tomcah pulled up. Ben came alongside him. "Must be the Holister place," he said hurriedly. "We'd better move!"

Both men dug spurs into their mounts and started galloping along the river trail. It was several minutes before they came upon Libby, her hands in the air, motioning them to stop. Ben came up, his face unable to conceal his shock at the sight of Liza and Tad. "My God!" he began. "What's happening here?"

Libby almost pulled him out of the saddle. "Isn't it wonderful? They're back!"

Ben, staring about him, dismounted to embrace the children. "Where did you come from?" he wheezed as he hugged Liza.

Excited as the children were, they were alert enough to let Libby answer. "They just got here," cried Libby. "Isn't it wonderful!"

Ben, lifting Tad, continued to stare at Libby. "They came all the way here by themselves?" His voice was weakened by an edge of disbelief.

"Yes, isn't it marvelous?" Libby, anxious to delay them, kept repeating herself. But it was no use; she saw Tomcah studying the slashings on the tree, and Ben, putting Tad down, confronted her with a new look, one tinged with irritation.

"Just where did he go?" he asked in that no-nonsense way that so marked him.

"What does it matter? They're back!"

Ben heard the pleading in her voice, but Tomcah was pointing to the tracks that led up to the house and the barn. He remounted, his face firming up with lines of concern. "As long as he's running loose in this settlement, it matters. Don't forget he's a Comanche."

Libby wanted to hold them any way she could, but they went galloping up toward the house. Ben McCulloch was not an easy man to fool.

Jody didn't think Ben McCulloch could be quickly thrown off a trail, particularly with Tomcah at his side.

At the barn he took a moment to point upward to the small hayloft. Hears-the-Wolf knew what he meant and understood why Jody was taking the two horses out beyond the near field, trying to lose their trail or make it hard to follow in a tangle of woods he could see rising there. But he didn't like being closed in; almost immediately he felt trapped. Only the knowledge that he was deep in *tejano* territory, and his pony could never outrun the vigorous pursuit that was sure to come, made him chance this barn. But as he huddled above the very spot where he had waited last time to deliver Libby a death blow, he made a pledge not to be taken alive.

Jody raced across the field, circled quickly through a stand of trees and heavy brush, then raced back to the barn, this time approaching it from the rear. He knew Libby would be trying to delay Ben, but even so, he could only count on a few minutes at best. As he reached the entrance to the barn, he saw Ben and Tomcah leaving the trees by the river and coming toward him. On impulse he pulled the wooden beams he had been working on to where he could set them against the door, making it difficult to enter. He tried to look like a man involved in his labors, but Ben was frowning peculiarly as he rode up. "Nothing stops you from working, does it, Jody?"

"Never get finished if you don't stay with it."

Ben rose up in the saddle and looked about him. "I don't suppose you heard a shot here a while back."

"A shot?" Jody shook his head. "Nope, didn't hear any shots."

"Mighty funny; Tomcah and I did. Take it you didn't see anyone either."

"Fact is, Ben, I've been inside the barn, haven't seen anyone, but thought I heard someone riding off in that direction." He pointed to the far woods beyond the field.

Both Ben and Tomcah could see tracks heading that way, but Ben's expression lacked conviction, and the smile he gave Jody had nothing to do with humor.

"We'll take a look," he said laconically. "Just don't forget you're fooling with Comanches. Any more trouble and you might have plenty to answer for."

When Ben and Tomcah disappeared in the woods beyond, Jody signaled Hears-the-Wolf down. Pointing south, he showed by quick gestures how the Indian could circumvent his pursuers and be free to travel west again. Hears-the-Wolf didn't need any urging; his grimmest fears had almost been realized. As he hurried away, his mind kept turning over a quandary that had begun in the hayloft. Was being a chief really worth all this?

Jody watched him go, then raced down to meet Libby and the children coming up from the bower. They were still excited, but Jody raised his hands for them to listen. "Get ready, I'm getting the wagon out. You children are going home!"

Blue Hawk and Black Tail, Blossom and Bright Arrow between them, rode into the Tenawa village, trying to ignore the uncertain reception they were receiving. Black Tail, who had already set up a tepee for their use, threw a few words of explanation to a passing Tenawa chief, one whose friendship he had won by giving him a large knife he had taken from a burning warehouse in Linnville. Later he tried to explain *Isi-man-ica*'s absence to a council by showing them Blue Hawk's children, which the war leader had been away rescuing. The missing white captives, Liza and Tad, were more difficult to explain, but he and Blue Hawk had agreed to say the captives had managed to escape, and *Isi-man-ica* was now trailing them in an effort to bring them back.

While the Tenawas said little, the Penatekas took all this in with skeptical looks. A few rose to remark on the unlikelihood of the young captives, who hardly knew the country, getting away with a skilled tracker like *Isi-man-ica* on their trail. "We'll believe you when he brings them bound to our fire," said one.

"Why were they not kept here in camp where captives belong?" demanded another.

Black Tail argued the captives belonged to *Isi-man-ica*, and Blue Hawk, as his squaw, could take them where she pleased. But he knew such explanations were not enough, and his words could easily be weaving a net around Blue Hawk and himself, for their story, once told in council, could not be changed. Who knew what eyes might have glimpsed *Isi-man-ica* riding east with his captives? Hunters and scouts were forever roaming the countryside. Every encounter was remembered and, in time, reported.

Back in the tepee, he regarded Blue Hawk gravely. "It is not good," he said solemnly. "We must count on *Isi-man-ica* returning soon."

"He will come when the spirits will it."

"Then may they will it quickly." He looked down, rubbing his hands together nervously. "We must think of something to distract the people. They are restless and given to angry thoughts. It is a bad time; your man may be in danger."

"And we are not?"

Black Tail sighed quietly, settling on a robe and reaching for a pipe before saying, "We will share his fate."

Blue Hawk remained silent for long moments while she studied the sky through the open flap. "What if he returned with an offer of peace from the *tejanos*?"

Black Tail drew a mouthful of smoke from the pipe and released it before replying, "Is that what you hope?"

"He wants to be a chief; he must do something to win that honor."

Black Tail shook his head. "Our people were raised on war; they are resigned to it. They remember their last efforts for peace. Such talk will not console them now."

"Black Tail, you have heard their thoughts. What are they?"

"They are angry at their great losses, they are angry that the *tejanos* surprised them, and they are angry that they had too few guns to save themselves on the Colorado."

Blue Hawk looked at him intently. "You don't think a time of peace would serve them well? You don't think *Isi-man-ica* could bring this peace to them?"

Black Tail's face looked weary and void of hope. "Blue Hawk, *Isi-man-ica* is not a man of peace."

Blue Hawk sighed and dropped her eyes. "True, his strengths are the strengths of a warrior. We will just have to make them do."

Puzzled, Black Tail waited for her to look up. "Do what?" he asked.

She folded her hands before her and tilted her head as though peering into a far distance. "Make him a chief," she said softly.

Jody moved the wagon ahead at a good clip. The children could have gotten there quicker on horseback, but he wanted Libby to be on hand when they were united with their parents, and Libby could not leave Lance alone. He asked Liza and Tad to stay back in the wagon, for as they passed through the center of the settlement, they found chance faces staring at them, some with looks of surprise settling into scorn. Jody and Libby sitting in front ignored them, but Liza and Tad, sitting inside with Lance, peeked out and couldn't help giggling to themselves as they saw they were getting close.

The Chauncy farm was a mile east of the mission, just off the trail leading to Lavaca Flats. Jody pulled into the dirt lane that led up to the house. He slowed the team and let them walk the remaining hundred yards, whispering back to the children to get ready.

They were still twenty-five yards from the house when Buck appeared on the porch, a rifle in his hands and his mouth twisted up like a man ready to spit. Jody stopped the team, and Buck, his eyes riveted on Libby, took a step off the porch and one toward them. "You've got one helluva nerve . . ." he began. But the children could wait no longer; they jumped out of the rear of the wagon and ran to him, screaming, "Daddy! Daddy! We're back!"

Buck looked like a man stuck with lightning. For a moment he stood frozen with shock, but as he saw his children racing toward him, alive and well, his eyes went to the heavens and he flung the rifle as far as he could to sink down and embrace them. Tears fought their way into his eyes and then ran down his cheeks in a steady stream. Libby couldn't help it; she began crying too. For a full minute Buck and his children hugged each other and tried to prove by kissing each other's faces that they were really together again. In the excitement only Jody noticed Lucas guiding his mother through the door and out onto the porch. Maude's eyes looked haggard and dulled beyond care. But Lucas kept pointing at his brother and sister and shouting at her. The children, seeing their mother, ran to her. But as they grasped her, Maude collapsed and they had to hold her up to embrace her. But this they did until she began to hug them back, feebly at first but with rising strength. Buck had still not recovered; he came with his tearstained face over to the wagon. "My God, however . . . how did you . . ." But he couldn't talk.

Libby reached down and put a hand on his shoulder. "Don't try to say anything now, Buck; this is a time for rejoicing. Go join your family. Maybe now we'll all know a little peace and happiness."

"I just can't . . ." he tried again, but still choked up.

Jody pulled the wagon away; he knew it would be a day or two before Buck or Maude could settle their emotions and talk rationally. The spiritual devastation they had been put through would take time to fade into painful memory, but he could see Maude, who was rising now, and whose arms were beginning to fly in every direction as she reached time and time again for her children, was showing a tiny spark of energy that instinctively he knew was a sign of returning health.

As they started back, Jody couldn't help smiling at his wife, who was still crying as she looked back at the joyous sight of the reunited Chauncys all going to their knees to thank God for the deliverance of their Liza and Tad. He put his arm around her. "Do you think letting that Indian brave go is really going to bring us peace, Libby?"

She snuggled close to him, rubbing her eyes and looking up at him. He had never seen her look more beautiful. "It's a start, Jody," she whispered. "God willing, it's a start."

Chapter 41

HEARS-THE-WOLF had a disquieting trip back. Time after time he encountered *tejano* scouts or patrols, keeping him aware these plains were falling to their enemies. He would have to find some way to drive the whites from this bountiful land his fathers had fought for, from its great buffalo herds, from his people's source of life. But the Penateka had suffered serious losses. Could they still command the numbers necessary for such a task? Dare they risk losing more? His mind resisted the sight of his tribe sinking to a pathetic remnant, like once powerful Apache bands before the Nerm swept them from the prairies. No, his people would need help; they would need the Tenawa, the Tahneema, and other kindred tribes to the north and west, even the Kiowas. But would they come for the Penatekas? Buffalo Hump failed to convince their chiefs; could Hears-the-Wolf? Ah, but he could do nothing until his people acknowledged him as a chief.

His mind turned to Blue Hawk. She had promised to show him the path to power, the way to become a leader of his people. He had run deadly risks for her, but now that he was back, her wisdom would serve his ambitions, her body his powerful male needs. So anxious was he to see her again that he nearly missed Black Tail's mirror signals as he approached the Tenawa camp. His friend was posted on a hill to the east of the camp, clearly awaiting his return. Several minutes later they met in a grove above the stream and he watched Black Tail approach with dark lines of distress trenched into his face.

"There is trouble?" said Hears-the-Wolf, the other's expression serving as his greeting.

Black Tail could only find his breath with effort. "We will need strong medicine today, *Isi-man-ica*; evil thoughts have taken the minds of our people."

"Evil thoughts?"

"Yes, they are angry, and their anger is like an enraged buffalo charging at you."

"They have found reasons for this?"

"Too many to recount."

Hears-the-Wolf rose up on his mount and looked in the direction of the camp. "Where is Blue Hawk?"

"She waits for you. When you arrive in the camp, you will be called before the council. She must speak to you first."

Hears-the-Wolf studied Black Tail's face, looking for something to pin hope on. "You have smoked with the Tenawa chiefs?"

"Only with one. He says the Tenawa will not come against you unless our own people do. But beware, our people are like raving dogs surrounding a wounded deer; you will not find friendly ears among them."

Hears-the-Wolf sat staring at the ground. He was afraid of this. He had been absent too long. Though luckily he had avoided the disastrous attack, his suspicious disappearance made it easy for people to blame him for their miseries. This was Blue Hawk's fault; but for her, he would not be facing this dangerous threat. Surely he could no longer hope for power; Black Tail's

eyes said as much, if not more. But now the damage
was done. His people, once aroused, were deadly and
difficult to appease. Was there a way out of this storm
gathering before him, this tribal anger that would confront him like a prairie fire roaring in from all directions?
If there was an escape from this wretched trap, his mind
could not summon it; he could only think of one direction in which to turn. He raised his eyes to meet Black
Tail's. "Where is Blue Hawk?" he said, resignation failing to cover the bitter rasp of his voice.

Blue Hawk was waiting for him outside the camp. He
came into her presence, not with the ardor he had
planned for days but with a look of sullen defeat, one
that warned her her task would not be easy.

They looked at each other for several moments before
she said, "It's good that you have returned; there is
much to be done."

"If there are answers to these evils, only you have
them. My heart tells me the people have prayed to the
spirits, and both have turned their faces away."

"This is not a time to speak to their agony but to their
need for revenge."

"Against me?"

"No, you idiot. What can they gain from vengeance
against you? In spite of your pretenses, you come before
them without wealth or even importance. No death they
could inflict on you can reduce their pain."

Hears-the-Wolf's face began to take on a quizzical
expression. "Blue Hawk, even if one such as I can grasp
this truth, will they?"

"You will make them grasp it."

"You want me to turn their vengeance toward the
tejanos!"

"No, *Isi-man-ica,* you cannot defeat the *tejanos*. Use
your head; you must turn them to where their vengeance
will be rewarded."

Hears-the-Wolf's face finally began to take on the

contours of a slow awakening. "The *Mexicanos*," he breathed. "You want me to lead them against the *Mexicanos*! Does Blue Hawk already know this to be their wish?"

"Of course I don't. But they are miserable in defeat. Not only hundreds of lives, but honor, was lost on the Colorado. They were massacred and left impoverished. Their pride keeps telling them that had the *Mexicanos* given them decent rifles, they could have fought the *tejanos* off. Wise ones among the Tenawa don't believe this, nor do I, but the Penatekas want to believe it; no"—her hand sliced through the air—"they desperately need to believe it, and that should make them soft clay easily molded by the hands of a clever warrior.

Hears-the-Wolf gathered his arms about him and looked away in dubious thought. "Blue Hawk, will this not require strong medicine from the spirits?"

"No, it will require listening to me."

Hears-the-Wolf hung silent for a long moment, his troubled eyes asking for and receiving strength from the firm countenance of Blue Hawk. Finally he sighed and raised his head to peer in the direction of the camp. "I am ready," he whispered. Then, pulling her to him, he embraced her tightly.

Ben McCulloch and Tomcah finally picked up the trail again and followed it back to the barn. The Holister wagon was gone, and with it all those left at the farm. Ben was strangely silent, but they rode down to the river and stopped at the bower, where he pointed to the slashings on the tree. "What does all that mean?" he asked Tomcah.

Tomcah stared, puzzled for a moment, but finally said haltingly, "It says they equal . . . no longer in each other's debt. It is the kind of thing that passes between chiefs."

Ben couldn't help smiling. He understood it and realized Liza and Tad had been brought back because

Libby had taken in and protected those two Comanche kids. Still smiling, he shook his head. It was a strange world.

Nevertheless, it dawned on him that this might put down the potential trouble brewing in the settlement if word of it got around. Surely it would, at least, quiet Buck Chauncy and maybe a few others. He liked the Holisters, particularly Libby, and didn't want to see them leave. Nodding to Tomcah and putting spurs to his horse, he decided to get started on spreading the word at once.

Pete Spevy came that Friday morning smiling and doffing his hat like a politician seeking votes. "Got to tell you folks," he began with one foot up on the porch to balance himself. "They planning the biggest prayer meeting ever. Them Chauncy young 'uns coming home has got half the settlement quotin' Gospel. Figure you folks will be on hand, seeing as how you had a hand in fetching 'em back."

"Thanks for telling us," said Jody, picking up the shovel he had put down when Pete arrived. "Well, I got to finish digging that drain; could be some rain coming up."

Pete's face registered disappointment at this response to what he felt was a dramatic announcement. Privately he was expecting great excitement and a warm reception, one that would lead to an invitation for coffee and maybe breakfast. But he was confronted with Jody's back as the young Holister headed for the barn, and Libby, standing inside her door, where her voice just reached him, saying, "How's Maude?"

"She's mighty improved," reported Pete, obviously anxious to say more.

"I'm glad," replied Libby. But then he saw her stooping down to pick up Lance and, rocking the baby in her arms, move away.

"You folks hear President Lamar is a-coming this

way?'' he called out. He thought he heard Libby saying, ''No,'' but he wasn't sure. Finding himself alone, he slapped a hand on his knee, mumbled something under his breath, swung into his saddle, and rode off.

As he disappeared, Libby, Lance in her arms, came out again and walked over to the barn. Jody was digging steadily, but seeing her, he put the shovel aside and stood up.

''What are we going to do?'' she asked.

Jody rubbed his hand across a moist brow and peered toward the river where Pete had disappeared. ''Don't know. Maybe nothing. Maybe just do our praying here.''

''That's not what you said last time,'' she replied quietly. ''I'd like to hear some preaching, someone reading from the book. Just seems like you're closer to God when Gospel is being talk on.''

Jody bent over and reached for the shovel. ''Ain't right when a man goes to meeting and gets threatened with gunplay.''

''Jody, I'm sure Buck is a different man now that he's got his young 'uns back.''

Jody pounded the shovel against the earth. ''It wasn't only Chauncy; there was Jess and plenty of others a-settin' up for trouble.''

Libby buried her face in Lance's neck and rocked with him for a moment, then she said, ''All right, Jody, we'll just set here and await the Lord's will.'' She started back to the house, but then turned to him again. ''Didn't Pete say the meeting was day after tomorrow . . . or don't you remember?''

''I don't,'' he snapped.

The young men came adorned in their buffalo-horned helmets, their faces and bodies painted in garish yellows and reds; every forehead showed streaks of black. The reed flutes could just be heard above the throb of drums and the ring of tiny bells, and the clatter of rattles became a haunting beat behind the deepening pound of feet.

Hears-the-Wolf watched the fire leaping higher. He knew he had been brilliant before the council, spitting back every charge against him with stinging remarks about this assuaging of pride by attacking him when those who had betrayed the Penaketa, had brought them humiliation and defeat, were sitting amidst plenty, chortling over the success of their sins. At Blue Hawk's repeated advice, he kept shouting about the wealth of the weak *Mexicanos*; their pastures were full of horses, their villages storehouses of blankets, knives, and the many things the Panetekas now lacked. So loud did he describe the plunder awaiting them, and the slaves all knew every foray produced, that the young men of the Tenawa began to gather about the council fire, reacting to his words with smiles of approval. While there was little enthusiasm to go against the stubborn *tejanos*, a raid into largely unarmed and poorly defended Mexico was another matter. Soon the Penatekas, seeing the Tenawas nudging each other about the prospects *Isi-man-ica*'s repeated boasts were mounting, suddenly started shouting back at him to stop talking and lead them to this cornucopia of plenty that would restore their power to exist as a proud people again, and know the respect of fellow tribes of the Nerm.

Blue Hawk's wisdom extended futher than he knew. Word of this raid spread to the Tahneema, and many of their young men, knowing spoils were all but assured, appeared ready to take part. Hears-the-Wolf was to discover that greed drives more men to war than all the noble causes springing from the mind of man.

It was the night before his departure and four hundred warriors were dancing a wild dance of anticipation, many calling upon the spirits to journey with them and arm them with strong medicine. Hears-the-Wolf finally danced too. As he whirled about, stabbing the earth with his lance, the warrior in him swelled his heart and the taste of battle rose like a pungent spice in his mouth. Now he was truly happy, a warrior leading a fighting force to crush an enemy, and a sensual woman waiting to enclose his manhood on his return.

Blue Hawk and Black Tail watched him from a distance.

They had stood for a while in silence, but Black Tail, happy for his friend, could not restrain his joy. "He is a great fighter; he will soon make us proud."

"Proud of what?" asked Blue Hawk.

"That he has restored pride to our people."

Blue Hawk seemed to study the night sky. When she did not answer, Black Tail went on. "You have taught him much; now he will surely be a chief."

"I have taught him how to achieve power, but what he really needs, I cannot teach."

Black Tail let several moments go by, but he was too curious to remain silent. "And what is that, Blue Hawk?"

"Wisdom," she said, half to herself, glancing with weary eyes at the sky.

Chapter 42

THE STORY TRAVELED quickly through the settlement, for in spite of its origins, people wanted to believe it, even where deeply held convictions fought against it. With the volatility of all issues fueled by emotion, it wove its way in and out of credibility. But whether believed or not, the tale of Libby and the Chauncy children spread irresistibly, for it raised the hope of change. People, under the draining brooding stoicism of that summer, were war-weary. It had been too long since they'd had a tomorrow with joy and peace in the air, too long since nightfall was simply a time to rest under peaceful sprays of stars. Women were deathly sick of facing the future with fear, or the fall of darkness with dread. Many were privately praying that Libby's experience was a harbinger of returning sanity, perhaps promising a new life when crops could be safely harvested, and children raised in the harmony of happy homes. Ben McCulloch, nodding firmly at every mention of Libby, did nothing to discourage these hopes.

No household was more affected than the Chauncys'.

A steadily increasing glow seemed to have struck them all. The torment of their separation, for a time burdened with the finality of death, had driven home their importance to each other, and affection the hardworking Chauncys once thought it feckless to express now poured forth on every occasion. Maude's recovery was miraculous. For the first two nights she slept between Liza and Tad, rising early to sit and look lovingly at their heads half-buried in their pillows. Buck, before he did chores, would come in to hug her silently before another glorious day began.

Pete Spevy's visit was a disturbance not easily resolved, for they drew from his comments the Holisters might not be coming to the big prayer meeting slated for the following day. Libby Holister's name had been on their lips and in their prayers for some time, even making Buck stand quietly in the fields, asking God's forgiveness for his deeds and thoughts over the past weeks. But more than just the Chauncys felt the claw of guilt. Becky and Kate had confided to each other their shame at not showing greater understanding for Libby, for letting Jess and Race lead them into acts they now regretted. But Becky was not one for self-delusion. "Damn it, we did it! We blamed her for not hating the redskins as much as we did! No point in trying to make it look different. All of us folks listened to the Gospel, but only Libby, by God, heard it!"

Liza and Maude, seeing how troubled Buck was, suggested they might all feel better if they had a chance to ask Libby's forgiveness in person. "Want me to go alone?" he asked, looking wan at the prospect.

"No, I want to go," said Maude. "Twice that woman has risked her life for me, and got damn little thanks. If I had the means to, believe me, I'd build her a church."

In the end they all decided to go.

At the mission they ran across Becky and Jess. On

hearing they were headed for the Holisters', Becky said she and Jess would go along. Jess at first seemed reluctant, even faintly defiant, but Becky wouldn't give him time to talk. "You're going straight out there, Jess Bishop, and I have half a mind to make you take that candle mold with you. Land sakes, it's time we did something decent around here!"

Dale Sutter watched them go by, pretending he had not been able to gather from their comments where they were heading. But after they disappeared, he mounted and set off behind the mission on a short cut to home.

At the new general store Ben McCulloch was showing Jack Hays and Matt Caldwell what new supplies were now available from Houston and points east. The two Ranger captains were in the settlement to meet President Lamar, who was going to be stopping off at Gonzales on his way to Austin, his new capital. They were to act as an escort for the last and most dangerous leg of his journey. They were the only ones to know that Lamar, who was far more popular out here than he was back east, wanted to address the people of this settlement while he had the chance. Fiery by nature and dreaming of Texas one day extending to the Pacific, he was also acutely aware that the redoubtable Sam Houston was going to run against him for the presidency in the coming election.

Libby and Jody had spent another day thinking about their future. There were few alternatives open on that harsh frontier, and though neither mentioned it, returning to Missouri no longer seemed, even to Libby, the sanctuary it once appeared. Missouri was behind them now like their childhood. There was something about this border country that, in spite of its perils and trials, grew on you. Maybe it was its rawness, its implicit challenge to build it into something majestic, something that would call forth loyalty and pride.

Maybe it was its bigness that made one feel it had
room for the wildest dreams.

In the restive tide of such thoughts, they puzzled
through the day, stopping occasionally to stare at horizons that instilled in young minds visions of heady freedom and limitless space. By late afternoon they were
sitting on their porch watching V-shaped flights of birds
heading south. It was that hour of the day when a curious
lull struck the land. A deer with its grown fawn was
standing just visible at the edge of the woods beyond
the fields; somewhere a sandhill crane was crying a lament, its affliction unknown but pulling Libby's attention to the river. As she did she saw a wagon coming
down the trail with several riders moving about it, and
tried to make them out.

It was Jody, joining her, who offered the first recognition. "That's Becky riding in front," he said, rising
on his toes to see farther, "and I believe that's the
Chauncys in that wagon."

"Goodness, where could they be going at this hour?"
Libby was standing beside him holding one hand to her
throat. "That must be Jess . . . and I guess the Chauncy
children."

Jody put a hand over his eyes to ward off the declining sun. "By God, Libby, I believe they're coming
here!"

In the next minute it was clear Jody was right.

The wagon turned in to the trail leading up to the
house, and now they could make out the faces of
Buck and Maude, sitting in the wagon, and Becky
and Jess, and the older Chauncy children, riding
alongside.

"What will we do?" breathed Libby.

"Nothing! They're certainly coming here for a reason; we'll just wait and hear it."

The wagon stopped a hundred feet from the house and
Buck climbed down. Maude was climbing down, too,
but Buck came forward without her. He carried his hat

in his hand and looked troubled, almost ill, as he approached Libby. "I've got a piece that needs saying, Mrs. Holister, if you'll let me."

Buck was obviously a man humbled to the point of physically suffering at this pitiful need to show contrition. Libby's eyes could not conceal a rising sympathy for him. "Of course, Buck. Whatever you want to say, I'll be glad to listen, but please, won't you sit down?"

"No, best I just stand here." Maude had moved up to stand beside him, but he seemed unaware she had entwined her arm with his. "I reckon I owe you more than an apology," Buck began haltingly, "maybe more than I got words to say, but I had to tell you I know now you were right, there has to be a right and wrong or nothing a decent man does or even thinks makes sense. I guess I forgot that. But the Lord has punished me, and I got to believe it's only because of you that I received His mercy. Believe me, Mrs. Holister, I won't forget it again. I've said a lot of things about Injuns and I can't take them back, but after all this time, my children are back safe and sound. They can't all be killers."

Maude moved forward and, looking up at Libby, who was standing on the porch, managed a smile that told Libby more than anything else could have, that this woman was once again in touch with Life. "Libby," she said, refusing to allow the cold ring of "Mrs. Holister" to remain, "you've made us so deliriously happy, we just had to tell you we're praying for your happiness too. Please come to the prayer meeting tomorrow. I know it was terrible for you last time, but I'm sure a lot of people would feel blessed if you'd give them another chance to pray with you."

"I'm one of them!" said Becky, coming up.

Libby looked at Jody, but Jody's expression signaled it was Libby's response they had come to hear. Libby had to blot her eyes before she could speak. But then she said in a strained voice, "I have my own reasons to be thankful to the Lord. If He spares me, likely I'll be there."

There were murmurs of assent, but the moment was over. All of them turned and started back. At the river they met Kate and Race coming upstream. Becky stayed behind to speak with Kate for a few moments, but then all disappeared and the Holisters were alone once more.

"What do you think?" asked Libby, after several minutes went by and the visitors could no longer be seen.

Jody couldn't help smiling. "I think my wife has solved our problem."

"How?"

"By being a heroine and getting all these sinners elbowing each other out of the way just to pray next to you."

"Oh, Jody, stop! I'm not that special or that popular."

"The heck you're not. When they turn this settlement into a town, just because I've got you for a wife, I'm gonna be elected mayor."

Libby punched him, but he held her playfully and kissed her. Moments later they were on the bed in each other's arms. Their sudden lovemaking was spontaneous, wild but good. It left them spent yet comforted, both feeling they were once again where they belonged, once again part of this demanding, daunting, but exciting life.

Libby sighed as she heard Lance gurgling, an unfailing signal he was about to awake. "I wonder what happened to that Indian warrior," she whispered resignedly as she pushed her hair back in place and straightened her clothes to get up.

"We'll probably never know," answered Jody, remembering he still had chores to do. Somewhere a coyote howled and was answered by its mate in the woods beyond. The Holisters turned to the many

tasks that made up their lives, both quietly wondering
what awaited them at the campgrounds on the morrow.

Three hundred miles to the west, Blue Hawk and
Black Tail stood listening to runners coming back from
Mexico. The raid had been an awesome success. Captain
Flack, a military observer, would report: *In October
1840, more than four hundred warriors penetrated into
Mexico some four hundred miles, and killed, scalped,
burned, and destroyed everything they could; their
tracks could be traced for miles by the burning ranches
and villages.*

The poor *peóns* and *campesinos* paid dearly for
Canilizo's perfidy. Authorities in Nuevo León and
Coahuila would count almost fifteen hundred dead,
many women captured, and thousands of horses and
livestock stolen.

It brought joy to the Penatekas, who knew the tribe
would now be enriched by these great spoils, yet
Blue Hawk sat pondering the setting sun, her mind
seeming adrift like one who sees beyond the day.
Black Tail, buoyed by the word pictures messengers
were carrying back, settled beside her. "Surely he is
now a chief!" he said, satisfaction bringing an easy
roll to his voice.

Blue Hawk looked at him, her smile distant, uncertain.
"Yes, he is now a chief; there will be great excitement
on his return, but little more can be gained from raiding
the *Mexicanos*."

Black Tail turned to her, her tone if not her words
serving to sober him. "You speak of the *tejanos*?"

"Yes."

"You think they will come again."

"As surely as the sun will rise."

Black Tail sighed. "Perhaps they will give him
peace."

"Yes, one day they will."

Black Tail, his interest rising, turned to her. "You think a day will come when they will offer him peace? What would he give them in return . . . more land?"

"No, on that day there will be no more land to give."

Black Tail looked almost afraid to ask the inevitable question. "What then will he give?"

"His life."

The day broke clear with one dark cloud rolling in from the west. Jody was up before dawn. It was he who found the rig sitting next to the barn, the candle mold on the front seat. He smiled grimly. As unpredictable as redskins were, the whites were worse. Standing in the cool of morning, he couldn't help but sense how much emotions dominated the minds of men. Love and hate both bypassed reason, for one spawned the other. For humans to love meant hating what harmed or destroyed that love. As with so many things, it left him casting about in confusion; only Libby seemed free of these quandaries. Only Libby stood on this sanguine border of belligerents without an enemy. What's more, only Libby saw violence begetting more violence, yet accepted the deadly risk of standing against this lunacy as the price of peace. Was it possible to love this remarkable girl more? He didn't think so, but he was sure going to try.

They decided to go in the rig, something Jody wondered at. He was not as quick as his wife to overlook Kate's rude abandoning her when Libby needed her most. But Libby, with that strange wisdom of hers, just smiled at him. "If she sees us in her rig, she'll know she is forgiven, and that will spare us both a scene whose pain might keep us remembering these horrible days. Kate is a good person. We were once close; we will be again. Why burden our friendship with something as silly as spite?"

As they made their way to the campgrounds, Lance slept in the space behind Libby's seat. That dark cloud was finally joined by one or two others, and a few drops of rain sprinkled down. But the weather was ignored at the campgrounds, where scads of people were milling about, talking in large groups and gesturing to each other excitedly. Almost immediately the Holisters heard President Lamar was on hand and would speak before the Reverend Bumeister led them in prayer. In spite of the excitement, Jody noticed people were nudging each other and smiling as their eyes fell upon Libby. They left Lance in the rig with some teenaged girls who were tending children, and made their way to the rear of the assembly. But now the crowd opened up, and as though being beckoned from the speaker's hill, Jody and Libby moved forward until they were flush in front of the little dais set up for Lamar. Keeping their eyes down and feeling strangely embarrassed at this silent homage being paid, they settled on the ground, and immediately several people moved in to settle around them. When Libby finally looked up, she realized the Chauncys, the Bishops, and the Sutters were grouped beside them, as though being close to Jody and Libby were a privilege only they could claim.

The clouds passed over and the sprinkling rain stopped, the sun began to blaze through, and everyone knew the weather from now on would be fair. The Reverend Bumeister introduced President Lamar with what amounted to a speech, but Lamar was no amateur. He knew such a meeting as his presence made this was the event of the season for people cut off from their government in faraway Houston. They heard news about their nation, even in these fateful times, only when it was weeks old. He had prepared himself well. The evening before he had spent with the Ranger captains, whom he greatly admired and who told him the story of Libby Holister. He had been deeply impressed. This might offer a partial solution to his Indian problem, an issue his administration was anxiously studying, for his present policy of force was drawing dangerous if misguided criticism.

Finally Bumeister wound down his eulogy to this distinguished bearer of temporal power and Mirabeau B. Lamar, second president of the Republic of Texas, hero of San Jacinto, dashing cavalry leader and dreamer of empires, stood up. He did not disappoint the eager and attentive faces. His speech was passionate and dramatically revealed the struggles for survival that went on at all levels for their Lone Star nation. The people, westerners who lived by the word "struggle," listened, rapt by the import of his words, the deep resonance of his voice, and the crusading energy and exalted purpose with which he imbued his office.

But Lamar also knew these people had come there to pray, and he had prayers of his own to offer, not to improve his image but because he was truly grateful for those who fought and sacrificed for the republic he loved. "I give thanks to God," he said, "for recent developments along our border. But we must remember the Lord granted us victory because we produced men like Jack Hays, Matt Caldwell, and Ben McCulloch." A round of applause started somewhere in the rear and rippled through the crowd. The three Ranger captains, sitting behind the dais, looked away shyly, Jack Hays finally glancing up and searching the now pure blue sunlit sky as though it offered an escape. Lamar waited for silence to return before he went on. "But let us also remember that the Lord, weighing us in a far sterner set of scales, must have felt we were worthy of victory, worthy of ruling this fair land, only because we produced women with the vision and spirit of Libby Holister, the vision to rise above the bitterness and fury of conflict and the spirit to point us to a righteous, honorable, and lasting way to peace!"

Applause this time began around Libby and Jody, but

spread immediately throughout the crowd; like an on-coming ocean breaker, a great roar began to engulf them. Libby only knew Jody had his arm around her, pulling her closer, hugging her. The last thing she saw was the three Ranger captains on their feet applauding, then tears filled her eyes, and looking through them, all she could see was the sun's rays pouring down, bathing the earth in gold.